Praise for the novels of Alexandra Hawkins

### A Duke But No Gentleman

"The attraction between Blackbern and Imogene is intense."
*—Publishers Weekly*

"4.5 stars. The first of the Masters of Seduction series will more than satisfy those who savor a dark, richly woven romance."
*—RT Book Reviews*

"This edgy historical will appeal to romantic-suspense readers looking for darker layers in a Regency love story."
*—Booklist*

"5 stars. This book is everything that a historical romance novel should be."
*—The Reading Wench*

"Sensual and filled with plenty of surprises, *A Duke But No Gentleman* is an excellent summer read."
*—Romance Reviews Today*

"5 stars. The reigning authority of charismatic Regency rogues."
*—Jenerated Reviews*

"A fantastic start to a seductive series."
*—Night Owl Reviews*

"A-review. A very good book."
*—Bodice Rippers, Femme Fatales and Fantasy*

"5 stars. A smart, wicked,

### *All Night with a Rogue*

"Hawkins's first Lords of Vice tale calls to mind the highly sensual reads of Bertrice Small and Susan Johnson."
                                                    —*Romantic Times*

"Brimming with witty repartee, well-drawn characters, an intriguing plot, sizzling sensual love scenes, and innocence, this story is a delight."
                                            —*Romance Junkies* (4.5)

### *Till Dawn with the Devil*

"*Till Dawn with the Devil*'s romance is first-rate with unusual characters and an underlying mystery that will intrigue readers."
                            —Robin Lee, *Romance Reviews Today*

"Hawkins cements her reputation for bringing compelling, unique, and lush romances to fans eager for fresh storytelling."
                                    —*RT Book Reviews* (4½ stars)

"*Till Dawn with the Devil* promises an intoxicating journey, and delivers with an exciting series of twists and turns that leave the reader disoriented and begging for more."
                            —Melissa Kammer, *Fresh Fiction*

### *After Dark with a Scoundrel*

"Hawkins's talent for perfectly merging Gothic elements into a sexually charged romance is showcased along with the marvelous cast of characters taking readers on a thrill ride."
                            —Kathe Robin, *RT Book Reviews*

"I would recommend this story to anyone who loves an amazingly written romance."
                            —*Night Owl Reviews* (5-star Top Pick)

"Alexandra Hawkins has just cemented herself a place on my 'must-read' author list."

—Chrissy Dionne, *Romance Junkies*

"Poignant, sweetly romantic, and sexy as can be."

—Joyce Greenfield, *Reader to Reader*

### Sunrise with a Notorious Lord

"Simply spectacular from front to back!"

—*Fresh Fiction*

"Regency fans will enjoy the bold heroine and rakish hero."

—*Publishers Weekly*

"Charming, fun, and sexy."

—*RT Book Reviews*

"*Sunrise with a Notorious Lord* is a fun and lively story."

—*Romance Reviews Today*

### All Afternoon with a Scandalous Marquess

"Desire in disguise was never so sweet or passionate, and Hawkins hooks readers and draws them in all the way to the perfect ending."

—*RT Book Reviews*

"A good solid choice for historical romance fans."

—*Night Owl Reviews*

"Hawkins creates strong characters and dramatizes high emotion along with sensuality. Fans of Stephanie Laurens and Jo Beverley will enjoy this series."

—*Booklist*

"Easy reading and fascinating characters make *All Afternoon with a Scandalous Marquess* a light-hearted read."

—*Romance Reviews Today*

***Dusk with a Dangerous Duke***
"Another fantastic read in the Lords of Vice series."
—*Single Titles*

"Alexandra Hawkins never lets a reader of historical romance forget how wonderful she is at creating characters with depth and a romance between them that brings a tear to your eye." —*Mary Gramlich Blog*

***Twilight with the Infamous Earl***
"Fans of the series will relish this last book, bringing all the characters back together for one last stand."
—*RT Book Reviews*

"A story filled with laughter, devotion, and overcoming society's perception of a person."
—*Romance Reviews Today*

"The chemistry and family connections are Hawkins's strength and show well in this adventure." —*Booklist*

"I enjoyed every page of this book. Absolutely devoured it. Alexandra Hawkins is a very talented writer. She knows how to create a great story that will pull the reader in and make them curious about what will happen next."
—*Night Owl Reviews* (4.5 stars, Night Owl Top Pick)

"The characters are strong and easily likable."
—*Fresh Fiction*

## Also by
### ALEXANDRA HAWKINS

*A Duke But No Gentleman*
*Twilight with the Infamous Earl*
*Dusk with a Dangerous Duke*
*All Afternoon with a Scandalous Marquess*
*Sunrise with a Notorious Lord*
*After Dark with a Scoundrel*
*Till Dawn with the Devil*
*All Night with a Rogue*

# You Can't Always Get the Marquess You Want

Alexandra Hawkins

St. Martin's Paperbacks

This is a work of fiction. All of the characters, organizations, and events portrayed in this novel are either products of the author's imagination or are used fictitiously.

YOU CAN'T ALWAYS GET THE MARQUESS YOU WANT

Copyright © 2016 by Alexandra Hawkins.

All rights reserved.

For information address St. Martin's Press, 175 Fifth Avenue, New York, NY 10010.

ISBN: 978-1-250-06473-8

3 1703 00622 0232

Our books may be purchased in bulk for promotional, educational, or business use. Please contact your local bookseller or the Macmillan Corporate and Premium Sales Department at 1-800-221-7945, ext. 5442, or by e-mail at MacmillanSpecialMarkets@macmillan.com.

Printed in the United States of America

St. Martin's Paperbacks edition / April 2016

St. Martin's Paperbacks are published by St. Martin's Press, 175 Fifth Avenue, New York, NY 10010.

10  9  8  7  6  5  4  3  2  1

Pleasure's a sin, and sometimes sin's a pleasure.
—Lord Byron

# Chapter One

*Black Goat Tavern, 1816*

"You astound me, Fairlamb. Most days you are not so careless. Nevertheless, I am not one to question my good fortune. Seeing that I have gained the advantage and your attention, are you prepared to offer an apology?"

A wise man would have nodded and apologized. With his arms wrenched and pinned behind his back by an unknown foe, Mathias Rooke, Marquess of Fairlamb, clearly was at a disadvantage as he watched through his narrowed gaze while a familiar dark-haired gentleman with the build of a pugilist approached him with an air of confidence that revealed he reveled in having the upper hand.

Mathias was expressionless as he stared at the man, silently noting his disheveled evening attire and the clumsy retied cravat. Oliver Brant, Earl of Marcroft, appeared to have spent his evening fighting or in a brothel. Not that he was particularly concerned if Marcroft caught the French pox from an unfortunate harlot. The ladies of the ton had a high opinion of him, considering him fashionably handsome with his square jaw and prominent cheekbones.

All Mathias saw was the burning hatred in the man's hazel gaze.

He had only himself to blame for his current predicament. After all, it had been at his suggestion that he and his companions delayed their journey home by stopping at the tavern for a few pots of ale. He had also been the one to send his friends off to see to their horses as he settled the bill. Otherwise, he and Marcroft might not have crossed paths this day.

It was unfortunate for all involved that his decisions had placed him in the same room with Marcroft, since this particular gentleman tended to bring out the devil in him.

Mathias squared his shoulders. "Apologize for what precisely? My comment regarding your mistress's equine features was not meant for your big ears, Marcroft. If you take offense to an honest impression of the wench, then present your complaints to her mother and sire. It is not my fault you have appalling taste in—"

Pain burst like fireworks in his brain as the earl's right fist connected with Mathias's left cheekbone. His head snapped to the right, giving him a shower of bright sparks in his left eye and an instant headache.

Mathias shook off the pain as if he had been doused with a bucket filled with water. He smiled in a contemptuous fashion, deliberately baiting the man. "A respectable punch, Marcroft, I will grant you that. Order your mongrel to release me, and let us see how you fare when your opponent is unfettered—or do you take after your sire . . . striking only the defenseless?"

"I am my own man," the man holding him in a ruthless grip growled into Mathias's ear.

The Earl of Marcroft's thunderous expression revealed Mathias had struck a definitive blow without using his fists. Although he was not personally acquainted with the earl's father, the Marquess of Norgrave, he had heard all kinds of nasty rumors about the gentleman's misdeeds his entire life, which included goading unskilled opponents into duels for amusement. He had also heard that his father, the Duke of Blackbern, had once called the marquess his dearest friend, though Mathias believed such a close connection was an exaggeration. Even if the duke had confirmed the rumor was true, he would have never believed it. His father was a decent, honorable gentleman. He was nothing like Marcroft or his immoral sire.

"Release him!" the earl curtly ordered.

*About bloody time,* was Mathias's savage thought.

Before his arms were released, Marcroft drove his large fist into Mathias's stomach. He doubled over, his internal organs shifting in silent protest at the abuse while he struggled not to throw up the ale he had imbibed with his friends.

The earl clapped his gloved hand on Mathias's shoulder and lowered his head until their gazes were level. "I grow weary of listening to your brazen tongue and dull wit, Fairlamb. Before you disgrace yourself further, I shall accept your apology so you may take your leave."

Mathias slowly straightened, scowling as he noted that Marcroft mimicked his actions. By Christ's holy hand, he despised the dark-haired tyrant. "Why would you wish for me to leave when you put so much effort into gaining my interest?"

The slight furrowing of the earl's forehead revealed that subtlety was lost on the heavily muscled brute.

Mathias pursed his lips together and kissed the air. "Tread carefully, good sir. Else your passions will be the death of you." To emphasize his point, Mathias drew his finger across the front of his breeches and then his throat.

The tavern's patrons quieted as a look of incredulity flashed across Marcroft's face before it was swiftly replaced by outrage at the unspoken accusation. The earl's companion, who was standing behind Mathias, murmured something, but the only words he could discern were "courting" and "death."

In the next breath, Marcroft lunged for him.

The casual observer might have deduced from Mathias's relaxed stance that he was too inebriated to defend himself. Admittedly, once he had noticed the earl's presence, the ale that he had imbibed might have influenced his reckless decision to provoke a confrontation. Nevertheless, there was a reason why his family and friends affectionately called him Chance.

Luck was often on his side.

Mathias did not brace himself for the impact of Marcroft's charge. Instead, he seized the man's expensive coat at the waist and allowed the momentum to pivot them as if they were dance partners. Halfway through the graceful turn, he released his hold and sent his angry companion into the nearest wooden post. The brutal collision caused everyone in the public room to wince as the post shuddered but held firm.

The Lord Marcroft fell to his knees and then toppled over onto his side. He made no attempt to sit up. Or move. Several men rushed to the earl's side to assess the extent of his injuries.

The blond-haired man who had been so helpful in restraining Mathias earlier took a menacing step in his direction. "You will pay for what you have done."

Mathias was unimpressed. "Don't fret, you miserable flea-bitten cur. I always settle my accounts. Besides, I highly doubt that mild tap has put a dent in your friend's thick skull."

The man's cheeks puffed as he expelled a hot impassioned breath. His face was a mottled red as he raised his fists as if to exact revenge in Marcroft's behalf. A soft shuffling sound caught his attention, and his gaze shifted from Mathias's face to its source just over his shoulder. The man halted so abruptly, he skidded the final inches.

"It took you long enough," Mathias said, not bothering to glance back at the two gentlemen who flanked his sides. The arrival of his cousin Lord Kempthorn and their good friend Lord Bastrell meant his exchange of pleasantries with Marcroft had come to an end. "As you can see, during your absence I was outnumbered and quite defenseless."

"So I see," his cousin said as he grabbed Mathias's chin and tugged to get a better look at the bruise forming on his cheek. Satisfied that any damage was minimal, he dropped his hand and squinted down at the unconscious man on the floor. "Good grief, is that Marcroft?"

"I am afraid so," Mathias said, trying to sound as if he regretted the outcome of their skirmish. "I do not think he likes me very much."

"No, he does not," Christian Lyon, Viscount Bastrell, concurred. Everyone called him St. Lyon because there was nothing saintly about the charming gentleman when it came to his dealings with the ladies of the ton. His handsome features could have been made of chiseled stone as he glared down at Marcroft. "I doubt this latest encounter will improve his opinion. By the by, the horses are ready. Perhaps we should depart."

"A prudent decision," Mathias replied. He opened his coin purse and retrieved a guinea. Addressing the gentleman who claimed to be the Earl of Marcroft's friend, he said, "I regret we must take our leave before your companion recovers what little sense he possesses, so let's settle our account."

With a careless flick of his thumb, he tossed the coin in the air. When the other man stepped closer to snatch the coin out of the air, Mathias rammed his right fist into the man's soft belly. He caught the gold coin and watched dispassionately as the man groaned and doubled over.

Mathias slipped the coin into the small pocket of his waistcoat. "That was for binding my arms. You are learning some very unsporting tactics from Marcroft. In a moment of quiet contemplation, you might want to ponder the benefits of your friendship with the earl. Or else, the next time we shall meet will be on a grassy commons at dawn."

Mathias glanced up and noticed the amused expressions of his companions. "Our bill is settled. Shall we depart?"

No one spoke as the three gentlemen strode toward their awaiting horses.

Mathias placed his gloved hand on the pommel of the saddle and tried to slow his breathing as his companions gracefully mounted their horses. His shoulders ached from the rough restraint, and the abdominal muscles protecting his organs were sore from Marcroft's abusive fist. He quietly wondered if he could climb onto the beast without assistance.

"How badly are you injured?" his cousin asked in subdued tones.

"I'm fine, Thorn," Mathias said, using his cousin's nickname. He still made no effort to mount his horse.

St. Lyon also looked unconvinced. "We leave you alone for ten minutes, and you manage to find the one person who would happily wipe that smirk from your face. What the devil happened? From the look of things, Marcroft did more than add a little color to your face."

"Oh, you know how Marcroft is. Why throw one punch when there is an opportunity to deliver several. Cease fussing over me, I will recover." Mathias grimaced as he placed his foot in the stirrup. He sucked in his breath, quickly swung his leg over the back of the horse, and planted his backside on the saddle.

"Why didn't you send a servant for us?" Thorn demanded, sounding furious in his cousin's behalf. It was probably a blessing that the man's identical twin brother, Gideon, was out of the country. Together, the brothers could be rather formidable against any adversary.

Not that he needed any assistance when dealing with a member of the Brant family.

"And frighten Marcroft off?" Mathias snorted. "I was counting on him taking advantage of the odds that were deliberately stacked in his favor."

Understanding gleamed in the viscount's dark blue eyes as he slanted a glance at Mathias. "So that's why you sent both of us out of the tavern," St. Lyon said, shaking his head in amazement. "I suppose there was a good reason why you wanted the earl to practice his pugilist skills on your face."

He touched the swelling on his cheek and winced. "Now you are just being insulting. Lest you forget, I was not the one who was lying unconscious on the dirty floor of the tavern."

"Damn me," Thorn muttered. "You baited him into attacking so you could hit him?" His cousin sounded a little appalled by Mathias's strategy.

He shrugged. "I did not say it was a wise plan. It is not the first time I have lost my head around Marcroft. I truly despise the man."

"It is the one thing you and the earl have in common," St. Lyon dryly observed. "I have no great love for the scoundrel either, but you would do well to avoid him."

Mathias had been given similar advice on numerous occasions by his parents, the Duke and Duchess of Blackbern. His family and Marcroft's parents, the Marquess and the Marchioness of Norgrave, had some unpleasant history between them that had taken place long before his birth. Although he was not privy to all the details, one fact was apparent—the Brant family was his enemy.

"Excellent advice, but nigh impossible. Marcroft has been a barb in my arse since all of us were boys. His temperament has not improved with age."

He and Marcroft had been trading physical and verbal blows since their first meeting. He was not overly optimistic about their future encounters. Nothing short of a sword or bullet in the earl's heart would prevent the obnoxious gentleman from meddling in Mathias's affairs.

"Speaking of Marcroft's infamous temper—perhaps we should leave before he awakens," Thorn said, tipping his head in the direction of the tavern. "As it is, your father will be upset when he learns that you were attacked by a member of the Brant family so close to home."

Mathias tightened the reins in his grip. "How many times must I say it? I was not attacked. And I was the victor, by my account." He sighed. "Let us leave the retelling of this tale to me, eh?" He spurred his horse forward.

St. Lyon snickered behind him. "Lies will not work, my friend. How are you going to explain your face to your family?"

His companions' laughter muffled Mathias's creative curses as the distance increased between him and his enemy.

# Chapter Two

Several hours later, Mathias was alone when he strolled through the front door. St. Lyon and his cousin were tarrying at the stables while he smoothed things over with his mother and father. He quietly pondered the most expedient excuse he could offer his family for not finding his way home until now. He was several days late, and he had missed breakfast by three hours. Since he had reached the mature age of two-and-twenty, he thought it rather unfair that he was forced to suffer the indignity of presenting himself to his parents as if he were an errant child. Nevertheless, if all went according to his plan, this would be the last time he would be required to do so.

"Good morning, McKee," he genially greeted the butler, handing the servant his hat and gloves. The man had been in the Duke of Blackbern's employ long before his father had married Lady Imogene Sunter. The man could have retired with a generous pension and his parents' blessing, but the elderly servant considered it his duty to watch over the Rooke family. His dedication had made him part of their family.

"Always, Lord Fairlamb," McKee replied as if Mathias's statement had been a question. "Cutting it a bit short, are you not?"

Mathias chuckled, assuming the mild censure was in regards to his lateness. "Always."

His mother liked to tease her husband by telling him that he only had himself to blame for siring a son so much like him. Mathias viewed any comparison to his father as the highest praise. He had earned the nickname Chance before he spoke his first words. Later, his not-so-innocent exploits at the gambling tables and other reckless adventures with his friends had ensured that use of the name extended beyond his family.

"I hope Cook does not mind filling a few more stomachs," he said, mindful to keep the bruised side of his face hidden from the butler's keen gaze. "Thorn and St. Lyon have followed me home. We are planning to return to London together."

"I shall have their rooms prepared immediately," the butler said, the lines in his face becoming more pronounced when Mathias edged away from him. "How long will Lord Kempthorn and Lord Bastrell be staying with us?"

Mathias had private reasons why he was eager to return to London, but he had no intention of sharing them with McKee. He could have pushed onward to London, but he had not seen his family in a month. He missed his beautiful mother and his overly protective father. They had privately argued about it before he departed for one of their northern estates, and he regretted they had parted so formally. And then there were his younger siblings: Benjamin, who was twenty and also feeling the weight of their father's watchful eye; Honora, who at seventeen years old was looking forward to being presented at court; fifteen-year-old Mercy, who was less enthused about entering London's polite society; shy twelve-year-old Frederick, who preferred animals and books to people; and little Constance, who was seven years old and the youngest in the Rooke family. He had not realized how much he missed them all.

"We haven't decided. It could be a few days or a week."

McKee nodded, unruffled by Mathias's vague reply. "Good. Your mother lamented that your absences grow closer together. She will be pleased to have you and your friends seated at her table."

"Unless my mother and father have changed their plans, I shall see them in London," he said, uncomfortable with the twinge of guilt that crept into his chest and squeezed.

"Your mother and father have not altered their plans. However, priorities shift, and a man's amusements differ from those of his family."

"How did you—?"

"Who do you think looked after your father after his parents were lost to him? He was younger than you when he inherited the title, so I assume he knows better than most that a young gentleman craves his freedom."

He wondered if his father had turned to the old man for advice after his departure. Had he hurt his father's feelings? Distracted by the thought, he let down his guard and lowered his head.

It was all McKee needed. Mathias winced at the strength of the butler's hard grip as he forced his face to the side so he could get a closer look at the bruises. "You were brawling," the butler said flatly. "Were you fighting with your cousin? Lord Bastrell?"

"No!" Mathias shook off the butler's grip and stepped out of reach. "I was not even brawling. There was a minor incident at a tavern."

"Who? Your father will want to know."

That was a conversation he intended to avoid at all costs. If he mentioned the name Brant in his mother and father's presence, the consequences would be on his head. His father was not quite rational when it came to the Marquess of Norgrave. Mathias understood. There was something about the man's son that provoked him to violence. Perhaps it was something in the blood, passing from father to son.

"No one. I walked into a man's fist. The public room was crowded. It happens all the time," he said, ignoring the disbelief on the older man's face. "I would appreciate it if you did not mention this to my parents."

McKee chuckled. "You think you can keep this from them?"

Mathias strode to the large rectangular mirror on the wall and peered at his reflection. He poked the slight swelling at his cheek and grimaced. In the passing hours, the bruises had darkened. Although Thorn and St. Lyon were aware of the animosity between the Rooke and Brant families, he nonetheless reminded them not to mention Marcroft's name in his father's presence. With luck, he could bluster his way through a reasonable excuse for the injury that would satisfy his concerned family.

"The bruises are not so bad," he lied, and the butler snorted behind him.

"I shall have Cook prepare a poultice to see if we can get the swelling down." McKee turned in the direction of the kitchen. "Before you head upstairs to your bedchamber, stop by the library and greet your mother and father properly."

Mathias frowned. He was not prepared to face his family or explain away his injuries. "What about the poultice?"

"You cannot get miracles from a poultice, my lord. Or hide from your mother. Go to them. I shall see to it that your friends are comfortably settled into their rooms."

"You are not being helpful, McKee," he muttered.

"Do you hear me mentioning the name Brant?" The shrewd old servant nodded when Mathias flinched. "I thought as much. Off with you. And you might want to walk slowly to give yourself more time to come up with a better tale than walking into a man's fist."

Although the butler's amusement was deserved, Mathias's pride felt as bruised as his cheek. He also heeded the man's advice and took his time as he made his way to the library. Unfortunately, it was a short walk as he strolled across the freshly polished patterned marble floor. When he reached the entrance to the library, he noticed that someone had neglected to close the double doors. The two-inch gap gave him a restricted view of the interior. He reached for the gleaming brass doorknobs, but the sound of his father's voice gave him pause. How many times as a young boy had he faced these doors with his heart filled with dread and remorse over some minor offense? Too many to count, he thought. In hindsight, his father had dealt with him fairly, even though the child had viewed the various penances differently. How little had changed when the sound of his father's voice could summon the feelings of the boy he thought he had left behind a long time ago?

His grim musings faded at the soft breathy sound of feminine laughter. His mother. Imogene Rooke, Duchess of Blackbern. Just hearing her voice eased some of the tension in his shoulders. The daughter of a duke, she possessed a natural grace and diplomacy that complemented his father's strength and arrogance. If anyone could prevent the males in her life from pounding their chests as they competed for dominance, it would be his mother.

However, as he leaned forward, Mathias watched

through the gap in the double doors and noted almost immediately that his tardiness was not prominent in the duke and duchess's thoughts. His father circled around his desk, intent on reclaiming some small trinket hidden within his mother's hand. Even from his position, Mathias could sense the duke's interest was focused on the flirtatious lady who believed she was evading him. He knew his father was toying with his quarry. Anyone who was acquainted with the Duke of Blackbern knew he was wholly smitten with his duchess. Mathias and his younger siblings had spent their whole lives watching his mother and father play this particular game. In the end, the duke always caught his lady.

Perhaps it was impolite for him to notice, but his mother was not really putting too much of an effort in resisting her husband's advances. Twice around the desk, and once around the overstuffed sofa, and his father had already caught his duchess by the hips.

"Now are you prepared to be reasonable about this?" the Duke of Blackbern said, pulling his wife so she was pressed against him.

"Absolutely not!" the duchess said, keeping her closed fist behind her back. She kissed her husband's chin and used the distraction to slip from his grasp.

Laughing, she ran for the desk. Amused, Mathias shook his head as his father gave chase. The Rooke family had a position to maintain in the ton. It was apparent that any sense of respectability had been given the day off. No one would ever guess that his father would be celebrating his fiftieth birthday next year. Especially when the man was behaving like a lovesick youth.

Mathias glanced in the direction of the front hall when he heard the sound of the door opening and male voices echoing as Thorn and St. Lyon greeted McKee. It would be a matter of time before his friends would seek him out, so he might as well get any unpleasant business with his mother and father out of the way.

Mathias grasped both doorknobs and widened the gap so he could enter the library. He took two steps and froze. While he had been distracted by his friends' arrival, his father had managed to place his duchess in a very compromising position. His elegant mother was splayed across the desk; her usually neat coiffure had partially come undone as his father threaded his hand through her hair to deepen their passionate kiss.

Since he had five younger siblings, he did not want to bear witness to the making of a sixth. Out of respect for his mother's modesty, Mathias glanced down and discreetly coughed into his fist.

His head lifted at his mother's soft gasp. She had to tilt her head back to verify that it was her firstborn son standing near the doorway.

"Mathias!" The Duchess of Blackbern tried to push her husband away, but he only laughed at her flustered expression. "Let me up, you scoundrel," she said, sending their son an apologetic look. "We were not expecting you."

The duke sent Mathias a mischievous grin. "There is no need to fret, love," he murmured, gallantly helping her off the desk. He gave the front of her bodice a playful tug. "This isn't the first time one of our children has caught us kissing, and it won't be the last."

"Could you at the very least be a little repentant when it comes to scandalizing the children," she muttered as she picked up a hairpin on the desk and used it to secure a loose strand of blond hair. She walked toward her son, but he met her halfway.

"It is good to have you home again," she said, embracing him. When he lowered his head, she kissed him on the cheek. Still off balance, she did not focus her eyes on his bruised cheek right away. But then her gaze narrowed as she lightly inspected the swelling with her fingertips. "Good grief. What have you done to yourself?"

"If I had done this to myself, it would not have hurt so much," Mathias teased, meeting his father's amused gaze. "It is nothing to worry about, Mother. I barely notice it." He sent a desperate look to his father, silently pleading with him to come to his rescue. "I realize I am late, and I also have rotten timing when I do get around to presenting myself. My sincere apologies to both of you."

"Nonsense," his mother protested, moving aside so her son could greet his father properly. "I wish to learn more about what happened—"

"Let the lad catch his breath, Imogene. Apology accepted," his father said smoothly as the two men clasped hands. The duke winked as he placed his other hand on Mathias's shoulder to draw him into a brief embrace. "However, your timing was quite exceptional. A few more minutes, and your mother and I—"

"You will be sleeping in the stables if you finish that sentence, Your Grace!" his mother warned, the color in her cheeks deepening at her husband's teasing. Adept at changing the subject, too, she touched Mathias on the arm. "So . . . have you come alone or have you brought me guests?"

"Thorn and St. Lyon," he replied. "I promise we will not trouble you for long."

His mother wrinkled her nose, and she dismissed his vow with a wave of her hand. "Stay as long as you like. Nevertheless, we are already making preparations to travel to London. If you wish, you and your friends may travel with us."

"Darling, I doubt Chance, Thorn, and St. Lyon want to be slowed down by the family." The duke gave him a measured stare. "I assume you are eager to continue your journey to London once we've discussed estate business."

Mathias was, but he swallowed his agreement when he noted his mother's disappointment. "We plan to stay a week, and then we are returning to London."

"Returning?" she politely inquired.

His father's gaze sharpened at his slip of the tongue. Mathias winced and casually reached up to rub the back of his neck. "We, uh, I made a brief stop in London before heading home."

"What was so important that it could not wait?" the duchess asked, sounding perplexed by his decision. "Is that where you had trouble?"

Trouble? Mathias scowled. Ah yes, his face. He had no intention of mentioning Marcroft. Ever. "No, not London. I was at the Black Goat Tavern and—never mind. It was a slight misunderstanding."

"I see."

Unfortunately, all he was proving was that his mother had managed to muddle his thoughts as he tried to come up with a proper lie to explain away his bruises. He kissed her on the cheek. "Quit fretting. It was a minor incident. Happens all the time." At her appalled expression, "Or not at all. Forget I said anything." Mathias sighed.

His father laughed. "Imogene, you are embarrassing the lad. No one dies from a few bruises." To take any sting out of his mild rebuke, he placed his arm around her. "I'm certain Chance had business in town that could not wait. Am I correct?"

"Yes." Mathias nodded, grateful for his father's assistance. "Nothing too important, but it gave me the opportunity to inspect the premises and hire some staff."

"A sweet gesture, but there was no need—your father wrote his solicitor over a month ago to let him know of our arrival," the duchess explained.

"Forgive me, I meant the other house." He glanced at his father. "Instead of renting rooms, I've decided to open up your mother's old house." There was subtle tension creeping into the room that made his neck itch. "You offered me the house last season, Father. Have you changed your mind?"

The Duke of Blackbern shook his head. He stepped forward and deftly urged his son toward the door, placing distance between Mathias and the duchess. "No, of course I haven't. The house is yours to do with as you like."

Mathias cast a wary glance at his silent mother. "St. Lyon and Thorn are waiting for me. Shall we discuss business after supper?"

"We can talk about the estate tomorrow," the duke said easily. "Why don't you run along and see to your friends."

His father did not give him any choice. The door was closed in his face before he could speak another word to his mother. Mathias took a deep breath and slowly exhaled. The worst part of the visit was over. With a smile forming on his lips, he walked off to look for his friends.

Inside the library, the Duke of Blackbern turned away from the door and headed back to his wife's side. "How angry are you?" he quietly inquired.

The question cleared Imogene's unfocused gaze and brought her chin up. "Why would I be angry?"

"That I offered Mathias use of the house without telling you. I would have mentioned it earlier—" He swallowed the rest of his excuse when she abruptly raised her hand to silence him.

She turned away, wrapping her arms around her waist in a small gesture of comfort that cut him to the quick.

"I should have burned the house to the ground."

The emotion in his voice caused her to look at him. Imogene sat down on the sofa. With her arms still crossed, she stroked her upper arms with her fingers. "You made that offer to me twenty-four years ago. If you recall, I turned you down."

Tristan moved to the sofa and dropped to his knees in front of her. "This is hurting you."

She shook her head in denial, but her eyes were wet with unshed tears. "It is a house. Just a house."

Helpless, he did not know whom she was attempting to convince. "I could rescind my offer. I could tell him that I have already rented it."

That earned him a wry smile. "You rarely rent the house. Besides, he has already inspected it. He will know you are lying to him, and he will begin to question you about it."

"The lad will have other things to worry about if he challenges my dictates," Tristan said gruffly. He was furious with himself. In spite of her assurances over the years, he should have known that the thought of any of their children residing in that particular house would be upsetting to her. "Forgive me." He lowered his face to her skirts and inhaled, drawing comfort from her scent. Tristan shut his eyes at her touch.

"There is nothing to forgive, love. We discussed this years ago, when it was so obvious that Mathias was craving his independence. He is spending less time with us, so I knew—" She trembled.

Tristan lifted his face from her skirt and clasped her hands.

"It is merely a house. Has allowing it to stand empty year after year changed the past?"

Old hate simmered just beneath the surface. "No. Still, it's not too late to burn the damn house to the ground."

A soft laugh or sob escaped her lips. "I believe you,

but my feelings haven't changed. That house was your mother's legacy to you, and now you will pass it to our son. Besides, the property is too valuable to torch it because I was startled by Mathias's announcement."

Tristan reached up and cupped her face. "You were more than startled, love."

Imogene did not bother to deny it. "We cannot watch over him as we did when he was a boy. I worry that . . . someone might say something to him."

"It has been twenty-four years, Imogene. There is no reason for anyone to dredge up the past."

Tristan pulled her onto his lap and she offered him no resistance as he shifted his position to make her more comfortable. Imogene wiggled closer until her face was pressed against the side of his neck. Neither one of them spoke, but his thoughts drifted to the house he had inherited from his mother. The old place was a stately relic of his wild youthful indiscretions and painful memories. Twenty-four years ago, he wanted to raze the damn place. One night, in a fit of drunken anger, he had set fire to his mother's old bedchamber, and the east wing of the house was destroyed in the fire. Imogene had not questioned his motives. It was at her insistence that the wing had been rebuilt. To this day, his wife had never returned to the house. Tristan avoided it as well.

He must have been foxed when he invited Mathias to use the property as he saw fit.

Tristan tightened his hold on his wife. He was willing to let her have her way about the house, but if the situation became too upsetting, he intended to do something about it. Mathias could make other arrangements.

His thoughts took a decidedly darker turn as another name drifted into his mind like musty air in a room that has been locked for years. More than the house, this individual was the source of Imogene's concerns. This angered

Tristan more than he was prepared to reveal to his wife. It was also a reminder that he had failed her once. Never again. Not her. Not his family. If *he* dared to approach Mathias or any other member of his family, the bastard was a dead man.

# Chapter Three

Lady Tempest Elizabeth Brant could not have imagined a more perfect day. The sun was unencumbered with clouds, the air was fragrant and pleasing, and the occasional breeze kept the temperature temperate. With her drawing notebook under her arm, she stood and shook out her skirts. Her brother Oliver had set up a chair and easel so she might continue working on the landscape she had sketched the other day. However, she had grown restless after an hour. She decided a walk would ease some of the stiffness in her limbs.

Her actions had not gone unnoticed by her younger sisters. Arabella glanced up from the book in her hands and squinted at her since the sunlight was in her eyes. At nineteen, she had grown into quite a beauty. Her blond hair and hazel eyes made people comment often on how much she resembled their mother. Beside her sat their ten-year-old sister, Augusta. The youngest Brant was lying on her stomach as she examined an ant or some other insect that had caught her attention. Sitting in a nearby chair was their chaperone, Mrs. Sheehan. The thirty-two-year-old widow had been hired to chaperone the Brant girls six months earlier.

"And just where are you going, Lady Tempest?"

Mrs. Sheehan inquired without glancing up from her sewing.

"Not far," she replied, patting her notebook. "I thought I would explore a bit to see if there are any interesting plants to sketch."

Augusta smiled up at her. "Are you going to pull off your shoes and stockings to wade into the river?"

"Certainly not," Tempest replied, knowing it was precisely what Augusta would do if left alone. The small river was scenic, but too shallow for anything but small boats. "I have little desire to have mud drying between my toes for the rest of the day."

Augusta giggled because she sounded haughty, even to her ears.

"Do you want company?" Arabella asked. "I can finish my book later."

Tempest shook her head. "No need. I am really just looking for an excuse to stretch my legs."

"Are you still mad at Oliver for abandoning us?" Augusta asked.

"I was not mad at him."

Tempest had been mildly vexed with her brother. He had been sullen for days, and was prone to lash out at anyone who deigned to speak to him. Details were scarce, but there was a nasty bruise on his forehead. Oliver had been fighting, which was nothing new. Although he was, on most days, an agreeable brother, he had the devil's own temperament.

He was not the only one in the family who was quick to anger. Oliver had been fighting again with their father, the Marquess of Norgrave. Her brother refused to talk about what he had done, but when the marquess ordered his son to watch over his sisters, Oliver had viewed the command as a punishment. Perhaps it had something to do with the fight. The particulars did not really matter, she supposed. Oliver had escorted them to the river. Once they had settled in, he unhitched one of the horses and announced that he would return in a few hours.

It was his way of obeying and yet defying their father.

Oliver knew his sisters would not say a word, and Mrs. Sheehan was too smitten with the young earl to betray him. Since her brother did not elaborate on where he was going, Tempest assumed he had left them to seek out his friends or one of the local women he was currently bedding.

Tempest was not supposed to be aware of such things, but she was two-and-twenty years old and the eldest daughter of the Marquess and Marchioness of Norgrave. It was astounding what a lady could learn if she paid attention.

"Besides, Oliver did not abandon us. He will be back."

"Of course he will," Mrs. Sheehan murmured, giving Tempest a quick assessing glance. "Aren't you forgetting something, lass?"

Tempest frowned. She had her sketching notebook and pencil. "I do not think so."

The older woman tapped her temple with a finger. "Your bonnet, love. You won't catch a fine London gent with your face covered in freckles."

Tempest walked over to her chair and retrieved her straw bonnet.

Augusta giggled. "I don't think my sister can run fast enough to catch a gent."

"Maybe I don't wish to catch one," Tempest said lightly.

Unwittingly, her younger sibling echoed a similar observation made by their father. Now that Arabella was old enough to enjoy the London season, her father had teased that his eldest daughter's prospects would be cut in half, since many gentlemen preferred young brides fresh from the nursery. The marquess had not intended to be cruel, but the comment cut her to the quick. Arabella was younger and prettier than she.

"Hush," Arabella said, giving their younger sibling a pinch on her leg.

Augusta squealed in outrage. "Mrs. Sheehan, my sister is a villain!"

The red-haired chaperone chuckled. "Is she now?"

"Quit teasing Tempest," Arabella ordered in harsh tones. "If our sister sets her sights on a gentleman, she is fully capable of catching him—even if she has a freckled face."

At the subtle reminder, Tempest grimaced and placed her bonnet on her head, but she did not tie the long ribbons. She walked away from her arguing siblings and Mrs. Sheehan, their voices fading as the distance between them increased.

Wading through some of the taller grass, she followed a small meandering trail that took her to the water's edge before it veered away to higher ground. She eventually came to a large flattened boulder. Overly warm from her exercise, she sat down and placed her sketch notebook and reticule beside her on the stone surface. She removed her bonnet and waved it in front of her face. The tall grass buffeted by the spring breeze provided the perfect blind. Unless someone floated by her on a small sailboat, no one would even know she was there.

Tempest stared down at her feet. Her shoes were slightly muddy, but they could be cleaned. She thought of Augusta and her taunt about wading into the shallow water.

*Should I?*

Charlotte Brant, Marchioness of Norgrave, would not approve of such unladylike behavior. Tempest sat quietly for a few minutes and contemplated the odds of being caught. They were practically zero. Grinning, she quickly removed her shoes. She lifted her skirt and petticoat high enough for her to reach her garters and untied them. Finally barefoot, she held on to her skirts as she cautiously walked to the edge of the water. The water still held a chill, but it felt absolutely wonderful.

Tempest closed her eyes and tipped her face upward, enjoying the contrasting heat on her face and the coolness of the water. It was a decadent feeling as she defied convention. Her father had high expectations for his eldest daughter, and so far she had managed to disappoint him. Last season, her father thought he had found the perfect gentleman for her. What Lord Rinehart lacked in good looks, he had gained in title and wealth. The marriage would have provided the marquess with certain political advantages, and Tempest had been agreeable to her father's plans.

There had been only one problem.

The gentleman fell in love with another lady and banns had been posted before the Marquess of Norgrave could interfere.

Naturally, her father had laid the blame at her feet.

Tempest managed to roll her eyes, even while they were tightly shut. Her hair had been too dark because the gentleman had preferred a fair-haired lady. Her tongue was too sharp, for what man desired a lady more intelligent than himself. Then there was her height. She had been precisely three inches taller than her prospective husband, which her father claimed had much to do with her choice of shoes. It was ridiculous, but she had held her tongue. There was no point in arguing with her father when disappoint weighed heavily in his heart. He proposed that she slouch the next time she encountered a gentleman shorter than she. After last season, she doubted she could do much worse to embarrass her father.

Her eyes snapped open at a shout of surprise. Instinctively, she backed away from the water. The shout was followed by masculine laughter. Were they laughing at her? No, she was being foolish. If she could not see them, then they were unaware of her presence. Pushing deeper into the grass, she realized that she was standing on a finger of land that jutted out, bending the river and obscuring her view of the other side. As quietly as she was capable of, she walked to the other side. Tempest winced at the occasional sharp rock and sticks that scratched and tried to poke holes into the soles of her feet. She used her hand to sweep aside some of the tall grass, but what she glimpsed made her drop to her knees and hold her breath.

There were three half-naked men on the other side of the river's bank.

"It's freezing, you arse!" the dark-haired gentleman who was submerged to his neck complained to his companions.

Shirtless, the man with dark blond hair sat near the water's edge as he removed his boots and stockings. "You should never have accepted the bet!"

Another gentleman stood between his two friends. Wearing only buckskin breeches, he was slowing working his way into the deeper portion of the river. "Stop complaining, Thorn. You should join us, Chance. The water is quite invigorating."

"If freezing your testicles off is your definition of invigorating!" the man called Thorn shouted back, causing his friends to erupt in laughter.

Tempest was not offended by their coarse talk. She had heard worse from her brother and father when they were unaware that she was listening. From her view, she could distinguish that all three gentlemen were young and possessed well-formed physiques. The heat blooming in her face had nothing to do with the sun.

"Damn me, Chance, you are a braver man than I," the brown-haired man said as he moved closer to the fellow who had lost the wager.

His comment made little sense to Tempest until she noticed the man at the riverbank was removing his breeches. He turned to discard his clothing and presented her with a nice profile of his backside. She hastily covered her mouth to muffle her high-pitched squeak of surprise and averted her gaze away from the gentlemen.

Her heart received another shock when she saw Arabella standing behind her. "Dear heavens, you gave me such a fright. What are you doing here?" Tempest whispered furiously.

"I thought you might like some company," Arabella replied, her eyes narrowing at her sister's dirty bare feet and the high color in her cheeks. "What are you doing? And why are we whispering?"

"It is better if you do not know," Tempest said. *Better for me.* How could she explain away that she had been watching three half-naked gentlemen? Worse, Arabella might tell Mrs. Sheehan. Or her mother. "We should leave."

"No," her sister countered. Arabella moved closer and crouched down so their heads were level. "Not until I see what you are looking at. Is it a rare bird?" Her eyes widened as she peeked through the tall grass. A soft noise that sounded like a hiccup escaped her lips. She clapped her hand over her mouth and glared at Tempest.

However, she was not looking at her younger sister. Through their natural blind, she was disheartened to see that they had been discovered. The three gentlemen were staring back at her, their expressions of various levels of surprise and indignation as they realized that they were not alone. The man called Chance quickly covered his genitals with his bare hands.

"You there! Come out!" the dark-haired one demanded. He stood, revealing more of his torso.

"Good grief, he is planning to swim to this side!" Tempest scrambled to her feet and pushed her sister forward. "Hurry, before they catch us!"

Thankfully, Arabella was obedient, and the two women retraced their steps out of the grass. At the boulder, Tempest slipped her feet into her shoes and grabbed her stockings. Her sister retrieved her sketching notebook and pencils.

"Keep to the trail, Arabella," she said, glancing back even while she nudged her sister forward.

"Do you think they are following?"

Poor Arabella was terrified. Tempest tried to think of something that would reassure her. "I highly doubt they saw anything more than a glimpse of clothing in this tall grass, and it would be foolhardy for them to pursue us without their clothes and boots. By the time they dress and retrieve their horses, we shall be gone. With luck, they will assume it was a few boys playing a prank on them."

"And what if they come across our little group? What are you going to say to Mrs. Sheehan?" her sister demanded, sounding winded from their hasty retreat. "Oh no . . . what will we tell Oliver?"

"Don't be a goose!" Tempest snapped. "If anyone questions us, we will lie."

"But—"

She gritted her teeth. "Do you want to be the one who explains this embarrassing debacle to father?"

"No," her sister replied, slowing down as she considered the possible punishments that they might receive for their outrageous behavior. "If father learns of this, he may not permit us to join him and mother in London."

It was an appealing thought. Tempest shook her head. "He will never know if you keep your mouth shut and leave the lying to me." As an afterthought, she added, "If it comes to that." Tempest abruptly halted and listened. A minute later, she asked, "Do you hear anything?"

Arabella listened. "No. What do you hear?"

She did not hear the sounds of three angry half-naked gentlemen thrashing their way through the tall grass in search of them. "Nothing. I told you that they wouldn't chase after us. Catch your breath while I put on my stockings. Mrs. Sheehan will have questions if she sees my bare legs."

Her sister sighed. "She wouldn't be the only one with questions. Do you want to explain to me why I caught you spying on three gentlemen?"

Tempest laughed. Arabella sounded peevish, but she could not muster a lot of guilt, because her own heart was pounding in her throat. She sat down and roughly pulled off her shoes. "What do you think I was doing? Our father has high expectations for me this season, so I thought I would try my hand at finding a husband. I don't know about you, but I think it went smoothly." She glared up at her sibling as she tugged on her stocking. "Any other foolish questions? No? Excellent!"

The brisk walk back to their camp was done in silence.

# Chapter Four

"A couple of wenches?" Thorn buttoned the front flap on his breeches. "Are you certain?"

St. Lyon chuckled and shook his head.

"I saw a woman with dark hair," Mathias muttered for the third time. He pulled his shirt over his head. "She was speaking to someone. I did not get a good look, but I suppose it could have been a man."

"Maybe it was a lovers' tryst?" St. Lyon suggested.

Mathias's gaze searched the riverbank for some sign that their unwelcome observers had returned, but they were alone. "I doubt it. All of us swam over and searched the area. The grass is rough and the ground uneven and muddy. No, someone was watching us."

And he intended to find out why. His confrontation with Marcroft and his parents' reaction to his announcement that he would be residing separately from the family had left him edgy for days. Oh, his mother and father had spoken enthusiastically about him claiming his grandmother's house and their plans for London, but something seemed off balance. Mathias could not explain to his friends the reasons for his unease, but he trusted his instincts.

He sensed his parents were keeping something from him.

"You think Marcroft had anything to do with this?"

Mathias casually rubbed some of the dried mud off his boot. "Perhaps." He grimaced. "Though it does seem unlikely. I can't see him skulking in the tall grass just to get a glimpse of our white arses."

Thorn laughed. "So do you want to ride on and see if we can catch up to our little mischief-makers or do you want to head home?"

"There is still plenty of daylight. I see no reason why we should not enjoy the day," he replied, but his friends were not fooled by his careless tone.

He was eager to catch up to their little spies.

Much to Tempest's relief, she and Arabella returned to the camp without incident. Mrs. Sheehan looked up from her sewing long enough to assess that the girls were unharmed before her gaze lowered to tend to her work. Augusta had fallen asleep on the blanket.

Everything seemed so tranquil. If not for her soggy hem and the streaks of dirt on her skirt, Tempest could almost believe she had just awoken from a bad dream.

"Not a word to anyone," she whispered to Arabella before she reclaimed her chair, which was positioned in front of the easel. Her sister returned to her book, content to forget the entire incident.

Tempest opened her sketching notebook to a blank page and retrieved the pencil that had rolled off her lap and onto the ground. She was too shaken to focus on her landscape, so she absently sketched while she tried not to count the minutes.

Fifteen minutes later, her heartbeat had slowed to its natural pace. The three men had allowed them to escape. There would be no awkward confrontation. What had occurred had truly been an accident. Tempest had been unaware of the men's presence until she overheard their laughter. Of course, it had been wicked of her to spy on them. She was confident she would have slipped away without notice if her sister had not startled her.

Almost an hour had passed when the last of the tension eased from her shoulders. Tempest and Arabella had been spared, and she silently sent her gratitude to the heavens. Her gaze lowered to the pencil drawing she had been working on. Her riverbank scene included three male figures. Their modesty remained intact from their varied poses, but even her rudimentary outlines revealed the men were unclothed. A half smile formed on her lips. The prudent thing would be to burn the drawing when she returned home.

The squeak of leather and a welcoming nicker from a horse heralded her brother's return. Tempest raised her head to greet Oliver, but the words dried in her throat. There were three gentlemen approaching them on horseback. At first glance, all three men were handsome in their own individual way, she thought, as they guided their horses away from the river's edge and toward Tempest. Their horses and the expensive saddles complemented the air of confidence that enveloped her even from a distance. Their visitors were noblemen, and that knowledge should have been a comfort, since she and her sisters were without their protector. Nevertheless, all she felt in her stomach was a growing dread. Earlier, when she had come across the three half-naked gentlemen in the river, she had not gotten a good look at their faces. The damp buckskin breeches two of the men wore were proof enough that she was about to meet the three men she had hoped to elude.

"Good afternoon, ladies." The blond gentleman she recognized as the one who had removed his breeches tipped his hat in greeting. There was no anger or suspicion in his clear gray eyes as he studied her as intently as she did him. Beneath his hat, she knew his medium blond hair lightened near his temples and the top of his head. His symmetrical features and strong square jaw added strength and character to his face. Otherwise, his features would have been too feminine. Her gaze did not linger on the bruises on his cheek. She was too familiar with unpredictable males and their desire to resolve most problems with their fists. They revealed that the man in front of her was not afraid to mar his handsome face or fight for what he wanted. It would be unwise to under-estimate this gentleman.

Tempest abruptly shut her notebook.

"Good afternoon, gents," Mrs. Sheehan said genially. "A lovely day for a ride, is it not?"

"Aye, madam," the dark-haired gentleman replied. His build was leaner than his friend's, but his dispassionate, almost bored expression hinted that very few things surprised him. His dark green gaze surveyed the area they had chosen for the afternoon. "It appears you ladies have claimed a pretty spot."

"Indeed." The whisper of fabric, and their chaper-one had put aside her sewing. Mrs. Sheehan rose from her chair and approached the three gentlemen. She placed herself in front of Tempest. "Have you traveled far?"

"A few hours," was the blond-haired gentleman's vague reply. Tempest wondered if he was their leader, since the other two seemed content to allow him to direct the con-versation. It was disconcerting the way his gaze kept returning to her. "Are you ladies alone?"

Before Mrs. Sheehan could reply, Tempest stood. "My brother is with us."

Three sets of masculine brows lifted at what they per-ceived to be an obvious lie.

"Of course, he is not currently present," she hastily amended. "He took one of the horses to explore the area.

Perhaps do a little hunting. We expect him to return at any time now."

It was her way of letting them know that they were not so vulnerable as they appeared. For protection, Mrs. Sheehan had a small pistol concealed in her sewing basket, which was doing her little good, since she had left the basket next to the chair.

The blond gentleman stared down at Tempest as if he could deduce the truth from her expression. She kept her face deliberately blank. Even if he suspected that she had been the one to spy on them while they bathed in the river, he had no proof.

Mrs. Sheehan moved closer. Boldly, she placed her hand on the neck of the blond gentleman's horse and stroked the animal. "And who might you handsome fellows be?"

Good grief, Tempest recognized that particular tone. Was their chaperone actually flirting with the men? Tempest glanced back at Arabella, who merely shrugged.

The blond looked at his friends, and the three of them exchanged grins. Clearing his throat, he said, "You may call me Chance, madam."

Tempest did not need to see Mrs. Sheehan's face to deduce she was smiling like a besotted fool.

"Chance." The widow sighed. "What a delightful name. And who are your companions?"

"They call me St. Lyon, ma'am," the dark-brown-haired gentleman to the right of Chance said, touching the brim of his hat. His dark blue gaze and engaging grin seemed sincere.

"I'm Thorn," replied the gentleman with the dark hair and dark green eyes. He appeared to be less friendly than the other two.

"May we be so bold as to inquire after your name, dear lady?" Chance solicitously asked.

"Mrs. Sheehan." Not wanting any misunderstandings, she added, "Recently widowed."

"Eight years, I believe," muttered Tempest under her breath, earning a sharp reproachful glare from the chaperone.

Thorn coughed into his fist. Was he laughing at her?

When Mrs. Sheehan shifted her gaze back to Chance, she had recovered her good humor. "It feels recent. The good ones are always missed."

Tempest could not understand why the older woman's fawning over the three handsome gentlemen annoyed her. It was none of her business whom the lady flirted with, but her simpering behavior was embarrassing.

For some reason, Chance's gaze switched to her. "Have you ladies done any exploring?"

"No," Arabella blurted out.

"Some," Tempest corrected, glancing back at her sister. Arabella was a terrible liar. "Although not too far, since this is one of my favorite spots."

She and Mrs. Sheehan both took a cautious step backwards when Chance dismounted from his horse. The other two gentlemen followed his actions. St. Lyon grabbed the bridle of Chance's horse.

"May I?"

Tempest was so flustered by his presence that she nodded. He was larger than she originally believed. He was an imposing figure as he turned to look at the landscape displayed on the easel, which she had been working on before her fateful encounter with the gentlemen.

He looked at her. "You did this?"

She did not quite trust her tongue, so she inclined her head to signal her acknowledgement.

Chance glanced back at her unfinished picture. "You have a good eye for scale and color. My younger sister has a capable hand for simple sketches but has never mastered watercolors."

Warmed by the compliment, she said, "Thank you, Mr. Chance."

Thorn and St. Lyon chuckled. She looked at them and wondered if she had misheard their friend's name.

"Just Chance, my lady," he said, bestowing upon her a quick grin that sent her pulse racing.

"Who are you?" Augusta asked, her voice groggy from sleep. She sat up and eyed the three gentlemen with curiosity. "Are you friends of our brother?"

"And who is your brother, little one?" Thorn asked, his face softening as he spoke to her younger sister.

"Och, where are my manners!" Mrs. Sheehan exclaimed. "Gentlemen, these are my young charges, Lady Tempest, Lady Arabella, and Lady Augusta."

They were miles from a ballroom, but the introduction compelled Tempest and Arabella to curtsy. Augusta yawned.

Her sister's laziness did not go unnoticed by their chaperone. "Present yourself, lass. Do not shame your sisters or your family." To prove she meant business, Mrs. Sheehan marched over to the youngest Brant and helped her stand. "Our visitors are Chance, Thorn, and St. Lyon. And what do you have to say for yourself?"

"Good afternoon, gentlemen," Augusta said sullenly. She curtsied, which prompted the gentlemen to respectfully incline their heads.

"Would you care for a glass of cider?" her youngest sister asked.

Tempest assumed Augusta made the offer because she was thirsty from her long nap.

"A grand idea!" The older woman clapped her hands together with enthusiasm. "The jug and spare cups are in the coach. Would you care for some, gents?"

"You are gracious hostesses, ladies. I will confess that my throat is a little parched. I wouldn't mind a cup." Thorn handed his reins to St. Lyon, who accepted his new role as groom with aplomb. Then Thorn walked over to Augusta and extended his arm. "My lady, would you accompany me to the coach?"

Her sister giggled with delight at the gentleman's attention. Whether or not he desired it, he had made a new friend. Augusta placed her delicate hand on his arm, and they followed Mrs. Sheehan to the coach.

"I wouldn't mind a glass," St. Lyon announced to no one in particular. When he noticed Chance was still staring at Tempest, he realized that he was on his own. "Uh, Lady Arabella. Perhaps you can assist me. Can you recommend a place for me to secure the horses?"

Arabella cast a wary glance at Tempest. Out of loyalty, she did not want to leave her sister's side, but she could not come up with a good excuse. "Yes, of course. If you need me, Sister, you only have to call out."

Uncomfortable with having attracted Chance's keen interest, Tempest watched Arabella and St. Lyon walk away with the three horses trailing after them.

"Your sister seemed distressed to leave you alone with me. I wonder why?" he whispered in her ear.

Tempest started at his unexpected closeness. Her lips parted as she was prepared to reprimand him for his impudence, but what she saw in his hand prompted her to swallow the insult.

Chance was holding her straw bonnet.

He should have been angry with her. Lady Tempest and possibly her sister had spied on him and his friends, but her woebegone expression when she noticed he was in possession of her bonnet was incredibly endearing. When he had stuffed it beneath his waistcoat, he had no idea if he would ever track down its owner.

Mathias had not expected their spy to be so attractive. With hair the color of rich coffee and skin as smooth and flawless as cream, she had large hazel-colored eyes and full pink lips. He was usually drawn toward more exotic forms of beauty, but he could not deny that he was intrigued.

Lady Tempest stared at it as if it were a viper. "Where did you find it?"

An unnatural pinkish tint was splashed across her cheeks and nose. Too much sun could be to blame because she had been deprived of her straw bonnet, or perhaps she was embarrassed that she had been soundly caught by him.

She was not the only one who was uncomfortable. It was disconcerting to know that he had shamelessly stripped down in front of her and she had gotten a good look at his cock.

The realization was enough to make him blush. "I discovered this rather charming item near a large boulder close to where my friends and I had decided to take a swim." He held out the crushed bonnet and she snatched it from his hands as if his touch had fouled it. "Since the bonnet belongs to you, I can only conclude that it was you who was concealed in the tall grass on the opposite side of the river. Mayhap your sister, too?"

In a nervous gesture, Lady Tempest grabbed her long braid and pulled it forward. The dark glossy braided rope beckoned like a spoken invitation for him to stroke it. However, when he reached out to test the weight of her braid, she slapped his fingers. His mouth thinned with annoyance. "The grass did not entirely conceal your dark hair. So do not bother to deny that you were there. What did *you* see?"

Mathias preferred petite ladies who were soft in all the right places. Tall, gangly-limbed females were often awkward creatures who seemed uncomfortable in their own skin, but Lady Tempest was not clumsy or too thin. She was only five inches shorter than his admirable stature of six feet, and her confidence hadn't faltered until he presented her with her lost bonnet. It was a relief that he did not have to strain the muscles in his neck to observe her reaction to his question. Her inability to look him in the eyes and her visible distress told him that whatever explanation she was about to offer was more than likely to be a clever lie.

"You can tell me the truth," he assured her, lowering his voice in an attempt to soothe her. "If you are worried about Mrs. Sheehan—"

"I am not worried!"

He smiled at her indignation. One could not help but admire her spirit. "I can be generous if you are honest with me. Your chaperone does not even have to know that you have been a very wicked girl," Mathias teased.

Impotent fury burned in her hazel eyes. "What are you implying? That I deliberately spied on you and your friends? Do you think so highly of yourself?"

Mathias scowled, but his fierce expression eased when he figured out the source of her outrage. "Got an eyeful for your mischief, eh? I'll wager you have never seen a naked man, let alone three."

"Ugh, you are vile and arrogant! What gentleman removes his breeches in public with no regard to whoever might have been passing by, I ask you?" she demanded, shaking her crushed bonnet at him.

"No more arrogant than the lady who hid in the grass to watch three men disrobe. Did you turn away in disgust or did you call to your sister and invite her to watch the spectacle?"

Her eyes widened. "It wasn't like that at all," she said, her eyes bright with heat and shame. "I thought I was alone when I sat down on the boulder. I took off my shoes so I could wade into the river. Then I heard laughter."

Mathias had not set out to make her cry, and Lady Tempest had the look of a lady who was struggling to tether her tears. "You were curious," he said, trying to soften the misdeed.

She exhaled slowly. "At first, I was merely curious about the source of the laughter. I had no wish to intrude, and since I was alone, it seemed prudent not to reveal my presence. I pushed my way through the tall grass and it was then that I realized that you and your friends were—" She fluttered her hand since she had no intention of speaking of their nakedness.

"But you stayed?"

"No!" Worried that their discussion might be overheard, she glanced at the coach in the distance. Satisfied that no one was paying attention, she continued. "I turned to leave, but my sister startled me. I didn't expect her to follow me. Arabella wanted to know what had caught my interest. She thought I had found a rare bird."

Mathias tipped his head back and laughed. Two innocent ladies had definitely encountered something rare. "Of course, you tried to stop her."

"Naturally. However, Arabella was insistent—Oh, you can figure out the rest. I panicked and told my sister to run when you called out to us. I prayed all the way back to our camp that you wouldn't pursue us."

He had no doubt. "My apologies for ruining your splendid escape."

"Arabella and I ran most of the way. When you took so long to find us, I thought we had eluded you."

He erroneously had concluded that their spies had

nefarious purposes. "You might have if I had not discovered your straw bonnet."

A look of disbelief flashed across her face. "You searched for us because of my bonnet?"

Mathias would not have been comforted by the motivations that had driven him and his companions to look for her. A lusty country miss would have soothed his wounded pride. "Partly. I will admit that I was curious about the owner."

Lady Tempest sighed. "I suppose I owe you and your friends an apology for my intrusion."

"Your remorse is enough. I will explain everything to Thorn and St. Lyon."

His generosity seemed to lighten her mood. "You have my gratitude, sir. If Mrs. Sheehan learned of this, she would feel it was her duty to tell my brother, and he would not find any of this amusing. I know my brother. He would find some reason to blame you and your companions for my blunder."

"The gent sounds like a charming fellow," Mathias said dryly. "Perhaps I know him."

Lady Tempest shrugged daintily. "He has never mentioned the name Chance, but Oliver does not feel it necessary to share his private life with his younger sisters."

"Oliver?"

"Oliver Brant, Earl of Marcroft." She had glanced away and missed the recognition and dismay in his eyes. His face was expressionless when her gaze switched back to him. "Are you acquainted with my brother?"

He could not believe his bad luck. Lady Tempest was a Brant. He could not imagine that she would be happy to learn that he was a Rooke. "I do not believe so."

She tilted her head to the side as she studied his face.

"I do not mean to be rude, but I could not help but notice that you have bruises on your face."

Mathias snorted. "Do I? So nice of you to bring them to my attention." *Particularly since it was your brother's fist that did the damage.*

Lady Tempest pursed her lips. "My brother has bruises on his face, too."

He had already deduced that the lady was intelligent. Nor was he pleased with her connecting him with her dastardly brother. "Bruises are as common as birthmarks, my lady."

She ignored his dismissive tone. "Are you positive that you do not know my brother? He won't speak of it, but it's obvious that he was in a fight. Is that how you received that colorful bruise on your cheek? Were you brawling?"

A cold wind blew up his spine. Lady Tempest had mentioned that her brother would be returning. He had no intention of waiting for Marcroft or any other member of the Brant family to appear.

"Your brother is a stranger to me, my lady. I prefer to keep it that way. Now, if you will excuse me, my friends and I have a long ride home." Mathias formally bowed and walked away from the bemused young woman.

He could not have been more stunned if the lady had punched him in the face. Marcroft was her brother. The Marquess of Norgrave was her father. Mathias was so angry, he was tempted to march back and shake her for being related to his father's enemy. His enemy. Lady Tempest was his enemy.

By God, he wished he had never met her.

# Chapter Five

Mathias waited several miles before he revealed to his companions that Lady Tempest was one of the infamous Brants.

"Come on, Chance. This is a jest. The pretty chit is not Norgrave's get. I refuse to believe it," Thorn said, assuming Mathias was amusing himself at their expense.

"Believe it, Cousin. Lady Tempest mentioned that her brother, the Earl of Marcroft had bruises similar to mine." He gritted his teeth as he recalled their conversation. "She didn't ask me outright, but it was apparent that she wondered if I was responsible for her poor brother's injuries."

"You were," St. Lyon added, sounding too cheerful for the occasion.

"This is quite unexpected," Thorn said, still not convinced Mathias was telling the truth. "What are the odds of meeting a Brant out here?"

"Better than one might assume, considering that we spent twenty minutes with three of them," Mathias muttered.

"And yet, Norgrave's progeny were well-mannered and nary a hint of fang or tail," St. Lyon observed, unable to resist poking Mathias about the notorious feud between the Rookes and Brants. "Aside from Marcroft, of course."

"Of course," Mathias echoed in a light mocking tone.

The news that Lady Tempest and her sisters were Brants had unsettled him. Over the years, he had heard that the Marquess of Norgrave had sired numerous children, both legitimate and baseborn. He cast a side glance at St. Lyon. There had been rumors that his friend's mother had been one of the marquess's countless lovers, and the speculation within the ton was that Norgrave was the sire of her husband's heir. The earl and the countess fervently worked to quell such whispers when they surfaced from time to time. However, no one could deny that St. Lyon could have been mistaken for one of Marcroft's distant cousins. If there was any truth to the gossip, St. Lyon was content to ignore it.

Thorn guided his horse closer so he did not have to shout. "Do you think the ladies will mention us to Marcroft?"

"It's a possibility, though Lady Tempest seemed more worried about her brother finding out that she was caught spying on half-naked men," Mathias said as he reflected on the fear she'd tried to conceal from him. "The Brants may litter the countryside with bastards, but their females are protected from their baser instincts."

"More's the pity," said St. Lyon with an exaggerated sigh escaping his lips. "If I had known who was watching us, I might have removed my breeches, too. You certainly made an impression on Lady Tempest."

Had he? The viscount was being ridiculous. "It was nothing like that. The chit could barely look at me once she realized who we were."

Mathias could tell Lady Tempest was embarrassed by the incident and her own unladylike behavior. Given her family name, he should assume that she was adept at deception, but her discomfort and remorse appeared genuine. He had been prepared to be magnanimous and forgive her until she revealed the name of her brother.

Her family name.

Christ, what a muddle!

"That lady knew exactly who we were when she saw us." St. Lyon chuckled. "Not surprising, since she glimpsed every inch of us. The only thing she hasn't figured out is that you are one of those awful Rookes."

Mathias's lips twitched as he tried not to smile. "We Rookes are not awful."

"I'll wager the Brants say the same thing."

"Well, they are wrong. There is no such thing as an honest Brant," he said, mentally banishing the vision of Lady Tempest's guileless face.

"I have to disagree," Thorn confessed. "Lady Arabella and Lady Augusta were rather sweet and welcoming. Out of loyalty, our family has never associated with Lord and Lady Norgrave, but I have no quarrel with the daughters."

Mathias almost choked on his own spittle. "If you value our friendship, I pray you will not confess your new affection for the Brant daughters to my father. I would hate to give my own cousin the direct cut."

The viscount shifted in his saddle. "Your father is not that bad."

"Yes, he is," Mathias and Thorn said at the same time. He added, "My father has never faltered in his hatred for the marquess. Over time, his resentment has extended to the man's family."

"Have you ever asked his reasons for it?" St. Lyon asked.

"Of course. My father refuses to speak of it, but I assume it has to do with some slight or debt."

"I once asked my mother about it," St. Lyon admitted. "No one really speaks of it, not even the gossips. Nevertheless, it is rumored that your father and Norgrave both coveted your mother."

His father had commissioned a painting of his mother

after their wedding. The new Duchess of Blackbern had been nineteen years old and recently had given birth to him, although any signs of the pregnancy had been discreetly omitted by the artist. He had no doubt that her beauty and generous heart had enthralled countless gentlemen. It was plausible that the Marquess of Norgrave had fallen in love with her.

"I had guessed as much even as a boy. It must have been a bitter parting when my mother chose my father over the marquess."

"And thus a feud was born. I cannot fathom fighting with either of you over a woman," Thorn said.

"Nor I," replied St. Lyon. "One wench is as good as another."

"My father would heartily disagree." Mathias scratched his bruised cheek. "I think it best if we do not mention our encounter with Norgrave's daughters."

"I agree, though you will owe me another favor," Thorn teased.

St. Lyon grinned. "I'll add this one to my tally, too." His smile faded as he thought of something unpleasant. "What will you do if Marcroft learns that you spoke to his sisters and decides to challenge you?"

Mathias was not worried about the earl. "I will accept his challenge. Your appalling taste in lovers has ensured that I practice regularly."

The viscount growled, "I resent that charge. It isn't *my* fault that they don't always tell me they have a husband."

"I do not fear Marcroft," Mathias continued, ignoring his friend's outburst. "It seems inevitable that I will put a bullet in him someday."

"A pleasant thought," his cousin said wryly. "And what about Lady Tempest?"

"What of the lady?" He was slightly baffled by the

question. As far as he was concerned, there was nothing to be done.

"Are you telling me that you were not aware of the attraction between you and her?"

"There was no attraction, Cousin," he quickly denied. "Unlike you and our good friend, I do not pursue every lady who has fluttered her eyelashes at me."

"Ho, what boldface lie, my good man, but we shall save that debate for another day. Assist me, St. Lyon," Thorn entreated. "Tell me that you noticed it, too."

"Why do you think I looked after our horses? The lady saw no one but our lad Chance." The viscount shook his head. "It was truly quite tragic, but she must have seen something about you that she liked."

"You're both wrong," Mathias said, stubbornly refusing to acknowledge that he had felt anything at all besides mild annoyance and curiosity. "The lady was grateful. If we had revealed her mischief to Mrs. Sheehan, the widow would have told her brother. The poor girl would have received a sound beating from that scoundrel."

"Damn me, you believe Marcroft is capable of raising his fist to his own sisters?"

"I have seen nothing in the man's character that would dissuade me from thinking anything else." He could not recall a single encounter with the surly gentleman in which he did not employ his fists. "With a brother like that, the most spiteful action I could take is to pursue the chit."

Thorn and St. Lyon did not have a clever response.

"So no more talk about Lady Tempest. If fate is kind, we shall never meet again. We are leaving for London in a day, and I intend to dedicate my time there to more pleasurable pursuits."

Thorn cleared his throat. "Lady Arabella told me that her family will be residing in town this season."

Mathias stifled an oath. "Lord and Lady Norgrave

come to London each year. The Brants and the Rookes have managed to avoid any public confrontations. This season will be no different."

"It was simpler times when it was just the Norgraves and the Blackberns. These days, you and your brother Benjamin spend more time in London. How old is your sister Honora?"

"Seventeen," he replied, sensing the direction of his cousin's thoughts. "As well you know."

"Soon she will enter society. And let's not forget the Brants have Marcroft, Lady Tempest, and Lady Arabella," Thorn pointed out. "With more members of the Rooke and Brant families wandering about London this season, it is inevitable that the occasional confrontation with occur."

"God help us all when the rest of the Rooke brood is old enough to enter polite society!" St. Lyon teased, hoping to ease the tension between the two cousins.

Mathias knew Thorn was correct. He just didn't want to admit it. "Let's hope the younger Brants have the good sense to stay out of our way."

The viscount looked startled by his friend's harsh tone. The feud between the Rookes and Brants was none of his business and easy to ignore since he did not have any affection for the Norgrave heir. However, the man would draw the line at being cruel to innocent young women. "Marcroft is a lost cause."

"The earl can go to the devil. If he has any love for his sisters, he will keep them away from me and my family," Mathias said, his face grim and his heart icing as the image of Lady Tempest faded from his mind.

His loyalty belonged to the Duke and Duchess of Blackbern. No one could sway him to betray his family.

Before the evening meal, Tempest eschewed the drawing room for a stroll in the garden. She had spent the entire afternoon in Arabella and Augusta's company, and she was in no mood to listen to her mother's expectations for her when they journeyed to London. The quiet and the beauty of the gardens soothed her. Her thoughts kept returning to what she glimpsed at the river and the curious exchange she had had with Chance. The gentleman had seemed friendly, even though he had thought she deliberately spied on him and his friends. Even flirtatious—that was, until she mentioned her brother.

Chance had denied knowing Oliver, but she suspected the man was not being truthful.

Or perhaps it was the bruises. She had implied that he had been brawling. Had she insulted him by pointing out his injuries?

"Good heavens, I cannot believe I even mentioned it."

"Mentioned what, brat?" asked Oliver as he closed the distance between them. He had changed into fashionable evening attire. However, even his skilled tailor could not conceal her brother's rakish nature.

She wondered if he had dressed for dinner or was planning to depart for the evening. Their father had left the house over an hour ago.

"I thought I am too old to be called brat," Tempest said, holding her hand out. She was pleased when he grasped it.

He pulled her closer and kissed her on the cheek. "I disagree. You have definitely not outgrown all your annoying habits."

"Annoying, you say?" She huffed in feigned outrage. "I take exception to that remark. If you persist in calling me brat, I recommend not doing it in Augusta's presence."

"Why is that?" He held on to her hand as they walked the gravel path.

"She has laid claim to the endearment, and her feelings would be hurt if she thought she was not worthy of a special name," Tempest explained. "With all this talk about London, Augusta is feeling left out."

"No one is leaving her behind," Oliver argued, sounding mildly exasperated.

As the Marquess of Norgrave's heir, he had never been excluded from anything. Even as a child, he had often joined their father in his travels, while his sisters were expected to stay home and tend to their studies.

"Augusta will not be included in many of the amusements when we arrive in London," she said, gesturing toward the marble bench. At his nod, they left the main path and sat down. "Mama has been distracted with all the preparations, and we have seen so little of Papa."

"He has his own distractions," Oliver said, almost sounding amused by his explanation. "Father and I shall be leaving for London a few days before you."

"I am aware of this. If you have a moment, you should visit with Augusta before you depart. It's a small gesture, but she will feel like she is important, too."

It was one of the reasons why she had suggested the afternoon outing with her youngest sibling. Not that her sister was particularly appreciative of their efforts until Chance and his friends had intruded. Augusta had brightened when Thorn paid attention to her. Her reaction was a subtle reminder that their brother had been slowly withdrawing from their lives. They would see less of him in town because he insisted on setting up his own household. Next he would take a wife and fill the house with children.

Tempest softly laughed at where her fanciful thoughts had taken her. In truth, she could not see her brother marrying for a very long time. He was too young, and too much like their sire in temperament. Their father would agree. The marquess had always been quite vocal on the subject of marriage, particularly when it came to his heir.

Nor had their father softened the unpleasant fact that he had married Lady Charlotte Winter out of duress. Her family had insisted on the marriage because they had learned of her affair with the marquess and that a child had been conceived. In uncouth moments, when their father was drunk and full of bitterness that Lady Charlotte had trapped him into marriage, he referred to Oliver as his "child of lust."

Her father called her the "child of duty." Tempest assumed he thought another male child was in order to protect the title. Her mother had given birth to a boy after Arabella, but the child was stillborn. There were three other pregnancies over the years, but none of them had come to fruition until Augusta. If her father had names for her sisters, he kept them to himself.

"Care to share the jest?"

Tempest used the toe of her shoe to nudge some of the gravel. "Just an idle thought. I was thinking of our father."

"Is he lecturing you about last season?" Oliver asked gently. "Or his expectations for this one?"

His attempt to be delicate about the subject revealed that he was well versed in the details. She glanced away to hide her grimace. "Not recently, but I predict he will summon me to the library before he leaves for town. For now, he has left the duty to our mother."

Oliver was broad shouldered, so there was not much room for her on the bench. So when he affectionately bumped against her with his arm, he almost knocked her off her narrow perch. Laughing, he caught her before she landed on her backside. "You have my sympathies, Pest."

Tempest grinned at the old nickname. "You haven't called me Pest in ages."

"I recall the last time I uttered that name, you retaliated by sinking your teeth into my forearm. I had an imprint of your sharp teeth on my arm for months," he said, absently rubbing the abused forearm.

"I highly doubt it was months, Brother. Besides, you were being unkind when you said it." She grasped the edge of the bench and leaned back slightly as she tried to remember more details. "Oh, what were we fighting about? It seemed important at the time."

"Everything is important to a twelve-year-old."

Oliver was nineteen months older than she, and the closeness in their ages meant that he had been her best friend and her worst enemy. When they were younger, they had often quarreled over trivial things. They had managed to put enough scrapes and bruises on each other that their mother had had to separate them while they waited for their father to decide their punishments. Oddly, it was their shared fate that had brought them together again. Frightened, they had put aside their petty grievances and aligned themselves against their mother and father. Even the punishments were more bearable, knowing she was not suffering alone.

Tempest missed the boy who had been her friend and confidant. Once Oliver was sent away to school, everything changed.

She gave him a sidelong glance. "Why are you here?" she asked, keeping the anger from her voice. Oliver wanted something from her or he was here to do their mother's bidding. "You could have stayed with us this afternoon, but chose to dally with some tavern wench."

"What makes you think I was dallying with a tavern wench?" Oliver sounded curious, not angry at her charge.

"The bite mark on your neck."

His hand automatically went to his neck. He was in full evening dress, and the mark in question was concealed by his cravat. "There is no mark."

"I disagree, my dear Croft." She smiled, using the abbreviation of his title. "When you were hitching the horses to the carriage this afternoon, you loosened your cravat. That's when I saw a very large bite mark."

"Maybe it was a scratch?" he suggested, clearly uncomfortable with the subject.

"Your tavern wench has a mouth like a fish." She paused, her eyes twinkling with mischief. "A very large fish."

Oliver reached for her, but she squealed in feigned fright and leaped up from the bench before he could grab her. She picked up her skirt and dashed down the gravel path.

Tempest glanced back, and to her dismay, her brother was catching up quickly. She veered right and ran across the freshly mown grass.

Oliver scooped her up into his arms and spun her about. "I should throttle you, you little pest!" He allowed her feet to touch the ground, but he wrapped his fingers around her shoulders so she could not escape him. "Didn't anyone tell you that a lady should not notice such details as bite marks on her brother's neck?"

She stuck her tongue out. "No, I believe Mama skipped that particular lecture."

He laughed at her unrepentance. "Well, oblige me and do not mention the mark to our mother. I would like to avoid her usual lament about how much I remind her of our father."

His inflection was light, almost teasing; however, she was surprised there was a hint of old pain reflected in his gaze. It was gone before she could comment on it.

Oliver tapped her on the tip of her nose. "And for the sake of honesty, it wasn't a tavern wench. She was a dairymaid."

Tempest rolled her eyes. It made little difference to

her. Due to his youthful good looks and his title, Oliver had half the parish chasing after him. Regrettably, it never occurred to him to refuse any offer.

"Fine. You have my promise," she said, giving in easily since she was feeling generous. "Not a word about your large fish."

He laughed with her, but his expression sobered as his fingers cupped her shoulders. "I did wish to speak to you in private. About what happened this afternoon during my absence."

Tempest shrugged away from his grip. "Mrs. Sheehan told you." She took a step back when he moved closer. "Of course she did. How long did she wait before she tattled to you and Mama?"

Her brother gave her a level stare. "I thought it best that Mrs. Sheehan not speak of it to our mother. I assured her that I would handle this on my own."

"Brilliant. So now you have the right to lecture me?" she said, feeling foolish and manipulated.

He was standing between her and the house. If she tried to slip by him and run to the house, she would lose.

"No lectures, Tempest. I thought you might want to tell me your side of the story," he said, calm in the face of her distress.

"Have you questioned Arabella and Augusta, too?"

Oliver's forehead creased in puzzlement. "Should I?"

Tempest shook her head. She doubted Arabella would have told him about what they had seen at the river. Oliver was too calm to be aware of her accidental encounter with Chance and his friends. "No. Leave them alone. There is no reason to bully them when I am standing right in front of you."

"I am only asking questions. So far, you have not given me any answers."

She sighed. "I suppose Mrs. Sheehan told you that we had visitors this afternoon."

"Yes, she mentioned that three gentlemen were riding along the riverbank and approached when they saw you and the girls." He stared at her with a thoughtful expression that she found unsettling. "More to the point, why didn't you tell me?"

Tempest shrugged. "It slipped my mind."

"Truly? That doesn't sound like you." A half smile softened the hard lines of his mouth. "The girl who can recite portions of her favorite books."

She bit her lower lip as she weighed how much trouble the truth would cause her. "You are correct. The gentlemen didn't slip my mind. I even told Mrs. Sheehan *not* to mention their visit, because I thought you might conclude the gentlemen had approached us for sinister reasons, which was not the case. We offered them cider and exchanged pleasantries, and then they were on their way."

There was no need to mention to Oliver that the three gentlemen had been searching for the person who had watched them as they cooled off in the river.

Or that she had seen Chance without his clothes.

Oliver scowled down at her. "That's all that occurred?"

"Yes. What else did Mrs. Sheehan tell you?" she asked, wishing she had the power to sack her traitorous chaperone.

"The widow tells the same tale."

Tempest tried not to visibly react to his words. "Then you are satisfied. Perhaps we should return to the house."

"Not quite," Oliver said, his low voice sharpening as his eyes narrowed. "Mrs. Sheehan noted that you and one of the gents spent a considerable amount of time talking. In her opinion, there was a familiarity between you. She was concerned that you have met this gentleman before. Perhaps in secret."

Her lips parted in surprise. "I beg your pardon? That's utter rubbish!"

"Is it?" Her brother came closer, and she didn't back away this time. "Mrs. Sheehan thinks otherwise."

"Well, Mrs. Sheehan is wrong. She was either drinking something stronger than cider or she needs a new pair of spectacles." Tempest grasped the front of her skirt and tried to walk by her brother, but he blocked her exit by stepping in front of her. "What else do you want me to say?"

"The truth, damn it! Who is this man? How long have you been meeting him in secret?" Oliver demanded.

"You are the Brant with the secret trysts, Brother." Her hazel eyes darkened and sparked with anger. "Not I." Tempest had had enough. She stepped around her brother and headed toward the house.

His next words caused her to halt. "It will get worse for you if Father learns about it."

She turned around to confront her elder sibling. "Are you threatening me, Croft? Seriously?"

Oliver smoothed back a lock of hair that had fallen in front of his left eye. "Just tell me the truth. Who is this man to you?"

"Why do you keep insisting that Chance means something to me? I told you, I just met him this afternoon. If Mrs. Shee—"

"Chance," he said, cutting her off. "The gentleman Mrs. Sheehan thought you had formed an intimate connection with is Chance."

*Oliver didn't know their names.*

Tempest wished she could howl in frustration at her mistake. She had assumed the chaperone already told her brother the names of the three gentlemen.

"How many times do I have to tell you that I don't

have an intimate connection with the man? Or any of the men?" she asked, her voice lowering into a furious growl.

"What were the names of the other two?"

"See here, Oliver—"

"Names," her brother said, his calm demeanor melting like late winter ice on a hot day. "I want them now."

There was something in his eyes that told her she would not like the consequences if he learned that she had lied to him. "Uh, Thorn . . . and the other one called himself St. Lyon."

She was unprepared for him to grab her by the shoulders and lift her up so that only her toes touched the ground. "Chance, Thorn, and St. Lyon. You little fool, do you know who they are?"

"Oliver, you are hurting me," she said, despising the slight tremor in her voice.

He released her so swiftly, she stumbled to catch her balance.

Tempest eyed him warily. "I wasn't lying. I don't know these men. They didn't even stay long enough for a formal introduction."

"So they didn't know who you were?" He swore when she winced.

"I asked Chance if he knew you." Suddenly the man's reactions all made sense. "I told him your name."

"And what was his response?"

She stared at her brother with an unreadable expression. "He denied knowing you. I assume that was a lie."

"That man who introduced himself as Chance is Mathias Rooke, Marquess of Fairlamb."

Tempest felt the blood drain from her face. "He's a Rooke. Are you certain?"

"Of course I'm bloody certain, Tempest!" Oliver paced in front of her. He tapped his forehead. "Who do you think is responsible for my bruises? The bastard rammed my head into a wooden post."

Tempest resisted pointing out that Chance did not walk away from their skirmish unblemished. "I swear I didn't know he was a Rooke. Were the other two his brothers?"

Her brother shook his head. Had there been a tree nearby, he looked furious enough to punch it. "St. Lyon is Viscount Bastrell. Thorn is the Earl of Kempthorn. He is related to Fairlamb. I believe they are cousins."

"I didn't know."

Tempest glanced down at her hand and realized it was shaking. She was stunned that the gentleman who had flirted with her was a Rooke. Chance had not seemed like a Rooke at all. Not that she knew what a Rooke looked like. The way her father spoke about the Duke of Blackbern, she was expecting the man's heir to be an ugly hunchback creature with blackened teeth and eyes that burned with hellfire. Her family and the Rookes did not share the same social circles. She could have passed the entire Rooke family on the street and never known it.

Good grief—and she had seen a Rooke naked!

Her growing panic must have shown on her face, because her brother pulled her into his arms and hugged her.

"I didn't know."

"I know," he murmured into her hair. "Fairlamb has gone too far. I will call him out for this insult."

Tempest drew back so she could see her brother's face. "No. You cannot."

He laughed evilly. "It will be a pleasure."

"Oliver, he didn't know." She didn't understand this side of her brother. He looked positively bloodthirsty. "Listen, Lord Fairlamb did not know I was a Brant when he approached us. He must have been as stunned as I am now when I told him that my brother was Lord Marcroft."

"It doesn't change anything."

"How can you say that? Of course it does," she argued, assuming she was the only one present who was planning to be sensible about it. "Oliver, once he heard your name, Chance and his friends left immediately. He had no interest in speaking to a Brant."

He had left so abruptly that her feelings were hurt.

"Bastard."

She hadn't known Chance and Oliver shared a history. It was obviously an unpleasant one.

"You cannot challenge him."

Her brother snarled, "Don't be so certain. Fairlamb hates our family. I would not put it past him to have deliberately sought you out."

"No, Oliver—"

"Yes, damn it. You do not know him like I do. If he could hurt our family through you, he would seize the chance."

"You can't blame Chance for this."

"Stop calling the man by his nickname." His brows lowered as if he hoped to intimidate a confession out of her. "Unless there is something else you'd like to confess?"

She clenched her teeth and fought down the urge to scream at her elder sibling. "Lord Fairlamb is not to blame. It is my fault that he was searching for me."

Oliver brought his fists to his temples. "Tempest, you are not making any sense. Do you know him or not?"

"I do not." She held up her hand to signal that he would learn more if he did not interrupt her. "He was looking for the person who was spying on him and his friends."

Her poor brother looked confused. "What?"

Tempest took a fortifying breath. "It was accident, and

I really didn't see too much, since two of them were already in the river."

"Too much of what?" he thundered at her.

She sent him an apologetic glance. "Ah, flesh. Did I forget to mention that the gentlemen were undressed when I stumbled upon them?"

"Tempest!"

"So you can see why you can't challenge Chance—uh, Lord Fairlamb," she amended hastily when her brother growled. "Or mention any of this to Father and Mother or to anyone. Please, Oliver, my reputation would suffer if word got out that I was spying on half-naked gentlemen. Think of the scandal. I can't afford another unremarkable season in London."

"For the love of—!" Oliver marched over to the bench they had abandoned earlier and sat down before his knees gave out.

# Chapter Six

Tempest should have lied to her brother about her encounter with Lord Fairlamb and his friends.

Although Oliver had dressed for an evening out of the house, he announced to their mother's delight that he would be joining her and his sisters for the dinner. Tempest despaired when she heard the news. His sudden desire to spend the evening with the family had nothing to do with feeling exhausted as he had claimed, and everything to do with her.

As usual, Cook had outdone herself, but Tempest barely sampled each course on account of Oliver. Her beastly brother managed to distract their mother with witty anecdotes while he glared at her from over the rim of his wineglass. Arabella was aware of the discord between the elder siblings and tried to engage their brother, but his attention always seemed to shift back to Tempest. Augusta was the only one at the table who seemed to thoroughly enjoy the cook's efforts, as she happily shared scraps of meat with the marchioness's pug.

Tempest endured her brother's brooding stare and disapproval in martyred silence. Her stomach felt like it was in knots the entire duration of the meal while she waited for him to tell the marchioness that Tempest had not only flirted with a member of the Rooke family, but also managed to admire his naked backside. Oliver's furious expression revealed he was tempted to expose her foolishness. All she could do was sit there and wait for him to deliver the news that would either end with her being banished to one of their father's smaller estates or subjected to a painful whipping delivered by their father. Maybe both, since the Marquess of Norgrave would view her consorting with his enemy's heir as an unpardonable sin.

When the marchioness stood and announced they should adjourn to the music room, Tempest asked to be excused. She told her mother that she felt unwell and planned to retire to her bedchamber. Oliver's gaze had followed her movements as she left the dining room. If he intended to betray her to their mother, he was not going to have the satisfaction of her being present for it.

With her maid's assistance, she undressed and prepared for bed. She dismissed the young maid and told the servant that she would not need her for the rest of the evening. Unfortunately, it was still early and sleep eluded her. She sat down at her small writing table and opened her sketching notebook. Drawing always soothed her when she was troubled, and it would give her something to do in the quiet passing hours.

Two hours later, a soft knock at the door disturbed Tempest's self-imposed solitude. Rising from her chair, she shut her notebook and then walked to the door to let Arabella into the chamber before her mother discovered that she was still awake. Her sister had a kind heart, and must have guessed from Oliver's demeanor at dinner and Tempest's distress that he had learned of their uninvited visitors this afternoon.

Tempest turned the doorknob and prepared to greet her sister. She opened the door. "Oliver," she said, unable to hide her surprise. "This is unexpected."

Balanced in his right hand was a small tray that was covered with a white cloth. "May I enter?" he politely asked, his expression giving her no hint to his current mood.

"Of course," Tempest said, stepping back so he could enter her bedchamber. She waited until he stepped into the middle of the room before she closed the door.

Oliver glanced at the bed. The maid had pulled back the bedding, but it was obvious from the unruffled pillows and sheets that she had not been sleeping. "Mother chastised me for our afternoon outing."

"Why would she do that?"

"Your lack of appetite and request to retire early have her concerned. She blames me for overtaxing your delicate system."

"I suppose you denied her claims."

"I told her that you have always possessed a healthy constitution," he replied, moving to her writing table. With his free hand, he slid her sketch notebook to the side and set down the small serving tray. "I did, however, suggest that, like all vain females, you might be fretting about fitting into the new dresses our mother has ordered for London."

Forgetting that she should be kind to him, Tempest marched over and pinched Oliver on the arm. "How dare you imply I am too fat to fit into my dresses!" There was nothing wrong with her body. She was neither too fat nor too thin.

Her brother rubbed his sore spot and chuckled. "I never said that you were too fat. Merely that you might be worried about the fit of the dresses. My explanation for your odd behavior this evening was less upsetting than the truth, I daresay."

"So you did not make a grand confession to Mother?"

"I thought about it," he admitted, and his stern expression revealed that he was still angry. "However, who will keep you out of trouble if you are banished to the country while the rest of the family is in London?"

Tempest nodded at the covered tray on her writing table. "What did you bring me?"

"Beef tea and buttered toast," he said gruffly. "I told Cook that you were feeling poorly this evening and to prepare something light for your stomach. You need to keep up your strength."

His thoughtfulness was unexpected, and she was touched by the gesture.

She leaned around him to remove the cloth covering from the tray. A silver lid covered the beef broth and she left it undisturbed. Instead, she picked up a slice of buttered toast and took a bite.

"A truce offering?" she asked while chewing and swallowing the piece of toast in her mouth.

"Not precisely." He pulled out her chair and invited her to sit down. When she did, he dragged another chair closer so they could sit side by side. "Think of it as a small bribe."

Her right eyebrow arched. "Very small, indeed. If you think to bribe me, you should have also brought me dessert."

Tempest was teasing, but his glare told her that her brother found nothing humorous about their situation. He reached into his evening coat as if to search for something. Her eyes widened as he retrieved an apple from a pocket and placed it next to her tray.

"Dessert."

"Why, Oliver, you do still love me!" Tempest leaned over to kiss him on the cheek, but he stiffened and pulled away. She sighed and tried not to feel hurt by his rejection. "Or perhaps I am wrong. You spoke of a bribe."

"Fairlamb."

Ah, so her brother was not finished berating her about Chance and his friends. "Why are we speaking of him again? Oliver, I told you the truth. I was unaware that the gentleman I spoke to this afternoon was a Rooke."

His expression lost some of the harshness. "I know. As I watched you sulk at dinner, I thought about our conversation in the gardens and realized that I owe you, Arabella, and Augusta an apology."

Again he'd surprised her. "For what?"

"For leaving you and the girls unprotected." He lowered his gaze to his large bare hands, which bore evidence that he did not always wear gloves to protect his skin. "I was annoyed that I had been given the task to watch over you when Mrs. Sheehan was wholly capable of seeing to the task. If I had stayed, you would not have gotten into mischief at the river. If Fairlamb had still wandered into our camp, then I would have been there to deal with him."

"It would have been three to one, Oliver," she reminded him.

"You underestimate my skills and my hatred, dear sister."

In spite of the heavy shawl draped over her shoulders, she shivered. Tempest did not understand why her brother despised Lord Fairlamb so much. Then she recalled the marquess's reaction when he discovered that she was one of those dreadful Brants. Any warmth he had displayed toward her and her sisters vanished as he bade them farewell. It appeared there was hate in his heart as well.

Tempest nibbled on her toast. "I do not want to be responsible for you challenging Lord Fairlamb."

"That is why I wished to speak with you privately. When the family resides in London, there is a chance that you might encounter him again."

She wrinkled her nose. "Highly doubtful. I did not meet him last spring." She was positive she would have remembered a handsome gentleman such as the Marquess of Fairlamb.

Her brother gave her an impatient look. "Father saw to it that another gentleman was occupying your thoughts last season."

"Yes, so kind of you to remind me of my failures, Brother," she muttered, dropping her half-eaten toast onto the plate. "Unfortunately for everyone involved, the Marquess of Rinehart fell in love with someone else."

Oliver swore under his breath. "Rinehart was a fool!"

"Papa thought he would make me a tolerable husband, but he would have been a highly valuable son-in-law." She said lightly, "I believe our father still mourns the loss."

Tempest's pride had taken a mild blow because Rinehart's affections were bestowed to another lady, but she had never allowed herself to fall in love with the gentleman. Perhaps her heart had figured out before her head that she and the marquess were not the best match when it came to temperament.

He reached over and clasped the hand she'd rested in her lap. "Did Rinehart break your heart, Pest?"

No one in the family had thought to ask her that particular question. Especially since their father had such high expectations for the betrothal.

She shook her head. "It would have been grand if I had fallen in love with the gentleman our father had hand-picked for me. And yet, I felt nothing akin to love. A mild fondness . . . yes. He was a kind man. There was no ground swell, no spark, or music in the air." She paused and moistened her lips. "I have a confession. Promise you will not tell anyone?"

"I promise."

Tempest avoiding looking her brother directly in the eye. "I often wonder if the lack is within me, Oliver. Perhaps I am unable to fall in love."

"Nonsense," her brother protested. "You are placing too much value on the sentiment. You love your family, do you not? There is room in your heart for another."

Oliver did not understand. She turned his hand palm up and casually traced the lines she found there. "Would you say that there is love between our mother and father?"

"I have never given it much thought."

No, it was not something anyone discussed.

"There is duty and perhaps a degree of affection because they have been together for so long." Tempest frowned in concentration as she tried to put order to her thoughts. "However, I would not describe what they share as love."

"Whatever they have, our mother and father are satisfied." Oliver stilled her fingers by covering her hand with his. "Tempest, what has brought on such deliberation?"

"Expectations, I suppose." She carefully withdrew her hand. "I am not like Arabella, who can always discover new friends in a crowded ballroom filled with strangers. I assume love will come as easily to her. I am just not fashioned that way."

"A degree of caution can be an asset," he said, his gaze narrowing. "As for turning strangers into friends, do not think I have forgotten that you managed to befriend the son of one of father's enemies."

*Not this again.*

"It was an entirely different situation. I was so worried that Lord Fairlamb and his friends would figure out I had—" Noting her brother's thunderous expression, she swallowed her words. "Nevertheless, I was not flirting with those three gentlemen. I was being polite."

"Being polite to a Rooke is not acceptable, Tempest. If Father ever learns—"

She trembled at the thought. "I have no intention of telling him or Mama. Will you?"

His silence and measured look were enough to make her squirm in her chair. Finally, he said succinctly, "No."

"Thank you, Oliver," she said, resisting the urge to embrace him. "You do not have to worry about me speaking to Lord Fairlamb again. If, by chance, we encounter each other in London, I swear I will turn about and head in the opposite direction."

He was not entirely convinced. "What if he approaches you?"

"I will give him the direct cut," she said decisively. "However, the question is moot. The marquess will not deign to speak to me, now that he knows I am a Brant."

Oliver slowly nodded, and he seemed satisfied with her answers. "You will come to me if Fairlamb bothers you, yes?"

"Of course," she lied, crossing her fingers that were hidden by her skirt. Tempest would heed her brother's warning about the marquess, but she would not be responsible for the two gentlemen fighting.

If the occasion arose, she would deal with Lord Fairlamb by herself.

# Chapter Seven

*Three weeks later*

Mathias never thought he would develop a sudden passion for songbirds.

It had been his third night in London when he was introduced to Miss Clara King. Although the woman was two years older than he, the petite curvaceous soprano had a youthful appearance and hesitant manner of speech that gave one the impression that she had escaped the care of her governess. Nevertheless, there was nothing remotely infantile about her talent or her appetites. Since her arrival in late April, her performances had filled the theater, and she had become quite popular in certain circles of the ton. It was rare for her not to be surrounded by male admirers, but the fair Clara had made it clear that he was one of her favorites.

He understood the clever lady was savoring her success. She wanted to be wooed by her legions of admirers, and by a process of elimination she would select a lover or two who favored her with expensive tokens of affection.

Mathias was confident that he and Clara would be lovers soon. His calculated efforts would earn him more than the few kisses they had shared. She was already favoring him with special considerations. Whenever he called on her in her dressing room, she always requested that everyone else leave so they might have a private moment.

Mathias wondered if this was the evening he would coax her away from the theater and into his bed. He reached into the small pocket of his waistcoat and checked his timepiece. Miss King had already performed, and was likely holding court in her dressing room. As he sat with his friends, a half smile played on his lips as he considered abandoning them so he could ply his skills of seduction on the lady who had captured his interest.

"No."

Mathias glared at the back of the head of the gentleman who sat in front of him and slightly to his left. "Did you say something, Your Serene Highness?" he said, deliberately using his friend's royal title with enough of a sneer in his voice to gain the man's attention.

"I did. You are not leaving us so you can flirt with your little actress, Chance."

Antoine Rolland Sevard, exiled Prince of Galien, shifted in his seat so he could casually recline his arm against the top of his chair and the next. His female companion seated next to him did not mind using the prince's arm for support, especially when he traced the line of her neck with his finger. The lady shivered.

"How the devil did you know?" Mathias demanded, annoyed that he had been so obvious. "You were not even looking at me."

His friend winked and tapped the side of his nose. He laughed when Mathias glowered at him.

The prince had been just under a year old when his mother and father were swept up in *la Grande Terreur* and executed without the benefit of a trial. The small principality of Galien had been seized by the French, and the little prince would have been executed if he had not been smuggled out of the country by several nobles loyal to the late king and queen. It had taken another year before his friend had stepped foot on English soil. The orphaned child was embraced by the royal family, and Mathias's father was one of the noblemen who had offered his support. In England, his friend preferred to be addressed by his lesser title, the Duke of Rainbault. He only used his royal title at court or when he was conversing with people he disliked.

"Your lust makes you fidget, my friend," the duke said, his blue green eyes twinkling with merriment.

"At least you are not sitting next to him," St. Lyon drawled. "Stallions paw the soft earth with less enthusiasm."

"A charming description of our friend's predicament. I shall have to write it down in my next letter to Gideon," Thorn said, speaking of his twin brother, who had abandoned them to travel the world. "Why don't you just bed the wench and be done with it."

"I agree. Miss King is leading you and the rest of the fools who are pursuing her about on a string, Chance," declared St. Lyon, not paying attention to the lady who was seated beside him.

"I am surprised you have not put your head through her noose, St. Lyon," Mathias muttered, not caring that he sounded churlish.

The viscount cast a quick glance at his companion, who happened to be the daughter of one of his parents' good friends. She was distracted by the bulldogs performing tricks on the stage below. The man was a consummate rake, but for his family's sake, he could exercise a degree of discretion.

He leaned toward Mathias. "If I were interested, I would have tied the wench up with her leading string and tired myself out between her thighs. "However, Miss King is a bit too small for my tastes, if you want to know the truth."

"I don't," Thorn interjected. He and Mathias had not invited ladies to join them in their private theater box.

His friend was not boasting. For some unfathomable reason, ladies seemed to love him.

"I like a bit more . . . here," St. Lyon said, briefly gesturing chest high with his hands before he lowered them. The slight cupping needed no explanation. "And rounded just so."

"That is quite enough," Mathias said, refusing to be amused.

Rainbault laughed. "St. Lyon, have mercy on our friend. We are well aware that your cup runneth over and over. You are an inspiration to us all."

Mathias noticed that their discussion had not interrupted the prince's slow seduction of his female companion. Rainbault brought the lady's hand to his mouth and rubbed his lips lightly across her gloved knuckles. Her attention was wholly focused on the man sitting beside her.

So far, the women in his and his friends' lives had been nothing more than passing fancies. They were young, so their selfishness could be forgiven by family and friends. The women who sought them out and shared their bodies were not looking for husbands. These women wanted a lover and a protector, but they valued their freedom as much as he and his friends did.

Watching Rainbault and his soon-to-be lover as they anticipated the bed they would later share, Mathias's thoughts returned to Miss King. There was a reason why they called him Chance. He liked taking risks, and most of the time, he was rewarded handsomely for his efforts.

Mathias stood.

The prince groaned as his lady kissed the line of his jaw. He surprised Mathias by grabbing his hand. "Stay.

If you are bored, we can go to one of the taverns or a gaming hell."

"I vote for the gaming hell," Thorn announced to no one in particular.

St. Lyon cleared his throat to gain Mathias's attention. He gave a slight nod to the lady beside him. "I must stay until the end, but I can meet you later."

Mathias understood St. Lyon had to fulfill his obligations to his family. There would be other evenings when he would have similar restraints himself.

His gaze shifted back to Rainbault. "Our evening plans stand. You can do without me while I offer my congratulations to Miss King. The lady is expecting me and would think something was amiss if I did not stop by her dressing room."

The prince's wolfish grin revealed the gentleman heartily approved of Mathias's unspoken intentions. "What if your songbird is amenable to more than a lingering kiss?"

"I will send word if I am delayed." He clapped his hand on Thorn's shoulder and nodded to St. Lyon as he slipped by him and his companion and left the private theater box.

Mathias made his way down the crowded dimly lit corridor and headed toward the staircase. This was the third incarnation of the theater building. The earlier buildings had been destroyed by fire. The pungent fragrances of animal flesh, dung, hay, and sweat became more pronounced as he descended. Ladies and gentlemen held scented handkerchiefs under their noses as they climbed the stairs with the hope that the air improved in the upper tiers.

His gaze casually glided from face to face, and he politely nodded to the few he recognized. The slow-moving congestion of pedestrians did not permit any discourse, which was a blessing because he had tarried too long with his friends. Miss King's affections were fickle, and his rivals were benefiting from his absence.

Lost in thought, he was not certain what initially had caught his attention when his gaze locked on to one of the ladies walking toward him. In the gloomy interior, her lace frock worn over a white satin slip gleamed like muted moonbeams. The square bodice and the short sleeves revealed its owner was artfully formed as he appreciatively noted the graceful slopes of her shoulders and the fine line of her neck and profile. The lady was speaking to her friend, so her face was partially concealed by her fan. Her maid had pinned her dark brown hair and tucked most of it under a *toque à la Reubens* headdress that was decorated with precious stones and white feathers. She was not the only one who was flaunting her wealth, but this part of town was at the edge of respectability.

Was she a foolish chit or a prosperous courtesan?

If his meeting with Miss King was short, perhaps he could persuade the mystery lady and her companion to join him and his friends for the evening. As if sensing his perusal, the woman lowered her fan and met his gaze.

Recognition lit her eyes, which he knew were a hazel with tiny amber flecks.

Lady Tempest Brant.

Mathias's jaw tensed as her surprise gave way to dismay.

*When did she arrive in London?*

She whispered something to her companion, whom he now recognized as her sister, Lady Arabella. Delight brightened the other woman's face as she saw him, but her enthusiasm dimmed at what he assumed was her sister's hasty explanation of why he should be avoided at all costs.

*Yes, ladies, I am one of those dreadful Rookes!* he longed to shout at them.

He should have found their reactions amusing, but all he felt was annoyance. He bowed as he passed the Brant sisters, and Lady Tempest did not disappoint him. Her stubborn chin shot up and she glanced away as if the very sight of him offended her.

Lady Arabella offered him a weak smile, but she allowed her sister to lead her forward. It was then he noticed Mrs. Sheehan, who was lagging behind her charges.

"Why, Chance, how are you, my good sir?" the widow said, glancing over her shoulder, since she was unable to stop her ascent.

"Very well, ma'am," he replied. He saw no reason to be rude to the woman. It was not her fault that her employer was a blackguard. "Enjoy your evening."

Belatedly, Mathias wished there had been time to warn Mrs. Sheehan to be on her guard. Lady Tempest and her sister were ripe for the plucking if they encountered an unscrupulous fellow who coveted their jewelry.

Why the devil he should care one way or the other was something he did not wish to examine closely.

It was *him.*

Chance . . . no, Lord Fairlamb, Tempest silently rectified her error. There could be no familiarity between them. One polite exchange did not make them friends.

*Nor did it make him my enemy,* was her traitorous thought.

No, her brother was correct. Her father would not approve of any association with a member of the Rooke family. It was her duty to stay away from the marquess. She owed her family her loyalty, and if his cool mocking glance was any indication, Lord Fairlamb considered her his adversary, too.

"Why did you discourage me from speaking to Chance?" Arabella whispered to her. "It was obvious from his expression that our lack of civility offended him."

Tempest frowned and resisted the urge to rub her forehead. The headdress was beginning to give her a headache. "He will recover from his disappointment. I doubt this is the first time Chance has received a less than cordial greeting from a lady."

She silently wondered if his friends were joining him this evening. Allies of the Rooke family were not to be trusted as well.

Tempest regretted that she could not tell her sister the true reason why they could not associate with Chance or anyone associated with him. The evening Oliver had paid her a visit, he persuaded her not to reveal the gentlemen's names and their connections to the Rooke family to Arabella and Augusta out of concern that one of them would tell their father and mother. At the time, she thought her brother was being unreasonable. The odds of seeing Lord Fairlamb or his friends again were slight, since they had failed to run across each other last spring. However, Oliver had disagreed and it vexed her that he had been right to be concerned.

"Hurry, lasses, we are missing the performances," Mrs. Sheehan complained.

Much to their brother's chagrin, the streets were heavily congested with coaches and carriages as they journeyed to the amphitheater, and it had taken them longer than expected to reach their destination. Arabella had read in one of the newspapers that one of the main acts this evening was an equine melodrama. She had begged their mother to allow them to attend the performance. Lady Norgrave eventually agreed so long as Oliver joined them, and afterwards escorted her and Arabella to Lord and Lady Oxton's ball.

Tempest had expected her brother to protest, but Oliver appeared to be resigned that he would be called on to look after his sisters. Or perhaps he expected them to encounter Lord Fairlamb, which if that was the case, she was happy her brother had been delayed by several friends. He had ordered their chaperone to escort them to the private theater box and promised to join them later.

Once they were settled in their seats, she would warn Arabella not to mention that they had encountered the gentleman she knew only as Chance to their brother. Knowing Oliver, he would hunt the marquess down and challenge him for breathing the same air as his sisters or some other nonsense. She refused to allow her hotheaded sibling to ruin their evening out of the town house.

Their first week in London had been filled with dress fittings and shopping. The Oxtons' ball would be Arabella's first glimpse of the ton and a second chance for Tempest. She was determined not to disappoint her family.

By the time the trio had reached the fourth tier, there was only one seat available in their designated theater box.

"This is dreadful," Arabella complained to Mrs. Sheehan. "There was supposed to be more than one seat."

The horses were already circling the ring below. It seemed unfair to leave when the act Arabella was looking forward to was being announced. "You take the seat," Tempest murmured to her sister. "Mrs. Sheehan, perhaps you could take a position near the partition so everyone will know she is not without friends."

Mrs. Sheehan was not pleased with their predicament. "And what will you do, my girl?"

"I will remain here and wait for my brother," Tempest replied. "He should be joining us soon, and perhaps he can secure another box for us."

Mrs. Sheehan surveyed the crowded theater. "It's doubtful there are any spare seats."

Tempest silently agreed, but she did not want to ruin her sister's night. "Run along. Perhaps I will be able to convince one of the gentlemen to surrender his seat."

The realization that no one was meeting her gaze did not bode well for her.

Mathias presented his calling card to the male servant guarding the entrance to Miss King's dressing room, who immediately handed it to the lady's maid. Since he was late, he expected Clara would make him cool his heels so he would be properly repentant when she finally invited him to join her. He could hear male laughter coming from the room, which warned him that if she was truly vexed with him, he might be returning to his friends earlier than he had anticipated.

Ignoring the male attendant, who had a knowing smirk on his visage, Mathias turned his back on him as his thoughts returned to Lady Tempest and her sister. It was a rowdy crowd this evening. The ladies' elegant attire hinted that they had plans beyond the theater. Mathias wondered which ballroom they would patronize after the final performance. His butler had delivered half a dozen invitations for the evening. However, he had barely glanced at them because he and his friends were seeking other amusements.

Lady Tempest would be lucky if she was not robbed of her headdress and jewelry before she left the theater or later when they sought to find their coach. Mrs. Sheehan and her two charges would not be a match for a determined footpad.

Mathias glanced up at the sound of a disturbance at Miss King's door. Two gentlemen were discussing their evening plans as the pair exited the room. Three more gentlemen followed in their wake, and fifteen seconds later, another man crossed the threshold. He nodded to Miss King's servant and then noticed Mathias.

"Good luck," the man said before he walked down the narrow corridor that would lead to the stairs.

"Miss King will see you now, Lord Fairlamb," the servant intoned, gesturing him to enter.

Mathias found his little songbird perched in front of her dressing table. She observed his entrance as she admired her face in the small square mirror that was mounted to the table.

"Lord Fairlamb," she said, adding a touch of color to her lower lip. "I almost had given up on you."

"We are beyond titles, are we not? At our last meeting, you called me Chance." Confident that she would not turn him away, he strode toward her dressing table. "Forgive me, sweet Clara. I did not arrive at the theater alone."

She rose from her chair, and he noted that she had changed her dress. Earlier, she had appeared like an angel in white when she walked onto the stage. The dress she selected for the evening was scarlet. With her black hair unbound, she looked positively delectable.

He bowed formally and she curtsied. Neither one of them broke the connection of their gazes.

"I pray your companion was not a lady," Clara said, her eyebrows lifting in an unspoken challenge.

"Just St. Lyon and a few other friends you have yet to meet," he said, closing the distance between them. "I would have asked them to join me, but I was not in the mood to share you."

"A wise decision," she replied with a saucy swing of her hips. She held out her hand and he did not hesitate to clasp her fingers. "I dismissed the others so we might enjoy our time together in private."

Clara led him to the dark blue chaise longue that was

partially hidden by a four-panel dressing screen adorned with a floral tapestry and walnut frame. She drew him closer so they were concealed from view.

"I have missed you, my lord," she said, staring up at him with guileless green eyes that always stirred more than his protective instincts. In fact, when he thought of Miss King, his thoughts turned positively wicked.

Mathias sat down on the chaise longue and impulsively pulled her onto his lap so he did not have to strain his neck when he kissed her. Clara expelled a soft pleasing sigh and gracefully settled into his arms.

"Did you receive my flowers?" he asked, his fingers stroking her arm in a possessive fashion.

"Yes. Your generous bounty filled three large vases." She smiled coyly at him. "I have yet to thank you properly for your gift."

With her curvaceous backside pressing against the front of his breeches, there was nothing he could do with his unruly body. His cock thickened as she lifted her mouth to his in a silent invitation and the heavy floral scent clinging to her filled his nose. The male servant had closed the door when Mathias entered the room. With the privacy of the dressing screen, he had the sudden desire to undress her until she was gloriously naked as she reclined against the dark blue cushions and he was filling her with his cock. The only thing that made him hesitate was that he was not seeking a hasty coupling. He wanted to take his time as they learned each other's bodies.

"Will you not kiss me?" she whispered seductively.

He cupped the back of her neck and pulled her closer as their mouths collided. His kiss was carnal and possessive. He tasted the Madeira she must have enjoyed after her performance as she flirted with her male admirers. She wiggled closer and opened herself to his slow exploration of her mouth. It was another sign that she was eager to take their friendship to a more intimate level.

Mathias groaned as Clara slipped her hand under his waistcoat. Perhaps their first time together would be on the old and worn chaise longue. The lady seemed as hungry as he was. His hand at the nape of her neck slid forward and his fingers caressed the gold and ruby necklace she was wearing.

The moderately expensive necklace reminded him of Lady Tempest and the small fortune she was displaying in public. Christ, why was he thinking of *her,* of all people! He finally had Clara warm and soft in his arms, and if he was reading her intentions accurately, she was a willing participant in her seduction.

Clara moaned when he put a little too much enthusiasm into his kiss. His cock was folded into an uncomfortable angle in his breeches, and the thickening flesh throbbed. If he unfastened the buttons to give himself some relief, the lady in his arms would end up flat on her back, his cock buried deep within her.

Mathias doubted the haughty Lady Tempest had ever sat in a gentleman's lap. He stilled at the thought. What was wrong with him? It was none of his business what the lady did or whom she did it with.

"My lord—Chance?" Clara asked, bringing his attention back to her face.

Miss King was exactly the kind of distraction he was seeking while he resided in London. She was beautiful, comfortable with her body, and willing to share it with him. When they parted company, there would be no expectations or tears.

Unlike Lady Tempest Brant. There was nothing about her that wasn't complicated. It was guilt, he thought. His instincts had warned him that the lady and her companions were courting trouble, and he had turned his back on them. She was not his responsibility. More important, he was not interested in offering a Brant his protection.

His cock withered as his desire fled.

Damn Marcroft! Where the devil was her brother? He was the one who should be watching over his sisters. Not him!

Clara could sense that his thoughts were elsewhere. "Chance, have I done something wrong?"

Mathias claimed her mouth again. It was not much of an apology, but he refused to leave her believing she had offended him. "No, my sweet lady. You are enchanting and perfect. I am mad with desire."

"But?"

He brushed a quick kiss against her pouting lips. "I have to leave you."

"What?"

He gently slid her from his lap and stood.

Clara remained seated on the chaise longue, which gave her a level view of the front of his breeches. There was no sign of his earlier desire, and the realization distressed her. "Where are you going?"

"I forgot that there was—" He could not admit that he was going upstairs to search for another lady. "—I have an appointment. A very brief meeting. It won't take much time at all. Can you wait for me?"

"Wait for you," Clara echoed his words, and her darkening complexion warned him that she was unused to being rejected by any man. "After the last performance, I am supposed to attend an intimate gathering at a nearby hotel."

Clara did not sound very welcoming, but he seized the

chance to make amends. "I should be finished before the final act. I will return to the dressing room. If it pleases you, I can escort you to the hotel."

Perhaps he could secure a room and offer her a private apology.

She gazed at him with stormy green eyes. "If you are certain that you will return—"

"I am." Once he found Lady Tempest and her sister, he would take them to Thorn, St. Lyon, and Rainbault and leave the ladies in their care. His friends would see to it that they were safely escorted to their coach. Then he could banish the Brant sisters from his thoughts and enjoy the rest of his evening.

She inclined her head. "Then I would be honored to have you join me at the hotel."

Mathias was grateful for Clara's understanding. "You will wait for me."

A demure smile brightened her expression. "Of course."

# Chapter Eight

From the back of the theater box, Tempest watched as her sister leaned forward and clapped at the spectacle in the ring below. She could not see much from her limited view, so as the minutes passed, she had grown bored.

What was delaying her brother? She was going to throttle Oliver for abandoning them. Again.

None of the gentlemen seated thought to offer her their seat. It was horribly rude for them to ignore her. If she ever recognized one of them in a drawing room or ballroom, she fully intended to give the unfortunate man the direct cut.

Tempest was not the only person who was standing. The private box was overflowing with people. So much so, she had been nudged farther away from her sister. For the hundredth time, she flexed her cramped toes because her shoes were pinching her feet. While her elegant attire was lovely, the longer she stood in the gloomy theater box, the more uncomfortable she became. Her feet hurt, her back itched, and the headdress was threatening to list to the right. If not for Arabella, she would have told Mrs. Sheehan that she was ready to depart. Standing beside her mother was preferable to remaining a minute longer in this hot, smelly theater.

Most of all, she hated that her circumstances had

reduced her to whining. Tempest despised complainers. They were unhappy people who loved to share their misery with others. Tempest straightened her spine and was determined to persevere.

*Blast it all, where is Oliver?*

A burst of laughter erupted in the theater. She had only her imagination to deduce what those clever horses and their riders were doing below. Something wonderful, she thought dourly. The couple in front of her shifted and she had to take a step back to avoid colliding into them.

The step nudged her out of the private theater box entirely.

Tempest lost sight of Arabella and Mrs. Sheehan. "I doubt this evening could get worse," she uncharitably muttered.

Five minutes later, she would come to regret those words.

As she tried to peer over the heads of the other spectators, she felt a masculine hand curl around her left upper arm and responded to the heat of his body. Tension slid into her muscles and then it eased. No one but her brother would dare to touch her so intimately.

"So nice of you to join us, Oliver," she said without looking at her errant elder sibling. "Arabella and Mrs. Sheehan are toward the front. Perhaps we can ask someone to get their attention."

When her brother didn't reply, Tempest turned her head to address him and gasped. The man standing so close was definitely not Oliver. This man was three inches shorter and from his grip she deduced his extra weight gave him the advantage. He was older than she by ten or more years, and his reddened nose and bloodshot brown eyes suggested he had been drinking.

"Who are—oomph!"

For a drunkard, he was agile. Before she could finish

her question, he pulled her away from the entrance to the private box, pushed her against the wall, and slapped his hand over her mouth.

"You're a pretty one, eh?" The man leaned closer so she could smell gin on his fetid breath. He turned her head from side to side to examine her face. "Are you looking for a friend?"

Tempest nodded, but the gleam of excitement in his eyes revealed that she had given him the wrong answer. She furiously shook her head. He was not asking if she was looking for *her* friend, but rather he wanted to know if she was looking to make a new friend.

Him.

"What? You aren't the friendly sort?" He sounded disappointed.

Tempest glanced to the right and left, but the narrow passageway was empty. The shouts and laughter coming from the various theater boxes guaranteed that no one would hear her cries of help. Not that she would permit herself to be deterred by any obstacle. The first in gaining her freedom was to convince the man to remove his hand from her mouth.

Her wide eyes and muffled protest reminded him that he was preventing her from speaking.

"If I take my hand away, you won't cause a fuss by screaming, will you?" he asked, squinting up at her.

Tempest swallowed and slowly shook her head. Any man who grabbed an unwilling lady was not exactly harmless, but his drunkenness might have made him bold. The private box was in sight. If she could catch the man off guard, she could push her way inside or alert one of the gentlemen within that she needed some assistance.

Her companion eased his hand away and then thought better of it. She groaned when he pulled her farther down the corridor and away from her sister. It was darker in this section, so if anyone approached them, the person might assume she was willingly keeping this man company.

"This will do us nicely, don't you think?" Again he eased the hold on her mouth. "No screaming or I'll knock you out with my fist. Do you understand me?"

Tempest nodded.

She sagged with relief when his hand fell away. When she wasn't so frightened, she had a quick mind, and she could put it to good use if she remained calm.

"Thank you, sir," she said, and tried to smile. Her lips trembled, but she doubted the man noticed.

"What's your name, pretty?"

"Elizabeth," she replied, giving him her middle name.

He grinned. "Does your family call you Bessie?"

Not a soul, but that kind of reply was not very sociable. "How did you know?"

He was still crowding her and blocking her way to the theater box. "I've a cousin named Bessie. And I've known a few maids with the name."

Tempest nodded approvingly. "And might I know your name, good sir?"

The man inclined his head. "You can call me Archie."

"A pleasure to meet you, Mr. Archie." If she curtsied, there was a chance her body would rub against him, and she did not want to encourage him.

"Mr. Archie," he said, testing the name. "I like it."

Her unwanted admirer wore a brown suit, but it smelled of stale sweat. He touched the lace at her shoulder. "Such a fine dress. I have never seen one so white. Even the hem of your skirt is clean," he said, marveling that she had managed not to spill anything on her clothes.

"I arrived in a coach with my family." She cleared her throat. "My brother and sister are waiting for me in the private box. Perhaps you would like to meet them."

He ignored her offer. "And look how your fancy hat glitters when you move your head." He said, tilting his head to observe how the stones winked in the shadowed passageway, "Are those stones real?"

"Just paste," she lied. "There is no point in wearing jewels I can't admire."

He laughed and she flinched when he pounded the wall near her head. "I can't fault your logic, Bessie. Now, why don't you give me a kiss and then we can go find a quiet place to have a drink."

She would rather kiss a mangy wet cur than him.

"I can't leave without telling my brother, Mr. Archie," she said gently. Tempest loathed to touch her odorous companion, but she tried not to grimace as she patted him on the arm. "We can have that drink if you permit me to pass."

Archie stepped in front of her to block her escape. "There's no need to trouble your brother when all we're doing is being friendly. If he's your brother at all. Now, why don't you give me that kiss, Bessie darling?"

Tempest was getting nowhere with the unreasonable drunk. The way he was touching her arm and dress, she doubted a single kiss would satisfy him even if she fancied kissing him. Which she didn't.

"There will be no kisses, sir," she said coldly. If kindness did not sway the man, then it was time to try another approach. "You have detained me long enough, and now I intend to return to my family."

Tempest knocked his arm aside and managed three steps before he grabbed her by the waist and half dragged her down the passageway. Her headdress fell to the floor. She screamed and fought him, but he was too strong. No one seemed to hear her over the music and the laughter. It appeared Archie had changed his tactics, too.

"Hush, Bessie!" He pulled her close so her back was

flush against his front. "I don't want to use my fists on you. Not yet, at any rate."

She screamed and drove her elbow into his chest. He held her tighter as if he hoped to squeeze the breath out of her.

"I do beg your pardon." The male voice caused them both to cease their struggles. "I hope I am not interrupting anything."

When Tempest recognized the gentleman approaching them, tears blurred her vision. It was Lord Fairlamb. She had never been so relieved to see a familiar face in her entire life.

Archie held her as if she were a shield. "That you are, sir. Can't you see me and Bessie wish to be alone?"

"Bessie, you say?" His lips quirked as if he was tempted to smile. "A dreadful name, my dear. You have my sympathies." He touched his hat as if he was prepared to leave her to her fate.

Tempest felt a chill waft through her. Before she learned he was a Rooke, she had thought him a decent gentleman. Did he hate her family so much that he would walk away?

"Blast it all, Chance, you cannot leave me!" she shouted at him. If she had to cast all pride aside, she was willing to beg.

"Do you know this fellow, Bessie?" Archie peered at the marquess. "Are you the brother?"

"Yes!" Tempest said, not waiting for Lord Fairlamb's response. "He's my brother. Now, let me go before he challenges you."

Her would-be rescuer appeared offended by the question. "Are you drunk? Do I look like her brother, you filthy twit?"

The anger in the marquess's voice befuddled the drunken Archie. "Then who are you?"

There was a mischievous glint in His Lordship's eyes. "I'm the gent who is stealing the lady from you."

Tempest's eyes widened in surprise as Chance loosened the fist in his right hand and the walking stick he had concealed slid down the length of his arm to the floor. Before her captor could react, the marquess lunged forward as if he had a sword and stabbed the tip into Archie's shoulder.

The man released her and staggered back into the wall. Tempest moved toward Chance, but he walked around her and struck the edge of the walking stick against Archie's head. Dazed, the drunk slid down the wall until his backside hit the floor.

"Are you hurt? Do you want me to summon the watch?"

Tempest started at his harsh tone. "I—I do not know. I suppose we should or he might do this to another lady."

She groaned, wondering how she was going to explain to her brother what had happened. Oliver was not going to be reasonable when he recognized Chance. Nor would he thank the man for rescuing her from the clutches of a drunk.

Archie decided to take his fate out of their hands. When Chance looked away, the man climbed to his feet and swaggered toward the stairs.

"Let him go," she called out before the marquess could give chase. The man had frightened her, but he hadn't had a chance to rob her. Or kiss her. "I am unhurt."

Tempest brought her hand up to her mouth, and tears threatened to fill her eyes. The harsh lines of his face faded and were replaced with concern. He opened his arms and she stepped into his embrace. She pressed her face into his evening coat and tried not to cry.

"There, there, Bessie," he lightly teased. "All is well." A soft choking noise bubbled in her throat and she shoved him away. "Do not call me by that awful name." Tempest made the mistake of looking at his face. "And no laughing. The man ruined my perfectly terrible evening."

"My apologies, Lady Tempest," he said, trying to sound sincere. "Why did your friend think your name was Bessie?"

"I told him my name was Elizabeth. He dubbed me Bessie," she explained. Tempest touched her hair with her fingers and remembered that her headdress had fallen to the floor. Espying it several yards away, she marched over to retrieve it.

"What were you doing out in the corridor alone with a drunken stranger?"

With her headdress clasped to her breast, she walked back to him. "We arrived late, so there was only one seat left. I told Arabella to take it while I intended to stand in the back," she said, knowing she sounded defensive. "When more people arrived, I was sort of nudged out into the passageway."

"Nudged?"

"Well, I didn't go willingly," Tempest snapped at him. "Before I could return, Archie grabbed me."

"And then he tried to kiss you." His lips thinned with displeasure and he glanced at the doorway that led to the stairs as if he was planning to follow the man.

"At first, I thought he was just a harmless drunk." She nibbled her lower lip. "Then later . . . I don't know what he would have done if you hadn't arrived. And here, I haven't even thanked you properly."

She must have been more unsettled than she thought.

His gaze studied her face as if he needed to be reassured that she was indeed unhurt. "You're welcome." He tucked his walking stick under his arm and tugged the headdress from her boneless fingers. "Here. Allow me to assist you."

Chance brushed bits of debris from the lace cap and

adjusted the plumes. "Lean forward." When she obeyed, he placed the headdress on her head. Satisfied with the results, he lightly combed the curls around her face. Their gazes met as she raised her face upward and accepted his ministrations without complaint.

"Much better."

Tempest straightened. "Thank you."

Chance reached into his waistcoat and produced a handkerchief. He pressed it into her hand. "You might want to wipe the smudge of grime from your chin." Without any warning he tugged the linen from her grasp. "On second thought, let me do it."

She was grateful for the gloomy interior because it hid her blush.

He tilted her chin with a touch of his fingertips, and he used the handkerchief to wipe the dirt away. "You and your sister need more than my remarkable instincts for sensing trouble and Mrs. Sheehan to look after you in a place like this."

She winced at the anger in his voice. After her encounter with Archie, she had to agree. "We are not so foolish as to arrive without an escort. My brother is with us."

"Is he? So where is this brother of yours?" he demanded. "He was not with you when I passed you on the stairs. Nor was he here while you were fighting off the amorous advances of a drunk!"

"I don't know!" she said, embarrassed and grateful that Chance had been there for her when her own brother was absent. "He told us that he would meet us, but something has detained him."

"Or someone. Lord Marcroft is selfish to put his needs above his sisters when they are under his protection."

Even she could not offer a defense for Oliver. "So now you admit that you are acquainted with my brother. The day we first met, you denied it, Lord Fairlamb."

His jaw flexed as he ground down on his back molars. "Then you know who I am."

"Not really."

Chance appeared surprised by her honest answer.

"I know only that you are a Rooke, and that I am to avoid anyone bearing that name." Tempest expelled a soft sigh. "I should return to the private box before my sister or Mrs. Sheehan notice that I am missing."

"Is my name the reason why you and your sister refused to acknowledge me on the stairs?" he asked.

She tried to quell the guilt rising within her. Arabella had been correct when she said that the marquess had been offended by their rude behavior. Still, he had put his injured feelings aside to rescue her. His noble actions only managed to confuse her. "In part. My sister is unaware that you are a Rooke. Only I know the truth."

*And Oliver.*

He captured her hand to prevent her from leaving. "Do you know why our fathers are bitter enemies?"

It was an unexpected question. Tempest shook her head. "No. My father never speaks of the past."

"Neither does mine. Unfortunately, I have been acquainted with your brother since I was a boy. I can assure you that he has earned my hatred. Marcroft is an arse."

Tempest smiled at his coarse language. "I would not have used that particular word, but I am familiar with my brother's stubbornness." Her smile faded. "I am truly grateful for what you have done, but I want you to leave. I do not want my brother to see you. If he saw us together, he would use it as a reason to challenge you."

"Lady Tempest, your brother and I have been fighting since we were boys. I doubt—"

"He knows we met by the river that day," she blurted out. "I have spoken privately with him, and he has sworn not to mention it to my father."

Chance sneered. "And you believe him."

"Not for you, Lord Fairlamb. He keeps silent in my behalf." She hesitated. "Oliver protects me from our father. Even you must know that he can be quite unreasonable about your family, and I would have been punished for speaking to you."

The marquess took a moment to ponder her words. " 'Unreasonable' would apply to my father as well."

"Then we are in agreement, my lord. We will not speak of this meeting to anyone."

He cocked his head to the side. "I liked it better when you called me Chance."

Tempest gave him an exasperated look. "I will not be calling you anything, since we shall not meet again."

"Do you want to wager on it?"

The man was hopeless. For both their sakes, she walked away.

"No?" He followed in her wake. "Permit me to escort you to the entrance of the private box."

"There is no need." Tempest halted abruptly and turned to confront him. "Please. I do not wish to be responsible for you and my brother fighting."

"My dear lady, Marcroft and I rarely need a reason to pummel each other." Chance shackled both her wrists to prevent her from entering the box. "Nevertheless, if given the opportunity, I would challenge him for leaving you and your sister alone."

She was touched by his offer to defend her, but it was unnecessary. "I am fully capable of making my brother suffer for his sins."

"I would enjoy watching such a spectacle," he said, and the humor she had attributed to him at their first meeting gleamed in his eyes. "I will take my leave on one condition."

"I owe you a boon for your timely rescue. All you have

to do is name it," she said, eager to see him leave before her brother sought her out.

"A kiss."

Tempest's lips parted in amazement. "Is this some kind of prank?"

"When I came upon you and your drunken fellow, you appeared to be resigned to your fate." He released her wrists and awaited her reply.

The gentleman was addled. "I most definitely was *not*!"

"You are no coward, my lady. Bestowing a chaste kiss . . . naturally, on the lips," he swiftly amended so she could not find a means to escape his demands by kissing the air or his hand.

"One kiss."

"It will be painless," he promised. He leaned on his walking stick and stood there as if he were prepared to remain in front of her for the rest of the evening.

"Oh, very well," she grumbled, and took a step closer before she took the coward's path and ran from him. "You are a fool to kiss me, Lord Fairlamb."

Chance grinned. "You do know how to charm a gent," he teased.

Tempest placed her hand on his shoulder and rolled onto her toes to reach his lips. Her mouth pressed against his. She closed her eyes, counted to five, and then quickly withdrew.

Her heels touched the floor and she looked up at him expectantly, feeling awkward and embarrassed. If her brother had discovered them, Chance would have taken a bullet for that kiss.

The marquess stared at her as he stroked his lower lip with the pad of his thumb. If he dared to tease her about her inexperience, she was uncertain she could stop herself from strangling him.

"Your boon is accepted, Lady Tempest," he said at last. "Quite unexpected. I will bid you a good evening."

Chance bowed and strolled off. He did not glance back to see if she entered the theater box.

Tempest touched her fingers to her lips. For some reason, she sensed that Lord Fairlamb had granted her a small reprieve. No man would have been content with the chaste kiss she had given him.

She also had a disconcerting feeling that he was not quite finished with her.

# Chapter Nine

It had been unsporting of him to demand a kiss from Lady Tempest.

The chaste peck on his lips should have amused him. He had kissed his sisters with more enthusiasm. He could almost hear the silent counting in her head before she swiftly pulled away and braced for his mockery.

He could not decide if the manner in which she kissed him was deliberate or if she was that naïve.

Even she was aware that she deserved to be ridiculed for that paltry reward.

However, he let her walk away, her dignity intact. It was safer than revealing the truth. Her pitiful kiss had almost brought him to his knees. The second her soft, invitingly warm lips connected with his, the spark of attraction crackled beneath his skin like a summer thunderstorm. It flickered and playfully danced across his flesh, causing a chain reaction of awareness, sending a lightning bolt straight down to his cock. Lust coiled and rumbled within him like thunder. The ground beneath his feet seemed to give way, but not the need to press her against the nearest wall and kiss her until she was as breathless and yearning as he.

Lady Tempest was unaware of the internal battle he fought. She stared up at him, her expression a combination of wariness and hopefulness that he would be satisfied. It was apparent that she was unmoved by their kiss. He wanted to shake her until she lost some of that immeasurable control.

For leaving him wanting her.

The lady was a Brant, he reminded himself. Off-limits. Forbidden. Mathias was not interested in dallying with a virgin. Complicated females were not challenging. They were a royal pain in the arse.

His walk to the bowels of the theater was unhindered. Mathias was a practical man. It mattered little that Lady Tempest had inspired the lust churning in his gut like a caged beast. Another female was waiting for him. Miss King would not question his eagerness. She would lie on her old worn chaise longue and pull up her skirt and petticoat to entice him with her well-shaped legs. Clara would not blush when he unfastened his breeches or complain that he was not gentle when he covered her with his body and buried his cock in her womanly sheath. She would embrace the pleasure of their coupling, hold him to her breasts as he pulled out of her and spilled his seed against her thigh. It would never occur to her that while he was thrusting within her, he saw another lady's face in his mind.

Even if she suspected, Clara was too shrewd not to use his weakness to her advantage.

Of course, Lady Tempest would be scandalized if she knew her kiss was about to drive him into the arms of another woman. Or perhaps she would be relieved. Allowing herself to be seduced by Blackbern's heir was the stuff of nightmares, he thought mockingly.

Miss King's male servant was no longer guarding the door. There were no lingering male admirers milling about to chase away or hinder his efforts to claim her as his mistress.

Mathias raised his hand to knock, but decided against it. He preferred to surprise Clara. He silently turned the doorknob and opened the door several inches. What he saw within the room froze him in place.

Clara was not alone.

"You cannot leave me like this," she huskily pleaded.

"I am already late. I am supposed to escort my sisters to the Oxtons'." There was a rustle of fabric, and her male companion groaned. "Christ, Clara, you make me lose my head when you touch me like that."

It appeared the woman Mathias viewed as his soon-to-be mistress had decided not to wait for him after all. She had invited another gentleman into her dressing room while she waited for his return. The man had wasted no time on pleasantries. Oblivious to everyone but themselves, his little songbird was perched on her dressing table with her legs wrapped around the man's hips. From his position, Mathias could hear her soft gasps as the man rhythmically stroked the heated flesh between her legs. Just by listening to her breathy escalating cries, he knew she would soon experience the cresting pleasure as her wet channel tightened around the man's fingers.

If Clara's goal was to make him jealous, she had unwittingly selected the perfect gentleman for the task.

Mathias did not need to see the man's face to recognize the Earl of Marcroft.

Instead of looking after his sisters, the scoundrel was seducing the woman Mathias intended to make his mistress for the season. He was furious. Not for having Clara stolen away from him, but for Lady Tempest. If Mathias had not thought to check on the lady, the drunken fellow who had accosted her might have done more than frighten her.

Mathias quietly shut the door. If Clara had hoped for a confrontation between him and Marcroft, she would

be disappointed. His pride was bruised by the mere fact
that Marcroft was involved. By God, he truly despised
the gentleman. However, no lover had ever been worth
shedding a single drop of blood. London was filled with
beautiful women, and he would simply find another to
share his bed.

*So Lady Tempest and her sister are attending Lord
and Lady Oxton's ball?*

The lust that drove him straight to the duplicitous Miss
King had been inspired by another lady. Why should he
not seek her out?

*Hmm, could I?*

He was mad to contemplate it.

Lady Tempest was a Brant. She was complicated and
an innocent. Not really the sort of female that appealed
to him.

Or perhaps it was the risk of getting caught that he
found so tantalizing.

Still, there was no doubt the lady needed someone to
watch over her while she fluttered around London.

Why not him?

The added benefit was that Marcroft would be positively apoplectic if he caught Mathias even glancing in
Lady Tempest's direction.

Mathias grinned at the pleasant vision of the earl
frothing at the mouth. And if the man was foolhardy
enough to challenge him to a duel, then he would put a
bullet in him for being a rotten brother. As for Lady
Tempest, it was not as if he planned to seduce the
chit. He had not completely lost his mind. Although he
had to admit his thoughts about her were not entirely
honorable.

He would kiss her again. Next time, he would show
her how to kiss properly. His hands trembled in anticipation of another taste of her succulent lips.

Mathias had suddenly developed a craving for sweets—and forbidden fruit was the sweetest of all.

"Did you fall asleep during one of the performances?"

Tempest glanced at her brother, who sat across from her in the coach. Taking up more than half the seat so there was little room for Arabella, Oliver had a languid, indulgent expression on his face. The fact that he was oblivious to her barely suppressed annoyance at him just vexed her all the more. If this was her brother's attempt to tease her into forgiving him for abandoning them for most of the evening, then he would have to do better than insult her.

"Why do you ask, Brother?"

He raised his hand and used two fingers to gesture at her head. "One of your white plumes is bent and it's listing to the right."

With a growl of frustration, she pulled the headdress off her head. "I lost the pins anchoring it in place."

"How did you manage that, brat?" The corners of her brother's mouth curled upward.

Mrs. Sheehan took the headdress from her to inspect the damage. "It is a fine piece, and a shame some rude fellow knocked it off your head and stepped on it," the widow said, echoing the explanation Tempest had given the two women. "Once we arrive at Lord and Lady Oxton's town house, I should be able to mend it."

"Don't tease, Oliver," Arabella admonished. "Tempest was kind enough to allow me to have the remaining seat in the theater box." To her sister, she said, "I feel just awful that you were so miserable."

"I managed through it," she murmured, thinking of how heroic Lord Fairlamb had been when handling the drunken Archie. Tempest deliberately refused to ponder her brazen behavior, allowing him to taunt her into kissing him. "Oliver, you never really did explain where you were for most of the evening."

Her brother's unrepentant grin revealed everything she had deduced. The scoundrel had been up to no good. "I had my hands full with several distractions, dear sister," he drawled, likely slipping a double entendre into his explanation. "I have already apologized. How long do you intend to be vexed with me?"

"Don't let my annoyance trouble you, Brother," Tempest said briskly. "Once we part ways at the Oxtons', you will not have to concern yourself with my feelings."

Oliver groaned. "You can be a heartless creature, Tempest."

"I have learned from the master, Brother," she replied, her spiteful comment startling everyone in the coach. Including her, though she preferred to bite off her tongue rather than apologize for her cutting remark.

No one felt inclined to speak again until they had reached Lord and Lady Oxton's town house.


"Tell me again why we have delayed joining St. Lyon and Rainbault," Thorn asked after they had paid their respects to the Earl of Oxton and his countess.

"This stop will be brief," Mathias promised as he stepped into the ballroom. "And you are not missing anything. Did you see the look on Rainbault's face? He will insist on escorting the lady home, and we shall likely be waiting at the club for him to join us. As for St. Lyon, it will take some time for him to untangle himself from his family obligations."

Thorn stood to Mathias's left, and he inclined his head as he recognized an elderly couple. "St. Lyon barely glanced at the chit. Who was she?"

"I have no idea. I missed the formal introductions, and our friend was determined not to offer the shy lady any encouragement," Mathias said. A slight frown thinned his lips, as he could not find the lady who had brought him to the Oxtons'.

"It seemed out of character for St. Lyon to behave himself. Some nights he is worse than Rainbault."

"Not when the lady's parents are close friends of his." He had noticed the lady seated beside their friend discreetly observed the viscount when he was not paying attention to her. It was the same expression every female had stamped on her face when St. Lyon was around. One that was wistful and adoring. Most of them were half in love with the gentleman within minutes of an introduction. "His family would like to see him married off this season, but they are bound to be disappointed."

"How so?"

He motioned for his friend to walk with him. "I love the man like a brother, however, St. Lyon would make any respectable lady a dreadful husband."

"On what grounds?"

"Fidelity," Mathias said absently. "He has been incapable of being faithful to a single mistress. Since our arrival in town, I have seen him in the company of at least four females."

Thorn chuckled. "So he likes variety."

"I agree." He flashed a quick smile, knowing the same accusation could be leveled at all of them. "Nevertheless, a wife tends to disapprove of that kind of behavior."

"St. Lyon's family will not give up easily," the earl predicted.

"Neither will St. Lyon. Or he will do something outrageous to discourage them."

"Which should be highly entertaining," Thorn replied, likely contemplating how he might profit from the viscount's impending antics. "Although I cannot decide if his family is eager for him to settle down or hope a good marriage will put an end to the speculation that he might be Lord Norgrave's natural son."

Mathias's brows came together. It was rare for any of them to mention the old gossip. "You are lucky St. Lyon isn't here. The last man who brought up the subject was reward with a broken nose for his efforts."

"Have you not considered it, or does your father's hatred for Norgrave and his family prevent you from considering the possibilities because that would make St. Lyon your enemy as well?"

"Don't be an arse," Mathias snapped. "St. Lyon could be related to you and your brother, and I would still call him my friend."

"Very amusing," Thorn drawled as he leaned against the wall. "If it isn't for St. Lyon, then do you want to explain why we have ventured into enemy territory?"

"You have become very jaded about the ton if you view a ballroom as a hostile place," Mathias teased.

"Then it is mere coincidence that Lady Norgrave is present?"

"Is she?" he asked, trying to sound innocent. "For obvious reasons, I have been deprived of a formal introduction. Which lady is she?"

Thorn was not fooled. "Look for a lady in her forties. Blond hair. To your right, about halfway across the room. She is wearing a dark copper dress with a matching turban. The lady next to her is wearing blue."

The copper dress the marchioness was wearing caught Mathias's eye almost immediately. More startling was that he recognized the blonde, who had to be close to his mother's age. Not that he had ever been introduced, but on a few occasions when they attended the same ball, he had noticed her cool regard. She would not have been the first older lady who had approached him with the invitation of a casual affair. However, Lady Norgrave had kept her distance, and pursuing a lady with a jealous husband held little appeal for him.

Mathias and Thorn accepted glasses of sparkling wine from a footman. "I did not realize she was Norgrave's wife," he murmured, taking a contemplative sip from his glass. He grimaced at its sweetness. "Any chance we can trade this wine for brandy?"

"I expect Lord Oxton would accommodate us," Thorn replied. "Unless you have seen enough and we can leave."

"I—"

A young lady in a white muslin dress with shoulder-length curly hair the color of chestnut approached them, but her gaze was locked on Thorn. Her blue eyes were bright with joy. "Gideon, I cannot believe it is you! Why didn't you tell anyone that you would be in town? In your last letter, you did not mention your return."

Annoyance flashed across Thorn's face as his dark green gaze raked the woman. "The simplest answer is because I am not Gideon, Miss Lydall."

The lady flinched at his friend's harsh tone, but she was not intimidated by his temper. "My apologies, Lord Kempthorn," she replied, her initial open friendliness shuttered. "I was under the impression that you detested these affairs, so naturally I mistook you for your twin."

"An understandable mistake, Miss Lydall," Mathias said smoothly. Thorn could be blunt, but he was rarely rude to beautiful ladies. The man deserved an elbow in his ribs for the manner in which he was glaring at the young woman. "I have known Thorn and Gideon for years, and I still have trouble discerning the difference."

"You are too generous, my lord," Miss Lydall said, her troubled gaze still fixed on the earl.

"Lord Fairlamb." Mathias bowed. He might as well have been talking to one of the potted plants. Neither the lady nor his friend was paying attention to him.

"I was unaware that you and Gideon corresponded while he's been away," Thorn grumbled.

Miss Lydall shrugged. "Your brother is my friend and a gentleman."

Mathias blinked as Thorn took an intimidating step toward the lady. "What precisely are you implying, Miss Lydall?"

"Why, nothing at all, my lord." There was a blank politeness masking her face as she curtsied. "Forgive me for interrupting your evening, Lord Fairlamb . . . Lord Kempthorn."

"That was certainly unpleasant," Mathias muttered.

Thorn glared at the departing Miss Lydall. "I wasn't rude."

"The devil you weren't," he countered. "Who is she?"

"A neighbor of sorts." Thorn rubbed his jaw as if it ached. "As a child, she was always underfoot, chasing after us. Gideon had a bad habit of encouraging her, so it is no surprise the chit is in love with him."

Understanding crept into Mathias's expression. "So she is the reason Gideon left—"

Thorn shook his head. "No, that was another lady, and a long time ago. I fear Miss Lydall might try to get her sharp tenterhooks into Gideon's heart when he returns. He always had a soft spot for the girl, though I cannot fathom why."

"Would that be so terrible?" He hesitated. Thorn could be very prickly about his brother. "Especially with what drove Gideon to—"

"Yes," his friend said with his usual bluntness. "Miss Lydall is precisely the opposite of what my brother needs. Now, if you will excuse me, I think I need a glass or two of that brandy we discussed. Care to join me?"

There was no reasoning with Thorn when it came to his twin. Miss Lydall had walked away with her feelings hurt, but if she expected an apology from the earl, she would be disappointed. Mathias let the subject drop.

"I suppose I should. Coming here was a mis—" From the corner of his eye, he noticed that Lady Arabella was embracing Lady Norgrave. Several yards behind her, he spotted Lady Tempest as she chatted with two ladies who had delayed her arrival.

"I shall meet you in the library."

Thorn glanced over his shoulder to see who had caught Mathias's attention. He snorted when he recognized the Brant sisters. "You are courting trouble, my friend."

"Nonsense," he replied, anticipation rising in his chest at the sight of Lady Tempest. "It could be mere coincidence that we happen to be attending the same ball."

It was exactly what he planned to tell his father and mother if they learned of it.

"Not likely," the earl said, unknowingly ruining what Mathias thought was a reasonable explanation. "Chance, I know you are seeking a way to strike back at Marcroft for seducing Miss King."

Mathias scowled at the reminder. He still could not fathom why Clara had chosen Marcroft instead of him. "She would have made an admirable mistress."

Thorn sighed. "So you remarked several times in the coach. Nonetheless, I strongly object to you taking your frustrations out on those ladies."

His eyebrows pinched together as his frown became more prominent. "Does it count that I am interested in only one of them?"

Thorn rolled his eyes. "If you are hoping to provoke Marcroft into a murderous rage, then seducing one of his sisters will guarantee that you will succeed."

"I said nothing of seduction," Mathias mildly protested. "I simply want to test the waters with Lady Tempest."

He idly wondered if he could lure her away and coax her into kissing him again.

"And Marcroft will drown you in those deep waters if you try. Leave the lady alone. Come have a brandy with me before we depart and join our friends," Thorn softly entreated.

"Run along," Mathias said, ignoring his friend's groan of frustration. "I will not be long. I shall pay my respects to the lady, and then we can leave."

"I will tell the footman to send for our coach." Thorn started to walk away. "Just in case Marcroft is in attendance."

# Chapter Ten

"Tempest, what happened to your headdress?"

"Good evening, Mama." She curtsied, resisting the urge to touch her hair. "Oliver sends his apologies, but he was late for an engagement."

The marchioness's hazel eyes chilled at the announcement. "Of course he does," she said, displeased that her son had done his duty but offered nothing more. "You have yet to explain why you are not wearing the headdress we selected for that dress."

"It was a small mishap," Arabella interceded in Tempest's behalf.

She sent her sister a grateful smile. "The crowd at the theater was . . . uh, rougher than we had anticipated, Mama. In the crush, the headdress was trampled before I could rescue it. Arabella and Mrs. Sheehan attempted to repair it. However, once we removed the broken plumes, an imbalance was created—so I thought it best to do without it this evening."

"Did you?"

Tempest hid her wince at her mother's censorious tone. Her brother's absence ensured that the marchioness's ire was focused wholly on her. "There will be other nights to wear the headdress once it is repaired."

"What do you think of Tempest's hair, Mama?" her

sister asked, quietly distracting their mother by changing the subject. "One of Lady Oxton's maids was an absolute godsend, and she possessed a genuine talent for the current hair fashions. We shall have to make certain one of us passes our thanks to the countess."

"Naturally," the marchioness said to Arabella before she turned her critical eye back to Tempest's coiffure. "I concur, Daughter. The maid does have an adequate hand, and we do owe Lady Oxton our gratitude. Tempest, you should thank her personally."

"Of course, Mama," she said, impulsively glancing about the ballroom in search of their hostess. Her impersonal gaze passed over a gentleman sipping sparkling wine near one of the broad columns and traveled a few feet farther before she abruptly halted her search.

No, it could not be *him*.

Tempest's attention returned to the gentleman. Chance silently saluted her with his wineglass.

Good heavens, she could not allow her mother to see him.

She touched her mother on the arm and lightly guided her so that the marchioness's gaze was directed away from the marquess. "Mama, is that Lady Oxton in the silver dress?"

Lord Fairlamb shook his head, clearly amused by her subterfuge even though he was too far away to overhear their conversation.

Arabella noticed Tempest's distress, but she could not find the source as she looked around the ballroom.

"No," her mother said, peering at the woman Tempest had pointed out. "No, that is not her. The countess was wearing an uncomplimentary green dress this evening. I cannot fathom why Sarah allowed the seamstress to talk her into such an unflattering color."

Tempest signaled for the marquess to leave.

The scoundrel had the audacity to grin at her.

"Daughter, are you unwell?" She stiffed in surprise when her mother touched her cheek. "There is too much color in your face."

"Too much rouge," she confessed, clasping her mother's hand and drawing it away. "How clumsy of me."

Arabella looked baffled. "You are not wearing—eee!" she exclaimed when Tempest pinched her just above the elbow. She rubbed her arm and glared at her sister.

Lady Norgrave stared at her daughters. "Is there something you wish to tell me?"

"No," Tempest hastily replied. She nudged her younger sister. "Is that not so?"

Why was Chance here? Had he followed their coach? She raised her hand to motion Lord Fairlamb away, but she quickly changed directions and touched her hair when her sister noticed her gesture.

"Arabella?" her mother pressed.

Her sister had no idea why Tempest was behaving so strangely, but she was loyal. No doubt, she would have questions when they were alone. "Nothing, Mama. We are so happy to join you at the ball. Is Papa here, too?"

The marchioness's lips pursed in irritation at the mention of her husband. "No, like your brother, your father had other plans for the evening."

Amused, Mathias observed from afar as Lady Tempest distracted her mother and sister from his presence.

Intriguing.

Why was she protecting him? He did not require her assistance, but it was endearingly sweet of her not to cause a minor uproar by telling her mother that she was being pursued by one of those loathsome Rookes.

And he was definitely stalking her.

How had he not noticed her last spring? Even without

her jeweled headdress, she was not the kind of lady who blended into the scenery. It was not simply her beauty that appealed. There were many lovely ladies in the ballroom who drew a man's eye, including her younger sister. Something about Lady Tempest called to him. He had yet to figure out what it was about her, but he was content to ponder the puzzle at his leisure.

The lady herself had seen to it that he was left unmolested by her kinsmen.

And where was her devoted brother?

Knowing Marcroft's selfish nature, he likely abandoned his sisters at the Oxtons' front door so he could return to Miss King. Lingering resentment toward the man burrowed under Mathias's skin like an intrusive vine. He was still annoyed that the earl had snatched Clara away from him. There was nothing preventing him from returning the favor. The little jade was unaware that he had observed her tryst with Marcroft. He could leave Lady Tempest alone and renew his pursuit of Miss King. She would enjoy having two gentlemen fight over her.

Mathias had no intention of telling her that she was little more than a means to take a poke at the earl. Her greed had reduced her to such a lowly state. She deserved his ire more than the lady who was casting wary glances in his direction did.

"So it is true. I did not credit it when Thorn told me you were in the ballroom chasing after some chit," said a familiar male voice.

Mathias turned his back on Lady Tempest to address the gentleman to prove that the accusation was warrantless. "Vanewright, this is the last place I would expect you to be."

Christopher Avery Courtland, Earl of Vanewright, inclined his head in acknowledgment. He was as tall as Mathias, with intelligent blue green eyes and straight black hair that had been recently trimmed. The two men had crossed paths at school, but that was not where their friendship originated. It was at the House of Lords, where they had stood on opposing sides of several vigorous debates in which they had managed to find some common ground.

"My mother was unwell this evening, so she asked me to escort my sister in her stead. Have I introduced you to Lady Ellen?"

"Is Lady Netherley conspiring to marry the chit off this season?" At Courtland's knowing grin, Mathias shook his head. "Do not be offended if I politely decline your generous offer. My mother is already lamenting that I spend too much time in my clubs. If she learns that I was speaking with your sister, she might get the mistaken impression that I am seeking a wife."

"I can sympathize, my friend," the earl said. "My mother will not be happy until she sees all her children married off. Unfortunately, my sister is rather stubborn and claims to be content with her life. God willing, Ellen will provide enough of a distraction this season that my mother will be too busy to worry about finding me a bride."

"To my regret, my sister Honora will not be so useful this season. If you are still unmarried next spring, I would be pleased to make the proper introductions to your mother," Mathias teased.

"You are an evil man, Chance," the earl said, his friendly demeanor contradicting his words. "So if you are not hunting for a bride, why are you drawing the attention of every marriage-minded matron in the ballroom?"

"You are exaggerating."

Courtland's right eyebrow kicked upward.

Mathias laughed. "Thorn and I just arrived," he protested.

The earl shook his head at his friend's ignorance.

"When you have a matchmaking mother, as I do, you learn a few things. Trust me, your presence has been noted by every lady who has a young daughter, and it is only a matter of time before someone begs Lady Oxton for an introduction."

He cast a frustrated glance at Lady Tempest. She noticed his regard and tipped her head to the side as if to encourage him to leave. He had to admire her persistence.

"Thorn and I aren't staying. St. Lyon and Rainbault are waiting for us," he said, frustrated that he might have drawn more attention to himself than he had assumed.

"So Kempthorn is wrong when he says that you have taken an unhealthy interest in a certain lady."

"Thorn worries too much—and my interest is unhealthy only if her family learns of it."

"Tread carefully, my friend," Courtland warned, glancing back and noticing that Mathias was not the only one who was curious. "Marcroft fought two duels last month. He would not hesitate to challenge you, considering the history between the Rookes and the Brants."

"Marcroft should be concerned about the hole I put in his arrogant hide," Mathias said coolly.

"Then I wish you luck," Courtland said, resigned that there was nothing that would dissuade Mathias from his path.

"Luck is something I have always had in abundance, Courtland," Mathias said with a touch of arrogance. "However, I would appreciate some assistance if you have a few minutes."

Chance was leaving with Lord Courtland.

Tempest felt an unnecessary frisson of disappointment at his departure. Lord Fairlamb was respecting her wishes. She should be relieved that he had given up on his fool's errand to speak with her. The why of it, she could not fathom.

*I should not have kissed him.*

If he had been encouraged by her recklessness, she hoped there would come a time that she could correct her mistake. She did not want him to think that she went about kissing every handsome gentleman who demanded a kiss from her.

"My lord, may I present my daughters, Lady Tempest and Lady Arabella," her mother said, compelling Tempest to concentrate on the gentleman standing in front of her. He arrived in London less than a week ago, and for some reason, Lady Norgrave was thrilled that he had deliberately sought her out when he entered Lord and Lady Oxton's ballroom. "Daughters, may I present Thaddeus Tayer, Marquess of Warrilow.

"A distinct pleasure, ladies," the twenty-six-year-old Lord Warrilow genially replied. His bow was executed with admirable grace in a gentleman who was slightly over six feet in height.

She and Arabella responded in kind with a curtsy.

His casually studied both her and her sister with quiet approval in his blue green eyes. "The recent acquisition of the Warrilow title has broadened my circle of friends. However, I am pleased to call Lord Norgrave a close and dear friend. I must say that I am honored to have been afforded the opportunity to meet his greatest treasures . . . his beautiful wife and daughters."

"Nicely done, my lord. You flatter us," the marchioness said; her voice alone revealed that she was impressed by the gentleman's speech and manners. "If you do not mind me inquiring, how long will you be remaining in London?"

"As long as it takes, madam," was his enigmatic reply.

"For what reason, my lord?" Tempest asked, since Arabella could not stir herself to speak.

"Did your father not tell you?" At the abrupt shake of her head, the marquess replied, "I have come to town to seek a wife. Permit me to explain. I was a barrister before I inherited my cousin's title. For most of my life, I believed the line secure and never contemplated a day when the burden—nay, the sacred duty—would fall upon me. Needless to say, I was overwhelmed. It was your father who wisely suggested that I take a bride who could assist me, and shoulder the responsibilities of the household while I adjust to my new station in life."

"My husband is a clever man," Lady Norgrave said diplomatically.

What was left unsaid was that her father had high hopes of securing a match for one of his daughters. Lord Warrilow had come to London to inspect Norgrave's daughters, and if he found them lacking, the members of the ton would eagerly assist in his quest for a marchioness.

She had no doubt the gentleman would achieve his set goal with resounding success.

As a potential husband, the Marquess of Warrilow was an impressive candidate. Not only was he good looking with his dark hair, soulful eyes, and the subtle dimple in the middle of his chin. He was also polite, articulate, and educated. Tempest glanced at Arabella, who only seemed capable of gaping at the gentleman. If the marquess required a bride, her sister would be an advantageous match for him.

Tempest looked up and was startled to see that Lord Warrilow was staring at her with a contemplative expression on his face.

"I hope I am not interrupting?"

Tempest met the amused gaze of Lord Vanewright. Only minutes earlier, she had observed him departing the ballroom with Lord Fairlamb. When had he returned? She had had enough surprises for one evening. If her mother were to announce that it was time to leave, she would gladly say her farewells without complaint.

"Lord Vanewright," her mother said, extending her hand. The earl clasped her fingers and bowed. "Where is your delightful mother? I have yet to greet her this evening."

"I fear my lady mother is unwell this evening." At the marchioness's soft sound of dismay, he added, "It is nothing serious. In fact, I suspect Lady Netherley may have exaggerated her symptoms so I would attend the ball in her stead."

He winked at Lady Norgrave and she laughed before she could take offense that the man had called his mother a liar.

"You are a scoundrel, my lord. Small wonder your mother must scheme to gain your cooperation," her mother replied. She had two handsome bachelors within reach, and she was not about to waste such an opportunity. "Lord Warrilow, are you acquainted with Lord and Lady Netherley's heir, Lord Vanewright?"

"I am, madam," the marquess replied, nodding curtly to the other gentleman. "Vanewright."

"Warrilow." The earl dismissed the man with a subtle shift of his shoulders. "Lady Norgrave, with your permission, I would like to invite Lady Tempest to join me and my sister for a walk in the gardens."

"Lady Ellen is here?"

"Yes, madam," he said, disconcerting Tempest further by meeting her wary gaze. "When I told her that your daughter was present this evening, she begged me to find her immediately so they could renew their acquaintance."

Arabella looked askance at her, but Tempest was hardly in a position to reply. They had been introduced to both of Lady Netherley's daughters. Lady Ellen had been amusing and kind. However, their friendship was not so close that they corresponded through the post.

"Naturally, my daughter would love to see Lady Ellen again," her mother replied when she sensed hesitation within her eldest daughter. "Lord Warrilow, you do not mind keeping us company."

"Not at all, my lady," was the marquess's swift reply.

Tempest felt the heat of Lord Warrilow's gaze as she allowed Lord Vanewright to escort her toward the open doors of the Lady Oxton's gardens.

She did not anticipate any trickery until she stepped outdoors and saw Lord Fairlamb standing under the light of one of the torches.

# Chapter Eleven

The red highlights in Tempest's hair were noticeable as the light of flickering flame danced over the top of her head. Her face was composed and unreadable, so Mathias could not decide if she was pleased to see him again.

"So this was a ruse?" she asked Lord Vanewright. "Lady Ellen isn't here."

"My sister is in the cardroom, Lady Tempest. She would be pleased to see you again if you would care to join her later." The earl looked pointedly at his friend. "Do you know what you are doing?"

"You needn't worry, Vanewright."

"Very well. You are on your own if Lady Norgrave decides to play whist." The earl bowed and strolled off in the opposite direction.

Mathias offered Lady Tempest his arm. "I thought you might appreciate some fresh air."

She hesitated and glanced at the open doors she had walked through. There were several couples enjoying the night air. If she decided to flee, he would do nothing to stop her from leaving.

"It is a walk, my lady. Nothing more." Mathias gave her an exasperated look. "If I were planning to have my wicked way with you, the dark corridor of the theater would have better served my purposes," he said, infusing a hint of annoyance in his voice to gain her capitulation.

"Oh, very well." She slipped her hand through his, and he wasted no time in moving away from the other couples.

Lady Tempest had been seen entering the gardens. When she returned to the ballroom, it would be on Vanewright's arm. No one within the room would be aware that she'd switched escorts on the terrace.

The torches had been placed close enough to provide ample light throughout the back gardens. There was a slight chill to the air, but it felt good against his skin after spending time in the stuffy ballroom.

"Is Marcroft here or did he abandon you once again?"

She bristled at his question. "My mother asked Oliver to escort us from the theater. He never intended to stay."

In hindsight, he should not have attacked her brother. Marcroft was practically a saint in his sister's eyes, and his inquiry provoked a vigorous defense. Mathias decided to switch tactics. "Have you recovered from your ordeal?"

"Which one? The fumbling drunk or the kiss?"

Mathias grinned, thoroughly enjoying her spirited retort. "If given a choice, I prefer to discuss the latter."

Lady Tempest held her chin high, and she strolled with him fearless down the garden path. By God, the chit had cheek. Another lady might have fainted after being pawed by an ardent admirer. "I prefer not to discuss what happened at the theater at all."

"Very well." He sighed. "Let us discuss Lord Warrilow. What business does he have with your family?"

"None."

"None," he echoed. "Now, that is not precisely the truth. Your mother practically embraced him like a son when he greeted her."

Lady Tempest turned her face away, but he noted her irritation at his observation. "My father and Lord Warrilow are friends," she explained in a cautious manner, as if she was concerned about revealing too much.

"Warrilow recently inherited the title. I assume he looks on your father as some sort of mentor."

"I suppose," she replied, glancing at him. "My father has encouraged him to seek a bride."

"Ah, I see," Mathias said, sending pea gravel across the path with a sudden fuming kick.

Her family had brought her and her sister to London with the ambition to match them with titled gentlemen with prosperous estates. His family would eventually do the same for his sisters. He could not explain why he found the cold reasoning of the annual practice repugnant.

"So you would be content to marry a marquess?"

She gave him a long contemplative look. "I suppose. I have not really thought about it. Does the title matter?"

Warrilow was older, and he had been a respected barrister before inheriting the title. The lands and wealth that came with the title would polish away any rough manners or gaps in his education. "To some. It depends on the lady's aspirations."

"Well then, if it is based on a *lady's* aspirations, then wouldn't she choose a gentleman she could come to love and respect?"

He had discovered since he bedded his first woman that they were mercenary creatures. "What about title and fortune?"

She did not seem to notice the cynical edge to his voice. "Ah, now you speak of a father's aspiration. A man wants his daughter protected and well cared for, do you not agree?"

"Your father believes Lord Warrilow is worthy of you?"

She halted, surprised by the question. "Perhaps. Although I doubt my father had a particular daughter in mind when he encouraged the marquess to present himself to my mother." She cleared her throat. "To be honest, I did not fare well last season when compared to other young ladies close to my age. It is quite possible that Lord Warrilow will find my sister more to his liking."

He scowled, the small flicker of jealousy abating. Did she not see her own value? "I disagree."

He could see that she was delighted by his response.

"It is kind of you to say so, but you do not know me, my lord. I have many qualities that many gentlemen view as flaws." There was no sorrow in her expression, simply acceptance.

Mathias caressed her cheek with his knuckles. "Name these imaginary flaws."

She wrinkled her nose. "They are too numerous to recite. Suffice it to say, the man who marries me will have to be tolerant."

"Or so blinded by love that he cannot see any flaws." Mathias instantly regretted his words. He did not intend to offend her.

Lady Tempest astounded him by laughing. "If you know such a man, you have my permission to give him my name, though I doubt he exists."

"You are too young to be so jaded."

"I am two-and-twenty, Lord Fairlamb. I have seen enough of the world to understand that love is an indulgence, and in rare instances, a gift. A farmer may fall in love with a dairymaid and marry without any thought to himself or his family. However, a marquess's daughter must be practical out of necessity."

Lady Tempest baffled him. What lady did not seek love? Her views were full of contradictions. "So you would be happy with any gentleman, so long as he elevates you above his favorite hound," he said, unable to keep the pity from his voice.

There was little doubt that his father must have contemplated the advantages of marrying a duke's daughter, but that had not driven him to offer for her hand. His father had married Lady Imogene Sunter because he fell in love with her.

Mathias expected to do the same one day.

Unaware of his brooding thoughts, Tempest teased, "What lady could compete with a favored hound?"

Her smile coaxed from him a reluctant half smile. His mouth twitched. "Fine. I will concede that there are gentlemen who would choose a dog over a wife."

"Not you?"

He slowly shook his head. "I prefer a woman in my bed."

Lady Tempest gaped at him, speechless.

Mathias cursed his unruly tongue. He could not take back his words, so he tried to soften the brazen image he had placed in her head. "Dogs have foul breath."

She clapped her hands together and laughed at his pantomime.

Enchanted, he thought of another reason just to make her laugh again: "And they are far too hairy for kisses."

"I shall take your word on it," she said, seeming more relaxed with each corner they turned. The gravel path was designed like a large rectangle with intersecting paths for those who preferred shorter walks. If they followed the perimeter, they would eventually find their way back to the terrace.

Mathias encouraged Tempest to take the next turn. If he had his way, their walk through the torchlit garden would be the longest ever traversed.

"Is your family good friends of Lord and Lady Oxton?"

Content to set aside their conversation about Warrilow

and marriage, he shrugged. "The earl and his countess have attended several of my mother's balls. What about yours?"

"My father enjoys hunting with Lord Oxton. They make use of the earl's hunting lodge in the north."

It never ceased to amaze him how many families connected them, even though it was rare for a Rooke and a Brant to share the same room.

The wall of hedge opened up into an alcove, and he was about to ask Lady Tempest if she would prefer to sit when he noted to his great amusement that the marble bench was occupied. Arms entangled, the man and woman were too lost in their kiss to notice them. At his companion's soft gasp, he glanced at her to see her reaction. Instead of being offended or embarrassed, the lady stared at the young couple with curiosity and amusement. She met his gaze and smiled.

Mathias placed his hand on her waist and nudged her forward. She covered her mouth with her hand and tried not to laugh. Neither one of them spoke until they were certain the couple would not be aware of their presence.

When it was safe for her to speak, Lady Tempest pulled her hand away and giggled. "I think I know the lady."

"Do you?" he replied as they circled around a large fountain.

She nodded, and he longed to pull her into his arms and kiss her until the mischievous expression on her face sharpened into hunger.

"And that gentleman was not her betrothed."

Lady Tempest must have sensed his intent because she quickened her pace until she was out of reach. "What are you about, my lord? Did you follow me to the Oxtons'?"

"And what if I did?"

"You shouldn't have, Lord Fairlamb."

"You have called me Chance. There is no reason for formality between us."

"No reason." She raised her hands upward as if she were imploring the heavens to side with her. "Your family name is reason enough for formality. I should not even be speaking to you."

"Or kissing me."

She held her ground as he walked to her. "Stop!" Lady Tempest glanced down and moistened her lips. "You asked for a boon. I should have refused."

"And yet you didn't," he murmured, tucking his finger under her chin and lifting it until she meet his gaze. "Why is it that I want to kiss you again, even though the first one was quite abysmal?"

Lady Tempest was so anxious on account of his proximity that it took her a few seconds to comprehend his words. Her expressive hazel eyes widened and then narrowed, reminding him that she was related to a gentleman who would happily shoot Mathias if she asked. "What did you say?"

"Perhaps 'abysmal' is too strong a word," he said, knowing he was courting danger by teasing her, but her indignation was a temptation he could not resist. "It was probably your first, and no one gets these things right on the first try."

"Abysmal, he says," she muttered to herself. "My first kiss. I will have you know that I have kissed dozens of gentlemen, and not a single one ever complained, you arrogant muttonhead!"

Feigning disappointment, he shook his head with dismay. "Lying is a sin, you know. If you are looking to practice on someone, I would happily volunteer for the task."

Lady Tempest rolled her eyes and walked away without bothering to respond.

Chuckling under his breath, he followed on her heels.

"Aw, come now, Lady Tempest. You cannot be angry over a little kiss. A kiss, I might add, that you did your best to ruin."

Forgetting that she was not speaking to him, she said, "I did no such thing, Lord Fairlamb."

Mathias caught her arm and pulled her to a halt. "A lady who has kissed dozens of gents would have been more adept at kissing." He lowered his head until their foreheads almost touched. "Tell the truth. You were frightened to kiss me because I bear the Rooke name. You were worried you might like it." He pinched his finger and thumb together. "Maybe just a little."

"Don't be ridiculous. Have you considered that I didn't want to kiss you?" Lady Tempest hissed, tugging her arm free. She rubbed the spot where he had touched her. "Or is your opinion of yourself so bloated that you believe all ladies long for your kisses?"

"It is not what I believe—it is what I know." He took a menacing step closer. "You are afraid."

"I am not!"

"You are," he said, keeping his voice level. "That afternoon by the riverbanks . . . you felt it. An awareness between us. Attraction. Even St. Lyon and Thorn noticed it."

"You are wrong," she whispered.

"And then you kissed me," he continued, ignoring her denial. "Chaste. Brief. Painfully pathetic."

Lady Tempest brought her hand to her mouth, and the noise she muffled sounded like a cross between a sob and laughter.

Mathias wrapped his fingers around her delicate wrist and pulled her hand away from her mouth. "And still that simple chaste kiss struck me like a bolt of lightning. It split my skin, cleaved through muscle and bone, and touched my soul."

She would have staggered backwards if he had not held on to her wrist. "This is some kind of prank, is it not? You cannot possibly mean—"

"Do you honestly believe you are the only one who has something to lose?" His fierce gaze swept over her. "I love my father. I am loyal to my family. I could have my pick of any lady in London, and here I am, consorting with my father's enemy."

"I am *not* your father's enemy," she spit through clenched teeth.

"Nor am I yours, Lady Tempest," was his cool reply. "And yet, we have a problem, do we not?"

She and Mathias stared at each other, both of them feeling the weight of the attraction she stubbornly refused to acknowledge. He had not followed her to the Oxtons' to confront her, but he could not dredge up any regret about it.

"It is a problem only if we allow it to be," she said finally. "We will just stay away from—"

Mathias silenced her by covering her mouth with his. She had devastated him with a chaste kiss. Now he would show her the unplumbed depths of passion. He devoured her lips, breathing her in as if the taste and scent of her were paramount to his existence.

"Open your mouth," he murmured, placing tiny kisses on her pliant lips.

To his wonder, Lady Tempest complied. His tongue caressed the seam of her lips and slipped inside. She moaned against his lips as the edge of her tongue tentatively touched his as she swayed closer. For several minutes, he lost himself in the seductive duel, savoring the taste of her.

Her eyes fluttered open the moment he ended the kiss. She had no idea how beautiful she looked. Her hazel eyes were dark and heavy with desire, her lips reddened and slightly swollen from his kiss.

"Chance," she said, staring at him with a bemused expression on her face, as if she were truly seeing him for the first time.

"You are a very dangerous lady, Tempest," he said, kissing her again because he knew she would not push him away. "Fortunately, I like to court danger."

"But—"

Mathias kissed her again to silence her protest. "Hush. I am not asking for anything but a chance to spend time with you."

Her hazel eyes were gradually clearing of the passion he had stoked within her. "What you are asking for is impossible. My family—"

"Our families," he corrected, wanting her to understand that she was not the only one taking risks, "are not part of this. We can be friends. What harm does it cause any of them?"

She studied him in the darkness. "Is that what you want from me? For us to be friends?"

Mathias was reluctant to put a name to his feelings or what he would demand of her before they parted ways. "Would it make you feel better if I called us friendly enemies?"

"No." She stepped away from him. "It only reminds me of the consequences if my family catches us together."

He was confident he could handle Marcroft or her father if they decided to interfere.

Mathias tangled his fingers with hers. "Then we will have to make certain we do not get caught."

# Chapter Twelve

Tempest swallowed the sharp rising urge to scream when she opened the door to the library and was confronted by an unknown man.

"Zounds girl, you cannot go about frightening people," the sixty-year-old gentleman with more hair on his chin and eyebrows than on his head scolded as he worked his way around her. "I have a bad heart, you know."

"I beg your pardon, sir." She curtsied and turned to the side so she could offer him a clear path. "No one told me that my father had a visitor."

"Tempest, is that you?"

"Yes, Papa," she called out, and she turned back to the man she had practically collided into. "I—"

Tempest saw a parting glimpse of his back before the door closed. She walked into the room and glanced to the right. Her father was returning a book to the shelf. He opened his arms and she rushed up to him. The familiar weight of his arms wrapped around her as she pressed her face into his frock coat.

"Good afternoon, Papa," she said, soothed by his scent and warmth. "I hope I am not interrupting anything important."

"Oh, do you mean Mallory? No, he was only delivering some papers that I had requested." Lord Norgrave pulled away and studied his daughter's face. "I hear you had an adventurous evening."

Her stomach clenched and immediately her thoughts centered on Chance. She forced herself to relax. It was absurd, really. There was no possible way her father could have learned of her walk with Lord Fairlamb or their illuminating kiss.

"Which part? Being trapped in a coach with Oliver? The awful crush at the theater, which meant I spent the entire time standing in the back so I missed all the performances? Or Lord and Lady Oxton's ball?"

The marquess pinched her chin. "You look quite happy in spite of your misadventures."

Tempest followed him as he returned to his desk. She sat down in one of the chairs positioned near it. "Well, I am your daughter. I am made of sterner stuff than that."

He slipped on his spectacles and swiftly inspected a letter before he put it aside. He glanced at her over the lenses. "I was actually referring to Lord Warrilow. Your mother tells me that he insisted on an introduction."

"An introduction likely orchestrated by you, I would guess," she teased.

Her father's unabashed grin revealed all she needed to know.

"I thought so. I suppose Mama told you that the marquess was a perfect gentleman. He flattered Mama—"

"Which positively delighted her," murmured Lord Norgrave.

"And Arabella and I accepted his invitations to dance." She leaned forward. "I can attest that he is a competent dance partner. He stepped on my toes once."

"So you liked him?"

Amused by her father's nonchalant demeanor, she said, "Lord Warrilow appears to be very likable. So much so, I predict every matron who has a daughter will be inviting him to call on her household."

"Invitations he would ignore if I could give the young man some encouragement that he would be welcome in our house."

"I cannot speak for Arabella—"

"I am not asking for your sister's opinion. I would like to hear your thoughts."

"Lord Warrilow left a favorable impression, Papa," Tempest replied sincerely. "There was little opportunity to speak when we danced, but he seemed earnest in his quest for a bride this spring, so there is little doubt that Arabella and I are on his list of prospective candidates."

Lord Norgrave removed his reading spectacles. "My friendship with Warrilow has put you and your sister at the top of his list."

Tempest was not surprised by the news, yet her heart plummeted to her stomach. Last year, her father had taken great pains to ensure that she was at the top of Lord Rinehart's list, and the results had been disastrous.

"What? You have nothing to say? No words of thanks for your dear papa?"

"Naturally, I am grateful, Papa," she began.

"Good God, you are not thinking of debating me on the issue. Not after what happened with Lord Rinehart."

"Lord Rinehart is precisely the point," she argued, her courage wavering when she noticed his stern look. "You cannot govern another's heart. Warrilow will not marry me because it is the outcome you desire."

"You think not?" He leaned back in his chair and studied her. "Is that why you chose to walk in the garden with Vanewright?"

How did he know of her walk in the Oxtons' gardens? Her mother? Tempest frowned. When Lord Vanewright had invited her to join him, he told her mother that it was to see his sister, Lady Ellen. After her walk with Chance, the earl had kept his promise and escorted her to his sister. She had a pleasant visit with the young woman, who seemed unaware of her brother's machinations with Lord Fairlamb. However, if her father was aware she had been in the back gardens, then someone had been watching them.

What else had his spy glimpsed?

"You are well-informed. The walk was nothing more than a slight detour so I could admire the Oxtons' gardens."

"Vanewright would not have been my first choice if you hoped to catch his interest. He is a bit of a scoundrel, you know."

"Oh." She pursed her lips as she contemplated this bit of news. "I found his manners above reproach." Well, so long as she overlooked the fact that the earl had lied to her mother and handed her off to the son of her father's enemy. In that light, Lord Vanewright was a very wicked fellow. "Nor am I casting any aspirations in the earl's direction."

Her father gave her a look of approval. "It is just as well. Vanewright is enjoying his bachelorhood too much to be content with a wife, and his family's influence has diminished since Lord Netherley has withdrawn from town life."

Tempest had heard last season about Lord and Lady Netherley's tragic loss of not just one son, but two. Of Lord Netherley's inconsolable grief and his frustrations with his current heir. However, that was the problem with gossip. It was a mixed bag of truth and speculation. Such things did not matter to her father. He weighed the value of a prospective son-in-law by his family's influence and what benefits he could achieve from the alliance.

Some might view it as coldhearted, but it has served

her father well, since his marriage to her mother had been approached in a similar manner.

"My conversation with Lady Ellen did not include her brother or her family beyond the usual pleasantries," she said lightly as she rose from her seat. "Suffice it to say, Lord Warrilow did precisely what you asked of him."

"I will have your word that you will not discourage the young marquess."

"Heaven forbid." Tempest leaned over the desk and kissed her father on the cheek. "I shall not keep you. Harriet should be arriving soon and I must change my dress before we leave."

"What do you and your cousin have planned for the afternoon?" he asked, rising from his chair and following her to the door.

"A little shopping while I run a few errands for Mama," she said, her attention switching to which carriage dress she intended to wear. She waved and headed for the grand staircase.

Lord Norgrave's smile had a hint of indulgence as he watched his eldest daughter mutter to herself about the weather and dresses. She was a sweet, kindhearted girl who was determined not to disappoint him this season. He intended to make certain that nothing spoiled his plans for her to marry Warrilow.

"Did she admit that she and Lord Vanewright were in the gardens?"

Tempest was no longer in sight, but he could not resist sending his wife a censuring glance. "She explained everything." Noting his marchioness's doubt, he added, "The girl has no propensity for deceit. Unlike her mother."

"Or her sire," Charlotte replied crisply.

Norgrave inclined his head in an abbreviated bow. "Just do your part, Wife. Warrilow is ripe for the picking. I will have him for one of my daughters."

His wife frowned at this revelation. "I thought he was meant for Tempest."

"Naturally, she is my first choice, since she is the eldest daughter," he conceded. "However, the debacle with Rinehart proved that there are advantages to having more than one daughter."

"Such a clever man," she softly mocked, curtsying. "You have thought of everything."

Charlotte was baiting him, but he resisted the urge to punish her for her impudence. "I do what I must."

"This is not precisely how you expected to spend your afternoon."

Mathias shrugged at his mother's observation, neither confirming nor denying it. Seated beside his sister Mercy, they sat opposite their mother and Honora in the family's barouche-landau. His mother's note arrived while he was eating breakfast, asking him to join her and his younger sisters on a shopping jaunt. To indulge her, he'd canceled his appointments for the day.

"Why would I deny myself the pleasure of spending the day with three of the prettiest ladies in London?" he said, tickling his fifteen-year-old sister under the chin to make her giggle. "If you had not sent a note, I would have been forced to come up with an excuse to visit."

"You do not need excuses to visit your family, Mathias," the duchess said, her dark blue eyes vibrant with amusement, aware that her eldest son was deliberately flattering her. "You and your friends are always welcome."

"Just another reason why my friends are in love with you," he teased. "If you were not already married, I fear I might have to fight St. Lyon and Rainbault to protect your honor."

"Oh, Chance," the duchess sighed, though it was obvious she was not offended.

Honora rolled her eyes and turned her head so she could watch the pedestrians that strolled by them. Their carriage had slowed because several barrels had fallen from a wagon and now blocked a portion of the street.

Mercy tapped him on the arm. He stared at her and marveled how much she looked like their mother. "What would St. Lyon and the prince want with Mama?"

The duchess laughed when he appeared incapable of answering his sister's question. "Oh no, my dear boy, you are on your own," she said in response to his silent plea for assistance.

"I was merely teasing, honeybee," he said, the endearment a long-standing reference to her honey and golden locks. "Our mother is so beautiful that every gentleman she meets falls instantly in love with her."

The duchess poked his leg with the end of her unopened parasol. "Does that tongue of yours ever stop waggling?"

"Now, look what you've done. You have made Mama blush," Mercy said, enjoying the exchange between mother and son. "Though if the prince cannot have her, then maybe I should marry him. After all, I would be a splendid princess."

"The Prince of Galien would never marry a child," Honora said, dashing her younger sister's ambitions without even glancing in her direction. "Besides, he is *old*."

"He is not," Mercy said, sliding into a slouch as she crossed her arms over her breasts. "And I am not a child. In a few years, the prince and I could marry and then you would have to curtsy whenever I entered the room."

Outraged at the very thought, Honora's blue gray eyes narrowed as she glared at her sister. "You will never marry the prince, so I will never have to curtsy in your presence. Never!"

"Honora and Mercy, I have heard quite enough from

both of you," the duchess said sharply. "Honora, I expect better manners from you . . . and Mercy, you might as well put aside your aspirations to marry Rainbault. The gentleman is too old for you."

"How can that be? Papa is seven years older than you, and yet you were permitted to marry him," Mercy argued with the passion of a child who would not be denied. "The prince is older than I by only six years."

The duchess was momentarily silenced by her daughter's argument. To her credit, she recovered rather quickly. "His age does not matter. Even if Rainbault were the same age, he would still be older than you."

"But, Mama—"

"Not another word on the subject." Her measured stare swept over all three of her children. "Have I made myself clear?"

Mathias winced as his sisters glowered at each other. His mother was correct. Rainbault was a rogue and not a worthy suitor for any of his sisters. He would have to warn Rainbault of Mercy's lofty ambitions. Over the years, his friend had done nothing more than casually tease the girls as if they were his sisters, but Mercy had clearly developed an affection for the gentleman. He met his mother's mildly disapproving gaze and noted the increased color in his mother's cheeks. "Too much sun, perhaps?"

"You are your father's son," his mother replied. "You are capable of charming and annoying females of all ages with little effort. I almost pity the young ladies who capture your interest this season."

He raised an eyebrow. "Almost?"

"Well, I am your mother," she said dryly. "For the sake of my future grandchildren, it would be best if you marry their mother."

"You will forgive me if it takes a few years to find this

paragon," he said, always appreciative of his mother's wit. "If you need to play matchmaker, you might consider finding a good woman for Thorn. He seems a bit lost without his twin brother."

Her expression softened with concern at the mention of their cousins. "Eight months have passed since I received a letter from Gideon. I pray he has been more dedicated in his correspondence with his brother."

"I doubt it," he confessed. "Thorn doesn't complain, but I swear his temperament darkens with each passing year. In fact, I—"

A lady wearing a French cambric round dress with a blue and white checked pelisse scattered his thoughts. Her leghorn bonnet prevented him from seeing her face, but there was something familiar about her, he mused. If they were not at the mercy of the traffic, the carriage would already have passed her and her companions, and he would have been able to solve the mystery of her identity.

The lady obliged his curiosity by glancing over her shoulder, and he realized it was Lady Tempest. She was not alone. Their small party consisted of her chaperone, another lady, and a footman. He watched as two gentlemen and another lady caught up to them. Lady Tempest embraced the young woman and was genuinely pleased by the interruption.

*Who the devil were those two fellows?*

"Mathias," his mother softly called. When his gaze switched back to hers, she smiled. "You were saying?"

"What? I do beg your pardon," he said, resisting the urge to glance in the direction of Lady Tempest and her party. "I have forgotten what I was going to say."

"Chance was staring at the ladies," Honora tattled, noting the direction of his gaze. "Though, I must say his taste is improving. Whoever they are, they have paid a small fortune for those dresses."

"I was not staring," he mildly protested at his mother's questioning glance. "Not precisely. I thought one of the gentlemen chatting with the ladies seemed familiar. Perhaps someone I encountered at one of my clubs."

When his mother and sisters turned to take a closer look at the gentleman he claimed to know, Mathias groaned. He doubted his mother would recognize Lady Tempest, but he had no desire to put his assumptions to the test.

"Close your mouth, Honora," Mathias snapped. "Do you want to swallow a fly?" He tapped his walking stick against the bench to gain the coachman's attention. "Any way around this tangle, or should we disembark?"

Even as he asked the question, the coachman signaled the horses to move forward. "We should be fine now, milord. Don't ye worry."

He discreetly glanced at Lady Tempest as their carriage rolled by her and her friends, but she was unaware of his presence. After the kiss they had shared in the Oxtons' gardens, he had been considering how he might see her again without gaining the scrutiny of her brother or the rest of her family.

Mathias smiled at his mother.

*Or mine.*

Not that Lady Tempest had been particularly encouraging when she strolled away from him with Lord Vanewright at her side.

Still, the lady had kissed him and she had enjoyed it.

If given the opportunity, he would do it again.

# Chapter Thirteen

"You have a new admirer," Harriet whispered in her ear.

Tempest grinned as she accepted the small paper-wrapped package that contained several pairs of gloves and a fan she had impulsively purchased. Lady Harriet Caspwell was a year older than Tempest and a distant cousin. She also considered herself an expert on gentlemen, since she had been raised with four older brothers and had recently become betrothed to Lord Medeley.

"Pray tell me your gentleman does not possess a fickle heart," she teased, knowing the young earl was wholly smitten with his lady. If Harriet's mother had not insisted on their being wed at St. George's, Tempest was certain the couple would have headed north to Gretna Green the second her cousin had accepted his offer of marriage.

Confident in herself and the gentleman who loved her, Harriet gave her a playful nudge as they headed toward the open doorway where Lord Medeley, his sister, and Lord Chandler waited for them.

"You know I speak of the viscount. He sees no one but you, Cousin."

Tempest could not disagree when the gentleman they were discussing was indeed watching their approach. The same age as she, Anthony Warren, Viscount Chandler, was the Earl of Eyre's heir. Her father did not have a high opinion of Lord Eyre, and dismissed the son as too young and weak for his daughter. She doubted a year had altered her father's opinion, but the viscount was a handsome devil, and his interest was flattering.

"Poor Lady Joan," Harriet murmured with pity lacing her voice. "It is obvious that she adores Lord Chandler, and feels intimidated by your presence."

"I have been nothing but kind to her," Tempest protested.

"She fears you will steal her beloved viscount from her. It is the only reason why she did not join us. It is rather pathetic how she simpers and guards him like a faithful hound."

"Be kind, Harriet," Tempest replied, pasting a smile on her face so their waiting companions would not deduce that they were being discussed. "You have found your true love and he returns your affection. Not all of us are so fortunate."

"If you are referring to you and Rinehart, your argument has no merit," her cousin argued, forcing her words through her clenched teeth as she smiled at her earl.

"How so?"

Without looking at her, Harriet tipped her chin high. "Your father was the one who was in love with Rinehart."

It was such an outrageous statement, Tempest burst out laughing.

"Care to share the jest?" Lord Chandler said, easily transferring her small package from her hands to his. His uninvited courtesy earned him a frown from Joan.

Tempest glanced at her cousin, which caused both ladies to giggle. She shook her head. "My cousin likes to tease those she loves. Lord Medeley, you have my sympathies."

The twenty-eight-year-old earl was not as handsome as the viscount, but there was love and kindness in his vivid blue eyes when his gaze settled on Harriet. "I look forward to the time when I can listen to her laughter each day. Perhaps we should elope, my love."

While Harriet explained yet again how disappointed her family would be if they ran off to be married in Scotland, Tempest shared a commiserating glance with Lord Chandler. There was nothing so wonderful or annoying as a young couple in love.

The viscount tucked the package under his arm so he could offer his elbow. "Where shall we go next, Lady Tempest? I am yours to command."

"I wish to visit the bookseller's shop," a very disgruntled Lady Joan murmured behind them.

The wooden walkway was congested with pedestrians, and there was barely enough room for a strolling couple; otherwise, Tempest would have encouraged Lady Joan to walk beside them.

"How fortuitous! I would like to visit the bookseller, too," Tempest said, turning back and smiling at the dour Lady Joan.

Something akin to hatred burned in the other woman's eyes. Tempest glanced away. She had no reason to dislike Harriet's future sister-in-law, but the lady's friendly demeanor had chilled the moment she realized that she had competition for the viscount's affections.

"An appreciation for the written word," Lord Chandler said, oblivious to the tension between Tempest and Lady Joan. It only increased at his next observation. "Just one more thing we have in common."

With an air of impatience, Mathias slipped his pocket watch back into its pocket in his waistcoat. He stood outside the dressmaker's shop while his mother and sisters admired the recent fashions and fabrics. Since his interest in a lady's attire was limited to how quickly he could relieve her of her dress and underclothes, he announced that he would wait for them outdoors. His position also gave him the opportunity to observe Lady Tempest's progress.

"There you are," his mother said cheerfully. The footman behind his sisters had his arms filled with several large boxes. "How bored are you?"

"Not at all," Mathias said, offering the duchess his arm. "Although I was thinking that our next stop should be the bookseller's shop."

"When do you read?" Honora asked bluntly.

"I have intellectual pursuits," Mathias said, trying not to sound defensive when confronted with his sister's disbelief. "I will admit that I have little patience for novels like that romantic drivel recently published by Lady Caroline Lamb. However, I do find a quiet moment to read on occasion."

"No one is certain who published *Glenarvon*," the duchess said, striving to be diplomatic, though the three-volume tale had caused quite a stir among the members of the ton.

As they crossed to the other side of the street, he said, "Mother, everyone knows who authored the damn books. Just as no one is surprised that the lady waited until Byron departed England before she dared to have it published."

Honora giggled. "I have enjoyed Lord Byron's literary efforts. Perhaps I should read *Glenarvon*."

"No, you will not," the duchess said sharply. Her lips trembled as she tried not to smile when her gaze locked with Mathias's. "Always causing mischief, my boy. Come, Honora and Mercy. Let us see if we can find something less scandalous to read."

Her Grace and his sisters headed left while Mathias lingered near the entrance of the shop. He did not want to be obvious in his search for Lady Tempest, nor did he wish to alert the lady to his presence immediately.

There.

His breath caught in his throat as his mother and sisters approached Lady Tempest. The duchess was speaking quietly to Mercy, so there was no hesitation in her step as his mother and two sisters strolled by Norgrave's daughter. Lady Tempest glanced up from the book in her hand, but there was nothing but mild curiosity in her gaze before she returned her attention to the open pages.

She stood several yards away from two of her companions. On closer inspection, he recognized the gentleman. Lord Chandler. His head was tilted to one side as he listened to the lady standing next to him, but his attention was solely focused on Lady Tempest. Mathias wondered if she was aware that the viscount was in love with her. With some amusement, he noted that Chandler's companion was aware of his attraction and she was not happy about it.

The other couple had distanced themselves from their friends. The gentleman was Lord Medeley. Someone had placed a wager in the betting book that the earl and his betrothed, Lady Harriet Caspwell would not wed on the date set by the family. By their flirtatious glances, Mathias doubted the man desired to escape his matrimonial fate. He was so certain the marriage would take place, he intended to place his own wager on the couple the next time he visited the club.

Keeping track of his family, Lady Tempest, and her friends, Mathias picked up a book and casually strolled about the shop. His course to the lady was indirect. He halted at each table and feigned interest in the various books, deliberately keeping his back to Lady Tempest so she would not recognize him until it was too late to avoid him. Nor did he wish his mother and sister to figure out that something other than his appreciation for the written word had lured him into the shop.

Lady Tempest sensed his presence when he had finally positioned himself on the opposite side of the table of books she was inspecting. Her eyes flared in surprise and then narrowed in suspicion at his grin. Her swift glance in Lord Chandler's direction caused Mathias's eyes to narrow as well.

Worried about Chandler, was she? Perhaps he should give her an excuse to worry about *him*.

Mathias circled around the table until he and Lady Tempest were standing side by side.

With a book gripped in one hand, he picked up another and inspected its spine. "Miss me, darling?"

"What are you doing here?" Without giving him a chance to reply, she asked, "Were you following me?"

"Not at all," he denied, which was partially true. While he might have followed her into the bookseller's shop, he had not expected to encounter her this afternoon. "I am escorting my mother and sisters on their shopping excursion."

Lady Tempest swayed and Mathias worried for a second that she might faint. "Good grief, your mother is here," she whispered, obviously dismayed by the news.

His entire body tensed as he prepared to grab her if she tried to run for the door. "Calm yourself, my dear lady. If you flee, you will only draw unwanted attention to us."

She refused to look at him. Instead she shut the book she had been reading and selected another. "You need to come up with an excuse to leave the shop."

"The duchess has her heart set on purchasing a book. I cannot disappoint her by insisting that we depart immediately."

"I am not alone." She moved away from him.

Mathias took his time, but he slowly returned to her side. "Are you referring to Lord Chandler?" He turned, positioning himself so he was facing the opposite direction. "He is watching us."

"More reason for you to stay away from me," she hissed under her breath.

"When can we meet?" he abruptly asked.

Mathias had entered the shop with no firm plans beyond gazing at Lady Tempest from across the room. If an opportunity presented itself, he had hoped to speak with her. The viscount's presence and apparent interest in the lady had prodded him into more direct action.

"We cannot," was her flat reply. She moved on to the next table.

A few minutes later, they stood back to back.

"It is impossible," she murmured.

"Nonsense," Mathias countered. He searched the shop for his mother and noted that she was watching him. There was a quizzical expression on her face. Acknowledging her perusal with a nod of his head, he smiled and raised his hand. "I enjoy challenges."

"Have you found anything of interest?" Lord Chandler inquired, his approach ending Mathias's conversation with Lady Tempest.

"I have not made up my mind," she replied.

Mathias walked away, unable to discern if the words were meant for him or a sincere response to viscount. He glanced down at the book in his hands and suddenly grinned when he noted the title. It was perfect, he thought as he sought out a shop clerk.

Five minutes later, he returned to his mother and sisters. He gestured to the books in his mother's hands. "Are you ready to leave?"

"Yes, I believe so," his mother said, handing the books to him. "I noticed you found a beautiful young lady to amuse you while you waited for me to come to a decision."

"Did I?" he said, sounding amused. "Why would I bother when I am escorting the most beautiful woman in the shop?"

"And such a flatterer," the duchess replied, pleased but not fooled by his deliberate attempt to distract her. "Once the clerk has added the books to our bill, we can depart."

Tempest returned the book to the table as she discreetly observed Lord Fairlamb purchase the books for the Duchess of Blackbern. He had not made another attempt to speak with her again. Nor had he bothered to look in her direction. She should have been relieved that he had given up so easily. Lord Chandler had remained at Tempest's side, much to her dismay. Not to mention Lady Joan's. The two ladies stood in uncomfortable silence as the viscount took it upon himself to select a book for her. Her discomfort increased tenfold when a side glance revealed Lord Fairlamb's mother and younger sisters had to walk past her to reach the door. Perhaps it was her fanciful imagination, but she felt the Duchess of Blackbern's gaze slide over her. Seizing the nearest book, she opened it and practically buried her nose in the crease until she was certain Her Grace was gone.

"You will ruin your pretty hazel eyes if you persist in holding the book so close," Lord Chandler teased.

"What? Of course," Tempest said, lowering the book. It was then that she realized to her disappointment that Chance was no longer in the shop.

Her cousin and Lord Medeley joined their little group.

"I have found nothing that interests me," Harriet announced. There was a healthy amount of color in her cheeks, which revealed that the lady had spent most of her time flirting with her future husband.

"Shall I procure the book for you, Lady Tempest?"

She stared down at the novel she held in her hands.

Her unexpected encounter with Lord Fairlamb had distracted her, and she had yet to select a book. Since it had been her suggestion to visit the shop, it seemed foolish to leave without making a purchase. "It is kind of you to offer, Lord Chandler. However, it will take me only a moment to see to the matter."

Tempest separated from her friends and walked to the counter. She did not wish to encourage the viscount by allowing him to gift her with the book. Nor did she think Lady Joan would approve.

The male clerk smiled at her approach. "Good afternoon, my lady. Shall I add this to your other purchase?"

"My other purchase? I have no other," she said, frowning as the clerk handed her another book wrapped in brown paper and bound with string.

"Your husband told me to add all purchases to his account," the clerk said, not looking up from his task and missing the shock on her face.

"You must be mistaken. I have no husband."

Swiftly realizing his error, the clerk gave her an apologetic look. "Forgive me, my lady. I meant no offense. Lord Fairlamb spoke with such familiarity and fondness, I assumed you were his wife. Nevertheless, the gentleman insisted that I give you the book and I credit any additional purchases to his account."

He must have secreted a message within the book.

"Lord Fairlamb is very generous." She looked over her shoulder to make certain her friends had not eavesdropped on her exchange with the shop clerk. "He is an old friend of the family," she added to quell any speculation on why the marquess was purchasing books for a lady who was not a relative.

She need not have bothered. The clerk was too satisfied in gaining the additional sale to question a patron's motives.

"All finished." He handed her the other book. "I hope you enjoy the books."

"Thank you. I shall," she said, turning away and almost colliding with Lord Chandler.

"You bought a second book," the viscount said, his tone indulgent.

"The clerk recommended it," she said, feeling foolish that she was spinning lies about the book she was currently clutching to her bodice. "Shall we go?"

Several hours later, Tempest entered her bedchamber and shooed away her maid, telling her that she needed a moment of privacy. She wasted no time untying the string bow and unwrapping the book.

"*Poetic Trifles* by Ann of Swansea," she read out loud as she shook her head. "An unexpected choice, Lord Fairlamb. Unless you were as distracted as I was."

Tempest opened the book and thumbed through several pages until she reached the first poem. It was there that she discovered his calling card. She turned it over. In pencil, Chance had written the following command.

### Friday. Two o'clock. Egyptian Hall.

Perhaps she should be insulted by his high-handed manner, but with so many witnesses surrounding them in the bookseller's shop, there had been little opportunity for politeness or refusal.

In truth, she was intrigued. Tempest wanted to see Chance again. Meeting him would be not without risks. *Should I accept his invitation or reject it?* she silently wondered, tapping the card against her chin. She had three days. Her gaze finally focused on the title of the first poem and she laughed with delight as she read the line.

### *Tell me, is it love?*

Was she falling in love with Lord Fairlamb? It was too soon to tell, but she accepted the title of the poem as a sign from the heavens that she should keep the appointment with the marquess.

# Chapter Fourteen

"Any reason why you have a sudden interest to visit Egyptian Hall?" Thorn asked Mathias as they entered William Bullock's collection of natural history and curiosities. "We have already paid homage to Napoleon's carriage, and I have no intention of fighting my way through the crowd of spectators to view it again."

"I knew I should have invited St. Lyon," Mathias teased. "He is more agreeable."

"Why didn't you?" He surveyed the central hall with dismay. This time of day, the museum was congested with people as they navigated their way around taxidermy, large cases stuffed with artifacts, and statuary.

"He and Rainbault had other plans. Tattersall's, I believe," Mathias said absently.

"And this place was preferable?" His cousin sounded appalled. "Did you fall off your horse?"

Mathias shook his head. "Stop whining. As it is, we may not be here for long." In hindsight, he should have been more specific in his directions to Lady Tempest.

"Thank God! At last some good news," Thorn said, dutifully following Mathias as he searched the main hall. "When can we leave?"

"Soon." Mathias halted so abruptly, Thorn nearly collided into him. "She would have felt too exposed in this large hall. Perhaps she decided to wait in one of the small exhibit rooms."

"Who?"

"If she is courageous enough to meet me," he muttered more to himself than to his cousin. "The last time I saw her, she told me to stay away. You would not believe how stubborn she can be."

"No doubt," Thorn said dryly. "Do you mind revealing the name of this stubborn creature who has the good sense to avoid you?"

"Let's search the Roman gallery." When Thorn grabbed him by the arm, Mathias's eyes cleared, and he gave the man an impatient look. "Who? Lady Tempest."

His cousin tightened his grip and prevented Mathias from continuing his search. "Norgrave's daughter? What the devil are you doing? I thought you planned to stay away from her if you encountered her in town."

Mathias shrugged. "Good intentions, and all that. I guess I might have stuck to the plan if I hadn't kissed her."

Thorn swore under his breath. "Do you have an unspoken fancy to depart this world early, Cousin? Because Marcroft will happily oblige you and dispatch you to the nearest hellgate without hesitation. It is no secret that he will murder you if he catches you looking at his beloved sister. Just think what he might do if he learns you have put your hands on her. Not to mention what the chit's father will do if he learns that you are lusting after his daughter."

"Leave it alone. I have no intention of telling him," Mathias said, shaking off his cousin's grip and heading for the Roman gallery. "Can I count on you to keep your silence?"

"Out of loyalty to you and your family, I should head straight to your father and spare you from this madness that has overtaken your good sense," Thorn threatened, his words not louder than a whisper, but Mathias heard them.

He turned around and grabbed his cousin by the front of his coat. "If you speak of this to my father or anyone without my expressed permission, I will tear you apart with my bare hands. Have I made myself clear?"

"Christ!" Thorn knocked Mathias's hands away and smoothed the fabric of his coat. His expression was fierce, but he managed to keep his voice even when he spoke. "I would never betray you. Even if you are behaving like an arse. What about Miss King? Or have you forgotten about her?"

"I have decided to leave her to Marcroft's tender mercies," he said, striving to leash his temper. He did not want to frighten Lady Tempest off.

"So this is revenge," Thorn said softly.

Was he attracted to Marcroft's sister as a means to strike at the brother? *No,* he silently rejected the thought. If it were revenge, then he would have pursued both Lady Arabella and Lady Tempest. He sensed the younger sister would have given him less grief than the elder one.

Mathias grimaced. "My interest in Lady Tempest is not tainted with revenge. In fact, when I am with her, I try not to think of her brother at all."

Thorn grinned in sympathy. "Shrivels your cock, eh?"

"Because of him, I have been forced to embrace abstinence, which only makes me despise him all the more," he said crossly. Thorn's reminder that he had caught Miss King and Marcroft together did not improve his disposition. "If he learns that I have been courting his sister, it is the least he deserves."

His cousin did not conceal his shock. "You are courting the chit?"

Mathias shrugged carelessly. "For the moment." When

Thorn remained silent, he felt compelled to add, "I offer the lady only friendship. What harm can come of it?"

His cousin wisely held his tongue as they entered the gallery.

The room was sixty feet in length and a little more than twenty-five feet in width. There were three cupola windows overhead that illuminated the numerous vases, columns, marble sculptures, and tablets on display.

Mathias discovered Lady Tempest standing in front of a bust of a Roman emperor. Her dress was pale yellow with a dark blue spencer. She had not been watching the entrance for him. Instead, her head was bowed as she scribbled something into her journal.

Thorn had also noticed her distracted state. "The lady is obviously anticipating your meeting."

"Amused, are you?" Mathias grinned, unwilling to let his cousin sour his joy. Preoccupied or not, Lady Tempest was waiting for him. "Let us greet our new friend."

Lady Tempest sensed their approach and turned before he could touch her on the sleeve. Pleasure suffused her face, but there was a degree of wariness in her hazel eyes as her gaze slid from Mathias to his cousin.

"Lord Kempthorn and Lord Fairlamb, it is good to see you again," she said, shutting her journal and curtsying. "Have you come to see Napoleon's carriage?"

"Chance and I viewed the exhibit our first week in town," Thorn revealed. "However, our afternoon stroll through the museum has become more enchanting by meeting you again."

To Mathias's annoyance, his cousin moved closer and gently captured the lady's hand and bowed over it gallantly. Lady Tempest's lips quivered as if she fought not to giggle. As the man straightened, Mathias was tempted to cuff Thorn on the back of his head for showing off.

She extended her arm to Mathias and she looked at him expectantly. Not to be outdone, he bowed over her hand and lightly brushed his lips over her gloved knuckles.

"That was quite well done, my lord," she teased him as he released her hand. "A Rooke with manners. How unexpected."

There was no hint of insult behind her words. It appeared they were proving that a Rooke and a Brant could share the same room without coming to blows. "I rarely waste them on a Brant." He winked, drawing a reluctant smile from her. "Where is your chaperone?"

"Mrs. Sheehan?" Lady Tempest glanced around the room, but there was no sign of the widow. "Earlier she was complaining that there was a small stone in her shoe. There was a slight limp to her gait and she begged to sit down for a few minutes. I told her that I would be spending time in the Roman gallery. I thought she would have joined me by now."

"Perhaps Thorn could find your companion." Mathias looked pointedly at his cousin. "If her foot is still sore, he could sit with her until you are ready to leave."

Thorn cleared his throat. "I would be honored to take up the task."

Lady Tempest noted the silent exchange between the two gentlemen. "It does not seem quite fair for you—"

"Think nothing of it," his cousin said smoothly, dismissing her halfhearted protest. "Chance will keep you company while I search for your companion, since this will likely take a long time."

As Mathias and Lady Tempest observed Thorn's departure, she murmured, "That was rather clever of you to bring your cousin along to distract Mrs. Sheehan."

"I thought so," was his smug reply. "You never mentioned if your chaperone has been given my full name."

"No," she said quietly. "My brother thought it prudent not to reveal your name out of concern that Mrs. Sheehan might mention it to my mother and father. She does have orders to discourage any gentleman who lingers beyond a cordial greeting."

"Well, that does put a wrinkle in our afternoon outing," he said, not particularly concerned. Thorn was fully capable of distracting the widow.

"I thought so, too." Lady Tempest hugged her journal to her chest and turned back to the marble bust she had been admiring before his arrival. "That is why I put the stone in her shoe."

Lord Fairlamb's laughter surrounded her like a warm embrace.

"That was very wicked of you," he said, lightly touching her on the center of her back to guide her toward one of the benches positioned in front of the wall so spectators could sit and enjoy the numerous paintings displayed on the walls. "I shall have to remember that bit of trickery in the future."

"I highly doubt you are saddled with chaperones at your age."

"A man of my age would not think of a pretty widow as a burden," he pointed out, gesturing for her to sit.

"Very amusing," she said, settling down on the bench. Tempest stiffened, straightening her spine when the marquess sat down with only four inches separating them. "Do you believe it wise for us to sit so closely?"

"No one is paying attention to us, my lady," he said with an air of confidence that seemed to be as much a part of him as his good looks. "The public room will ensure that I will behave myself, though I give you permission to be as reckless as you desire."

Tempest smiled at his invitation. Before she met him,

she had not viewed herself as an adventurous person. "Why did you ask me to meet you, Lord Fairlamb?"

"Several kisses warrant a degree of familiarity, do you not agree?"

She inclined her head to acknowledge his mild chastisement. "Chance. Your nickname is rather appropriate."

"Just as I suspect that Tempest suits you as well."

"What? You do not like my name?"

"On the contrary, I adore it—just as much as I have always enjoyed the unexpected turns in life."

Tempest did not know how to respond to his remark.

Chance brushed his fingers against hers, bringing attention to the thin book in her hands. His light touch sent a wave of tingles up her arm, giving her gooseflesh on her upper arms. Fortunately, her sleeves concealed her reaction to his caress.

"Are you writing of our meeting in your journal?"

She covered her lips with her hand and smothered a giggle. "That would not be very prudent, since we went to so much trouble to meet in secret."

"Of course." He cleared his throat and looked mildly uncomfortable.

"Unless you feel this meeting is so important that it should be documented properly."

"Not at all—I only commented on it because it looked—" He noticed her smirk. "You are teasing me."

"A little," she said, opening the book. "You are correct. It is a journal, but I use it for quick sketches and notes of things that capture my interest."

Tempest turned a few pages until she came to her recent sketch. "As you can see, I was working on Nero's nose when you and Lord Kempthorn arrived."

Chance took the journal from her hands so he could inspect her work. He remained silent, and her nervousness increased with each passing second. "You have an extraordinary talent, Tempest," he said, not taking his gaze off the page. "Do you paint as well?"

His approval and genuine interest in her work thrilled her. "Most of my work is done in watercolor, but I have dabbled in oils."

The marquess lifted his gaze to hers, and the startling impact of the connection she felt did fascinating things to her pulse. "I imagine what you view as dabbling is rather remarkable."

"You flatter me."

"You are too humble," he countered. "You should solicit one of the members of the Royal Academy as a mentor."

It was unsettling to hear one of her private dreams spoken aloud. Especially by a gentleman she should be avoiding at all costs. Tempest shook her head. She was touched that he thought so highly of her work, but her father would never approve of her consorting with artists.

She retrieved the journal from Chance. "My skills are adequate, but not worthy of the Royal Academy."

"How do you know unless you seek out an opinion?"

Tempest rolled her eyes in exasperation. "Because I do," she said sharply. "A simple sketch of an emperor's nose does not mean that I should be pestering members of the Royal Academy."

"Tempest—," he began.

She shut the journal closed with muffled clap. "If you are planning to bully me into doing something I do not want, then we might as well part ways."

Tempest rose from the bench, but Chance captured her wrist.

"Stay. I promise to let the subject drop on one condition."

The marquess appeared to be contrite, but humbleness

did not suit him. She sighed loudly, knowing she was going to regret listening to his condition. "What is it?"

"Sit beside me and draw," he coaxed, already pulling on her arm so she had the choice of causing a scene or complying with his simple request.

Tempest sat down.

"You want me to sketch something," she said, convinced that he was merely indulging her so she would not leave.

"Anything you fancy," he replied, willing to use his considerable charm to sway her. "Your heart's desire."

She tilted her head to the side, giving him a quizzical glance. "And what will you do, my lord?"

"I will keep you company."

Tempest was wary of his motives, not that he could blame her.

It was difficult to put aside prejudices a villainous name could evoke, to ignore the guilt tickling one's conscience for even flirting with the enemy.

She was not his enemy any more than he was hers.

Mathias also was coming to the realization that the initial attraction he'd felt for the lady beside him was deepening. He knew Tempest sensed it as well, but she was still fighting it.

Her presence this afternoon was only confirmation that it was a losing battle.

Mathias admired her profile as she sketched in her little journal. He would have enjoyed thumbing through the pages to view her other sketches and little notes, but he had already pushed her enough for this day.

"I have met your younger sisters and regrettably Marcroft," he said, wishing to learn more about her life. "Do you have any other siblings?"

Lost as she was in her work, it took a few minutes

before she became aware of his regard. Straightening, she blinked several times. "You said something of my brother?"

"Not really. If it is all the same to you, I would prefer to forget he is related to you."

Tempest shifted on the bench, turning so her knees would have touched the side of his upper thigh if they were sitting closer. The new position prevented him from observing her work, but it did afford him an appealing view of her face.

"There are days when I would be happy to forget that Oliver is my brother," she said, smiling in coy manner that he found endearing. "Still, he is a good man."

Mathias snorted, but thought it best not to contradict her. Whether he liked it or not, Marcroft was her brother. Insulting her sibling would not gain him her trust. "I asked if you had other siblings besides the ones I have met."

Her gaze had dropped to the open journal again. "It is just Oliver, Arabella, Augusta, and I," she said, her pencil waving in the air as she sketched. "I was told that my mother had a difficult time when she was in confinement with Arabella. Everyone feared that she would lose the baby, and my mother almost died giving birth to her."

Since he was a bachelor, he could not speak firsthand of such matters. "It can be a difficult time for some ladies."

Mathias thought of his own mother. The Duchess of Blackbern had given birth to six children. From a young boy's perspective, his mother handled the changes to her life with graceful aplomb. It was only as he grew older that he became aware of how difficult these pregnancies were on his father. While the duke doted on and spoiled his wife, in unguarded moments, Mathias saw the strain on his father's face. The fear the man tried to conceal as he worried about the health of his wife and their unborn child. His mother had been fortunate. All her children were born healthy, and she had recovered from the childbed with minimal fuss.

"My sister was small when she was born, but she was strong." Tempest frowned at her work. "It took almost a year for my mother to recover. The next child she bore was stillborn. A boy, I was told. After that, three miscarriages. It was doubtful my mother would carry another child again, but years later, Augusta surprised everyone. What about you? In the bookseller's shop, I saw your mother—and I assume the two young ladies with her were your sisters."

Tempest had been more observant than he had realized. Though, he and his sisters did share similar characteristics if one looked closely. It was apparent that the lady had been curious about his companions.

The notion pleased him.

"Yes, my sisters, Honora and Mercy. I also have two younger brothers, Benjamin and Frederick, and the youngest is my sister Constance."

"Oh my, such a large family," she marveled. "How could you bear so many younger brothers and sisters underfoot?"

Mathias had not really considered it. "Normal, I suppose. Annoying at times. I spent part of the time away at school. I often traveled with my father as he taught me how to manage our estates, so I learned to appreciate the months all of us could be together."

Tempest raised her gaze and held his stare. "It was not better for those of us who were left behind. When I was younger, I missed my brother dreadfully."

"You and Marcroft are close?" he asked, hoping that was not the case.

Her expression grew wistful at the question. "We were

born eighteen months apart, so we were inseparable as children. However, it all changed when Oliver left the nursery and was eventually sent away to school." She shrugged, accepting the changes even though the thought of them made her sad.

To distract her, Mathias tapped the top edge of her journal with his finger. "You have been working so diligently. Can I see what you have been working on?"

Her hazel eyes narrowed and a mischievous grin brightened her face. "No." She moved the journal so it was out of reach. "I do not believe I will show you."

"Don't be cruel, darling," he coaxed, confident that he would get his way. "Art should be appreciated, and I am one of your most ardent admirers."

It was the same tone he had used when he was a boy to wheedle extra sweets from the cook. As a grown man, he had similarly seduced ladies into his bed.

Sticking her pencil into the crease of the journal, she closed it. "Absolutely not."

Tempest stood and Mathias mimicked her actions.

"A quick peek," he said, relishing their game.

"I think not," she said, strolling away.

She was not evading him so easily. It took only a few steps to catch up to her.

"What if I purchase the sketch from you?" he asked, choosing a different tactic. If they had not been in such a public place, he would have been tempted to kiss her until she surrendered.

"Don't be ridiculous," she said, continuing past the painting that depicted the judgment of the sons of Brutus.

A couple sitting on a nearby bench glanced up but quickly lost interest, since neither Mathias nor Tempest was looking to cause a scene.

Still, there was no reason not to revel in flustering a beautiful lady.

"Five pounds."

She expelled a ladylike snort. "No."

"Ten." He had no idea what she had been drawing, not that he truly cared. She could have drawn lines on the page, and he would have paid a small fortune just to make her smile.

"Stop it." She circled around to the other side of a large marble column. "I am not selling it."

He peered over the marble. "Just think of it," he argued. "I could be your first patron."

"You are a madman." She was grinning, obviously enjoying their verbal sparring. "Perhaps I could pay you ten pounds to leave me alone."

"You cannot afford my price, so you are stuck with me," he teased.

"Lucky me." Tempest moved to a pedestal that displayed a large vase.

With his arms crossed behind his back, he stalked her as she zigzagged from one sculpture to the next. She was not putting much effort in escaping him. He was not in a hurry to catch her.

For now.

The exhibit room was not so crowded as it had been when he and Thorn first entered it. No one stood between him and his quarry, and he lazily guided her to the far corner of the room, where a very plain-looking woman had been immortalized in marble.

Mathias noted Tempest's eyes were gleaming with anticipation, and she was slightly out of breath because of her stays, though it was impolite of him to notice as much.

She hid the journal behind her back. "Nothing you can say will change my mind, Lord Fairlamb," she vowed, but the smirk on her face dared him to try.

"Unpredictable and passionate," he said, keeping

his voice low and seductive. "Traits one expects in an artist."

The description also fit most of his lovers.

It was rather perverse, but he liked difficult females. Without asking permission, Mathias slowly stepped closer and reached around until they were almost embracing.

"What are you doing?" Tempest whispered, caught between his body and the statue. There was no place for her to escape.

"Satisfying my—" The front of his coat pressed lightly against the front of her bodice. When he stepped backwards, he held her journal in his hand. "—curiosity."

She bit her lip. The nervous gesture was innocent and enticing, and Mathias had to resist the urge to pull her back into his arms and kiss her thoroughly.

Instead, he opened the journal to where it had been marked by her pencil. His lips parted in astonishment. "You were sketching me."

Or rather, parts of him. While they were talking, she had drawn his eyes and eyebrows at the bottom of the page. Another sketch was a profile of his nose and mouth. The third was the beginnings of a full-body drawing as he sat on the bench. There wasn't much detail, but she had captured his casual slouch perfectly.

"Am I something you fancy, Lady Tempest?" he asked, recalling his earlier encouragement. He was impressed and amazed that she had managed to sketch him without overtly studying him.

Mathias expected her to deny it. She was a sweet-tempered lady who had been sheltered by her family. Such ladies were not encouraged to speak openly of their desires. However, even now, she managed to do the unexpected.

Tempest leaned forward as if to whisper her answer. "Perhaps," she purred, but the seductive ploy was spoiled by a strangled gasp. She plucked the journal from his hand and attempted to slip away.

He touched her on the arm. "What is it?"

"Mrs. Sheehan and Lord Kempthorn. I have to go," she said, the urgency in her voice heightening his concern.

"Wait," he said, tightening his hold on her arm. "When can we meet again?"

Tempest stared at him as if he had lost his mind. "I don't know. Please. You need to let me walk away. Mrs. Sheehan hasn't spotted me yet, but it is only a matter of time."

With his back to the entrance, Mathias was shielding her from discovery. "Return to the bookseller's shop. I will leave a message for you. Just give your name to the shop clerk."

"I may not be able to return to the shop right away," she said, her body tense and vibrating with distress.

He gave her an impatient look. "If I do not hear from you, I will send a messenger to you."

"Not to the town house!" Appalled by the brazen suggestion, she gripped his arm. "The servants usually give all notes to my mother."

"I was not planning to give your brother a reason to challenge me, Tempest," he said soothingly. "There will be other occasions for us to meet. If I cannot approach you, I will send someone to you."

"As you wish," she said, sounding distracted, her thoughts focused solely on her escape until he grasped her hand and brought it to his lips. Startled, she met his gaze, and her worried expression relaxed as she smiled. "Until we meet again, Lord Fairlamb."

She peered over his shoulder. Knowing Thorn, he was keeping the chaperone distracted so Tempest could walk away from Mathias unnoticed. She nodded and slipped away from him. He did not watch her departure. Instead he scowled at the ugly statue in front of him until he sensed his cousin's presence.

"Satisfied?" Thorn asked.

"Not in the slightest," Mathias growled.

# Chapter Fifteen

Tempest had ignored his last note.

A week had passed since their meeting at the Egyptian Hall. He had been disappointed when he returned to the bookseller's shop three days later, only to be informed by the owner that no lady had come for Mathias's note. He had been greeted with the same reply on the fourth, fifth, sixth, and seventh days.

Rejection, even if it was unintentional, was a ruthless, swift stab to the heart. Doubt left him wondering if Tempest was just a shameless flirt who had no inclination toward meeting him or if her family had learned of their meeting and she was presently locked in her bedchamber as punishment. Short of boldly knocking on the front door of the Brants' residence and leaving his calling card, Mathias was left with more questions than answers.

He was unused to waiting for a lady.

Most ladies adored him. They flirted back and encouraged his pursuit. He had bedded more than his fair share, and he considered many of them a friend. It was just Tempest who was destined to drive him mad with frustration and lust. His family name was an obstacle. She feared his family and was suspicious of his intentions.

*I should stay away from her.*

As he sat brooding in one of Rainbault's drawing room chairs, he muted the conversation around him as he silently puzzled out his next step with Tempest.

"I recognize that particular look." The amusement in the feminine voice prompted Mathias to glance up.

"Why, Mrs. Kitts, when did you arrive?" he said, stirring from his slouched position in the chair, but she gestured for him to remain seated.

"Thirty minutes ago, not that you noticed. By the by, when did you start thinking of me as Mrs. Kitts, you heartless rogue?" she replied, sitting down next to him on the embroidered footstool with cabriole legs carved from mahogany.

"When you married Mr. Kitts, I believe," he said, unable to keep from grinning. "How are you, Sabra?"

"I shall be splendid once you have given me a proper greeting," she said, her pout reminding him of a spoiled child—albeit a very pretty one.

"I see beauty improves with age, darling."

"I tend to agree," she said, leaning forward in anticipation.

Mathias saw no reason to deny an old friend. He shifted his body and met her halfway. She offered him her powdered cheek, but turned at the last second so his lips touched hers. Her hand lightly touched his cheek and she kissed him again. Each tender kiss was infused with affection and remembrance. One of his friends cheered in the background, most likely thrilled he was doing something other than brooding.

Sabra's blue eyes were damp with unshed tears when she stepped back and stared at him. "By God, I have missed you, Chance."

"It has been more than a year, has it not?"

She fluttered her eyelashes and looked heavenward

and offered a silent plea for patience. "Fourteen months, not that I was counting. Nor do you deserve it."

He had some history with Mrs. Kitts. However, it was years ago, when she was Miss Battle. She came from a family of wealthy merchants and was thus allowed to mingle on the fringes of polite society. Her respectable dowry drew the interest of fortune hunters and second sons, but the young lady had higher ambitions. He was sixteen years old when he was introduced to the nineteen-year-old Sabra at a large country house gathering, and was instantly smitten. Her pale blond hair, delicate features, and large blue eyes reminded him of an angel. Spending an hour in her company revealed that if she had come from the heavens, then someone had tossed her out. She was a very wicked minx. It took her only three days to seduce him in their host's orchard.

Sabra had been his first lover. She had been generous with her body and taught him how to please her. He was so blinded by lust that he had not given much thought beyond their next coupling. When her family discovered that she had seduced the Duke of Blackbern's heir, they had whisked her away to avoid any unpleasant confrontations. He had not been Sabra's first lover. She had collected quite a string of young noblemen before they had met, so her practical father knew the duke would not consider his untamed daughter a potential bride for his heir.

It was not until eight months later that Mathias had come across her again in London. They had a very pleasurable reunion. It was only afterwards that Sabra confessed that her father had married her off to the second son of a baronet. The marriage had paid off her husband's gambling debts and opened more doors for her and her family. It was a loveless marriage, but that had not swayed Mathias into continuing the affair. Even if she had spoken the truth, he doubted Kitts would have approved of his wife taking lovers. He and Sabra eventually had settled into a casual friendship, and three years later, word had reached him that her husband had died in a duel. Whether it was over gambling debts or Sabra's unfaithfulness, Mathias never bothered to inquire.

"What has brought you to Rainbault's door this evening?" he asked out of politeness.

"I encountered him at the park the other day. He mentioned you in passing, and I lamented that I had not seen you in ages."

"I was unaware that you were in town this month," he explained, placing his hand over the one she rested on the ornate arm of his chair.

"Not that you ever trouble yourself to find out." She was pouting again. It made less of an impact now that she was a twenty-six-year-old widow than it had when she was a nineteen-year-old.

"My darling Sabra, what you and I had is old history. You have been widowed for three years, and for all I know, you could be married again."

"Have you bothered asking anyone?" she huffed.

"Sabra."

His calm manner and patient expression reminded her that he was no longer that reckless, passionate boy she had seduced, and could bend around her little finger.

"Oh, very well. You are correct, of course." She sighed. "Perhaps it was vain of me to hope that you have waited for me."

Her outrageous statement was rewarded with a hearty laugh. "Just as you have saved yourself for me, Mrs. Kitts?" Mathias picked up his brandy from a small round table beside the chair. He took a contemplative sip as he studied her through his veiled gaze. "No, I think not. So why do you not tell me the real reason you have sought me out."

Ten minutes later, he held Rainbault by the front of his evening coat and was shoving his back against the wall just outside the drawing room. "You told Sabra I was looking for a lover," he growled into his friend's smiling face.

"I might have mentioned it." The prince did not appear to be troubled by Mathias's anger or his precarious position. "Releasing your seed into a willing woman does wonders for a man's disposition. From the perpetual snarl carved into your face, I would deduce that considerable time has passed since you've had the pleasure."

"Chance." St. Lyon placed his hand on Mathias's shoulder. "Rainbault wasn't alone that day in the park when he encountered Mrs. Kitts. I was there, and it was my suggestion that she join us this evening."

The prince glared at St. Lyon. "Don't steal all the credit, my friend. I thought it was a grand idea."

"Which one of you told her that I often speak of her fondly?"

Both his friends shrugged, or at least Rainbault tried. It was difficult to move since Mathias had him pinned to the wall.

St. Lyon said, "You may not have mentioned her of late, but I know you well enough to know that you are fond of the lady."

He could not believe that his friends had conspired to get him into Sabra's bed. "What I had with Sabra ended when she married Kitts. If I had wanted to renew my friendship with her, I would have comforted her when I heard the news that her husband was killed in a duel. Your meddling has placed me in an awkward position."

"How so?" Sabra demanded, standing in the open door of the drawing room. Inside, the room was silent as the occupants tried to eavesdrop on the argument in the passageway. "All you had to do is tell me the truth."

Her smile wasn't as bright as it had been when she first sat down on the footstool. "I think I will take my leave. Good evening, gentlemen."

Mathias scowled at Rainbault before he released his grip. "This isn't finished between us."

"Count on it," the prince replied.

"Sabra . . . wait," he called out, chasing after her. He caught up to her before she reached the front door. "I told you to wait."

"I do not answer to you or any man, Chance," she cried.

Mathias expected the anger, but her tears almost undid him. "I wish to apologize. For myself and my friends. Rainbault and St. Lyon are well meaning. Over the years, I have spoken of our time together because it was important to me. You were important to me. If you weren't, I would never have introduced you to my friends. My biggest regret is that their actions have hurt your feelings."

"I am fine," she said shakily.

"You used to be better at lying."

Mathias reached into an inner pocket and handed her his handkerchief. Sabra murmured her thanks and wiped the tears on her cheeks. He placed his arm on the small of her back and led her to one of the cushioned benches in the front hall.

He sat down beside her, waiting for her to compose herself. Much to his relief, it didn't take long.

"I feel foolish." Her slender shoulders trembled, but her tears had stopped flowing.

"You are not to blame." Mathias gently took her hand and clasped it within his. "My friends made some assumptions about you and what I might want. They were wrong."

"Chance, the only one confused this evening is you," she said, her lips curving into a smile at his surprise.

"Your friends might have been thinking only of your needs when they invited me here, but I was focused on my own when I accepted Rainbault's invitation."

"Sabra." He was uncertain how to proceed with her.

Her fingers threaded through his. "You were right when you said that you could have comforted me after my husband died. For the first few weeks, I thought you might call on me; however, you never did."

"I didn't learn of your husband's death until weeks after he had been buried."

She nodded, accepting the apology in his tone. "I was lost for a few months. My husband—Well, he was not my first choice, and then his family was difficult because of the circumstances surrounding his death."

So Kitts had challenged one of Sabra's lovers.

"I should have been a better friend and called on you."

"I never blamed you. I heard rumors that you were involved with an actress at the time." At his sharp intake of breath, she laughed. "I was in mourning, so friends would visit and share the latest gossip."

"I see."

"And you are embarrassed," she accurately deduced. "I would not have thought it possible."

"I did not realize my life had become gossip fodder," he muttered, grateful that he was not blushing like a virgin.

"To be fair, I did have a special interest in you," she said, enjoying his discomfort. "Lest you forget, I was your first lover."

Mathias glanced up, but there was no one in sight. He wondered how many of his friends were listening to their private conversation. "It is not something I am likely to forget, Sabra."

"Indeed not." Her face softened as she placed her other hand on his cheek. "I did not come to talk about the past.

I actually sought you out because I heard another rumor—that no lady has currently ensnared you this season."

Tempest's face shimmered in his mind.

"We are friends, Chance. Not good ones, I will admit," she said, bowing her head as she traced the length of his fingers with hers. "However, I long for us to be good friends again. The sort who turn to each other when the other needs comforting."

"Is that what you need, Sabra? Comforting?"

"There is a gentleman. An earl," she added. "He is much older than I, but he claims to adore me and he is quite wealthy. He hasn't asked for my hand in marriage. Yet. Nor has he pressed for anything more than a chaste kiss on my hand. My family is encouraging me to accept if he does."

"It sounds as if you know what you want," he said, feeling more confused than ever. Any man who claimed to understand how a lady's mind worked was a braggart and a liar.

"You first came into my life when I was on the verge of marrying another man." Sabra slipped her hands free and gestured at him. "And now that I am seriously contemplation marriage again, I am presented with the opportunity to see you again."

"If you need advice about marriage—"

Sabra giggled and wrinkled her nose. "Good heavens, no! I have plenty of married friends who can offer me advice. My offer is another kind of comfort. While I await my fate, I thought we might renew our old friendship. A man like you should have a small stable of lovers, and it troubles me and your friends that it remains empty."

"My bed is no one's business but my own," he said, anger sharpening his voice.

"True." She rose from the bench. "Nevertheless, I would

like to make it my business. Unless . . . there is someone else."

Mathias remained silent.

Her eyes twinkled with delight. "Ah, nothing to say. Now I am intrigued."

He stood and glared at her. "Leave it alone, Sabra."

"Dear me." She was unmoved by his temper, but her blue eyes did cloud with concern. "Could it be that you have finally fallen in love, Chance?"

"You behave as if I am incapable of such tender sentiment. Once I thought I was in love with you, Sabra."

"You were not in love with me," she said, dismissing the suggestion. "Although I do recall that you had a fondness for my body."

"There is no reason to belittle what we shared," he said, stiffening at her subtle mockery of their brief love affair. "It was a long time ago. My heart recovered and any hurt feelings have faded."

"Which is precisely my point, Chance," she argued. "A man in love does not recover so quickly. The pain may fade, but it is not forgotten. Or so my friends keep telling me."

"You do not love your earl?"

She shrugged. "I love the notion of becoming a countess, and I do love living comfortably. Perhaps I will come to love the earl as time passes."

It would be a cold marriage, he thought. She was such a passionate woman, her nature would eventually drive her into the warm arms of another man. "And when you were nineteen years old . . . did you love me, Sabra?"

Her blue eyes misted with old memories of the past. "We were young. You were so handsome, and the strength of your body still gives me shivers of pleasure when I think of our time together. I would have loved being your marchioness, and later, your duchess."

Mathias bowed his head. He had often wondered if his father had paid the Battles off to hasten their departure. Sabra was right. If he had truly loved her, he would have fought for her. He would have confronted his father with his unspoken accusations and then he would have searched for Sabra and promised to marry her when he was older. Instead, he had let her go. Her marriage to Kitts had given him an excuse to move on with his life.

"No, Chance, I did not love you. I was young. I did not want to marry anyone, but my father was determined to see me settled since I enjoyed the marriage bed too enthusiastically."

He nodded. "I remember."

Sabra laughed, and impulsively kissed him on the mouth. "I still do. Chance, if you ask me to go home with you—I will go. I am not asking for promises. Nor do I have any expectations. We could just amuse ourselves until it is time to say farewell."

Mathias lowered his forehead to hers. Her invitation was exactly what he had been seeking when he arrived in London. An uncomplicated dalliance. A few weeks or a month of mindless pleasure, and then they would part without bitter recriminations or tears. It was all Sabra could offer him, and a few months ago, he might have accepted.

Mathias pulled away and kissed her on the forehead. "Did you arrive in a hired coach? If you like, I could have my coachman take you home."

Disappointment cast shadows in her expression. "It is kind of you to offer. Yes, I believe it is time I should return home."

The need to apologize rose in his throat, but he swallowed it. "I will say my farewells to my friends, and then we can depart."

"Chance?"

"Yes."

She took a step toward him. "If it doesn't work out with your lady love, I pray you will reconsider my invitation."

Mathias raised his hand in acknowledgment as he walked toward the stairs. He no longer wanted to throttle his friends for their interference. If Rainbault insisted on an apology, he would receive it. He owed his friends that much.

This evening had been a test, and a revelation.

Sabra Kitts was everything he desired in a lover, and her invitation had left him cold.

Mathias was seeking more than a quick, emotionless gratification. Something he could easily do with his own hand, if his body needed a release. What he longed for was more elusive and was fraught with risks.

He wanted Tempest.

Just thinking of her sent his heart thundering in his chest and his loins heating with lust. He had never felt this way about a lady, and he wasn't comfortable with the notion that he was falling in love with her.

Their relationship was ill-fated, he brooded, because claiming Tempest would herald the day he would betray his family.

# Chapter Sixteen

"Are we missing anyone?"

"I do not believe so," Tempest replied, giving Lord Warrilow a weak smile as she straightened in her seat.

It was not the first time she had glanced over her shoulder and searched the faces of Lady Henwood's guests as they made their way from the drawing room and into the music room. There were so many people present, the three large doors separating the two rooms were to remain open so anyone who wished to remain seated in the drawing room could enjoy the concert. The countess had invited Miss Clara King to entertain them this evening. Arabella had informed her that they had missed her performance the night they had been caught in the traffic and Oliver had abandoned them for a few hours. It had also been the night Chance rescued her from the drunk and smugly demanded a kiss as his award. She had bristled at his arrogant taunt, and their kiss had been mediocre and uninspiring.

Kissing him had improved with a little practice.

Not that she had been given any opportunity to kiss Chance or anyone else. Although, if she wanted to kiss a gentleman, Lord Warrilow might be willing if she offered him any encouragement. He had been a frequent visitor to her mother's drawing room. This evening, he had been invited to sit with her family. It was a sign that the man was taking a closer look at her and Arabella for his bride.

Chance would not be pleased by this news.

Ten days had passed since he asked her to return to the bookseller's shop. Unfortunately, the task had been more difficult than anticipated, since her mother expected her to stay home and entertain Lord Warrilow and what appeared to be a constant stream of visitors. Her mother was enjoying the activity in the household, and Tempest had not come up with a good excuse to leave the house.

Tempest suspected Chance was not one to be thwarted, and that would make him reckless. The fine hairs on the nape of her neck tickled in warning. She half expected Lord Fairlamb to stroll through the door and sit down next to Lord Warrilow.

And would that not be courting disaster!

"You seem distracted this evening," the marquess observed, and Tempest suddenly felt guilty that she was thinking about Chance when she was sitting beside a handsome gentleman who had done nothing to deserve her rude behavior.

She compounded her guilt by lying. "I was looking for Lady Harriet."

"I was not aware our cousin would be joining us," her sister said, turning her head, but Tempest refused to meet her gaze.

"It was nothing certain, so it would be unfair to ask a footman to reserve a seat for her and any companions," Tempest explained, praying that God would not strike her dead for her lies.

It was Chance's fault, she silently fumed. She had been an honest person before she spied on him and his friends bathing in the river.

Tempest glanced over at her mother, who was standing

in front of a large mirror and speaking with one of her friends. The marchioness saw something in the mirror's reflection and visibly stiffened. Something or someone had caught her attention.

She prayed it wasn't Chance.

Tempest watched helplessly as her mother slowly turned and glanced at the other side of the room. Lady Norgrave's mouth thinned. Following the direction of her mother's gaze, she recognized the lady who had just entered the room with her children.

It was the Duchess of Blackbern.

Tempest had the sudden desire to melt into the floor.

"Is something amiss?" Lord Warrilow inquired, noticing that she was slouching in her chair.

Tempest straightened. "Not at all. Everything is just splendid."

Arabella kicked her in the shin. *What is wrong with you?* she silently mouthed.

The Duchess of Blackbern and Lady Norgrave in the same room. This was probably not the first occasion on which the two ladies were forced to deal with each other. From the corner of her eye, she watched the duchess greet a few friends before she and her three daughters sat down on the left side of the room toward the front. She seemed unaware of the marchioness's presence.

That fact clearly annoyed her mother. Ignoring her companion, Lady Norgrave was staring at the duchess.

"Tempest!"

"What?" Arabella and Lord Warrilow were looking at her with various degrees of puzzlement. "Forgive me, I was not listening. What did you ask me?"

Arabella sensed something was troubling Tempest, but she was uncomfortable demanding answers in front of the marquess. "You look unwell, Sister. Perhaps you should retire upstairs to the ladies' parlor before Miss

King's performance," she said pointedly. "I will tell Mother where you have gone."

Tempest seized on the excuse her sister provided, and nodded.

"Lady Tempest, I would be pleased to escort you," Lord Warrilow said, preparing to stand.

"That is unnecessary," Tempest assured the marquess. "I won't—"

It was then that she noticed Chance and St. Lyon standing near the middle door that opened into the drawing room. Chance crossed his arms and scowled at her. It was then that Miss King entered the music room from the back of the room. Oliver was escorting her to the front.

When had her brother met Miss King?

Tempest switched her gaze back to Chance. He had also noticed her brother's arrival, and his anger had been redirected. Most days, she would have been thrilled by this fortuitous development, but not when there were too many Rookes and Brants in the same room.

"Unnecessary, because I am staying." She smiled re-assuringly at Lord Warrilow. "I would be disappointed if I missed Miss King's performance."

Lady Norgrave wordlessly sat down next to Arabella. Tempest could feel her mother's anger rolling off her like churning waves. Her brother took a seat in the front row so he could be close to Miss King.

It would be a miracle if the evening didn't end with a brawl.

Mathias shared Tempest's gloomy thoughts.

He had initially been overjoyed when St. Lyon told him that Tempest was attending the concert. What elation he felt had waned when he saw Warrilow seated beside her.

Was the marquess the reason she had not gone to the bookseller's shop?

The man made the mistake of touching Tempest on the arm to gain her attention. Blind with fury, Mathias did not realize he had taken a step forward to rip the offending limb out of its socket until St. Lyon held him back.

He was so focused on Tempest, he had not noticed his mother's arrival with his sisters. Or Lady Norgrave's presence. The marchioness was not pleased he saw now, and the rigidity in Tempest's shoulders revealed she was aware that a confrontation between the two women was possible.

Why had Lady Henwood invited both ladies?

While he was mulling over his choices, Tempest turned her head and saw him. Her dismay was a blow to his stomach. She rose and he wondered if she was planning to confront him, and that was when Miss King and Marcroft entered the music room.

Marcroft was too distracted by his enchanting companion to notice anyone, but his presence was too much for Tempest. She took one look at her brother and promptly sat down.

"I was unaware your mother was attending this evening," St. Lyon muttered.

"As was I."

"Did it escape your notice that Lady Norgrave is also in attendance?"

Mathias exhaled noisily. "No, it did not."

"Then I do not have to mention Miss King and Marcroft."

He gave his friend a quelling glance. "Can you cease pointing out the obvious? I am not blind."

"You are when it comes to Norgrave's daughter," St. Lyon argued. "That lady has brought nothing but trouble to your life. If you persist, that brother of hers is going to put a bullet in your thick skull."

He lowered his voice when Lady Henwood began her introductions. "You worry too much, St. Lyon."

The viscount leaned against the wall and crossed his arms. "Do you want to leave before Marcroft stops thinking with his cock?"

It was a sound course of action, but Mathias shook his head. "I cannot leave. Not until I speak with my mother," he explained, cutting off his friend's heated response. "I highly doubt Lady Norgrave will cause a scene. She has as much to lose as my mother. However, I shall feel better once I have escorted the duchess and my sisters to their coach."

"And Lady Tempest?"

"My plans have not changed."

St. Lyon cursed. "How do you precisely intend to speak to the lady right under the noses of her family and yours?"

There was nothing humorous about his grin. "Fetch me a footman."

Tempest might be questioning Lady Henwood's good sense by inviting Lady Norgrave and the Duchess of Blackbern to the same gathering, but her instincts were correct when it came to hiring Miss King for the evening. The woman could have been one of Euterpe's handmaidens, for she possessed not only grace and beauty, but a voice worthy of Zeus's ear as well. Her brother was obviously enthralled, and had likely laid claim to the young songstress's affections. Nevertheless, Oliver had competition. She cast a look at Lord Warrilow. Her lips twitched with amusement.

Miss King's rendition of *The Fairy-Queen* had bewitched the marquess, along with the other gentlemen in the music room. A discreet glance at her mother eased the tension in her shoulders. In spite of the Duchess of Blackbern's presence, the music was soothing her mother's indignation. With any luck, she and Arabella would be able to coax the marchioness into their town coach before she remembered why she was so furious.

She turned her head away from the lovely Miss King at the light tap on her shoulder. Thankfully, it was not Chance or his friend St. Lyon, but rather one of Lady Henwood's footmen.

"I beg your pardon, my lady," the servant murmured in her ear. "Your presence is required in the front hall."

"What is it?" Tempest whispered back, annoying several of the people sitting next to her. She murmured apologies to everyone.

"Please, my lady. It will only take a few minutes."

Tempest nodded to the servant, and he immediately backed away since he was obstructing the view for several guests. At her sister's questioning glance, she whispered in her ear. "I will return shortly."

Arabella inclined her head to acknowledge that she understood, and Tempest rose from her seat. She ignored her mother, who had definitely noticed her eldest daughter's retreat, and exited the room as quickly as she could. It was not fair to ruin the evening for everyone else.

The only person arrogant enough to summon her in the middle of Miss King's performance was Lord Fairlamb. Since their mothers were currently sitting on opposite sides of the music room, it made sense for them to put their heads together and come up with a plan that would not involve bloodshed.

In the distance, she could hear Miss King sing "I Prithee Send Me Back My Heart" and wished the lady well when it came to her brother. Oliver's infatuations rarely lasted more than a few weeks. The emotion she infused into the ballad hinted that the young woman had dealt with a broken heart in the past.

As the door shut behind her, it was Lady Henwood's butler who was waiting for her. "Good evening, my lady. My apology for the interruption to your evening, but a message has arrived for you."

Tempest retrieved the note from the silver salver the servant presented. "Thank you," she said, dismissing the butler. She took a few steps away from the footmen standing on either side of the door and unfolded the note.

*Meet me in the blue parlor.—C.*

Although no one was observing her, she lowered her chin to conceal her grin. Anticipation blossomed in her chest, expanding until she thought she would burst from joy. Not wanting to waste a single minute, she hurried to the stairs. Tempest had no right to feel this way about the insufferable gentleman. There were moments when she resented her reaction to him. It soothed her pride that he appeared to be at a loss about her, too.

Her mother had been bringing her to Lady Henwood's house since she was a young girl. She and Arabella had explored the house from top to bottom, and she knew the shortest route to the blue parlor. Most of the guests were watching Miss King's performance, and she did not encounter anyone as she made her way upstairs.

Counting the doors as she walked by them, Tempest halted in front of the door to the parlor. In a moment of vanity, she readjusted the curls near her temples and ears. She took a deep breath and opened the door.

Before she could enter the room, a masculine hand shackled her wrist and dragged her into the parlor. She stumbled forward, but Chance caught her. Chuckling, he wrapped his arm around her waist and hugged her against his front while he shut the door and locked it.

"Chance!" Tempest struck his shoulder with her fist. "Are you trying to stop my heart? You frightened me half to death."

"Whom were you expecting?" he asked, taking his time in releasing her. "How many fellows have dragged you into an empty parlor?"

"Only you, Lord Fairlamb," Tempest replied. She was vexed with him, but he did not appear to notice. She placed her hands against his evening coat and attempted to shove him away. "Release me at once, scoundrel."

"In a moment."

Chance's words should have warned her of what was coming. One of his hands glided up her spine and cupped the nape of her neck. His grip tightened, tugging her head to fall back, and his mouth descended. There was nothing gentle about his kiss. It was wonderfully carnal, possessive and demanding. She felt light-headed, and held on to him when he ended the kiss.

"You are utterly mad," Tempest said, giggling as Chance tugged her hand and led her into the shadowed interior of the small parlor. Someone had taken the time to light several oil lamps by the tables positioned near the door, but no one had lingered long enough to illuminate the entire room.

"Mad for you," he said, halting in front of the sofa.

Chance seemed more fascinated with putting his hands on her again than lighting a branch of candles. He cradled her face in his hands and bent his head down until their foreheads and noses touched. "Do you know how many days have passed since I last saw you?"

"Ten," she whispered, touched by the ache in his voice.

He sighed. "It feels like a month. Where the devil have you been?" he demanded, giving her a little shake. "I left a note with the shop owner, but you never claimed it. Each day, I returned to the shop and waited for your response."

Guilt nibbled at the pleasure of their reunion. "I was unable to slip away. Mama was in the mood for company, so she opened the doors each afternoon. Naturally, my sister and I were expected to stay and visit with anyone who called on us."

"I assume you were entertaining more than your mother's old friends." He made a soft noise of disgust when she looked down at her evening slippers. "While I was worrying that your father had locked you away for speaking to me, you were flirting with potential suitors in your mother's drawing room." He pivoted and walked away from her.

Tempest followed him. "Chance, I had no choice. My father expected me and my sister to receive every gentleman who called on our household."

He abruptly turned and caught her by the elbows. "And the lapdog who was sitting beside you . . . was he one of the gentlemen who called on you?" he asked sulkily.

Tempest swallowed to clear the sudden dryness in her throat. The marquess was jealous. The realization was as astounding as it was frightening. She could not recall a single instance when a gentleman had desired her so much, he wanted to strangle her for it.

"Lord Warrilow is a friend of my father's. Of course he is welcome in our house," she said warily. She placed her hand over his heart and gently stroked his chest as if he were an angry beast that needed a calming hand. "Chance, I was not avoiding you. I am just not any good at subterfuge. As soon as I could have left the house, I would have gone to the bookseller's shop or I would have figured out another way to get a message to you."

Some of the tension left his body. "Did you miss me?"

She stared at her hand on his chest and nodded. "You know I did."

Chance used his fingers to tip her face upward and captured her lips with his own. His mouth was demanding, as if he were channeling all his frustration and longing into the kiss. When he lifted his head, both of them were breathless.

"I cannot stay long," Tempest warned, placing her hands over his and drawing them away from her face until there was a respectable distance between them. She was content to keep her hands clasped within his as they sat down on the sofa. "If Miss King finishes her performance before I return, my mother is bound to send someone to search the house for me."

"No one can search a locked room," Mathias pointed out, his humor restored now that he knew she had not been deliberately avoiding him.

"That is not precisely the point," Tempest said, turning her face away when he attempted to kiss her. What she had to say was important, and to her annoyance, he was not paying attention to the risks of their situation. "We have other concerns besides one of the servants catching us together. It is one of the reasons why I wanted to speak to you in private. Did you notice that your mother and sister are downstairs?"

"I did. It was rather thoughtless of Lady Henwood to invite your mother and mine on the same evening." He leaned forward and caged her with his arms by bracing one on the back of the sofa and the other on the armrest. "What do you propose we do? I have a suggestion."

His lecherous grin told her all she needed to know about his idea.

Tempest evaded his lips, so he nuzzled her neck. "How can you make light of the situation!" she argued. "Our mothers are in the same room. Not to mention my brother. Once Miss King finishes her performance, there is no predicting the outcome."

"Actually, there are some details that are quite predictable. For example, Miss King. Her performance will last precisely one hour. As for your mother and the duchess, St. Lyon is discreetly observing them. If a crisis arises, he will send one of the servants to find me while he intercedes in my behalf."

In this instance, his confidence was reassuring. She felt his lips brush a kiss against the side of her neck. "How do you know that Miss King's performance lasts one hour?"

Chance froze. "A guess?"

Tempest was unconvinced. "No. The word you used was 'precisely.' Are you acquainted with Miss King?"

"Well."

Of course Chance would know the beautiful Miss King. Like her brother, he was probably one of the numerous gentlemen who hovered around her dressing room in hopes of gaining a private audience.

He had gone to the theater to see Miss King on the evening he had rescued her. Had he returned to the young woman's side after they parted ways? With a sound of disgust, she shoved him off her.

Chance fell back against the cushions of the sofa, laughing. "Tempest."

"Is Miss King your mistress?" she asked.

"Are you jealous?"

"No!" Was she? Tempest ground her teeth together as she stood. "It must be dreadfully inconvenient to have my brother sniffing at her skirts. You have more in common with Oliver than I had imagined."

Chance's eyes chilled at her words. "Marcroft and I are nothing alike."

Tempest held her chin high as she lifted the hem of her skirt to step over his feet. "We shall have to disagree on this point. If you do not mind, I will take my leave. My mother—ooph!"

Without warning, he rose up and grabbed her by the waist, pulling her onto his lap. "I do mind," he growled into her ear. "Now, listen to me, my lady. Miss King is not my mistress. Nor is she my former mistress. Your brother is welcome to her."

Outraged by his rough handling, she wiggled in his lap in an attempt to free herself. "Let me go!" She kicked his leg with the heel of her shoe.

"You have a rather nasty temper when provoked," he said, and nipped her earlobe for her attack. His arms felt like bands of iron. "Ask me the name of the lady who has captured my fancy. Whose face haunts my dreams when I sleep?"

Her energy depleted, Tempest sagged against him. "Chance. If this is some sort of game, I prefer that you play it with someone else." Tempest did not think her heart could bear the disappointment.

"Is that what you believe—that I am playing games?" he said, his voice somber.

"I do not know what I believe," she confessed. "I just do not want to see my family hurt because you and your friends thought it would be a grand jest to flirt with one of Norgrave's daughters."

"Very clever of me, is it not?" he said, and his harsh mocking tone caused her to wince.

Tempest stirred to climb off his lap, but his arm tightened around her waist.

"I have chafed against my father's authority for years. Seducing his enemy's daughter would prove that I am a ruthless bastard and demonstrate my loyalty to the family. He might even reward me for my cleverness."

"You are not that cold," she cried out. "That cruel. It isn't you."

"How can you be certain?" he persisted, using that same mocking voice that made her want to shout at him. "After all, I am one of those awful Rookes."

"I don't think of you as a Rooke!" she blurted out, startling both of them.

Chance caught her chin, and their eyes met. Satisfaction flared in his light gray eyes. "Progress, indeed, if you can overlook my name. Let's see if you truly see the man."

When he crushed his mouth over hers, Tempest tasted the anger he was suppressing. It was simpler to accept the passion that blasted away all the good reasons why they were not a good match. He had deliberately goaded her, shattering her defenses. Her loyalties.

She did not want to feel this way in his arms.

Even as the thought shimmered in her mind, she saw it for what it was—a lie.

How simpler her life would be if she and Chance had parted amiably, if she had walked away and returned to the music room. Lord Warrilow was awaiting her return. She would smile at the marquess and do everything in her power to ensure her father's plans succeeded.

"Open your mouth for me, damn it," he muttered, lightly biting her lower lip.

Her lips parted in anticipation.

The room seemed to spin as she was slowly eased onto her back, cradled by his arm until her body was cushioned by the sofa. It was an impressive feat, since not once had his mouth released hers. Chance's tongue unfurled, flowing over her bottom teeth and stroking her tongue. Tempest moaned, feeling rather wanton. Her nipples constricted and ached beneath her stays. He had one knee wedged into the seam of the sofa and the other balanced on the front edge of the cushion as he caged her with his body. His body rubbed and heated hers without the full burden of his weight.

Tempest arched her back, prolonging the contact of the front of her bodice pressing against his waistcoat. She brazenly threaded her fingers into his hair at the back of his head, and pulled him closer. Kissing Chance was a wonderful and heady experience. She had never kissed a gentleman in such an intimate fashion. However, there was no awkwardness between them.

Only hunger.

Mirroring the flirtation of his nimble tongue, it wasn't long before they were both overly warm and shaking from their labors.

Chance broke their kiss. There was a feverish cast to his light gray eyes, and his lips were damp. His expression had her tugging on his hair so he would kiss her again.

"You will be the ruin of me," he murmured, kissing her again with a sweetness that had her heart fluttering. "And I will be the ruin of you if we continue."

"Just one more kiss," Tempest insisted, her hands sliding from his shoulders to the front of his evening coat. She gripped the edges to pull him closer.

Chance stiffened to resist her invitation. "Tempest, I—"

His knee on the outside edge of the sofa slipped from its moorings and he toppled over, taking her with him.

Tempest felt a burst of air from his lungs tease the curls around her face as they landed on the floor. "Are you hurt?" she asked, trying not to giggle and failing miserably.

"So you are amused?" was his dry reply.

She barely managed a high squeak when he abruptly

tightened his grip and rolled them so their positions were reversed. The thin rug offered little comfort as he covered her.

"Still amused, Tempest?"

"You are no gentleman, Lord Fairlamb," she said, attempting to sound as if she were vexed with him. Her smile ruined the effect.

"I never claimed to be one, my sweet," he replied, kissing her roughly on the mouth before he rolled off her. Chance sat up on his knees and offered her his hand. "And yet, I must behave myself this evening. Let's tidy your hair before you return to the music room. We do not want your brother to come looking for you."

Oliver was too distracted by Miss King to notice her absence. Chance deliberately mentioned her brother to hasten her departure. A frisson of annoyance chafed against her good mood. She placed her hand in his and allowed him to help her stand. "So . . . now that you have had your way with me, my lord, I am to be dismissed?"

With her head held high, she walked by him to the nearest mirror. A side glance revealed he was frowning at her, and when she peered at her reflection, she confirmed it. Good. Now they were even.

Unfortunately, the fickle Lord Fairlamb was correct. Her hair was disheveled from their frolic on the sofa and floor. Using her fingers, she repositioned the curls around her face. She moistened her lips and winced. Her lips were tender, and there was a slight plumpness. The subtle change was appealing, but anyone scrutinizing her face might deduce what she had been doing in her absence.

Chance startled her when he grabbed her upper arm and turned her to face him. Face-to-face, he appeared to be more than annoyed with her. He looked downright furious.

"If I had had my way with you, as you so indelicately described it, we would not be snapping at each other," he snarled.

Before she could respond, Chance had her pressed against the wall and was kissing her. Tempest forgot about her annoyance and kissed him back with utter abandon. Neither one of them felt like being gentle as their tongues dueled for dominance. She held on to large fistfuls of the back of his coat until her vision began to darken at the edges.

She had forgotten to breathe.

Chance released her, and she swayed unsteadily until he caught her around the waist.

"Damn," he swore. His thumb brushed her lower lip. "You might want to use your fan around your mother."

"Why?" She was still feeling a little dizzy and unfocused.

"One glance, and Lady Norgrave will conclude someone ravished you," he said bluntly.

Tempest was confident she could evade a close inspection from her mother. "I am not the only one who looks well kissed."

With a thoughtful expression, Chance touched his lower lip. He grinned at the noticeable swelling. "It is your fault, you know."

"My fault?" Tempest turned away and checked the damage done to her hair and lips. Chance was correct. It would be difficult to explain away the high color in her cheeks and the fullness in her lips. "How so?"

"You keep taunting me to put my hands on you." Chance stepped behind her and kissed her bare shoulder. "When can I touch you again?"

"I do not know." Tempest stared into the mirror, and their gazes locked. The blinding need that seemed reserved solely for him had cooled, giving her the opportunity to recall the dozen or so reasons why she should stay away from him. "Shall we try the bookseller's shop again?"

"Then I wait another ten days? I would rather not," he said, still annoyed about it.

"We could meet in the park?"

"Rotten Row is not a very discreet place to meet," he mused out loud. "Someone is bound to recognize us and share the good news with our families."

And then she would be beaten by her father and sent to one of the estates in the country until he could convince Lord Warrilow or some other gentleman to marry his reckless daughter. Tempest shook her head. "There are other places to meet besides one of the ton's favorite haunts," she said, stepping out of his embrace. "Unless you have a better suggestion."

"What day?"

"Three days," she said, picking the first number that came into her head.

"Two," he countered. "My patience does have a limit."

"Three o'clock?"

"Half past the one o'clock hour," he replied. "It will be too early for the fashionable to make an appearance. If you like, you could bring your sketching notebook."

She nodded, touched that he looked beyond his own needs. "I will." She offered him a shy smile. "I should go. With a little luck, Arabella and I should be able to convince our mother to leave after Miss King's performance."

Her mother would not seek out a confrontation with the Duchess of Blackbern in front of Lord Warrilow,

Tempest thought. Not that she intended to share her reasoning with Chance. She curtsied. "Good evening, my lord."

The marquess captured her hand and kissed it. "The very best," he replied as if she had asked him a question.

# Chapter Seventeen

Tempest slipped into the music room unnoticed. There were half a dozen of Lady Henwood's guests crowded near the door, so she threaded her way through them to find a place to stand at the back of the room. She was relieved everyone's attention was still centered on the raven-haired Miss King. The young woman was singing a sad ballad about unrequited love. The emotion vibrating in her voice and the grief twisting her face appeared sincere, and they stirred sympathy even in Tempest.

Chance had been smitten with Miss King.

She pouted at the unpleasant thought.

The marquess had not been immune to the woman's beauty; however, in his defense, Tempest doubted very few gentlemen were capable of resisting Miss King's charms when she cared to wield them. It was an enviable talent. Perhaps it was fortunate that the woman had abandoned her attempts to lure Chance into her bed and turned her attentions to Oliver.

She idly wondered if she should warn her brother, but dismissed getting involved. Oliver was not inexperienced when it came to affairs of the heart. Neither was Miss King.

It was Tempest who was in over her head.

She started as everyone applauded. The woman who

was the center of all the adulation curtsied and smiled demurely as Oliver presented her with a bouquet of flowers. One by one, guests began to stand and move toward the front so they could be introduced to Miss King. With so many people moving about the room, Tempest could no longer see a glimpse of her mother and sister.

It was going to be a long evening.

"Fancy meeting you here, Lady Tempest."

Her eyes widened as she recognized Chance's voice. Without looking at her, he stepped forward until he was standing beside her.

"What are you doing?" she whispered, resisting the urge to glare at him. "Are you trying to call attention to yourself?"

"Not at all," he replied, sounding too calm for their predicament. "It is going to be difficult to convince my mother to leave unless I find her first."

"Don't be obtuse." When she realized she was frowning, she took a deep breath and carefully blanked her expression. "Why are you standing next to *me*?"

"No particular reason, darling," was his casual reply. "The lighting in the parlor was meager, and I wanted to see your face. You look beautiful this evening."

His compliment deflated any annoyance she was feeling. "You are too kind."

She shuddered as he deliberately grazed the back of his hand against hers. "If I were kind, I would leave you alone," he drawled. "Two days, Lady Tempest. Do not disappoint me."

Chance strolled away without waiting for a response. Tempest looked around her, and no one seemed to have noticed her brief exchange with the marquess. Her shoulders sagged with relief.

Until she noticed that her mother was staring at her. *How long has she been watching me?* Her pulse quickened at the thought her mother could have seen her speaking to Chance. Several people crossed in front of the marchioness, momentarily obscuring Tempest's view, and by the time she did have a clear view, her mother had turned away to speak with someone.

She did not recognize the gentleman, nor did she care so long as her mother stayed away from Chance and the Duchess of Blackbern.

"There you are!" Her cousin enveloped her into an enthusiastic embrace.

"Harriet," she said, drawing back. "I did not expect to see you this evening."

"It was a last-minute decision," Harriet explained, looking exceptional in her green dress. "Mama was worried Lady Henwood would be offended if we did not make an appearance. I tried to tell her the countess would understand, considering the distressing situation."

She had mentioned Harriet to Lord Warrilow, but it had been lie. Had he said anything to Arabella or her mother? Distracted by her own concerns, it took a few seconds for her cousin's words to register.

"I beg your pardon. What distressing situation?"

Harriet looked over her shoulder at the small crowd gathered around Miss King. "Did your mother not tell you? My father has made a fool of himself over a certain lowbred woman."

Tempest could not fathom it. "Your father and Miss King? I do not believe it."

"Mama discovered a pile of bills from numerous merchants." Harriet's eyes were hot with outrage and pain in her mother's behalf. "When she confronted him, he naturally denied that the woman was his mistress. She threw him out of the house, and Papa has been sleeping at one of his clubs ever since."

Tempest watched her brother discourage one of Miss

King's ardent admirers with a dark glance. She could not imagine Oliver sharing his mistress with a gentleman old enough to be her father—not to mention a relative. "Perhaps your mother misunderstood."

"The deliveries were made to Miss King, and the bills were sent to my father. What other explanation could there be?" Harriet asked.

She clasped her cousin's hand. "I agree, it is damning evidence. However, I know your father. He is a good man. I cannot believe he would betray your mother and his family in such a public and humiliating manner."

"Then why is he renting a room at his club?" the other woman said.

"Well, your mother has a rather formidable temper," Tempest gently pointed out. "Gentlemen always make fools of themselves over women. It was a harmless flirtation that had already run its course when your mother discovered the bills on his desk."

"Harmless or not, when I marry Lord Medeley, I will not tolerate such deceit," Harriet vowed, her hurt and anger suddenly directed at her betrothed.

Tempest hoped the earl was not in attendance this evening, as he would be unable to avoid the sharp edge of his beloved's tongue.

"Would you?"

Tempest immediately thought of Chance flirting with Miss King. Her fingers tightened around her cousin's fingers until the other woman winced. She hastily released Harriet's hand. It was unfair for her to be furious about something that had occurred before he met her.

Unless he was not being completely honest with her.

"I would quietly murder my betrothed if he betrayed me." Tempest shook her head. Chance had not asked for her hand in marriage. Nor would he if she persisted in behaving like a woman scorned by her lover. "Nevertheless, I doubt your father betrayed your mother. Once your mother has calmed down, your father will be more inclined to offer apologies and an explanation."

"I hope you are right." She glanced again over her shoulder at Miss King. "Mama thought if she was absent this evening, there would be talk."

"There always is," Tempest said, her voice filled with sympathy. "However, the gossip will be speculation about my brother's relationship with Miss King."

His behavior this evening was likely embarrassing their mother.

"True." Harriet put her arm around Tempest's waist. "Remind me to thank Oliver later. You can always count on family."

"Speaking of family, perhaps we should rejoin them."

Harriet nodded. "By the by, I know it is none of my business, but I have to ask. Whom have you been kissing? Is it anyone I know?"

Tempest could feel the blood drain from her face. "Is it so obvious?"

"I'm afraid so, Cousin."

On the other side of the room, Mathias was also about to pay for his sins.

After he had walked away from Tempest, he headed for the general area where he had last seen his mother and sisters. Neither St. Lyon nor his family was in sight. He stared down at the empty chairs, but he was not worried. Lady Norgrave was still holding court on the opposite side of the music room. Or she was just minutes ago. There were too many people standing around him to keep track of her, and that was just fine with him. If she recognized him, the marchioness would be less than thrilled to see another Rooke.

It would be the least of her worries. Lady Norgrave

would require smelling salts if she learned about her daughter's latest mischief with him.

If the poor lady could glean his wicked thoughts about Tempest, she would lock her daughter away and take to her bed.

However, Tempest was safe, and she was returning to her family well kissed but otherwise untouched. Mathias was not ruled by his cock. He was not planning to give Marcroft a reason to call him out.

The thought brought him up short.

It seemed only weeks ago, he had been baiting the earl into a duel. Mathias still despised the man, but if Marcroft challenged him, Tempest would not be the reason for it. He intended to keep her out of his quarrel with her brother.

"They are probably waiting for the coach," he said, confident St. Lyon was protecting the duchess and Mathias's sisters.

He turned and halted when he noticed Clara King was standing in front of him. He hadn't given her a thought when he returned to the music room. When he wasn't paying attention, she had excused herself from her admirers—even Marcroft.

"My compliments on a fine performance, Miss King." He bowed, but did not step closer or attempt to kiss her hand. "I will leave you to your admirers."

Clara King was just as lovely as he remembered. The floral scent teased his nose as she closed the distance between them. "Why? Are you not one of my most devoted admirers, Lord Fairlamb?"

The impact of her liquid blue gaze could muddle a man's good sense. He had learned that lesson first-hand. Still, he was not completely immune when she was standing so close to him.

Then he recalled that Marcroft had bedded her, and

annoyance cleared his head. "Admirers can be as fickle as the lady they worship, Miss King."

She appeared puzzled by his statement. Or perhaps she was a better actress than he had credited. "I have been worried about you. You never returned to the theater, nor have you called on me at the hotel."

"I have no doubt you have found other amusements, Miss King," he said dryly. If he had not witnessed what a heartless jade she was, he might have felt obliged to apologize for his rude behavior.

The singer was visibly taken aback by his coolness. He gave her credit for her swift recovery. "The last time we spoke, you called me Clara."

A lot had occurred since that last meeting. He and Clara would have become lovers if he had not chased after Tempest. The decision had changed everything.

"I regretfully must take my leave," he said politely. "My family awaits my return." He turned to walk away.

"No, wait!" Miss King said, taking a step forward and then stopping when he halted. It was the first time he had seen her appear indecisive about her next move. "Will I see you again?"

"While you reside in London, your popularity with the ton makes it inevitable," he said, not unkindly. "There is no reason to pout, Miss King. After all, you still have Marcroft dancing on a leading string."

Mathias did not wait for her reply. He pivoted on his heel and walked away. Clara King might lament that a rich fish had slipped her hook, but she was wise enough to cut her loses. She was not in love with him any more than he had been in love with her.

He glanced up and to his chagrin, Tempest was heading in his direction. Their gazes met, but she deliberately slid hers and stared at something over his shoulder. Or someone. Clara King. Mathias silently cursed his rotten luck. Tempest had observed his exchange with Miss King and assumed that he had lied to her.

The pain in her gaze felt like claws digging into his gut.

Mathias ground his back molars together in frustration. He wanted to go to her and explain that the singer had approached him. Unfortunately, he was not in a position to offer explanations. Tempest was not alone. Lady Harriet was at her side, and from the corner of his eye, he saw Marcroft making his way toward his sister. The only thing that would make the situation worse was if Lady Norgrave tapped him on the shoulder.

It was definitely time to leave.

Switching directions, he strode toward the nearest door and exited the music room.

Charlotte stepped away from one of Lady Henwood's potted plants and into the brighter glow flickering from the wall sconces as she watched Blackbern's heir disappear around the corner.

*Yes, I know who you are, Lord Fairlamb.*

With two daughters ripe for marriage, she had made a point of studying potential husbands for them. Norgrave had selected his favorites for the season without asking her opinion. Not that he would have listened to her. Her husband handpicked gentlemen who fit his aspirations, confident that their girls would blindly accept his dictates. Last season's debacle with Rinehart should have been a hint of things to come.

The walking nightmare this season had taken the form of a Rooke.

It was enough for Charlotte to believe in curses.

In the last few years, she had observed Lord Fairlamb whenever fate was cruel enough for their paths to cross. It was obvious to her that the young nobleman had the look of his father and his mother. She knew precisely who he was before a friend confirmed her suspicions. From the gossips, she had gleaned that the marquess had inherited his father's carnal appetites. It was all Charlotte needed to know to condemn him.

When had Tempest met him?

Although Fairlamb and her daughter behaved in the music room as if they did not know each other, Charlotte had taken one look at them standing close together and she *knew*. Perhaps it was a mother's instinct. Her eldest child was in danger. Gently reared and spoiled by her family, Tempest believed in the good in people. She had no idea of pain, of cruelty . . . of the ruthlessness of a man's nature.

Something had to be done.

Her mind made up, Charlotte walked down the passageway. A footman stood near one of the open doors. He held a silver tray laden with sparkling wine. *Only the best for Lady Henwood,* she thought as she plucked a glass off the tray without slowing her stride. She continued down the hall until she came to the stairs.

"Up or down?" she murmured. Should she confront young Fairlamb with her accusations? No, he would only deny them. Men were such duplicitous creatures.

She sipped her wine to steady her nerves.

"Upstairs it is."

A lifetime had passed since she last sought out the company of this woman. Once she had considered her a friend. Later, she realized that she had been nothing more than a nuisance. She had been a naïve girl who had been merely tolerated by the people around her, who later stared at her with various measures of pity.

Only one lady knew her secrets, and Charlotte despised her for it.

She opened the door to the parlor their hostess was using as a private room for the ladies. The room was not empty. As she entered the room, a maid dipped into a curtsy and would have spoken to her if Charlotte had not dismissed her. Three ladies sat in a group and were chatting about their children. Another woman was partially hidden behind a screen as the harried maid she was berating was loosening her tight stays.

She discovered her quarry sitting in one of the chairs near the hearth. The Duchess of Blackbern had her back to the door, so she had not noticed Charlotte's entrance. However, her friend was more observant. The matron leaned forward and whispered something to the duchess. Although Her Grace was too polite to turn around, Charlotte took some pleasure in observing how the news of her arrival caused the other woman's shoulders to stiffen.

She took another sip of her sparkling wine and stared down at the woman who had played a role in ruining her life. "Good evening, Your Grace."

The Duchess of Blackbern slowly stood up and turned to greet her. Charlotte could not recall the last time she had spoken to the woman she had once considered a close friend. Time had been kind to the duchess. Her youthful features had matured, leaving her with an almost ageless beauty. It seemed unfair that this woman had been rewarded while Charlotte had been punished.

"Good evening, Char—Lady Norgrave," the duchess said, correcting herself. Too much time had passed for familiarity.

"Imogene," the duchess's companion entreated.

Her Grace turned away from Charlotte to address her friend. "Please, Ruth, I do not want to keep you. We will continue our talk later."

Charlotte finished her wine and walked around the chair so she could place the empty glass on the mantel. "Yes, do run along. Her Grace and I have some catching up to do."

"Watch your step, Lady Norgrave," the matron warned, shuffling her larger figure to avoid brushing against her. "The Duke of Blackbern will have something to say if you upset his lady."

Charlotte feigned a shudder. "I consider myself dutifully warned." She paused, waiting for the woman to leave the room. "How do you tolerate the meddling old harpy?"

The Duchess of Blackbern sat down and gestured for her companion to join her. "Lady Ludsthorp is Tristan's aunt. She is aware we haven't spoken in years. Needless to say, your decision to approach me concerns her."

Charlotte settled into her chair and nodded toward the door the countess had exited. "How much does she know?"

The duchess grimaced. No doubt she was thinking about the past. "Just enough to be concerned. Why are you here, Lady Norgrave?"

"After all we have shared, I believe we should set aside our formal titles. Once you called me Charlotte," she said, infusing enough of a dare in her tone to get a reaction from the other woman.

"And you called me Imogene."

She ignored the hint of sadness in the duchess's almost flawless face. If Imogene thought her regret would blunt Charlotte's anger, she was wrong. "I have not come to talk about the past, Your Grace. Nor do I wish to renew our old friendship."

"Then what do you want?"

"We share a common problem."

"What?"

"More to the point—whom," Charlotte said, watching the other woman closely. "Your son."

Surprise and curiosity flashed across the duchess's face. "Which one?"

"How blessed you are to be able to boast that you have more than one."

"It is not boasting to ask for clarification, Charlotte. Which son is troubling you?"

"You truly are unaware," she said, mildly amused. "I am referring to your husband's heir, Lord Fairlamb."

Charlotte thought the duchess was incapable of guile, but her expression blanked at her son's name.

"What has he done?"

Charlotte leaned forward. "Are you aware that I have three daughters? My eldest girl is a year younger than your son."

"No."

She smiled sweetly at the vehement denial. "Tempest is incredibly beautiful. Norgrave—" It was cruel of her to mention the marquess's name so soon, but she was curious in regards to the lady's reaction. Fortunately, the duchess did not disappoint her. "—and I have high hopes that she will marry this year. We have had a continuous stream of gentlemen who have visited our drawing room this month."

Imogene shook her head. "Are you telling me my son is calling on your daughter?"

It was a shame, really, she could not credit Fairlamb with such brazenness. She might have opened her drawing room to him just to see her husband's face when he learned of it. "No."

"What are you accusing him of doing?"

"I am not certain," Charlotte quietly admitted. "He is up to something. I saw them together this evening—"

"My son is here!" the duchess exclaimed, beginning to rise from her chair.

"Sit down," she said sharply, and was surprised when Imogene obeyed. "If you were unaware of your son's whereabouts, then it is apparent you and Blackbern are neglecting your duty."

"Our son is not a child, Lady Norgrave. He is a grown man and has his own residence," Imogene staunchly defended him. "St. Lyon—"

"Who is this St. Lyon?"

"A friend of Mathias's," the other woman said, dismissing the details with a wave of her hand. "I was unaware of his presence until he approached me and my daughters. He refrained from mentioning my son." She pursed her lips and pondered his deliberate oversight. "He offered to summon the coach and watch over the girls while I stopped to speak with Tristan's aunt."

"And pray, why would a son send his good friend to watch over his family when he was capable of seeing to the task himself?"

Both of them knew the answer, even if the duchess was reluctant to admit it.

"What proof do you have?"

"I saw them standing together at the back of the music room," she said, aware that her evidence was flimsy at best. "Something was going on between them."

"Charlotte, is it not possible that there is another explanation?" she asked gently.

"Tempest received a note from someone. She left the room during Miss King's performance, and the next time I see her, she is standing beside Fairlamb."

"I can appreciate your concern," Imogene said, carefully picking her words. "However, it is difficult to believe Mathias would approach your daughter."

The fight between Blackbern and Norgrave twenty-four years earlier and the reasons for it were a deep, dark unnavigable chasm between them. Neither Charlotte nor Imogene seemed willing to try.

"You do not believe me?" Charlotte dug her fingers into the armrest. "This is not the only occasion I have seen your son at the same function as my daughter."

"And I have noted Lord Marcroft's attendance at a few functions over the years, and never once did it occur to me that he was there to seduce one of my daughters. Let us speak frankly, Charlotte," Imogene said. "It was simpler for our families to avoid each other when our children were younger. Now that they are older, such accidental encounters are bound to happen. I think even you would agree that it is unfair for us to blame them for being curious."

"Does your son know?"

Charlotte stared at the other woman. She did not have to offer any explanation.

Almost immediately, Imogene's gaze dropped to her lap. "No. Tristan and I never speak of it." She swallowed. "And your children?"

"No. Your secrets are safe, Imogene. Ironic, is it not, that after all these years, my husband still protects you."

Charlotte regretted her waspish comment the second it was uttered. She watched as Imogene's face paled. It was the only sign she hurt her. The duchess was stronger than most people knew.

"You do not understand. I doubt Norgrave would have told you, but there is a good reason why my husband cut all ties with him."

"I know everything, Imogene." At the duchess's look of disbelief, Charlotte said, "It is you who possesses only half of the tale."

"Then tell me."

"Another night, perhaps." *Or never.* Charlotte stood, and was disconcerted that her hands were trembling. "I will concede that I may have misunderstood what I saw. Your son might very well be innocent."

"He is." The duchess stood. She looked as miserable as Charlotte felt.

"For the sake of our old friendship, I ask that you watch him. If you see anything that troubles you, I beg you to speak with Fairlamb and take steps to discourage him. Nothing good will result from your son and my daughter developing a tendre for one another."

"I agree." Imogene hesitated. "Thank you for sharing your concerns with me."

"I do this to protect my daughter," Charlotte said simply. "It might be prudent not to mention our little chat to your husband. Blackbern has proved to be quite unreasonable when it comes to those he loves. I will not have my family suffer for it again."

Imogene looked as if she wanted to argue, but she nodded her head. "I will ask Ruth not to speak of our meeting."

"More secrets?" Charlotte sighed. "Very well. What's a few more between old friends?"

# Chapter Eighteen

The knock at Tempest's door was not unexpected.

"Come in, Arabella," she called out.

"I was afraid that I might wake you."

"I am not tired," Tempest admitted. "I thought I might read, but I am grateful for the company."

Her younger sister was already dressed for bed. Her hair had been braided by one of the maids. Her white shapeless nightgown and the white mop cap on her head made her look younger.

Tempest placed her brush on her dressing table and rose from the small bench. She held out her hand. "We could sit on the bed and talk."

It had begun as a game to outwit their governess, who believed children should retire to their beds early. Often they were still too restless to sleep, so one of them would sneak into the other's bedchamber. Sometimes they were caught and both were thoroughly scolded for their disobedience. The poor woman eventually stopped trying to separate them, and Tempest had lost count of the nights she and Arabella had slept in the same bed.

Tempest pulled back the covers for her sister, allowing Arabella to climb into the bed first. She then walked over to her dressing table and picked up the unlit candle. Lifting the glass chimney off the oil lamp, she lit the candle and extinguished the lamp. She returned to the bed and placed the candle on the table.

"Move over," she said, and Arabella obliged her since she usually fell asleep first.

Tempest climbed into bed. She plumped her pillows and settled down next to her sister.

"Lady Henwood was wise to invite Miss King," she said when her sister remained silent. "I wonder if she shortened her performance for the intimate gathering or if she sang a different collection of songs at the theater."

"I never considered there could be a difference," Arabella replied, turning onto her side so she could look at Tempest. "I didn't come to discuss Miss King."

Tempest was content to drop the subject. In truth, she was still reeling from the sight of Chance speaking with Miss King. He was likely paying his respects, but his discomfort when he saw her had made her stomach ache. She had not thought herself capable of jealousy, and it shamed her that she had a few uncharitable thoughts about the woman as she and her cousin had walked by the couple.

"What did you wish to discuss?" She rolled onto her side so her face was inches apart from Arabella's. "Is this about Oliver? I know he—"

"Actually, I wanted to talk to you about the note you received from the footman," she blurted out as if she had been biting her tongue all evening.

Wary, Tempest brushed a stray strand of hair from her sister's cheek. "What about the note?"

"Who sent it?"

Tempest glared at Arabella. "Are you inquiring out of curiosity or for Mama?"

"Mama did not say a word to me," her sister replied, outraged by the question. "Neither did you, for that matter.

I cannot believe you thought I was spying on our mother's behalf."

Contrite, Tempest said, "I did not mean to—"

"Forget it." Arabella sighed. "I was worried, and I was not the only one. Lord Warrilow was concerned, too. You walked out of the music room, and no one saw you again until the end of Miss King's performance."

"I did return. Out of respect for Lady Henwood's guests, I chose to remain at the back of the room," she explained, sticking as close to the truth as possible.

"Whom did you meet?"

"Harriet," Tempest replied.

"So . . . she was the one who sent the note?" Arabella asked, sounding mildly curious.

"Of course. I told you and Lord Warrilow that I was expecting her."

"Ha!" Her sister slapped the palms of her hands onto the bedding and sat up. "You are lying! Harriet most definitely did not send you a note."

Somehow Arabella had deduced she was lying. Determined to brazen it out, she glared at her sister. "How do you know? Did you actually read the note?"

Her sister called her bluff. "If Harriet wrote the note, then you will not object to showing me the note."

"I lost it." This time she was speaking the truth. She must have dropped it when Chance had grabbed her and pulled her into the informal parlor.

"Why won't you tell me the truth?" her sister cried. "You are behaving oddly, even for you."

"First you accuse me of lying, and then you hurl additional insults at me." Tempest huffed. "I believe I have heard enough from you. Feel free to return to your bedchamber."

"Sister."

"I mean it," Tempest said, prepared to shove Arabella off her bed.

"Ask me how I know you are lying about Harriet," her sister demanded.

Kneeling on the mattress, Tempest sat down on her heels. "I returned to you with Harriet at my side. How dare you claim that I was lying."

"I never said that you were lying about Harriet's appearance," Arabella replied, clenching her teeth. "I am accusing you of lying about the note. Harriet did not summon you."

"How do you know?"

"Because I asked her when she first arrived." At her sister's shocked expression, Arabella smirked. "Oh, you were unaware that Harriet arrived during Miss King's performance. Our cousin and her mother were less courteous when they entered the music room. When Harriet sat down in your empty seat, I asked her about the note. She denied seeing you or sending a footman to you."

Tempest winced.

Her sister nodded. "Our cousin failed to mention that she spoke to me first. When I told her that you stepped out of the room, she offered to look for you."

No, Harriet had forgotten to warn her of the conversation she had with Arabella. It also explained why the other woman was so confident Tempest had been meeting someone in secret.

"Did you say anything to Mama?"

"No. I allowed her and Lord Warrilow to believe Harriet was responsible for your absence." Her stiff posture and the chill in her voice were proof that her sister was very cross with her.

"I apologize for doubting you," Tempest said, resisting the urge to hug her. Arabella was unpredictable when she was hurt. "And I regret lying to you. You are correct. Harriet did not write the note."

The coldness in her sister's expression vanished and she edged closer. "Who did?"

"First I require a promise," Tempest hedged, needing some assurance that Arabella would take her confession to the grave.

"I swear I won't tell anyone," she said, linking her fingers with Tempest's. "You can trust me."

Arabella was not the sort to tattle. Tempest swallowed and inhaled. "Do you remember Chance?"

For a few seconds, her sister looked puzzled by the name. Recognition washed away her blank expression. "One of our gentleman bathers? How could I forget him or the others? Oh, what were their names?"

She offered her sister a faint smile. "Thorn and St. Lyon. If you recall, we briefly encountered Chance again at the theater."

Arabella brought her hand to her mouth. "Good heavens!" She glanced at the closed door as if she expected someone to be listening at the keyhole. "Is Chance courting you?"

"In his own way, I suppose," was her weak reply.

Arabella gasped. "Is this why you have been so frosty to poor Lord Warrilow?"

"I have not been frosty!" she protested.

Her sister was not listening. "Mama and Papa will be thrilled when they learn that you have another suitor."

Tempest groaned and collapsed against the stack of pillows. "No, Arabella, they will not be pleased."

"Why not?" Her eyes rounded as she came to her own conclusion. "Chance is a fortune hunter."

"I fear it is worse than that, dear sister."

"Worse than a fortune hunter." She tapped her lower lip. "He is in trade? A gambler? A second son? The natural son of a nobleman? Oh, I surrender. Why do you not want our mother and father to know about Chance?"

"The gentleman who introduced himself as Chance is Mathias Rooke, Marquess of Fairlamb," Tempest said, feeling sick to her stomach. If her sister betrayed her, she would never be allowed to see him again.

"Lord Fairlamb."

Tempest watched with a dispassionate expression on her face as her sister finally connected Chance with his family. She leaned forward and covered her sister's mouth with her hand to muffle her high-pitched shriek.

"Are you trying to wake the entire household?" she hissed.

Arabella swiftly shook her head and mumbled an apology. When Tempest removed her hand, she said, "Chance is the Duke of Blackbern's son? When did he tell you?"

"He didn't. Oliver told me."

"I do not understand. The three gentlemen were gone before our brother's return. How did he know?"

"Oliver has some history with Chance, and none of it pleasant." When her sister covered her mouth again, Tempest braced for another stifled scream, but Arabella shook her head. "Our brother indulged in a bit of blackmail. He would not tell Papa and I promised to avoid Chance."

"You lied to Oliver."

From her sister's point of view, small mountains could be forged from her numerous sins.

"Of course I did not lie to Oliver. I fully intended to stay away from Chance, and then we encountered him at the theater. While you were seated in the private box with Mrs. Sheehan, I was accosted by a drunk. Chance rescued me."

Tempest decided to skip the kissing part of her tale,

since neither one of them had been impressed with her efforts.

"You were rescued by Lord Fairlamb." Arabella sighed. "Can you imagine anything more heroic?"

Her sister possessed a romantic heart. If she heard the entire tale, she might not have thought him so gallant. However, Tempest's opinion of her tarnished knight had improved with each meeting.

"At first, I was disheartened because our brother has burdened me with an impossible task. I cannot keep my promise and never see Chance again. I do not even want to."

Arabella clutched one of the feather pillows and hugged it to her breasts. "Are you in love with him?"

She evaded her sister's questioning look. "It is too soon for declarations." It was obvious that Chance was struggling with his feelings for her. Even if he did love her, a man in his position had too much to lose. He would never defy his family.

"Papa will never grant his blessing for the match."

Lord Norgrave would rather see her dead than in the hands of his enemy.

If she had any sense, she should cease struggling against fate. Her father had decided Lord Warrilow would be her husband, and he could be very persuasive. The young marquess had never encountered anyone like Lord Norgrave. "There is no reason to court Papa's approval. Chance has not proposed, and if his family is as difficult as ours, he never will."

"So you have given up?"

"Not in the least," she said haughtily. "We Brants have stubbornness bred into our bones."

Rainbault braced his forearms on the long wooden table and leaned forward. "Is St. Lyon exaggerating? Did you seduce Norgrave's daughter while the chit's mother awaited her return several floors below?"

Mathias glowered at the viscount, who responded with a shrug. "Your loose tongue is going to get me maimed by a sword or dueling pistol."

"Do not blame me. You are courting death, my friend," St. Lyon countered. "Dallying with a Brant will end with you staring at the wrong end of a pistol."

After he and the viscount had escorted his mother and sisters to their coach, the two men had joined Thorn and Rainbault at a tavern. The prince had been in the middle of a brawl when they arrived. The small cut near the corner of his mouth was still bleeding, but he had held his own against five men.

"I thought you were goading Marcroft into challenging you?" the prince asked, his tone revealing what he thought of such an action.

"If you are caught, who do you think will demand satisfaction?" Thorn asked, well on his way to becoming drunk. "The father or the son?"

"Both," Mathias replied without needing to think about it. He picked up the bottle of brandy and poured more into his cousin's glass. "And then you can count on my father finishing what the Brants started.

"A man does not murder his heir," Rainbault said, scoffing at the notion.

Mathias brought the glass of brandy to his lips and drank. "Blackbern would consider it a mercy killing if he suspected his heir suffered from lunacy."

A throaty laugh rumbled in Thorn's throat. "Well, as your cousin, I have often questioned your judgment."

Mathias knocked his cousin's feet off the bench, causing him to lose his balance. Thorn landed on his arse. "You're drunk. Your opinion does not count."

"No one is going to accuse you of lunacy, Chance," the prince persisted.

"My father would if I were foolish enough to get ambushed by Norgrave and his son," Mathias replied, rubbing his neck.

"Seducing Norgrave's eldest daughter would be proof enough," St. Lyon said, earning another glare from Mathias. "What? You and Lady Tempest missed most of Miss King's performance this evening. What were you doing? Counting her eyelashes?"

"Or her teeth," interjected Rainbault.

"This is Chance," Thorn said, climbing back onto the bench. "His face was buried in her muff."

Wicked, shrewd laughter filled the air.

Mathias grimaced at his friends' ribald teasing. He was surprised by his reluctance to discuss Tempest. None of them would understand. "All of you have spent too many nights in the stews to appreciate a genuine lady. Nothing happened," he said, unable to stop the grin from curling the corners of his mouth as he brought the glass to his lips again.

"Then Lady Tempest has my sympathies," Rainbault said, shoving his empty glass forward. Mathias obliged him by refilling it. "How long have you been plagued by impotence?"

Mathias choked on a mouthful of brandy. "Bastard!" He struggled to breathe. "Are you trying to kill me?"

"You can hardly"—more laughter—"blame Chance for his lack of concentration," St. Lyon staunchly defended his friend. "The Duchess of Blackbern and Lady Norgrave provided one hell of a distraction this evening."

Thorn's expression sobered. "I still cannot believe Lady Henwood invited both ladies. Are you positive there was no confrontation between your mother and the marchioness?"

"I watched over the duchess while our friend was failing to impress his lady." St. Lyon grinned at Mathias's growl promising retribution. "There was never a moment when his mother was alone."

"I agree," Mathias said, recalling his cordial conversation with his mother. She had been pleased to see him, but was unwilling to delay him from joining his friends. "The duchess would have mentioned exchanging words with the Marchioness of Norgrave."

"Well, well . . . brace yourselves, my friends. Trouble approaching," the prince muttered under his breath.

Mathias glanced to the right and sneered. Marcroft was heading toward their table. "If this continues, we are going to have to start drinking in taverns outside London."

In fairness, Tempest's brother did not seem pleased to see them either.

"Fairlamb," the earl said grimly. He placed his large hands against the rough surface of the table. "A moment of your time. We have private business to discuss."

Marcroft was not acquainted with civility. He bullied and blustered, but he had never been capable of intimidating Mathias. "You are mistaken. My family does not do business with the Brants or anyone who associates with them."

Mathias ignored the other man's sharp inhalation and his friends' murmurs that included warnings and disapproval.

"You have always had more courage than brains," Marcroft said silkily. "And while I thoroughly enjoy messing up that handsome face of yours, what I have to say should be done in private."

"I keep no secrets from my friends."

"Truly?" Marcroft raised his eyebrows in feigned surprise. "Then you are a bigger fool than I had imagined." He cast a contemptuous glance that encompassed everyone at the table. "Considering the history between our families, you are generous with your trust. Friends will betray you if there is something to profit from it."

Mathias abruptly stood, causing St. Lyon, Thorn, and Rainbault to freeze. A look in any of the gentlemen's cold gazes revealed that they were braced for a fight. His friends had proved their loyalty countless times, but he preferred to handle the earl on his own.

"Very well, Marcroft. I will humor you for a few minutes if it will hasten your departure." He bent down and murmured in St. Lyon's ear. "Make certain his friends do not follow us."

Marcroft smirked at the viscount's curt nod. Even if Mathias had not earned St. Lyon's loyalties, the two gentlemen would have never been friends.

Mathias was anticipating some kind of trickery from the other man, so he was on guard as they stepped outdoors and walked to the side of the building.

"You have my undivided attention. What do you want?" he asked.

"Ah, there are so many ways I could respond to your question," the earl replied, stroking his jaw. "Let's start with this."

Some things never changed. He hastily ducked and avoided the other man's fist. The burst of energy resulted in knocking Marcroft off balance, and Mathias took advantage of it. He shoved the earl into the wall of the tavern, twisting his left arm behind his back to hold him in place.

"Let go."

"I'd rather not," Mathias said cheerfully. "When given a choice, you always lead our conversations with your fists. So typical of a Brant."

"You deserve more than a bruise on your chin." Marcroft grimaced in pain as Mathias twisted the man's arm higher.

"Suffice it to say, I disagree." He leaned forward, savoring that he had his foe at a disadvantage. "Are we finished or did you have something to say to me?"

"Aye, I have something to say: Stay away from my sister, you bloody bastard!" Marcroft struggled against Mathias's hold, not caring if it increased his discomfort.

The genuine outrage in the earl's voice concerned Mathias.

"Which one?" he asked, testing the other man. "I believe you have three."

"There is no one here who is impressed with your wit, Fairlamb," Marcroft spit, his large body vibrating with rage. "No more games. I am aware you met all three of my sisters. I am also aware that Tempest has caught your eye."

It was a calculated risk, but Mathias released his grip on the earl and stepped back. He watched the other man roll his shoulders to ease the tightness and lingering cramps. Marcroft slowly turned and leaned against the outer wall of the tavern as he rubbed his abused arm.

"All your sisters are quite lovely, Marcroft," he said easily. "If you are aware of our meeting, then you also know it was coincidental."

There was no reason to mention that Tempest and Arabella had spied on them at the river's edge, or that the ladies had seen more than was proper.

"I was assured by Tempest that your meeting was an accident and that she was unaware of your identity since you had introduced yourself to her as Chance." The earl dragged his hand through his hair. "Do not play games with me, Fairlamb. I was told you approached my sister at Lady Henwood's house."

Mathias wondered who had tattled. Lady Norgrave would be his first guess, though the lady would have to be as ruthless as her husband to force a confrontation between him and her son.

"I encountered many of the countess's guests this evening. Your sister was one of them," he said, clearly exasperated with the earl and his undisguised hostility. Perhaps Marcroft had good reason to worry about Mathias's intentions toward Tempest, but he was not foolish enough to admit it. Most days, the man needed little provocation to annoy him.

"This may astound you, but I can be civil, even to someone who bears the surname Brant."

Marcroft's eyes narrowed. He took an intimidating step forward but Mathias refused to move. "Despise me all you want, but Tempest is to be left alone. My sister is not one of your ladybirds or merry widows. She is too innocent to comprehend the base and vile nature of a man like you."

"Or you," Mathias said softly.

"Aye, or a man like me." In the gloom, his eyes gleamed dark humor. "My sister deserves to marry a respectable gentleman who will treasure her, give her a home, and fill her arms with children. You and I know that you are not that man."

"You have no idea what I am capable of, Marcroft," he said, fighting back the temptation of driving his fist into the earl's smug face. "Though, I will admit that my friends and I do not sit around a table and lament over our bachelor lives."

"That's what I thought." The earl's fierce expression lightened into something akin to relief. "Then you have no reason to pursue Tempest."

"None," Mathias lied. He had many reasons, but he had no interest in sharing them with Tempest's belligerent sibling. "Does your sister know you are spying on her?"

"I am not—" Marcroft broke off and his jaw tightened to stop himself from revealing too much. "As her brother, it is my duty and honor to protect Tempest. Consider this a friendly warning. If we must meet again, it will be at dawn. Have I made myself clear?"

"Eloquently." Mathias inclined his head and began to walk away. He had never been one to brush aside threats, especially when delivered by Marcroft. "Is Miss King under your protection as well?"

The man's head snapped up. "Miss King?"

"Well, this evening, I spoke to her as well," he said, relishing the flash of jealousy that crossed the earl's hard features. "She was quite eager to renew our acquaintance."

Mathias tensed at the man's savage expression. He added fuel to the emotional conflagration by grinning. A gentleman like the earl would not willingly admit that he possessed tender feelings for his mistress.

"Do what you will with Miss King," Marcroft said gruffly. "Just leave my sister alone." The earl shouldered past him and disappeared around the corner.

It was unlike Marcroft to surrender so quickly. Mathias was almost disappointed. He wondered how Miss King would feel if she knew her lover's affection was so shallow, he would hand her off to another man. He could not summon much sympathy for the greedy wench. As far as he was concerned, Marcroft and Miss King deserved each other.

As for staying away from Tempest . . .

Mathias stood in the shadows, listening to the laughter and music drifting from the tavern. Now that he was alone, he could admit that even if he had sworn in blood to keep his distance, it would be a lie.

He could not explain how he knew. It was something he scented in the air, tasted on his tongue, and felt deep within the marrow of his bones—Tempest would be his lover.

# Chapter Nineteen

Attired in their carriage dresses, Tempest and Arabella had been waiting in the front hall for one of the grooms to harness two horses for their carriage when the butler told her that Lord and Lady Norgrave had requested her presence in the drawing room.

"Wait here," she had told her sister, and she headed up the stairs.

She had not realized how nervous she was until she noted that her hand slightly shook when she reached for the doorknob and opened the door to the drawing room. Her father was not at home in the afternoons usually, and seeing her parents together increased her distress.

Her mother sat on the sofa, and her father in one of the chairs. She had not interrupted them from any task that kept her mother's hands busy or challenged her father's intellect. The nearby tables were not cluttered with books, newspapers, or her mother's embroidery. No, her parents had been sitting in the drawing room, absorbed in their conversation. Unfortunately, she had a feeling she knew precisely the subject at hand.

Her.

Tempest swept into the room and curtsied. "Good afternoon, Mama and Papa," she said, hoping the expression on her face matched her cheerful tone. "Starling just caught Arabella and me before we departed for the park. You wished to see me?"

"Where is Arabella?" her mother inquired.

"In the front hall," Tempest replied, her gaze moving from her mother's face to her father's. "Is something amiss?"

"Not at all," her father said, rubbing his hands together as if he were pleased with himself or her. The insight immediately put her on guard. He rose from his chair and walked over to join her. Taking her by the hand, he kissed the top of it. With his head lowered, her gaze was drawn to the scar on his face. It was an old wound, beginning near the outer corner of his eye and traveling down his cheekbone. When she was a child, she had asked him about it, but her father told her various tales of its origin, from battling pirates to an escaped bear that had mauled him. Although her curiosity had not diminished, it seemed rude to press him for an explanation that he was reluctant to discuss.

She followed him to the sofa. At his unspoken invitation, she sat down, and the marquess sat in the chair positioned beside her. Flanked on either side by her mother and father, Tempest said, "Is there news? Should I go downstairs and ask Arabella to join us?"

"Your mother and I will not keep you," her father said. "I forgot to mention at breakfast that I saw your Lord Warrilow the other night."

"Papa, it would be presumptuous to refer to the gentleman as my anything," Tempest mildly protested, uncomfortable that her father viewed her connection to the marquess as a fait accompli. "Do you not agree, Mama?"

The fine lines around her mother's mouth became more pronounced. Tempest could not discern whether she was annoyed by the subject or by the simple fact that she was being drawn into the conversation.

"The frequency of Lord Warrilow's visits hint that he would welcome any encouragement from you," her mother replied. "However, your prudence is commendable."

"And highly unnecessary," Lord Norgrave argued. He withdrew his timepiece from his waistcoat and noted the time. "Even now, Warrilow is on his way to our house. When he learned that you and your sister would be at the park this afternoon, he insisted on providing an escort."

Tempest's heart sank at the news. While Arabella was willing to overlook meeting Chance at the park, she doubted Lord Warrilow would be so generous.

"Something wrong, Daughter?" her mother asked.

"Not at all," she replied, rising from her seat. It was too late to ask one of the lads working in the kitchen to deliver a message to Lord Fairlamb. There was also the risk that he might tell one of the older servants, who would feel obligated to share the information with her mother. "I will tell Arabella the good news."

Norgrave watched his eldest daughter hurry out of the drawing room as if someone had set fire to the back of her skirt. The girl was skittish, which was unlike her. Out of his three daughters, Tempest had the look of her mother, but underneath, she had more in common with him and her brother. She was cunning, and could be uncompromising when she set a task for herself. It was a pity that Tempest had not been born a male. He would have liked to have another son at his side.

Unfortunately, Charlotte had been utterly useless on that front. A stillborn son after Arabella, and three more failed pregnancies after that. For years, he thought his wife's womb was a grave, and then Augusta was born.

He had never been so disappointed.

His title and charm had guaranteed that there were

many women in his life. Before and after his marriage to Charlotte. Some of those women had given him sons, but he had no use for them. Marcroft was his heir, and most men would have been satisfied, but one son made him vulnerable. A careless accident or a miscalculation during a duel, and Norgrave would swiftly find himself without an heir.

He had contemplated divorce. However, her family was an obstacle. Her ruthless brothers had tied him to that miserable woman, and nothing short of her death would free him. Charlotte's death. It was a thought that gave him comfort in his darkest hours of despair.

"You are smiling," his marchioness murmured, and he turned his head to see that she was staring at him. "A rare occurrence when we are alone, so I assume that I am not the cause. I trust you are satisfied with the progress of this courtship?"

Norgrave shrugged. "Warrilow sees the benefits of aligning our families. He did express some concerns about Tempest's willingness." He stopped and waited to see if his wife would offer any concern or explanation. When he was met with silence, he continued, "You failed to mention that there was an incident at Lady Henwood's house."

"What incident?" The marchioness cleared her throat. "Oh, do you mean our son's blatant interest in Miss King? To be honest, it was embarrassing how he fawned over the woman. It was obvious to all that she is his mistress."

If he had not been carefully observing Charlotte, he would have missed the flash of panic in her eyes. Which was curious, since it had been a long time since he had managed to fluster her.

"I don't care about our son's flirtations," he said, dismissing the subject. Whatever Marcroft's latest sins, he was positive he himself had done worse. "Warrilow told me that Tempest excused herself during Miss King's performance, and she did not return until the end. He was concerned she invented some tall tale to avoid his company."

"Rubbish," Charlotte said, rising from her seat.

Norgrave caught her by the wrist, keeping her from leaving. Her reaction to the marquess's complaint about Tempest had been relief. Intrigued, he tightened his hold.

His wife glared down at him. "Your young protégé worries for naught. Tempest was visiting with Harriet. You know how devoted she is to her cousin."

"Perhaps you are correct," he conceded. His gaze locked on to hers. He offered her a genial smile when she winced as the pressure of his fingers increased. "So why don't you tell me about *your* evening at Lady Henwood's. It appears I missed something, but I am confident you will want to share every detail with me."

"You have made us late."

"Will you stop prattling on about it!" St. Lyon complained. "No man should appear too eager to see a lady. Have a little pride, for my sake."

Mathias chuckled. There was nothing his friend could say or do to ruin his good mood. The two men had arrived at the park on horseback. Although they had not discussed it, he assumed Tempest would travel by carriage to the park. He was even prepared for her not to arrive alone, which was why he had invited St. Lyon. The gentleman could coax a smile from even the dourest lady's companion. If he and Tempest could not come up with a plausible reason to take a short stroll together, he planned on riding beside her as the ladies' equipage rocked and rattled its way through the park.

"Do you think Lady Tempest might bring her pretty

sister with her?" the viscount asked, attempting to find a silver lining in what appeared to be a cloudy day.

"You are too old for Lady Augusta," Mathias teased.

"A delightful child, but I was referring to Lady Arabella."

Mathias sent a questioning glance at St. Lyon, but he was staring straight ahead. A troubling thought occurred to him as he studied his friend's profile. With the rumors whispered about his parentage, flirting with a lady who possibly could be your half sister would be frowned upon by even the most dissolute reprobate.

"You are too immature for Lady Arabella," he said, shaking off the gloomy thought. There was no reason to interfere unless his friend insisted on causing trouble.

St. Lyon's pursed his lips and contemplated his friend's opinion for a moment. He sighed. "Very true."

With his right hand holding the reins, he leaned forward and lifted his backside off the saddle in an effort to see beyond a large carriage in front of them.

"Well, not to ruin your good humor, but I believe I see a wrinkle in your plans, my friend."

Mathias directed his attention to the source of St. Lyon's concerns. Ahead he peered at the two carriages in the distance. He dismissed the first because he counted four passengers. He observed there were two ladies in the second one. Since both ladies wore bonnets, he could not identify them with any certainty. He guided his horse to the right and he immediately understood the reason for St. Lyon's remark. The ladies were not alone. A gentleman rode beside their carriage on horseback.

Lord Warrilow.

"I do not believe it," Mathias muttered.

The viscount's side glance was sympathetic. "Perhaps it is not her."

"Of course it is her." Her companion was likely Lady Arabella. "The marquess has been Tempest's most ardent suitor. Lady Norgrave invited Lord Warrilow to sit with the family when they attended Lady Henwood's musical recital."

St. Lyon recognized that particular expression on his friend's face, and tried to stave off a confrontation. "If the man is searching for a bride, it would make sense that he would court other ladies."

Tempest chose that moment to turn so he could see her elegant profile. Mathias's simmering temper threatened to boil over.

"Follow my lead," he said, nudging his horse to advance so they could pass the slow carriage blocking their path.

"This might not be a good day to pay your respects to Lady Tempest and her sister," the viscount said, but he dutifully followed behind Mathias. "Whatever you are planning, I beg you to reconsider."

"You worry too much," he said, urging his horse to quicken its pace.

"Chance!" St. Lyon called out, but he was already falling behind.

Mathias did not signal the bay to slow down until he had almost reached the rear wheel of the Brants' carriage. He could hear the hooves of his friend's horse crunching the gravel behind him, letting him know that St. Lyon had caught up to him.

However, he was too late to halt a confrontation.

Tempest must have heard the approach of the two riders, and she glanced over her right shoulder. She noticed his thunderous expression and winced.

*There was nothing I could do,* she silently mouthed.

For an apology, it was a lousy one. Tempest looked

quite repentant as she stared up at him with somber eyes and a hint of a pout on her lips. Warrilow had joined the ladies, but not at her suggestion. Some of the tightness in his chest eased. Then her sister laughed at something the marquess said, and the stir of sympathy for both ladies evaporated.

He touched two gloved fingers to the brim of his hat and acknowledged Tempest with a nod. Pressing his heels into the horse's flanks, he rode off without a backward glance. He wondered if St. Lyon would linger to offer apologies for his friend's rudeness.

When the viscount caught up to him, he was not pleased. "You are an arse!"

For once, Mathias did not disagree.

# Chapter Twenty

"It was so kind of you to escort me to the Karmacks' ball," Sabra said, hooking her arm through Mathias's as they entered the ballroom.

"I thought you were holding out for your elderly earl," he teased. Four days had passed since he and St. Lyon had ridden off and left Tempest and her sister in Lord Warrilow's capable hands.

Since he was brooding, his friends had dragged him from one gambling hell to the next. Rainbault, St. Lyon, Thorn, and he had gotten roaring drunk on cheap wine. He won at some tables and lost at others. There had been a few brawls, and Rainbault was challenged to a duel because he had fondled another man's wife. The details were a blur, but the prince had managed to charm his way out of his awkward situation without firing a single shot.

Mathias slept most of the day. When he awoke his manservant presented him with Sabra's invitation to join her. He felt bad about the way they had parted, so he accepted her offer as a way to apologize. They were good friends again, and now that his head was clear, he vowed never to drink wine of questionable vintage ever again.

"My earl is not in town," Sabra informed him. "It aggravates his gout. I believe it is just an excuse so he can remain in the country and fish."

He and Sabra had spent the last hour in the receiving line to greet the earl and countess. By all accounts, everyone was in attendance this evening. Earlier he had glimpsed St. Lyon as he followed a lovely blonde upstairs. Mathias just hoped for his friend's sake that it wasn't one of Lord Karmack's daughters.

"What do you want to do first? Dance or figure out where our host has set up the cardroom?" She leaned toward him, her mouth nearly brushing his ear. "Thorn's parents are standing near the window to the right of us. Knowing your cousin, he plans to remain in the cardroom to avoid the lady his mother and father will insist he should meet."

The thought of cards reminded him of the nights he had been out drinking. His sour stomach still ached from the abuse. Mathias shook his head. "We can cheer up Thorn later. I will be your dance partner. Do you think your elderly earl approves of dancing?"

Sabra responded with laughter. "As long as he does not have to dance, he heartily approves."

As they strolled toward the other dancers and orchestra, Mathias frowned. "It is not my place to judge, but will you be happy marrying a gentleman so sedentary? You have nothing in common with him."

Touched by his concern, she stroked his arm to soothe him. "He needs an heir, and I can provide him one. In return, he will give me a good life, Chance. I have not come to a decision, but I would be a fool not to accept."

Mathias was about to disagree when a lady attired in a white gauze and satin dress with wide rich green ribbons, fragile lace draperies, and silk roses gracefully danced by him with her male partner.

Tempest and Lord Warrilow.

Tempest appeared equally stunned by his presence. He was not aware that he had taken a step in their direction with the sole purpose of separating them until Sabra squeezed his arm.

"Is that her?"

His furious expression and need to commit violence were all the confirmation the lady required. "You have an affinity for earls. Lady Tempest collects marquesses." Mathias cursed, drawing scowls from several guests.

"Perhaps we should adjourn to the cardroom," Sabra suggested, tugging on his arm. "From the looks of Lord and Lady Karmack's guests, he likely has little competition at the table. Together you can recoup your losses from the other night."

"Who told you that I lost?" he sneered, insulted by the very notion that he could not play cards while he was intoxicated. "I never lose." He glared at Tempest and the marquess. "Come. We are dancing."

"Honestly, Chance," Sabra said, refusing to move. "This is not one of your better suggestions."

"I disagree."

It took every ounce of courage for Tempest not to flee.

She had been unaware that Chance was acquainted with Lord and Lady Karmack. She had arrived with her mother and Arabella, but they decided to start their evening in the cardroom. When the three ladies noticed Lord Warrilow standing in the ballroom alone as if he had been waiting for someone, Lady Norgrave had proclaimed it providence that Lord Warrilow was on hand to amuse Tempest, since she was not interested in playing cards.

Tempest knew her mother had conspired with the handsome marquess.

Lord Warrilow approached them before she could protest. It was not his fault that he required a bride and her family had decided she would be perfect for him. Just as during the carriage ride in the park, she was reluctant to make a fuss. He did not deserve her anger or her indifference.

Seeing Lord Fairlamb only compounded her guilt.

Until she noticed that he was not alone. The petite blue-eyed blonde in the crimson ballroom dress touched Chance with a familiarity that cut Tempest to the quick. As Lord Warrilow led her to the center of the ballroom, she could see the lady whispering to him.

Was she begging him to leave the room with her?

A few minutes later, Chance and the blonde joined the dancers.

Tempest had to look away, her eyes stinging from the threat of unshed tears. She was jealous, blast him! It was probably his goal, a bold reminder that he could claim any lady he wanted.

After seeing her with the marquess in the park, had Chance decided she was playing games with him? It didn't help that he never had a high opinion of her family. Perhaps he had thought it was time to put aside his feelings for her and find a lady over whom his family would not threaten to disinherit him if he continued to court her.

She choked on a soft sob.

"Has something upset you?"

Tempest pasted a smile on her face. "Just a little breathless," she said. It wasn't a lie. Seeing Chance holding another lady in his arms had squeezed all the air out of her lungs.

With her heart aching, she and the marquess danced, weaving their way through the other dancers. She saw glimpses of Chance and his female partner as she executed turns with her hand clasped firmly within Lord Warrilow's. The other couple was on the far side of the dancing area, and he seemed to be steering his companion near the garden doors.

Tempest thought of their stroll through Lady Oxton's gardens. Of the kiss she had shared with Chance. She almost cried out as she saw the couple disappear into the night. Lord Fairlamb was a horrible man. A thief of hearts. She despised him, and if given the opportunity she would happily murder him and dance on his grave.

Not paying attention, she stepped on the marquess's black evening pump and stumbled. Lord Warrilow caught her, and her front was pressed against his chest.

"Forgive me, my lord. I was careless," she murmured, and moved away. She winced.

"My lady, you are hurt," the marquess said, walking toward her.

"It is nothing. I merely twisted my ankle." Tempest grimaced in pain as she took another step.

"Allow me to assist you." Ignoring her weak protests, he placed his arm around her waist and helped her cross the ballroom. "I will send someone to inform your mother."

"No," she said, pulling the arm he had raised to signal a servant downward.

"There is no reason to disturb her or Arabella. The initial pain startled me, but it feels better. I will head upstairs and have one of the maids tend it. If I rest my foot for a while, it will recover quickly." She offered him a genuine smile. "Then Mama does not have to know how clumsy I am. How is *your* foot?"

He fought not to grin. "My foot is fine, Lady Tempest."

With her hand on Lord Warrilow's arm, she fought the

urge to limp to demonstrate that her injury was minor. They continued to the staircase in the front hall.

She released his arm and reached for the newel. "I can continue on my own, my lord."

Lord Warrilow glanced at her feet as if he could discern for himself the extent of her injuries. He nodded and his gaze lifted to her face. "I enjoyed dancing with you this evening."

"Even the part when I stepped on your foot?" she teased.

"I believe it was my favorite part," he shyly admitted, and grinned at her look of astonishment. "It gave me an excuse to hold you in my arms."

"Oh." Although it had been an accident, it was the first time he confessed that he desired a more intimate connection. "It was rather nice," she said awkwardly.

"Are you certain you do not want me to send for your mother?" He glanced away, looking uncomfortable. "I have another engagement, and I was planning to leave. I could—uh, stay."

Lord Warrilow had stopped at the Karmacks' for the opportunity to visit and perhaps dance with her. Of course he had other plans for the evening. Her father rarely attended balls, preferring his various clubs.

"No, there is no reason for you to change your plans. Go . . . enjoy your evening," she said, clutching the newel post. "If I need my mother, I will ask one of the servants to get her or my sister."

"Very well, then." He bowed. "I look forward to seeing you again, Lady Tempest."

"Good evening, Lord Warrilow." Her smile slipped when the marquess turned his back and headed for the front door.

When he was gone, she slowly made her way upstairs.

Her ankle hurt, but she could put her full weight on it. Tempest blamed her tears on her injury rather than the pain of Chance's rejection. With her vision blurred by her tears, it dawned on her that she did not know which room was being used by the Karmacks' female guests. She opened one door, and the interior was dark. The next door was locked. She wiped her wet cheek and tried the door across from the locked one.

She gasped as she collided with a blond-haired lady. The woman barely glanced at her, but she murmured an apology and strode away. Her hair color reminded Tempest of the lady with whom Chance had disappeared into the gardens. She covered her mouth with her hand and stepped into the room, only to cry out again when a familiar gentleman caught her by the arms.

"Lady Tempest."

She blinked and tried to clear her vision. Of all the rotten luck. She had run into Lord Bastrell, one of Chance's friends.

"My lady, are you hurt?" he asked, his hands impersonally checking her arms for injuries.

"I—I am fine, my lord," she said, her voice breaking into a sob. "You can leave—"

Most gentlemen avoided a lady's tears at all costs. Tempest expected him to flee with her blessing, but the viscount astonished her by pulling her into the room. Ignoring her assurances that she was fine, he led her to the sofa and produced a handkerchief.

She would have been impressed if she had not longed for him to leave her in peace.

Instead of sitting in one of the parlor's chairs or the sofa, the gentleman crouched down in front of her. Tempest refused to look at him. She could feel his worried stare as it lingered on her face.

"It is kind of you, but you do not have to stay with me." She wiped the dampness from her cheeks. "I just need a moment of privacy."

"Has someone upset you? Insulted you?" he softly inquired.

"Nothing so dire. I—I twisted my ankle, Lord Bastrell," she confessed, praying her honesty would hasten his departure. "I am embarrassed that I have troubled you."

"St. Lyon. You can consider me a friend, my lady."

The viscount's kindness ruined her composure. Her face twisted as the pain and grief of her loss rose up in her throat and threatened to choke her. Suddenly she found her face buried in the curve of St. Lyon's shoulder. He was on his knees and had pulled her forward to offer her comfort.

He was the second gentleman this evening who had offered her friendship and compassion while she cried over the man she could not have.

"There, there," he crooned as if soothing a child. "Can you talk about it?"

She felt like a fool. "I—"

Tempest started as someone enthusiastically slammed the door. She and St. Lyon separated, and she turned to see Chance stalking toward him.

"First Warrilow and now one of my closest friends," he growled as if she had betrayed him.

"Chance," the viscount began as he braced the palm of his hands on his knees and stood. "It is nothing like that."

"Not one word, St. Lyon," the marquess snarled, knocking the other man's hand away when he attempted to touch his shoulder. Chance glared down at her tearstained face. "Quite the little seductress. You certainly hoodwinked me. Then again, I would expect that from a Brant."

Tempest stood. Rage filled her, and her fingers twitched as if she longed to slap him.

Noticing that she had curled her hand into a fist, he tilted his chin upward. "Take a shot, darling. I dare you."

Her lips thinned at his tone. Oh, she longed to strike him down. If only she had been born a male.

St. Lyon grabbed his arm. "That is enough. What is wrong with you? Are you drunk?"

Chance's ire switched to the viscount. "And you, one of my dearest friends. Do you have to bed every wench who crosses your path?"

"Leave him alone," Tempest said, grimacing as she stepped closer to the two gentlemen. "Do not paint St. Lyon with the brush of your sins, Lord Fairlamb."

Chance had cured her of her tears. The vile scoundrel.

"What is she talking about?" the viscount asked. Baffled, his gaze shifted between her and his friend.

"Your friend favors evening strolls in the garden. A different lady each night," she said, her face twisted with disgust. "I'll wager you do not even know her name."

"Sabra," Chance impatiently snapped as St. Lyon groaned.

"You arrived with Sabra on your arm?" The viscount shook his head with disappointment. "Are you mad? Not a wise decision, my friend."

"Did I ask for your blessing?"

The mystery lady had some history with the gentlemen.

"I don't care who she is," Tempest said, the air hissing through her clenched teeth. "Or whom you stroll with through torchlit gardens, or—or whom you kiss. She can have you!" With her chin high, she marched toward the door. Her ankle hurt, so she did not bother to hide her limp.

"What the hell is wrong with your foot?" Chance yelled as he followed her to the door.

"It is none of your business, Lord Fairlamb," she tossed back.

St. Lyon pulled his friend back before he could put his hands on her. "She was upset when I ran into her. I intended to calm her and then look for her family. Before Lady Tempest's arrival, I had been visiting with a—uh—friend."

Tempest rolled her eyes. The viscount's friend had been straightening her clothing when she exited the room. She opened the parlor's door to leave, but Chance used the palm of his hand to shut it.

"I will scream if you stop me from leaving," she threatened.

"Where is Warrilow?" His harsh tone had her bristling. "Did he say something to upset you?"

"Did *he*?" Her eyes narrowed, and Chance and St. Lyon were intelligent enough to deduce that she was furious. Both of them took a step back. "I will have you know that Lord Warrilow is a consummate gentleman, and you, Lord Fairlamb, can go to the devil!"

No one stopped her when she opened the door. Tempest stepped into the hall and moved as quickly as her sore ankle allowed her. She was too upset with Chance to feel much pain. The man had crushed her heart, and then he had the audacity to be furious at Lord Warrilow for possibly upsetting her.

She was almost to the stairs when she felt a light tap on her shoulder. Blindly she struck out, but her arm sliced harmlessly through the air. To her shame, she had tried to hit Lord Bastrell.

"Forgive me, I thought you were—him."

The viscount held up his hands in surrender. "I told him to stay in the parlor while I spoke to you. Neither one of you is thinking clearly."

"Which has always been my problem when it comes to Lord Fairlamb," was her scathing reply, directed at herself. "Fortunately, I have come to my senses."

"Are you leaving?"

She nodded. "First, I need to find a servant. My mother and sister are in the cardroom. I need to let them know that I have twisted my ankle and plan to retire early."

"He did not listen to me when I told him that you were hurt," St. Lyon muttered.

Tempest frowned, not catching his all his words. "I beg your pardon?"

He grinned. "Nothing. Say, I have an idea. While you hunt for a servant and write a note for your mother, permit me to make amends for the misunderstanding I have created between you and Chance by loaning you my coach."

"It is unnecessary. Any misunderstandings are Chance's fault. You are not to blame," she said generously. "Nor do I care what he thinks." *Not after watching Chance flirt with that Sabra woman.* "And you do not have to escort me home. We arrived in the family coach. The coachman can return for my mother and sister later."

"Nonsense," he countered, smoothly taking her arm to make her descent down the staircase less painful. "This is likely the first of several stops for your mother and sister. Why inconvenience them, when I can do this small service for you."

"St. Lyon—"

"Think nothing of it," he said, sidestepping her protests. "It will be my honor to assist you. Not to mention, my chivalry will annoy Chance."

Tempest was still mad enough at the marquess that it

was the right thing for St. Lyon to say to gain her consent. "Very well. I will talk to one of the servants."

"The coach will be waiting for you when you are ready, my dear," St. Lyon assured her.

# Chapter Twenty-One

Tempest expected if St. Lyon had been kind enough to lend her his coach that he planned to join her on the drive home. Instead, he helped her settle into the coach and moved to shut the door.

She stalled him by placing her palm against the side of the door. "You are not coming?"

The viscount inclined his head. "Pray, forgive me for abandoning you. I confess that I have some unfinished business with that blonde. You know the lady—she was the one who was—"

"I am truly sorry about that," Tempest replied, not wanting any details. "You can offer my apologies to your friend as well."

St. Lyon wiggled his eyebrows in a leering fashion. For a rogue, he was quite charming. "I will," he promised, and shut the coach's door.

He glanced up at the coachman sitting on the perch. "Look after Lady Tempest, good man."

"Aye, milord," was the coachman's gruff reply.

With a final wave to St. Lyon, Tempest settled back against the richly appointed compartment to enjoy the drive home. Exhausted, she thought to close her eyes only for a minute.

Five minutes later, she was soundly asleep.

\* \* \*

Something soft tickled her cheek.

Without opening her eyes, Tempest slowly became aware that the coach was no longer moving. She yawned and straightened to stretch her back. It was then that she opened her eyes and gasped.

Tempest was no longer in St. Lyon's coach. Someone had carried her inside while she slept, placed her on a sofa and covered her legs with a blanket. The depth of her exhaustion and the trust she had unknowingly granted the coachman left her shaken. She glanced at her surroundings. The interior of the unfamiliar sitting room was illuminated by several oil lamps.

*This is not my father's house.*

She pushed aside the blanket and sat up so her feet touched the thick rug. While she was asleep, someone had removed her evening slippers. Before she could panic, Chance entered the room with a large pan in his bare hands.

"Good, you are awake," he said, kneeling down in front of her. "I was beginning to become concerned that you had not told St. Lyon the whole truth."

"About what?" she asked, not understanding how she was sitting in a stranger's house with Chance.

"The extent of your injuries," he calmly explained. "He told me that you had injured your ankle, but you barely stirred when I opened the door of the coach, I thought you might have bumped your head when I rolled one of the wheels over a particularly nasty hole in the street."

She sank back down on the sofa. "You were the coachman?"

"Yes." At her stunned expression, he hastily explained, "You were never in any danger. I have some experience handling the ribbons. St. Lyon, Thorn—all of us have had a turn or two on the perch. Sometimes we hold races."

She simply gaped at him. He ducked his head and repositioned the pan of water near her feet. "Never mind. Now, which ankle is hurt?"

"My left," she said, flexing her bare toes, and grimaced. "It's still sore, but it feels better."

"I heated some water. Bathing your ankle in salt water should ease the pain." He gently grasped her left foot and placed it in the warm water. "I also made enough if you would like some hot tea."

The warm water did nothing to alleviate the dread brewing in her stomach. "Is this your father's house?"

Chance shook his head as he fussed and repositioned her foot in the pan of water. "I told you that I no longer reside with my family. This is my house."

"Why am I here?" she blurted out. "What is going on, Chance?"

"No trickery, I promise," he said, drawing an X over his heart. At some point, he had removed his black evening coat and waistcoat. His cravat knot was still tied, but he had rolled up his sleeves when he pumped and heated the water. "Are you comfortable? I could light the coals if you are chilled."

"The blanket is enough," she said, silently wondering if she had struck her head. None of this made any sense. "You were very angry with me."

"And you thought about punching me." He made a soft scolding noise with his tongue. "St. Lyon claims you took a swing at him."

"I thought it was you," she muttered, still embarrassed by her behavior.

"Ah," he said, not sounding too upset that she had been provoked to commit violence. "Well, no harm done. God knows I had it coming if you had managed to hit me."

Suddenly it was too much for Tempest to take in. His

calm demeanor was too much at odds with his angry accusations. She brought her hands up and covered her entire face so he could not witness her tears.

"Tempest," he said, inching forward on his knees until he was close enough to peel her fingers from her face. "My love."

Without any hesitation, he pulled her into his arms, encouraging her to bury her face into his shoulder. Tempest felt his hands at her back. Chance held her close while she sobbed. "I am so sorry," he murmured into her neck. "I was jealous. It shames me to admit that I lost my head when I noticed you dancing with Warrilow. Not to mention how he ruined our meeting at the park. I was beginning to wonder if you had a hand in it, and I took it out on you. I wasn't being fair, nor did I give you a chance to explain. I said some awful things to you and St. Lyon."

"He loves you," she said, sniffing a little as she raised her head. Chance handed her a clean handkerchief. "St. Lyon obviously has forgiven you. Otherwise, he would have never helped you trick me into climbing into your coach and aiding you in my own kidnapping."

"I have not kidnapped you," he denied, plucking the handkerchief from her hands, and wiped away her tears. "Think of this stop as a delay. You can leave anytime you wish. All you have to do is ask. I just wanted some time alone with you so I could apologize to you properly. I was cruel and I deserve to crawl."

Chance looked so grumpy about the notion that she could not help but smile. "Are tending my ankle and the hot tea part of your repentance?"

He careless lifted his right shoulder. "I suppose. You never told St. Lyon how you injured your ankle, and you were so angry at me that I was worried you had made it worse."

"I was watching you and Sabra and not paying attention. I stepped on poor Lord Warrilow's foot and twisted my ankle," she explained.

"Sabra and I," he began, and took a moment to knead the muscles at the back of his neck. "I was sixteen years old when I first met her. She's a few years older, and for a few months, I thought I loved her."

"She's very beautiful."

"Yes, well . . . it ended quickly when she ran off and married someone else," he said, unhappy that he was dredging up a part of his life that he would prefer to forget. "She's been widowed for a few years, and now she has an elderly earl enamored with her."

Tempest did not know Sabra, but she had seen how the woman looked at Chance. She was in love with him. "You are no longer sixteen. This time you might be able to convince her to run off with you."

"Maybe."

He glanced away, and Tempest realized that Sabra had already tried to seduce Chance. Any sympathy she had for the widow faded. "Where is Sabra?" she asked, praying the lady was not waiting for Chance to return to her.

"I abandoned her in Lord and Lady Karmack's garden. We quarreled when I told her that I was planning to confront Warrilow, but when I entered the ballroom, both you and Warrilow were gone. I asked St. Lyon to see that she gets home," he said, refolding a portion of her skirt because a section of the hem had been sitting in the pan of water.

His lack of concern for his former lover's welfare should not have lifted Tempest's spirits, but she was a selfish woman. She silently rejoiced that the beautiful Sabra would be returning to her elderly earl.

"What happened to Warrilow?" He had kept his voice level, and infused a touching note of curiosity not to arouse her suspicion that her answer mattered to him. "It is difficult to believe he would have left you, especially when he was aware you were injured."

Ah, so that was the reason he was so angry when he had entered the parlor. Chance had expected to catch Tempest and Warrilow in a scandalous embrace. Finding his roguish friend alone with her had further ignited his temper.

"Lord Warrilow had other plans for the evening. He offered to stay, but I encouraged him to leave."

"I accepted Sabra's invitation to escort her this evening only because I did not want to spend another night drinking myself into a stupor so I did not have to think about you and Warrilow," he confessed, threading his fingers through hers until their hands clasped. "I was there as her friend. Nothing would have happened between us, even if we had remained in the garden."

Tempest held her breath when he lifted his lowered eyelids and held her gaze.

"There is only one lady I conspire to lure into a garden at midnight."

Finally remembering to breathe, she noisily exhaled. "Who?"

"Why, it is you, my darling girl," he replied, his eyes glowing with affection and humor.

"Does this place have a garden?"

He highly approved of her suggestion. She could see it in his expression, the way his mouth curved and his nostrils subtly flared.

Then he shook his head.

"No?" Tempest tried not to pout. "You disappoint me, Lord Fairlamb."

"You have a sore ankle, love," he reminded her as he unfolded his body so he could cage her against the sofa. Tempest fell against the pillows on the sofa. Her bare foot kicked the surface of the water, sending a liquid plume across the rug. "Besides, you are right where I want you."

"I am?" she coyly asked, but she was unafraid. It was when she believed she had lost him that her fears and regrets had tormented her.

"Yes, my lady." He leered, looking very much a scoundrel. His mouth hovered enticingly just above hers. "Do you welcome my kisses?"

"Ye—"

Chance crushed his lips against hers.

Hunger long denied collided with the growing swell of relief. Tempest welcomed the sharp sting from the edge of his teeth, and she wrapped her arms around his neck to draw him closer. She ignored the discomfort and teased him with her tongue. Using the nimble tip, she poked and stroked, testing the narrow part for weaknesses.

Abruptly he opened for her, allowing her to sink deeper into him. Her tongue curled and unfurled against his, giving him pleasure even as she laid claim to her own.

Tempest made soft sounds of surprise when he covered one of her breasts with his hand.

His mouth tore away from hers. "We should stop," he said, giving her another opportunity to push him away.

Chance had told her that she was free to leave. All she had to do was ask.

The fact that the choice had always been hers endowed her with a power she had been unaware she possessed. Tempest brazenly moved closer and played with the clever knot of linen at his throat. She could feel his heart thundering in his chest. "Do you truly wish to stop? Send me away when you went to so much effort to bring me here?"

"I want you to stay," he said, his eyes hot with desire. "Every time I kiss you, it is becoming more difficult to remember that you are an innocent. Every time I touch you, I am greedy for more."

"It is the same for me," she said, knowing her eyes reflected the same longing she glimpsed in his. "When we are apart, all I do is daydream of the next time we can be together." She pressed her face against his shirt.

"Tempest," he groaned, still fighting her.

Himself.

"I never thought wanting could hurt so much," she murmured against his chest and nibbled at the small button on his shirt. "You know how to ease it. For both of us. Show me. I want to give you pleasure."

"Just looking at your beautiful face gives me pleasure, Tempest," he said, capturing her chin and tilting her face until their gazes locked. "I would not ask more of you."

"You are not asking," she said, her voice low and seductive. She had never been so certain of anything in her life. "I am offering. I am aware that you have had other lovers."

Chance did not want to talk any more about his past. "I touch you, and former loves crumple into dust like ancient dried flowers that had been tucked away in a box that once held treasured memories. I feel my lips against yours, and I wonder how I could bear the loneliness while I waited for you to find me."

He took his time, worshipping her mouth.

"Have I thanked you for spying on me and my friends?" Chance playfully bit her lower lip. "I thank God every day for your curious mind."

Tempest laughed as she thought how fate had brought them together.

Of how her family had the power to tear them apart.

No, she would not dwell on her fears or the future. Why spoil the present when in the here and now, Chance belonged to her. Nor would she regret loving him. If she lost him, she would look back on moments such as this as a gift.

"You are the only lady who occupies my thoughts, Tempest." He kissed her lightly on the mouth as if to soothe away any jealousy or hurt she might have felt. "My heart belongs to you."

She stilled, aware of the importance of his confession.

"And your body?"

Hidden beneath his dark breeches and covered by her skirt, his thickening cock pulsed and strained, demanding that he free the unruly flesh and demonstrate his eagerness to claim her.

Mathias kissed her nose. Another kiss to her cheek. He wanted to explore every inch of her skin and revel in the scent that was uniquely hers.

"My body is yours as well," he said, continuing to struggle against the internal conflict between assuaging his lust and protecting her.

St. Lyon had told him once that a man resisting his true nature usually ended up destroying what he sought to protect. Embracing it gave him a measure of control and balance.

From the first day, Mathias had been fighting this unwelcome attraction for Tempest. Realizing it was mutual only fueled his resolve to resist her, and infuriated him when she still managed to slip through his defenses.

Her family's determination to bind her to Lord Warrilow was likely to get the gentleman killed. He had envisioned the marquess's death a thousand times.

Mathias wanted to kill him with his bare hands for contemplating marriage, knowing the lady could be Warrilow's and he had her family's blessing.

Christ, he was tired of fighting—her and himself.

Mathias rubbed the silky fabric of her bodice with his

thumb, unerringly finding her nipple, which was concealed by layers of fabric and whalebone. He longed to undress her and reveal the plump nipple, rubbing his lips against it until it swelled. He wanted to tease the flesh with his tongue until she begged him to stop.

And then he wanted to show her what would happen if she let him continue.

"Chance?"

Could she sense how close he was from surrendering to her?

She was the virgin, but it was Mathias who stood on the precipice, knowing that if they became lovers, it would change him. He had yet to decide if he would be better for it.

"Are you offering me your body, Tempest?" Her body tensed under his, but they had come too far for him to be subtle. "If you stay, we will become lovers. Will you let me touch you? Taste your breasts and the hidden flesh between your legs?"

Her breathy gasp revealed that her clever, talented mind had not pondered such an act. Now that he had uttered the enticing words, she would think of nothing else. She was wondering how his mouth would feel as he kissed her sensitive flesh, his tongue spearing into her.

His hand lightly slid down her body. Mathias was not even touching her dress, but Tempest stirred and arched, craving his touch. She could not fathom the pleasure he could give her, and he longed to show her.

"Let me love you," he said, taking her hand and brushing a kiss against her knuckles.

He could barely draw air into his lungs as he awaited her answer.

"Yes." Her soft, shy reply sent his heart tumbling over the edge.

The word had set both of them free.

# Chapter Twenty-Two

"This love you speak of," Tempest said, giving him an unsteady smile. "How does it begin?"

Chance leaned closer and brought their clasped hands to his chest. Over his heart. "Here. For us, it begins here."

"Not always?" she asked, and tilted her head to the side, thinking of her brother.

"No," he acknowledged. "Some men—Sometimes only the flesh is worshipped. However, that is not us."

Tempest had other questions, but all of them scattered like a flock of birds when he brought her hand from his chest to the knot of his cravat.

"Have you ever undressed a man?"

She shook her head. He released her hand and he tipped his chin upward to give her access to the knot. "I do not—I feel silly."

Chance was not laughing at her. "Here, allow me to assist you." Wordlessly, he began to untie the elaborate knot.

Once he had freed the two ends, Tempest took over the task, unwinding the length of fine linen wrapped around his throat. Chance grinned at her when she was finished. "Perhaps I should sack my valet and hire you," he teased. "Now unfasten the buttons on my shirt while I work on the ones on my waistcoat."

Tempest had never undressed a gentleman, and it was a novel experience. There was a heightened sense of intimacy, touching him in this manner. "Did you ask a maid to remove my stockings or did you see to the task personally?"

"The servants have retired for the evening," he said, meeting her curious gaze. "I promise I didn't peek at your legs. My concern was only for your injured ankle, but I didn't know which one, so I had to remove both shoes and your stockings."

Tempest had unfastened the three buttons on his white shirt. She watched as he removed and discarded his waistcoat. He moved from his kneeling position to the sofa, so he could remove his black evening pumps.

His side glance held a glint of mischief. "If you feel I was too high-handed, you can always untie my garters. You can even look at my calves." He wriggled his eyebrows in a leering manner to make her laugh.

Not waiting for her reply, Chance unfastened the buttons at the bottom of his breeches and tugged on the ties to loosen the garter on his left leg. Before he could untie the right, she bent down and did it for him. He finished the task by removing the stocking.

"You do have very well formed calves," she said, admiring his muscled contours and the soft dark brown hair that covered his legs. "I will have to make comparisons—"

Tempest squeaked, not expecting Chance to turn and pounce. Nervous giggles bubbled forth as they bounced when his right knee landed on the sofa cushion and his right hand grasped the high back and his left the armrest.

"From this day forth, you are absolutely forbidden to look at another man's legs or anything else below his waistcoat," he said, struggling to keep his voice stern.

Tempest's lips twitched. "And what will happen if I disobey?"

"This!" His mouth latched on to hers and they shared a slow, leisurely kiss. To chastise her, he lightly bit her lower lip. "And this."

Tempest gasped as he snaked one arm around her back and the other under her knees and picked her up. To keep from falling, she embraced him, locking her fingers around his neck. Chance nudged the pan of water with his bare foot.

"What are you doing, Lord Fairlamb?" she inquired breathlessly.

"Isn't it obvious? I am carrying you to my bed, where I plan to thoroughly ravish you." He bowed his head and kissed her sweetly on the lips. "If I keep you well pleasured, you will never look at another gentleman's shapely calves."

He raised her higher so her skirt would not catch on the sofa and carried her past the wall partition, revealing his bedchamber. She tightened her hold and glanced at the bed. It was no different from any other bed she had admired in other houses, but this one belonged to Chance.

"You must have been quite confident to have carried me upstairs to your private rooms," she said, the tremor in her voice betraying her apprehension.

"On the contrary," he said, carrying her to the side and placing her on top of the bedding. "I am not currently living alone. My cousin is in residence. With his twin brother out of the country, Thorn has been lonely and forlorn, though he would vehemently deny the suggestion. His family thought his spirits might revive with some companionship."

Tempest's eyes widened at the sight of Chance removing his shirt and revealing his bare chest. There was a light dusting of dark hair on his chest that matched his legs. His torso was flawless and beautifully muscled. If she'd had her sketching book, she would have asked for more light so she could draw his physique.

Chance absently scratched his flat stomach. "Then there are the servants. Not to mention any guests Thorn invited. Bringing you to my private sitting room seemed the most sensible thing to do."

Tempest rubbed her toe against the side of his leg. "Very clever of you." He could have brought her to another room in his house, but he had picked his bed-chamber because that was where he wanted her to be.

Chance sucked in his cheeks and exhaled noisily. If he dared to laugh at her, she intended to kick him.

"I thought so." He moved closer to the bed. "Now, be good and roll onto your stomach."

"Whyever for?" And then she realized he planned on unfastening the buttons of her dress. "Oh."

After a brief pause, she slowly rolled onto her stomach and elevated the upper portion of her body with her arms.

"You have done this before," she said before she could suppress the remark.

His touch was light and his fingers nimble as he freed her from her dress. "I would be lying if I said that I was unfamiliar with a lady's unexpressibles. However, my experience is not so boundless as you might imagine. Until I met you, my friends often marveled at my restraint."

She felt cooler air wash over her back. Next, he went to work on unlacing her stays.

"And now?" Tempest prompted.

Chance sighed. "Thoughts of being with you fill my days. I have lost count of the nights I have lain on this very bed and envisioned us together. Of the rightness of it."

Tempest squeezed her upper thighs together to ease

the subtle tension his words conjured between her legs. "It makes little sense." She glanced over her shoulder, and with light of the lamps flickering at his back, his face was cast in shadow. "Still, I feel it, too."

"Sit up and come to me, Tempest," he said huskily.

She obeyed, using her hand to hold her front bodice in place. If she moved her hand, her unbuttoned dress would fall down to her waist, revealing her stays and chemise. With her other hand, she touched her hair and pulled the small silver filigree combs from it. Her dark brown hair tumbled and cascaded over her shoulders.

Approval gleamed in Chance's eyes, and he moved forward to collect the delicate combs and place them on a small table.

"I have never seen your hair down like this," he said, captivated by its softness and thickness. He stroked her hair, following the length that almost reached her hips. "I cannot believe you have been hiding all this bounty from me."

"I wear it down on occasion," she said, amused by his reaction. "Or I braid it to keep it out of my way while I am working on a task."

"But you'll wear it down just for me," he said, kissing her temple.

"Only if it is appropriate."

He was standing so close, she could feel the heat of his body. The lingering masculine scent of the soap he used when his valet shaved his face. Freed from her stays, she felt her nipples pucker and swell until they ached. She swayed and instinctively leaned toward him.

"Look at me, my lady," he entreated, cupping her face with his hands.

Tempest stared into his gray eyes, which affirmed everything she needed to see—eagerness, desire, and love. She took a deep breath and released the clothing she had clasped to her breasts. Her dress and untied stays slid down her body, revealing her nipples through the thin material of her chemise.

Chance's eyes flared with excitement and hunger, and his hands moved from her face down to her waist. He eased the clothing over her petticoat-covered hips and stays, and dropped the dress to the floor. Without breaking eye contact, he reached around to the middle of her back and untied the strings of her petticoat. Another tug, and her drawers whispered down her legs.

Standing only in her chemise provided little modesty. Chance's hands moved from her hips to her buttocks. He gently cupped the rounded flesh and pulled her against his body. It was then that she felt a distinct hardness at the front of his dark breeches. His eyes closed and his head fell back as he nudged her closer, and the thick rigid flesh rubbed enticingly against her.

"I have waited so long," he said, his voice heavy and thick with longing. "I don't know if I can last."

Tempest did not understand the full meaning of his confession, only that it was heartfelt. She started when he unexpectedly grabbed the hem of her chemise and pulled the remaining underdress over her head.

He tossed it over his shoulder and smiled at her. "Now I know I won't last," he said, and she sucked in her breath sharply when his bare hands encircled her waist and he raised her high enough to sit on the mattress. "Lie back."

The large tester bed with its carved mahogany posts and thick drapes cast her in dark shadows that were untouched by the oil lamps in the sitting room. Tempest reclined as Chance had instructed and then wondered what she was supposed to do with her hands. It seemed foolish to fret about something so trivial.

Chance, on the other hand, was not watching to see if she had done as he asked. Instead, his head was bowed and he was unfastening the cloth-covered buttons on the front of his breeches. Absorbed in his task, he was unaware that she had braced her upper body with her bent forearms so her view was unobstructed.

With no hesitation, he pushed his breeches down his lean hips, baring his aroused manhood, thighs, and finally his legs. The Marquess of Fairlamb was an exquisite specimen of a male in his prime. The glow of the oil lamps turned his skin golden while shadows hugged and settled into the muscled contours of his limbs.

He abruptly glanced up and noticed her guileless regard and appreciation.

"Will you allow me to sketch you one day?" she impulsively asked.

Chance laughed and shook his head. "If you added me to your little book, then I would ask that you burn the page before anyone saw it, which would be an atrocity because talent such as yours should be shared. Still, I would never hear the end of it if my mother learned my bare arse was on display for all of London to behold."

Tempest giggled as she politely averted her gaze. "Well, from my view, it isn't your backside that is exposed."

He uttered a soft curse and climbed onto the bed. "Ah, well, it is a persistent condition since I met you," he said, obviously untroubled by his physical response.

In fact, he only seemed interested in her, and that brought her in close proximity to his manhood. Tempest was grateful the interior of the room was dark so he could not see the blush that likely covered her entire body. Chance had rolled onto his side, and as he caressed her shoulder and arm, she was wholly aware of every spot where his bare skin touched hers.

"I have never done anything like this," she softly confessed. "I—"

He pressed his forefinger to her lips, and then replaced it with his mouth. "Close your eyes. Let your fears and doubts slip away," he said, kissing the line of her jaw and moving down to her neck.

Tempest tipped her head to one side when Chance used his tongue to outline the graceful arch. He lightly bit her collarbone and she shuddered.

"That's the way of it," he murmured, placing a trail of kisses that led him to her breasts. "Just feel, my love."

Tempest gasped as his mouth closed over her left nipple. Her hands touched his broad shoulders with the half-formed notion of pushing him away. He was not supposed to kiss her *there*.

It was too intimate.

Her breasts felt heavy, and energy sizzled just beneath the surface of her skin as he suckled the swollen nub. Every time the muscles in his throat contracted, the dampening flesh between her legs pulsed. She pressed her legs together in an attempt to control it.

However, Chance wanted her to feel the storm building in her body. As his mouth moved to her other breast, his hand slid down over the soft curve of her belly and caressed her thighs. His fingers gently kneaded the tense muscles until she began to relax.

Her thighs parted, giving him access to the soft dark down between her legs.

"Easy, now," he murmured, his fingers lightly teasing the hidden feminine folds.

"You shouldn't," Tempest whispered, her mouth suddenly dry. "It isn't—"

"It is," Chance assured her. He adjusted his position so he could kiss her on the lips.

Her damp hardened peaks rubbed against his chest, causing her to moan. Everywhere he touched her, she ached. Her skin felt hot and sensitive, and she did not know if she could bear another minute of it.

Two fingers glided along the seam of her feminine folds and parted the yielding flesh.

"Chance!"

"Do you like how I pet you?" he whispered, his hot breath gusting across her skin. "Feel how wet you are for me, Tempest. It is a sign of your unspoken hunger for me."

She could not deny the wetness or fathom his interpretation of its meaning. From some hidden source, proof of her desire coated his fingers. Chance stroked her boldly, and the muscles of her abdomen tensed. His fingers pressed deeper and her body opened for him.

Tempest opened her eyes when his fingers abruptly withdrew and Chance covered her with his body. She felt his rigid staff brush against her belly as he adjusted his position until he settled between her legs.

With her eyes shut, she had not seen the lines of tension becoming more pronounced on his face. His gray eyes were dark and intense as stared down into her face. The time he had spent soothing her fears and heightening her desire for him had come at a price. It had eroded his restraint, as his needs demanded to be assuaged.

"Too fast," he muttered, struggling to maintain control of what he had begun. "I always seem to lose my head around you."

"Do you wish to stop?"

"No!" There was a feverish look in his gaze when he lowered his mouth to hers.

His hand slipped between them, and she felt him adjust his manhood. The blunt head pressed against her drenched folds, and he guided the rigid flesh deeper.

Instinct had her tightening her legs around him, but her action only increased the pressure as his arousal tried to meld into hers. Chance rocked against her, and suddenly her growing discomfort became a burning pain as her flesh enclosed his manhood and he possessed her fully.

She and Chance gasped. His head dropped until his forehead rested on her shoulder. She swallowed, and realized what discomfort she had initially felt had eased as his hard flesh filled and expanded within her.

Then he began to slowly withdraw. Tempest wondered if Chance was done, but he pushed into her and filled her again. His breath was ragged when he raised his head, but his hips seemed to move of their own volition. Soon the steady pace of his manhood thrusting into her created a new kind of tension within both of them.

"Do you feel it?" he asked, blindly reaching for her left leg and wrapping it around his hip. The slight change in position deepened his thrust, and the groan of pleasure vibrated from his chest and into hers.

A curious heat washed over her as Chance's pace increased, and a new tension was growing in her body. He must have been feeling it as well. His fingers dug into her buttocks and his thrusts lost their fluid rhythm. Two hard thrusts, and he collapsed against her, setting off a chain reaction of sensation within her.

Tempest arched against him, driving him deeper. Her soft cries mingled with his hoarse shout as his manhood expanded within her. Her inner muscles clenched around the pulsing flesh and she felt the warmth and wetness of his seed fill her.

They were both shaking from the pleasurable onslaught. Neither one had the strength to move. Tempest closed her eyes and fought back tears as her feelings overwhelmed her, knowing Chance would keep her safe.

# Chapter Twenty-Three

His heart was pounding so fiercely in his chest that he thought it might burst.

Mathias thought only elderly gentlemen risked death after a vigorous coupling, but if he were fated to perish in Tempest's arms, then he would die a very happy man.

"You almost killed me," he murmured, kissing the top of her head.

Tempest sniffed and hiccupped against his chest. "I am still trying to draw air into my lungs."

Already, he could feel his sated cock withering within her snug sheath, so he carefully pulled out so he wouldn't cause her further discomfort. He reached over and pulled the sheet over them. Tempest's skin was damp with sweat, but he thought she would appreciate a small gesture of modesty.

Mathias rolled onto his side and pulled her against him so he could see her face.

"You've been crying?" His heart stuttered in his chest. "Did I hurt you, darling?"

*I was too eager. Too rough. I deserved to be flogged for upsetting her.*

"No, I am fine," she began.

"Don't lie. There are tears on your cheeks, Tempest."

The sight of them offended him so much that he wiped them away with his thumb.

"Chance, you didn't hurt me." She hesitated, and bit her lip. "Well, maybe in the beginning it hurt a little."

Mathias didn't make a habit of debauching young innocents. Tempest turned out to be the exception to most of his rules when it came to women. He had taken her maidenhead, and he knew from a few casual conversations with his friends that some pain was to be expected with an untried miss. The knowledge didn't improve his opinion about his clumsy lovemaking.

"I will be more careful with you," he solemnly vowed.

"You were," she said, touching his face. "It was all a little overwhelming, that's all."

Mathias offered an unsteady nod. In the last few minutes, he could sympathize with her reaction. He slipped his arm around her shoulders and nudged her closer. She laid her cheek against his chest.

The thought of being the cause of her tears was enough to make him want to blubber.

"This changes things," he murmured into her hair.

She sighed. "You will want to do this again."

His cock stirred, reacting to her words.

*Not now, you greedy flockpate!*

Mathias placed his hand over the growing bulge under the sheet just in case she noticed his unruly body. "Have you in my bed? Yes, I could get used to cuddling with you in my bed."

Tempest traced the diameter of his left pap, and the flesh beneath her finger hardened. Everything she did tended to make him hard. "Just the cuddling part?" she asked, trying to appear innocent.

Mathias not-so-gently pushed her onto her back, and he moved on top of her. "No, you make me greedy. I want it all." He took her hand and brought it to his loins so she could feel the proof of his desire. "If you weren't sore, I would already be inside you."

"I don't feel too tender," she protested. "We could—"

Mathias shook his head. If he listened to another word, he would pull the sheet back and push his cock inside her. "No," he said, softening his rejection with a kiss. "I don't want to hurt you again. I can wait."

Now that he had been given a small taste, he knew he would have her again.

*And again.*

He rolled onto his back and tucked her against his side so he had the pleasure of holding her in his arms. His friends were likely to ridicule him for acting so besotted over a lady, but he would endure their teasing. Tempest was worth it.

"Soon I will have to play coachman again, and drive you home," he said, feeling too content to let it ruin his mood. As long as Tempest was tucked into her bed before her mother returned home, Lady Norgrave would never suspect that her daughter had spent the last few hours in his bed.

"So this will be our secret?" She raised her head from its comfortable perch on his chest and met his gaze. "You won't tell your friends."

Mathias raked his fingers through his hair. He did not keep secrets from his friends, but that was not her first concern. Tempest was worried that their families would learn of their relationship. This was their first night together, and he didn't want to ruin it with the truth.

Their families would eventually know about him and Tempest.

How could he be so certain?

Mathias planned to tell them.

\* \* \*

The next morning, Mathias was summoned to the Blackbern town house.

McKee opened the door and stepped aside so he could enter. "You are late, Lord Fairlamb," the butler said, confirming his statement by checking his watch.

"It couldn't be helped, McKee," Mathias said, handing the servant his walking stick and hat. "I had an appointment near St. Paul's that was imperative I keep. Where are my parents?"

"The drawing room," the elderly servant replied, favoring his right leg. "If you will follow me—"

"Rest your knees. I will show myself up," he said, overruling the McKee and heading to the stairs.

"Very good, my lord."

"Mathias!"

He looked up and saw his youngest sister, Constance, overhead. "Good day to you, runt," he said, increasing the pace of his ascent. "I thought Mother told you to stop climbing the stair railings?"

The seven-year-old girl gave him a broad grin that revealed she had lost a front tooth. It explained why her lisp had become more pronounced. "Mama says I can climb anything as long as someone is watching."

He plucked her off the sloped balustrade and tossed her over his shoulder. "The duchess was not giving you permission to fall on your head in front of spectators."

She giggled as he carried her up to the remaining stairs and continued to the drawing room. Mathias strode through the opened doors and grinned as his mother and father hastily moved apart.

"A thousand pardons for interrupting," he said, pivoting halfway so Constance could wave to their parents. "Look who I found on the stairs again."

"Constance!" the duchess said, rising from the sofa

and walking toward her children. "How many times have I told you that it isn't safe to climb the balustrade?"

"Is that how she knocked out her tooth?" Mathias teased, bouncing several times on his heels to make his sister laugh.

"Her face is turning red," his mother said, hovering nearby in case she needed to interfere.

Mathias rolled his eyes. "I'll bet the color is quite flattering." He had handled all five of his siblings in the same manner when they were younger, and he hadn't dropped anyone on their head.

"Chance, put her down before all her blood drains out of her ears," Blackbern ordered, leaning back on the sofa and enjoying the chaos of their arrival.

"Hear that, runt? Papa says no more dangling like a silly monkey." He gave her a quick hug and bent down so she could stand.

"No!" Constance wrapped her thin arms around his hips and leaned against him.

Mathias expelled an exaggerated sigh of regret. "Sorry, my girl. Papa's 'no' overrules yours."

The duchess sensed an impending tantrum for the youngest Rooke, so she immediately took charge of the matter. "Constance, McKee has been searching for you."

"What does he want?" Her dark blue eyes stared up at her mother with hurt and suspicion.

"You have to talk to him." The duchess leaned over and kissed her daughter's forehead. "However, I want your promise that you will stay off the balustrade as you search for him downstairs."

Constance pouted, proving that age didn't matter. Rookes did not like to lose. "Fine. I promise."

His mother nodded approvingly. "Good. Now, give your papa a kiss before you dash off to your next adventure."

His sister ran to the duke and kissed him on the cheek. She grinned up at Mathias as she passed him, and she disappeared through the open doors.

"Is McKee looking for her?" he asked his mother.

However, it was his father who responded. "The man dotes on her. If he doesn't have a treat tucked away somewhere, he'll have Cook prepare something special."

Mathias nodded and got down to business. "My apologies for being late. I had an appointment I could not cancel. Why did you summon me?"

"Problems?" His father sat up, suddenly alert.

He thought of the several hours he had spent at Doctors' Commons. And the importance of what he had procured. "Not at all. Just a little personal business."

Although he was bursting to tell his parents the good news, he was doing everything out of order. "Did something happen?"

"That's odd, I was about to ask you the same question," his father said, motioning to one of the chairs. "Sit down, Mathias."

His father usually called him by his nickname, so if he was using his first name, something had happened. "What's wrong?"

The duke glanced at his wife. Wordlessly something passed between them before his mother shook her head. She returned to the sofa and sat down.

"Chance, we have been hearing rumors," his mother explained.

Mathias glanced from his father to his mother. "When do either of you listen to town gossip?"

The duke's visage darkened. "Usually, I wouldn't give a damn about rumors. However, this one connects you with a certain lady."

Feigning disinterest, he touched his cravat. "Father, are you truly in a position to chastise me about my private business?" His eyebrows lifted. "Because if half the rumors about your wild misspent youth are true, I look forward to hearing every detail. Perhaps we should adjourn to the library and talk about this over some brandy."

His father glared at him.

"Tristan," the duchess murmured, placing her hand on her husband's arm. "Mathias, stop baiting your father. We are merely concerned. There are rumors that you have been seen in the company of Lady Tempest Brant."

Of course this was about Tempest. If he had been caught with a courtesan or if he had installed Miss King in his grandmother's town residence, his mother and father would not look half so worried as they did now.

"It is true, I have met Lady Tempest," Mathias said, deciding not to lie since Lady Norgrave had also seen them together. "What of it?"

"Are you courting her?" his father asked, appearing to brace himself for his son's reply.

"Do you require a reporting of my conversations with the lady?"

"To ease your mother's mind, it might prove helpful," was the duke's grim reply.

Mathias sent his mother an apologetic glance. "Well, I regret I cannot oblige you. However, I can assure you both that my exchanges with Lady Tempest have been respectful and above reproach."

An unbidden vision of Tempest spread out naked on his bed crept into his mind. Before he had driven her home, he showed her another way he could love her—with his face buried between her legs and his mouth kissing her so intimately that she screamed as her blinding release surprised her.

It was perhaps his favorite moment of the evening.

He did not know Thorn had returned home until his

cousin pounded on the door, demanding to know if Mathias had murdered the wench in his bed. Thorn was startled when he recognized the lady, but he recovered quickly. He apologized and closed the door. Poor Tempest had been mortified that their carnal mischief was no longer a secret, despite his assurances that his cousin would not tell anyone.

*Did Thorn tattle?*

"You may view this as a grand jest, but Lady Tempest is not one of your conquests," his father snapped.

The duchess appeared uneasy discussing her son's private life, and Mathias could sympathize. He was damn uncomfortable.

"Lady Tempest is not your concern," he said coolly.

"She is if you are thinking with your cock rather than your head!" The Duke of Blackbern stood up and glowered at his heir. "Don't give Norgrave a reason to confront you."

Annoyed, Mathias sneered, "Lord Norgrave doesn't worry me. Do you fear him, Father?"

His mother came to her feet. "Stop it. Both of you."

Rage filled his father's blue gray eyes. "Don't push me, Chance. You will not like the results." The duke's contemptuous expression was cutting as much as it was insulting. "Whatever you are doing with the lady, end it."

His mother often claimed he had inherited his temper from his father. Mathias arched his right brow. "And if I choose to ignore your sage advice?" he taunted.

"Then I will put an end to it," his father said with silky menace. "And neither you nor Norgrave will like my methods."

# Chapter Twenty-Four

"So what did Papa wish to discuss with you?"

Tempest and her sister had accepted an invitation to watch fireworks at Vauxhall with Harriet and her betrothed, Lord Medeley, his sister, and Lord Chandler. Since their arrival, their little group had increased in size with Lord Warrilow's late appearance. Even Oliver had stopped by to pay his respects while they had been enjoying their supper boxes. He had been alone, Tempest noted, but she doubted her brother would remain alone for long. If Miss King was not waiting for him, the gardens were filled with attractive young ladies who would be drawn by his handsome dark looks.

Unfortunately, the viscount was unhappy to have a new rival for Tempest's attention, but Lady Joan had not bothered to conceal her delight. Perhaps she had heard the news that Lord Norgrave was pressing for the marquess to make a decision soon.

"Lady Tempest promised to meet you," Rainbault reminded him. "You are too impatient. Stop pacing and join us. Drink some ale. If you persist in glowering at their little group, one of the gentlemen is bound to notice and wonder why."

"Let them wonder," Mathias grumbled. "I would be

happy to inform them that they are flirting with my lady. I'm not going to be cast aside like an unwanted suitor and let Warrilow hold her hand while they watch the fireworks."

St. Lyon blocked his path. "Chance, her friends are not the only ones to avoid. While I was chasing after a buxom brunette near the pavilion, I believe I recognized Marcroft."

"Are you certain it was him?" Mathias demanded.

The viscount's hands parted in surrender. "Like most of the gentlemen present—including us, I might add—Marcroft is wearing a mask. The gentleman I saw at a distance had the earl's broad shoulders and rude bearing. If it is Marcroft and he learns you are close, he will retrieve his sisters and stuff them in the nearest hackney coach."

Mathias cursed. When he received Tempest's note, he had not anticipated that she would be surrounded by friends and suitors.

"Lady Tempest knows you are here," Thorn announced.

"How the devil do you know?"

"When the others aren't paying attention, she keeps glancing in our direction," his cousin replied.

His calm demeanor infuriated Mathias. Just once, he'd relish observing Thorn lose his composure over a lady.

Rainbault selected a piece of chicken from the plate in front of him and popped the meat into his mouth. His brow furrowed as he chewed. "It is getting darker, Chance. Perhaps your lady is waiting for everyone to be distracted by the fireworks."

Five days had passed since he argued with his father. He had caught glimpses of Tempest twice, but there was no opportunity to pull her aside and talk to her. Kiss her. He needed to hold her and hear from her lips that she had not been deliberately avoiding him—or regretted gifting him with her innocence.

Thirty minutes later, Tempest and her companions abandoned their seats in the saloon and strolled away from the festive tents. With colored lamps illuminating from overhead, they enjoyed the music and the evening air.

"I am following them," he announced to his friends. He refused to give Lord Warrilow an opportunity to be alone with her.

"Do you want company?" St. Lyon asked.

Mathias shook his head. "If I don't return, walk over to the fireworks stage. It is likely their destination as well. I will find you."

Hand in hand, Tempest and Chance hurried down the narrower paths that diverged from one of the main walks where he had lured her away from her companions and into the thick grove. These less traveled paths were sheltered by the leafy canopy of large elm and sycamore trees that were strung with glass lamps. The paths themselves twisted and curved with no specific destination, but benches and tables were scattered throughout for anyone who wished to sit and enjoy their surroundings.

"What if Lord Warrilow finds us together?" she asked, feeling guilty that she had abandoned him.

"I watched him kiss you, Tempest." From his grim expression, Chance viewed the marquess's actions as a grievous sin. "And I am not feeling very forgiving about it."

"He surprised me," she tried to explain, but it was unfair for the marquess to bear all the blame. She had kissed him back because she didn't wish to injure his pride. "It meant nothing."

Tempest and Chance looked back at the first sounds of fireworks.

"I didn't realize it was so late." Many of the visitors would be drawn to the explosions and bursts of light in the night sky. "Should we head in that direction so I can return to my sister and you can find your friends?"

"Eventually," he replied, slowing his gait. The overhead lamps provided some illumination, but his expression was concealed in shadows. "Tempest, what if Warrilow proposes to you? Will you accept?"

"My father is eager for the match, but—no, I would not accept." She halted. Chance took several steps and then turned back for her. "I am not in love with him."

Tempest and Chance stared at each other. Neither spoke for several minutes. Music and explosions filled the air. Her nose caught a whiff of gunpowder.

"Whom do you love?"

Tempest crossed over to him. "You. I am in love with you, Chance." She blinked in astonishment as she noted his disbelief. "Don't tell me that you didn't know?"

"Brants don't fall in love with Rookes," he said hoarsely, his low voice rich with emotion.

"And Rookes don't fall in love with Brants," she replied. "So where does that leave us?"

"Together. In love. I love you, Tempest."

Warrilow and the fireworks faded into the distance as she and Chance kissed. Tempest slipped her hands under his evening coat and his arms encircled her waist. With their lips locked together, he guided her backwards until they were off the path. They were alone, but he wasn't taking any risks.

Suddenly, he pivoted and she gasped as he pressed her back against the trunk of a tree.

He broke off their kiss. "I want you."

"I want you, too." She grabbed his coat to pull him closer. "Kiss me again."

"Right this minute." At her blank look, he clarified, "I want to shag you here. Against the tree. Now."

Tempest admitted his frank words excited her, but she did not take him seriously. Even though they were alone, this was still a public place.

Surely, he did not mean for them to—

"Now, Tempest." Chance reached for the front flap on his breeches and unceremoniously unfastened the buttons.

He took her hand and brought it to the rigid length that was thickening at her touch. His manhood was hard, hot, and felt like silk against her skin. She measured the full length of him with her fingers. As her thumb rubbed the tip, a few drops of fluid leaked from the opening.

Her sheath contracted at the thought of him filling her. Of him taking her against the tree, out in the open with the stars glittering overhead.

Without waiting for permission, Chance began to push up the front of her skirt and petticoat. He made a soft sound of appreciation when he touched her bare thigh. "No drawers, Lady Tempest?" he drawled, and she could feel the heat of a blush. "Very naughty—and I know just how to reward you."

Mathias kissed her roughly on the mouth. Painfully aroused, he was feeling reckless. He could think of nothing else but claiming her. He pulled Tempest against him, letting her feel the relentless throb of his cock as the length of it pressed against her belly.

"What if someone comes down the path?" she whispered.

As far as he was concerned, a small crowd could

gather around them, and they could even watch, so long as they didn't interrupt him. He tried to think of something that would assure her. "If we are quiet, no one will know what we are doing."

Tempest was nervous, but he also heard the excitement in her voice. Sliding his hands around to her buttocks, he filled them with her soft curves and lifted her until the head of his cock found the soft yielding core. He dragged in a ragged breath as he eased her slowly down the rigid length, her sheath parting and closing around him until she was fully seated.

"Wrap your legs around my hips," Chance whispered, his face pressed into the front of her bodice.

The tightness of her sheath threatened his restraint, and he reveled in it. Using the trunk of the tree to keep his balance, he began to thrust deeply into her. Tempest could do little more than hold on. He felt her legs squeeze his hips as he quickened his pace, driving his cock into her over and over.

"Oh my stars," she gasped.

With his cheek rubbing against her bodice, he forged into her body. Each thrust was a test of balance and endurance, and within minutes his body was drenched in perspiration. He could hear the tempo of the firework explosions increase, and he matched it, driving them to the brink.

"Chance—I—oh God!" Tempest dug her fingers into his shoulders and cried out. Her head fell forward and she smothered strangled gasps by muffling them into his coat.

As she shuddered against him, her sheath milked his cock; he thrust deep and surrendered. His seed exploded from the head of his cock, followed by steady jets of milky fluid pumping into her. The sensation seemed endless, as if her body demanded every drop from him.

Chance staggered, but he regained his balance. His cock was still buried deeply inside her, and if they had not been outdoors, he could have happily remained in this position for the rest of the night. Preferably with them reclining on a comfortable bed.

Tempest gazed down at him in wonder. "That was incredible."

"Have I told you how much I adore brazen women?"

She grinned, and then she lowered her face until their lips met. In the aftermath, their kisses were leisurely and tender.

As much as he desired it, he could not steal her away. He would have to return her to her friends. To Warrilow. Chance loathed that part the most.

# Chapter Twenty-Five

It had been a grand night, even if it ended with Tempest bidding a reluctant farewell to Chance. His temperament had been mercurial during the brief hour she had shared with him. He was furious and jealous when she had first seen him with his friends; next he had been intense, protective, and ruled by lust and the thrill of the claiming; and finally, he had been tender, contemplative, and somehow resolved.

Something was troubling Chance. Or someone. Tempest discreetly glanced at Lord Warrilow as he entered the front hall of the Brant household with her and Arabella at his side.

"Good evening, daughters! And Warrilow, my good friend," Lord Norgrave said from the threshold of his library.

Her father had been drinking his favorite brandy this evening, and quite a bit of it, if his unsteady gait was any indication. He leaned forward and brushed a kiss in the air since he missed her cheek. Her father moved on to Arabella.

"Pretty, pretty Arabella. Give your father a kiss."

Her sister gasped when her father gave her a hard kiss on the mouth.

Her mother was noticeably absent. When her husband

was in one of his moods, the marchioness preferred to retire early. If Tempest tried the door, she would discover that her mother had locked it.

"I will bid you all a good night," Lord Warrilow said, already backing away. The gentleman had been acquainted with Lord Norgrave long enough to know how difficult her father could be when he had been drinking. "Ladies, it was a pleasurable evening."

Her father pinched his brow and shook his head to clear it. "Warrilow . . . wait." He swallowed the remaining brandy in his glass and handed it to Arabella. "Be a good daughter and fill another glass for your papa."

He pivoted halfway and walked back to the younger marquess. "You cannot end your evening with us. We have not celebrated the good news."

Tempest untied her bonnet and removed it. "What news, Papa?" She followed her father's gaze to Lord Warrilow.

"There was no opportunity to speak with your daughter, Norgrave," the younger gentleman said, his discomfort obvious. "If you prefer, I will call on you tomorrow afternoon."

"Why wait?" her father argued. He waved his hand carelessly at the staircase. "Make use of our drawing room. Tempest, go with your husband."

Tempest froze at her father's order. Arabella was standing in front of the library with their father's glass of brandy. Both women stared at Lord Warrilow.

Lord Norgrave slapped his hand over his mouth, causing him to sway. He chuckled as his hand fell away. "Not very well done of me, was it?" He staggered toward Tempest and placed his hand on her shoulder. "Don't dawdle, Daughter. You and Warrilow have much to discuss."

He gave her a little push when she didn't move.

"Come, my lady," Lord Warrilow said, taking charge

of the situation. "We can talk privately in the drawing room."

Tempest glanced over her shoulder at her sister. Arabella appeared as startled as she. It was no secret that Lord Warrilow had come to London to claim a bride, but until he kissed her at Vauxhall, she had been convinced the gentleman's feelings for her were lukewarm.

Her feelings for the marquess were equally uninspiring. Only Lord Norgrave appeared eager for the match.

Neither she nor Lord Warrilow spoke until they entered the drawing room. Tempest shut the door and almost locked it to keep her father out. In his current condition, his presence would be far from helpful.

She took a fortifying breath. "My lord—"

The marquess held up his hand to halt her speech. "No, allow me to speak first, Lady Tempest." He took her by the hand and led her to the sofa. "Please, sit down."

"My father is very drunk, my lord. When he awakens, he may not even recall this conversation," she said, praying the gentleman would not follow through on Lord Norgrave's demands.

"This is not about your father." Lord Warrilow sat down next to her. Discovering his palms were damp, he rubbed them on his thighs. "Forgive me, my lady. I suppose I should have requested a glass of brandy before I rushed you upstairs."

More brandy was not what this evening needed.

"We can discuss this another day," she said softly.

The marquess shook his head. "No, I have been working up the courage for days. I had hoped that we might speak earlier . . . in private. However, I frightened you with the kiss and you ran off."

And she ran straight into another man's arms. While the gentleman who wanted to offer her marriage searched for her, she had let Chance push up her skirts and ravish her against the trunk of a tree. It was wickedly wanton, and she had loved every minute of his wild claiming.

"My lord, your kiss startled me, but I do not fear you." She struggled to find the right words. "You are a good man. I know my father feels we would be a good match, but I think he is wrong. You deserve someone who—"

Tempest tried not to flinch when he claimed her hand.

"I confess I had my doubts at first, but I have changed my opinion." Lord Warrilow placed his other hand over hers. "My lady . . . Lady Tempest, would you do me the honor of becoming my bride?"

His words were everything Lord Norgrave wanted to hear. When Tempest tried to envision herself as Lady Warrilow, all she saw in her mind was gray fog. How could she love him when her heart and body belonged to another?

"You overwhelm me, my lord," she said, staring at their clasped hands. Tempest let her shoulders sag as she shut her eyes. "I was about to tell you that I needed a few days to give you my answer, but that is a lie. Lord Warrilow, I cannot marry you. You are a kind man, and I have enjoyed your company, but I am simply the wrong lady for you."

The marquess flinched and then slowly released her hand. He avoided her gaze. "Is there someone else?"

She hesitated. However, Lord Warrilow deserved the truth. "Yes."

"Does he—?" He cleared a blockage in his throat. "Has this gentleman declared himself? Are his intentions honorable?"

Tempest glanced forlornly at the door. They should have asked Arabella to bring up the decanter of brandy.

"He has not declared himself to my father." Nor would she ask him to, since it would result in Oliver challenging him. She and Chance would have to confront both families if they planned to build a life together. "There are a few obstacles."

Lord Warrilow gave her a pitying glance. "Of course there are, though I feel compelled to offer you some advice. A married gentleman rarely divorces his wife."

Tempest's head snapped up. "He's not married. It's—Oh, suffice it to say, my family will never approve of him."

"If it is hopeless between you and this fellow you love, then there is no reason why you couldn't marry me." The marquess's tone was light, but she sensed he was not teasing.

"Even if I had not met this other gentleman, I would still decline your generous offer. In truth, I look on you as another brother."

Lord Warrilow clasped his heart and chuckled. "My lady, you wound me."

"I care, my lord," she said, praying he would forgive her one day. "I care enough to reject you for your own sake."

"Another arrow pierces my heart." The marquess shook his head and wearily stood. "I cannot bear any more truths between us, my lady. I hope you understand."

"I do." Tempest said, rising.

She solemnly followed the marquess downstairs, where her father and sister waited for them to share their good news.

Lord Norgrave squinted at Tempest and then the unsmiling Lord Warrilow. "Well? Shall I have one of the servants wake your mother so we can have a proper celebration?"

The young marquess retrieved his hat and gloves from a narrow table. "Allow your lady to sleep. There will be no marriage."

"What?" Lord Warrilow's announcement momentarily sobered the older gentleman. "Of course there will be a marriage between you and Tempest."

"I cannot marry a lady who loves another." Lord Warrilow turned to her, and there was a glimmer of bittersweetness in his expression. "You deserve happiness, too, my lady. You will never achieve it if you are not honest with your father."

Tempest closed her eyes in despair.

Lord Warrilow bowed and bade everyone good night.

"Listen to your daughter, Norgrave," the marquess advised. "I will see you tomorrow at the club."

Arabella, Tempest, and their father remained frozen in place. The front door shut behind Lord Warrilow.

"Who?"

Her gaze shifted to Arabella's after her father's soft question.

"After all my efforts to secure you a husband, you refused him. I want the name of the gentleman who is behind your betrayal of me and your family," he said, his teeth snapping together.

"There is no reason to involve him," Tempest hedged. "I am not marrying him."

"Ah, so you have betrayed me for no reason."

His sudden calmness should have warned her. Lord Norgrave turned and slapped Tempest across the face, the force behind it knocking her to the floor. Her hand covered her sore cheek, but she did not make the mistake of rising.

"Tempest!" Arabella cried out, rushing to her side. "Papa, please . . . it is not her fault."

"Do not defend her!" he bellowed.

Her sister clapped her hands over her ears and buried her face into Tempest's shoulder.

"I want the scoundrel's name, Daughter."

Tempest glared at her father. "No! He has nothing to do with my decision to turn down Lord Warrilow."

With a roar of frustration, he staggered to Tempest and hauled her to her feet. Arabella began to cry as he shook his eldest daughter, her head snapping forward and backwards.

"A name!" he screamed into her face.

Tempest had never defied her father or her mother. She was terrified, but she refused to reveal Chance's name. She did not trust her father or brother not to hold him responsible for her defiance.

"I cannot," she whispered.

Lord Norgrave raised his hand again.

"I know who he is, Papa!" Arabella sobbed. "Please don't hurt my sister."

Burning with fury, his light blue gaze centered on Arabella. "Give me his name, Daughter, or I will take my whip to your sister's back."

Tempest shivered, but she refused to believe her father would whip her. "Don't, Arabella."

"Mathias Rooke . . . Lord Fairlamb," she confessed, unable to meet Tempest's gaze.

Lord Norgrave was so surprised, he released Tempest. She edged away from him and gathered her sobbing sister into her arms. Her father did not seem to notice. His lips parted as he shook his head.

"Fairlamb, you say." He rubbed his jaw and pondered the depth of his daughter's betrayal. "Blackbern's heir."

If he had struck her again, Tempest would have conceded that she deserved it. She would have accepted her punishment without protest.

Instead of attacking her, her father began to laugh. A snort became a few chuckles. His chuckles flowed into belly-shaking laughter that went on and on until he was gasping for breath. Lord Norgrave dragged air into his lungs and kept laughing.

Tempest had never been so frightened of her father.

Still holding Arabella, the two sisters moved away from him and escaped upstairs. Even behind her locked door, she could still hear her father's laughter.

# Chapter Twenty-Six

The rumors of a betrothal between Lady Tempest Brant and the Marquess of Warrilow reached Mathias's ears the following afternoon at one of his clubs. The unfortunate fellow who shared the good tidings swiftly regretted it once he was interrogated by Mathias. He heard the news again when he encountered a friend at his favorite tailor. When another acquaintance mentioned it when he was at Tattersall's with Rainbault and St. Lyon, he was too agitated to be near the horses.

Short of confronting Tempest directly, which his friends strongly discouraged, there was only one gentleman who could confirm if there was any truth to the gossip.

Marcroft.

After a few inquiries, Mathias knew where he could find the earl. This time of day, Marcroft often patronized a small tavern that was known for a private room that was off the main taproom where young nobles honed their pugilist skills with anyone willing to fight them. Rainbault and Thorn had witnessed several of the earl's matches as he tested his fists against hardened opponents who earned their living on the purses of such private fights, but Mathias had been reluctant to tangle with Marcroft in an establishment he often frequented.

"Have I mentioned what a terrible idea this is, Chance?" Rainbault asked when they arrived at the tavern.

"Once or twice," Mathias muttered. "Unless you and St. Lyon are planning to tie me to a wooden post, I highly recommend you cease wasting your breath arguing with me about it."

"I cannot fathom why you are obsessed with this chit," the prince said, sounding equally annoyed. "One is as good as any other."

Mathias seized his friend by the front of his frock coat and shoved him against the exterior wall of the tavern. "That is where you and I disagree. If you care about your unblemished chin, do not belittle a lady I hold in the highest esteem or I will put a dent in it."

"Good God, you are in love with her!" St. Lyon exclaimed.

Mathias abruptly released his friend's coat and took a step back. "I am n—Damn it all!"

"It is a reasonable explanation for your recent behavior." Rainbault used his hands to smooth away the wrinkles caused by Mathias's fingers. "Which even you must admit has lacked a degree of sanity."

Mathias gritted his teeth but did not argue. His life has been cast in turmoil since he first encountered Tempest. He was keeping secrets from his family and friends; his temper had been honed to a fine, dangerous edge; and the thought of Warrilow claiming Tempest as his bride was driving him to seek out a man he viewed as an enemy.

"Let's find Marcroft, and then we can leave." He entered the tavern, not glancing back to see if his friends followed him.

The earl was in the private room that was used for wagered fights; however, he was not one of the pugilists. He sat at a small table in a corner of the room with two friends. Both men stood when they noticed Mathias's approach with St. Lyon and Rainbault at his heels.

Marcroft did not appear to be concerned by their arrival. "Gentlemen, I was unaware you favored this tavern." He turned to address his companions. "A sign of the times, I suppose, when an establishment must open its doors to undesirables."

"Normally, I would enjoy trading insults with you, Marcroft," he said, bracing his hands on the table. It wobbled as he leaned forward. "However, for the sake of brevity, I prefer to get straight to my business with you."

The earl gave him an assessing look and sat back in his chair. "I would invite you to join me, but, alas, all the chairs have been claimed by my friends."

Mathias gave him a humorless smile. "I do not plan to share a pot of ale with you, Marcroft."

The other man glanced over Mathias's shoulder at St. Lyon and Rainbault. "And what of your friends?"

"They have no interest in drinking with you either," Mathias quipped. "I just need you to answer a few questions and then we will leave."

"It must be something awfully important for you to approach me, Fairlamb," Marcroft said, speculation gleaming in his eyes.

It was of the utmost importance to Mathias, but he was not going to admit it. "Warrilow. Has he offered marriage to your sister?"

Some of the amusement in the earl's gaze faded. "Which one? I have three sisters."

"Don't play games with me."

Marcroft's lips tightened at the unspoken threat. "And I have told you to stay away from Tempest. And yet, here you are, asking questions about her that everyone within hearing distance would agree are none of your business."

"Warrilow." Mathias ground his back molars to

keep from losing his temper. "Has he approached your father?"

The earl's eyes narrowed. "He has, and I believe my father has accepted. Why do you ask?"

His heart twisted painfully at the other man's response. It was followed by a burst of jealousy. "And your sister is agreeable to the match?"

Marcroft's eyebrows rose in disbelief. "I have no idea. What's important is that my father approves of the marriage. Any qualms my sister might have will be addressed once she and Warrilow have settled into their married life." The earl stood when he noted Mathias's fierce expression. "Fairlamb, you are not actually thinking of interjecting an opinion in this matter?"

"Why would he do that, I wonder?" Rainbault muttered.

"Tempest is not in love with Warrilow," he said flatly.

"No, I suppose she is not," Marcroft replied, sensing the internal struggle Mathias battled with his emotions. "Though, my sister is a dutiful daughter. Even if she had tender feelings for another gentleman, she would acquiesce to her father's dictates."

The notion that the earl was correct was a bitter realization. Still, he had a signed paper in his possession that would tip the outcome in his favor. "Care to wager on it?"

"Stay away from my sister, Fairlamb," Marcroft snarled. "My father has already taken steps to ensure that she is protected from you or anyone else who seeks to ruin her happiness."

"Norgrave is sending her out of town? When?" he pressed.

"As if I would tell you," the other man said, his voice dripping with scorn. "Whatever flirtatious game you were playing with my sister ends now. If you attempt to approach her again, I will challenge you to a duel.

Perhaps a bullet will spare other ladies your unwanted attentions."

"Consider this my acceptance in advance."

Before anyone could react, he punched Marcroft. His fist clipped the other man's chin and sent him sprawling into his chair. The wall behind him was the only reason the earl was upright. He looked as startled as everyone else by Mathias's unexpected violence.

"We can set a date when I deserve it." He turned and met Rainbault's admiring gaze. "I am finished here."

If Norgrave thought it necessary to send Tempest out of London, her departure was likely immediate, and he did not have much time to put his own plans into action.

"I am sorry you were caught up in all of this, Arabella," Tempest said as London vanished in the distant horizon.

Because of her, she and Arabella had been banished to the country by their father.

"You are not to blame," was her sister's generous reply.

"Aye, she is," Mrs. Sheehan said, adding an insulting snort. "Behaving like a brazen hussy as you traipse about town with that Rooke fellow. It is fortunate Lord Warrilow will take you to wife after all is said and done. To be certain, the gossips will be counting on their fingers to see how quickly your belly swells and you present your husband an heir. You should be thanking Lord Norgrave for protecting you from—"

"That is quite enough from you, Mrs. Sheehan," Tempest said, her tone sharp. It was so unlike her, the older woman swallowed the rest of her words and returned to her sewing.

In spite of her mother's pleas and arguments, Norgrave announced that Tempest and her sister would return to the country and remain there until her wedding to Lord

Warrilow. She had not even been allowed to bid her future husband farewell. Her father assured her that the young marquess would understand a man's need to protect his daughters from unscrupulous gentlemen.

There was only one gentleman her father needed to worry about, and he had taken steps to guarantee that she had been unable to send him word of her departure.

Would he attempt to find her, Tempest silently wondered. Or would he accept that what they had shared was over now that her father was aware of their friendship? Even if Chance was determined to pursue her, her impending marriage to Lord Warrilow would cool his ardor. He could not stand up against his father any more than she could defy hers.

In the quiet confines of their traveling coach, Mrs. Sheehan's sneering words about the gossips counting on their fingers tormented her. In their haste, neither she nor Chance had considered that a child might result from their passionate coupling. Even now, the notion of carrying his child did not strike fear into her heart as perhaps it should. Selfish or not, if she could not keep the gentleman she had fallen in love with, then she wished for his child. Her father would see to it that she and Lord Warrilow married quickly. If there was a babe growing in her womb, everyone would assume it was her husband's.

"All will be well, Sister."

Tempest started at the touch of her sister's hand covering hers. She did not realize she had made a soft mournful sob that alerted Arabella to her distress or the tears on her cheeks. Wiping them away with her fingers, she tried to smile in an attempt to reassure her sister.

"You slept only a few hours," her sister pointed out, since Tempest had cried for hours after her argument with their father. "Try to sleep. It will pass the time until we reach our destination."

Tempest closed her eyes, letting her sadness and fears slip away as the sounds of the horses and coach lulled her to sleep. It seemed only minutes had passed when she abruptly awoke to masculine shouts and pistols discharging.

"What is wrong?" she asked, instinctively reaching for Arabella's hand as the coach slowed. She must have slept for hours, because someone had lit the interior lamps, and through the window the sky revealed it was almost twilight.

"Highwaymen," Mrs. Sheehan whispered, her face ashen. "Three helpless women. They will murder us."

"Not if we give them our valuables," Arabella replied, keeping her voice low.

Tempest was in agreement. "We need to keep calm."

"Stand, good sir!" one of the thieves shouted to the coachman. "Set aside the ribbons and climb down from your perch."

Resisting the urge to press her face to the window, Tempest peered through the dusty glass and could discern at least two men on horseback. The door suddenly opened, and all three ladies shrieked in fright.

"What 'ave we 'ere?" A hooded man braced his hands on each side of the door to block their escape. "Three ladybirds in the cage," he called out to his companions.

"Comely lasses?" one of the men inquired.

A low chuckle rumbled from beneath the black hood. "Fair enough for us."

He reached for Tempest, who shrank away from his touch.

Mrs. Sheehan slapped the man's hand. "Leave my lady alone! These ladies are under my protection, and you will not lay a filthy hand on either one of them."

"Trouble?" a third male voice inquired, clearly amused.

"Nothing I can't 'andle," he replied, reaching against for Tempest. He grabbed her hand with the intention of pulling her out of the coach.

"No!" shouted Mrs. Sheehan.

Tempest took advantage of the man's distraction and sank her teeth into his forearm. He yelped in surprise and hastily released her. Outside the coach, she could hear the other men laughing.

"Sharp-toothed wench!" he growled before he roughly seized her by the arms. She cursed him and fought back, but he was too angry with her attack to be gentle. He pulled her out and shoved her into the arms of another hooded man. "Ye kin 'ave this one, and good riddance!"

The other man caught her and held her too close for decency. When she attempted to pull away, he raised his unencumbered hand to reveal the pistol he was holding.

Tempest immediately stilled.

Helplessly, she watched her sister and Mrs. Sheehan disembark from the coach. The highwaymen had the two women stand next to the coachman. Softly their chaperone sobbed into her handkerchief.

"Watch 'em," the man who had hauled her out of the coach ordered the man who remained on horseback.

"Aye. Nary a twitch or I'll shoot," the man said coldly.

No one moved as the thief searched the compartment for valuables. Tempest bit her lip to muffle her groan when the man revealed the pistol Mrs. Sheehan had concealed in her sewing basket. Chuckling to himself, he secreted the pistol beneath the fabric of his woolen cloak.

Thunder rumbled in the distance.

"Finished?" the man on horseback asked. "Best not get caught in foul weather."

Tempest's head lifted as she turned toward the man.

All three men were covered from head to toe to conceal their identities, but there was something about this man's voice that seemed familiar.

She flinched at the flash of lightning overhead.

"Give that back!"

Tempest looked away from the highwayman and switched her attention to Mrs. Sheehan, who was tussling with one of the highwaymen for her reticule. The widow cried out in despair as the man won the battle and searched the bag for valuables.

"Filthy blackguard!" Mrs. Sheehan sobbed as the man emptied the contents of her reticule on the road.

He held out the empty bag and motioned to Arabella. "Put yer baubles in 'ere!"

Silently, her sister obeyed his hoarse order. Anticipating that she was next, she hastily removed her earrings and a gold ring that her grandmother had given her. She dropped her jewelry into the reticule the moment it was pushed in her face.

"That's a lass," the man holding her murmured.

She shut her eyes and said nothing when he patted her on the hip.

"Tie those two up," the thief on horseback ordered, gesturing toward the coachman and their chaperone.

"See here, sirs," the coachman protested as his hands were secured behind his back with a length of rope the highwayman produced from underneath his cloak. "These are noble ladies. There is no need to truss them up."

Tempest glanced up at the darkening sky as she felt drops of cold rain strike her face.

Once the man was finished with the coachman and Mrs. Sheehan, he ordered them into the coach and shut the door. Next, he walked to Arabella.

"Wrists together, milady," he said gruffly. "As in prayer."

Arabella nodded and complied. Ignoring the widow's pleas for mercy, the highwayman led her sister to the man on horseback and lifted her up. The other man caught her by the waist and settled her on his lap.

Tempest tensed as the man approached her. A part of her wanted to flee their captors, but the prospect of getting shot in the back for her efforts forced her to stand still.

"Behave yerself, milady. Else I'll paddle yer backside fer biting me," the highwayman said, binding her hands. The man holding her handed over his pistol to his comrade so he could mount his horse. By the time she was settled on the highwayman's lap, it began to rain in earnest.

"Please, sir," Tempest said, keeping her voice low. "Let us go. You already have our valuables. Kidnapping my sister and me will slow you and your companions down in this foul weather and increase your odds for the hangman's noose."

It was a calculated risk appealing to a highwayman. The one who had held her had been gentle, and seemed kinder than the other two. If she could not convince him to release her and Arabella, perhaps he might protect them from the other two.

She stiffened in his arms as he pulled her body firmly against him. Belatedly, she realized his intentions as he pulled the edges of his cloak around her to protect her from the rain. She leaned into his warmth and inhaled. Her eyes widened as she took in his familiar scent.

His lips brushed against her ear, and she sagged against him in relief.

"I lost my head the moment I met you, Lady Tempest,"

Chance whispered into her ear. "I'll risk the hang-man's noose to keep you."

Altering his voice, he said to his friends, "We ride!"

Once they were several miles away from the coach, Mathias, St. Lyon, and Rainbault removed their dark masks but kept their hoods in place because of the steady rainfall. Tempest's sister had not screamed at her kid-napper when St. Lyon removed his mask, so Mathias as-sumed the viscount had already revealed his identity to put the lady at ease.

"I cannot believe you left the coachman and Mrs. Sheehan bound in our coach," Tempest muttered for the third time. Her relief at learning that she was ac-quainted with the highwaymen swiftly faded as she pondered the fate of the servants. "The poor woman was terrified."

"We had to be convincing," Mathias argued. "The coachman had his orders. As did your Mrs. Sheehan. Both servants were armed with pistols. Neither one of them was going to hand you over without a fight, and we did not leave them helpless. Rainbault took the time to pull the coach off the road and secure the horses. If the coachman doesn't free himself and the widow right away, they have shelter for the night."

"And you allowed Rainbault to rob Mrs. Sheehan." Tempest cuddled against him as he tried to shield her against the weather.

"He took only her pistol and her empty reticule. Everything else was returned to her sewing basket," he explained, annoyance edging his voice. "If you would prefer to marry Warrilow, I could always leave you and your sister at the nearest inn and continue on my way."

"How did you know?"

"Rumors of your impending marriage had already reached the gossips." He tightened his hold on her as he recalled seeing the darkening bruise on her cheek. "I assume your father learned about us."

Mathias had been assured by certain handsomely compensated individuals that they would be discreet. Nevertheless, he assumed one of them had gone to Lord Norgrave.

"Lord Warrilow deduced I cared for someone else and was willing to step aside. When my father realized that I harbored feelings for another man, he demanded that I reveal his name." Tempest shuddered. "Forgive me. My father—he had been drinking. I had to tell him the truth."

"Is that when he struck you?" he said angrily, incensed that the man had abused his daughter.

"No," she said softly. "That happened earlier. He laughed when I revealed your name."

"Did he frighten you?"

"Arabella and I have never been more terrified of him," she confessed.

Learning this, Mathias did not regret taking her sister with them. He had considered leaving Arabella behind with the servants, but he wanted Tempest to have someone she trusted with her. Without her knowledge, he had made decisions on her behalf that would change both their lives.

"Are you heading for an inn?"

Mathias knew both ladies were uncomfortable, but since he and his friends had disguised themselves as outlaws, it was not safe for them to rest until they reached their destination.

Instead of answering her question, he countered with one of his own. "Were you planning to marry Warrilow?"

Tempest buried her face into his dampening coat.

Finally, she said, "My father was determined to see me married to the marquess. I was willing to marry him if it meant my family would leave you alone."

He signaled his horse to halt.

Tempest pulled back to meet his livid glare. "What?"

"Have you so little faith in me?" he shouted at her.

"Chance?" Rainbault called out over his shoulder before he alerted St. Lyon to halt.

Rain flowed down her cheeks like tears. "Of course!"

"Then you think I am a coward?"

She shook her head. "No! I was trying to protect you."

"From whom? Your father? Marcroft?" He was offended that she believed her family could defeat him. "I could best any challenger."

"And you think that makes me feel any better?" she yelled back at him. "That my father or brother would be injured—or worse, die by your hand? That you were forced into a confrontation or hurt because I fell in love with you? There are no victors. Not when it involves you and my family."

"Chance, this is not the time—" St. Lyon raised his hand in surrender when Mathias scowled at him.

"If you weren't in such a hurry to marry Warrilow—"

"I did not want to marry him!" Tempest said, shouting over his words.

"—you would have realized that you had overlooked another way to deal with the situation."

"Oh really?" she said, lifting her chin so she could look down her nose at him. "And what, pray tell, did I overlook?"

"Marriage. To me," he said, resisting the urge to shake her for giving up on them so quickly.

"Marry you?" She seemed dazed by the very notion.

His temper receded at her bemused expression. His voice softened as he explained, "Thorn is waiting for us with a member of the clergy. I already have the special license. If you consent, we can marry this evening. You will be my marchioness—wedded and bedded legally—and our families will have to accept it."

*Eventually,* he silently amended. He was confident that he and Tempest could wear the families down with time and perhaps a few grandchildren.

"You want to marry me?" Tempest asked, her tears mixing with the rain.

Mathias cupped the side of her face with his hand. "I know. It surprised me, too. I could come up with a dozen reasons why this is madness. Why you were the last person in England that I should marry."

"A dozen? Truly?"

He grinned as her voice sharpened with annoyance. "There was one unassailable fact that defeated all my arguments—that convinced me to risk everything for you."

"And what is that?"

"I love you. You, my lady, claim my heart, my body, and my eternal soul. I would defy my family and lay down my life for you."

Ignoring his friends' groans, he claimed his beloved's mouth and poured everything he had into that kiss. He had yet to ask her if she could sacrifice everything for him, but he sensed her answer in the way she pressed herself against him and kissed him until they were both breathless.

"I was so miserable when I thought that the next time we would meet, I would be Lady Warrilow," she confessed, the wretchedness and humiliation of the day reflected in her gaze. "He is a good man, I believe. However, I do not love him."

Mathias despised the jealousy that surged in his veins whenever she mentioned the marquess, but he had found her before her marriage to the gentleman could take place. "Whom do you love?" he murmured against her hair.

"I—," she began.

"Chance, is it your intention to drown us all?" Rainbault complained, his patience coming to the end. "Gain your lady's consent and let us be on our way!"

"Aye, Fairlamb," St. Lyon added. "I prefer not to be robbed by a genuine highwayman."

Tempest glanced away in embarrassment at his friends' mild teasing. Nevertheless, the rain and the chill were adding to their discomfort. Mathias captured her chin and tipped her face toward his. "Marry me, Tempest."

He held his breath at her hesitation. After all his planning, he had never considered that she might refuse him.

"What of your family? Do not lie and tell me they approve of this match."

Mathias was reluctant to tell her that his mother and father were not any happier about his interest in her than her parents were. Of the angry words he had exchanged with his father and the pain in his mother's eyes when he told them that he planned to marry Norgrave's daughter.

"No," he conceded, because Tempest was the only one who could understand his guilt over putting his happiness above loyalty to his family. "In time, my mother and father will put aside the past. They will come to love you as much as I do."

Doubt still clouded her expression, but his response seemed to satisfy her. "Yes, Lord Fairlamb. I will marry you," she said before he pulled her into a crushing embrace while he struggled to keep control of his horse. "I love you."

"Thank God!" heartily exclaimed the prince. "Congratulations to you both. Now, can we be off!"

By ten o'clock, Tempest was a married lady. She stared down at the gold ring on her left hand, proof that she and Mathias Rooke, Marquess of Fairlamb, had exchanged marriage vows with her sister and his three friends as their witnesses. Although her hair had still been damp from their journey, she had to credit the Duke of Rainbault for being a thoughtful highwayman. Instead of searching for valuables to steal, he had managed to stuff several dresses and a few accessories into a satchel so she and Arabella had dry dresses to wear for the wedding.

Warming herself by the fireplace, she smiled up at Chance when he entered the bedchamber. He carried a candelabrum in one hand and a bottle of wine with two wineglasses in the other.

"Good evening, Husband," she said cheekily. Several flashes of lightning flickered through the thin gaps in the drawn curtains, followed a few seconds later by a crash of thunder. "Did you brave the cellar barefoot?"

The long ride had encouraged everyone to retire shortly after the wedding. Arabella had helped her undress before she wearily staggered to her own bedchamber, leaving Tempest to greet her new husband wearing her chemise and a wool blanket to cover her bare legs. While she prepared for her wedding night, Chance and his friends had celebrated their adventure as highwaymen and toasted the groom downstairs in the library. Along the way, her husband had lost his evening coat, waistcoat, stockings, and boots.

He bent down and kissed her on the mouth. "Good evening, Lady Fairlamb. I left the task of procuring more wine from the cellar to Thorn, since he had good news to share and it gave us something else to celebrate."

"More important than our wedding?" she teased.

Chance placed the branch of candles on the table, and he eased down on the floor beside her. "It is to my cousin." He laid one of the empty wineglasses on his lap so he could fill the other glass and hand it to her. Then he retrieved his glass and filled it. "Before Thorn left town to prepare for our arrival, he received news from a family member that his twin brother has returned to England."

"Why did he not join us?" Tempest was looking forward to meeting Gideon, since he and Thorn were now part of her family.

He took a sip of his wine and set the bottle aside. "Word has reached the family that his ship has arrived in port. My cousin has yet to present himself."

"I like Thorn," she said, privately pleased that Chance's gruff cousin had treated her and Arabella as beloved sisters. "Is Gideon very much like his brother?"

"In looks, yes. When they engage in a bit of trickery, it is difficult to tell them apart. However, Thorn and Gideon are as different as you are from your sister when it comes to temperament. I doubt the years apart have improved the situation."

There was more to the tale, but Chance seemed reluctant to continue the conversation about his cousins. He confirmed her thoughts with his next words. "Enough talk about my cousins. I am more curious about what you are wearing under that blanket, Lady Fairlamb."

Her eyelashes fluttered in a flirtatious fashion. "Why do you not see for yourself?"

Chance swallowed the remaining wine in his glass and placed it on the table. With their gazes locked, he took her unfinished wine and set the glass on the table. With the edges of the blanket tucked loosely around her waist, Tempest assumed he would grasp the edge and peel it back. He surprised her by inching closer. His hand stroked her unbound hair before he speared his fingers through the thick mass until she felt them at the nape of her neck. Slowly, he urged her to lean forward until their lips met.

His mouth tasted of the wine, and of the brandy he had drunk with his friends. Her tongue unfurled and teased his. He smelled of rain, wool, and smoke.

"It feels like it's our first time," she said, kissing the underside of his jaw. The lace strap of her chemise slid off her right shoulder. She felt his fingers skim her bare arm.

"It is."

Chance had removed his cravat; however, his shirt hindered her questing lips, and her trail of kisses had moved down the side of his neck.

Anticipating her request, he drew back and pulled his shirt over his head. Bare-chested, his skin appeared golden in the candlelight. Tempest sat up on her knees, allowing the wool blanket to slide lower as she shuffled closer. She kissed his collarbone and stroked the dark coarse hairs on his chest.

"Have mercy on me, Wife," he entreated, his husky voice thick with restraint. "I do not want to disappoint you on our wedding night."

Emboldened, she reached for the buttons on his breeches. A discreet glance at the front of his breeches revealed the proof of his desire for her. Tempest recalled how it had felt when Chance pierced her body with his manhood and filled her until she could barely breathe, and she shivered.

"Cold?" He urged her closer so he could warm her with his body.

"You," she whispered, opening his breeches and filling

her hands with his aroused, rigid flesh. Like the rest of him, the velvet length was hot to the touch and Chance trembled as her fingers stroked him.

The subtle musk of his arousal filled her nose and lungs. She sat on her heels and wondered how he might taste.

"Is anything forbidden?"

His heavy-lidded gaze widened as he sensed the direction of her thoughts. "Nothing. I am yours to command," he said, shoving his breeches down over his slim hips. He sat down on the floor to free his legs and tossed the breeches aside.

With a playful push to his shoulder, she silently encouraged him to lie down, and he eagerly obeyed. Jutting from the nest of hair between his legs, his manhood was thick and firm and rising as if begging for her touch. At its base, the texture of his flesh changed. Even so, it was no less sensitive to her exploration.

Her long brown hair pooled around his hips as she trusted her instincts and lowered her head. Chance tensed at her first tentative taste as she licked at the salt coating the head of his manhood.

"Do you like it?" she asked, curious about the tension in his body. Her husband was as tight as a bow.

"Yes," his reply hissed through his lips. "You can take more of me."

Intrigued, she lifted her head so she could see his face. "How much?"

"As much as you like."

The back of Chance's head hit the floor when she lowered her head and took the head of his manhood into her mouth. The salty taste increased as her tongue lapped at the trickle of fluid leaking from the opening. Her husband moaned and his hips lifted off the rug as if silently urging her to take more.

With her fingers curled around the base of his rigid length, her mouth widened and his manhood slid deeper. Sensing she was uncertain how to proceed, Chance guided her by showing her how much he enjoyed the feel of her mouth and tongue as the hot flesh slid deeper and retreated. She gagged a little when the thick head bumped the back of her throat, and the minor setback allowed her to set boundaries for herself and revealed the telltale signs of her own arousal.

As she suckled and teased the head of his manhood with her tongue, her nipples tightened as the swollen nubbins rubbed against his legs. Warmth flooded and expanded in her lower belly as wetness collected in the womanly folds between her legs.

Tempest moaned, drawing him deeper as she envisioned him filling her. She squeezed her thighs together in a feeble attempt to ease the heightening ache.

She needed him inside her.

Now.

Tempest released his manhood, the tip of her tongue licking her lower lip so she could savor the taste of him. Could a man release his seed in his lover's mouth, she wondered.

"Chance?"

His eyes snapped open at the need in her voice. His pupils had swallowed most of the gray color in his eyes until it was thin rings. Chance reached for her and dragged her up until she reclined on top of him. He rolled them until their positions were reversed and his manhood, wet from her mouth, pressed against her belly. He braced most of his weight on his arm and used his free hand to part her thighs. In her next breath, his hot flesh found the heart of her and filled her with a single hard stroke.

It was precisely as she had remembered.

The fullness of him expanding the inner muscles of

her sheath, which constricted around his manhood as Chance plunged wildly into her. Tempest tugged his head down to her breasts, which were still covered by her linen chemise, but the thin fabric was no hindrance to his hungry mouth. The fabric dampened as he roughly sucked on her nipples as he drove his flesh deeper into her. She writhed against him, silently demanding more. In response, he lightly bit down on one of her nipples.

Tempest cried out, but not from pain. The sweet agony Chance had created within her exploded and flickered madly as lightning crackled overhead. Her release rumbled like thunder vibrating her and the floorboards. She opened her eyes in time to see her husband rising above her like a pagan god, his gray eyes dark with lust and the clawing need for completion.

It was her name he roared as his tempo became more frenzied, and then he delivered one final thrust so deep, she was pinned to the floor as his seed burst out of him, filling her with thick steady pulses.

With their skin slick with sweat and her muscles trembling from the carnal onslaught, she had never felt so complete or powerful as in that singular moment.

She wished she and Chance could stay like this forever.

"No regrets?" he murmured lazily against her shoulder.

"Not at all." She sighed. "You?"

His labored breathing teased her neck. "Just one."

She stiffened, but he merely chuckled. He kissed her shoulder and gently withdrew his softening manhood from her sheath. His fingers teased and parted the womanly folds that were wet with her arousal and his seed. She gasped when he unerringly found the sensitive knot of flesh hidden within.

"I never got around to undressing you properly."

Chance picked her up and carried her to the bed. "Don't worry, darling. You will enjoy how I make it up to you."

Completely enthralled with each other, neither Chance nor Tempest thought about their families or the difficulties that would be waiting for them when they returned to London.

# Chapter Twenty-Seven

"My father will kill you."

His new bride's lack of faith in his abilities should have annoyed him, but the dark bruise on her cheek was a vivid reminder that Lord Norgrave was capable of violence. "You will not be wearing widow weeds, Lady Fairlamb. Your father might try to contest our marriage, but I assure you that our marriage is quite legal, not to mention fully and most pleasurably consummated. You are my wife in every way possible. He cannot take you away from me."

Tempest was too worried to be distracted by his gentle teasing. "Why are you convinced that my father will accept our marriage, when your own family is still struggling with it?"

Mathias leaned forward, prepared to refute her claims until his automatic defense of his family was overruled by the unpleasant reality of their situation. He sat back and rubbed the ache in his chest. "An excellent point."

His family's reaction to Tempest and their recent marriage had divided his loyalties. In his life, there had never been a moment when he was not secure in his father and mother's love and support. It infuriated and hurt him to learn that they were a lie. Their love did have conditions. They wanted him to sever his ties to Tempest.

*Never.*

"My father is blinded by the past. Whatever your father has done, my father seems incapable of forgiving him." Mathias sat back in the chair and scrubbed his face with his hands. "Has your father ever mentioned what happened between him and Blackbern?"

"Never." She crossed her arms and hugged her chest. "My mother never speaks of it either. Chance, you may have to accept that neither family may acknowledge our marriage or our children. Do you still wish to remain married to me?"

He leaned over and kissed her pouting lips. "Yes."

Tempest started at the soft knock at the door. She and Mathias stood, and she looked so frightened by the prospect of facing her father that he wanted to punch him for hurting her. However, fighting his new father-in-law was not part of the plan. He needed an ally if he and Tempest hoped to end the feud between their families.

"Enter," Mathias called out, and the butler opened the door.

"Milord, you and Lady Fairlamb have a visitor. Lord Norgrave. He claims to be your wife's father."

"Show him in."

"Very good, milord." The butler bowed and left. A few minutes later, he returned with their first guest.

He reached for Tempest's hand and threaded his fingers through hers to remind her that she was not alone. Her skin was cool to the touch as she visibly struggled to remain calm. "Remember, love, you are my marchioness. He cannot force you to leave with him."

She shut her eyes and shuddered. "I know," she whispered, her eyelids lifting at the soft click of the door.

"Lord Fairlamb, may I present Lord Norgrave." The butler backed out of the library and shut the doors.

An uncomfortable silence filled the room.

Tempest made no effort to embrace or acknowledge her father. Mathias understood her wariness, so it was up to him to make the first move. He released his wife's hand and stepped forward, as he inclined his head. "Lord Norgrave, we have not been properly introduced. I am—"

"I know who you are, Fairlamb," the marquess said, his light blue gaze conveying both intelligence and confidence. "I must admit that I was curious about the gentleman who kidnapped my daughter."

"It was hardly a kidnapping, Lord Norgrave," Mathias said, silently inviting her father to sit. "It took a little time to secure the special license to marry your daughter. Once I had it, I saw no reason to delay our marriage."

He walked over to a cabinet and opened the doors to reveal several decanters. "Brandy?"

"Yes, I wouldn't mind a glass. The occasion calls for it, do you not agree, Daughter?" the marquess asked, his gaze fixed on Mathias as he poured brandy into one of the glasses.

Tempest stared at her father. "Do not pour one for me, Chance."

"No celebratory toast, Tempest?" Norgrave lightly mocked while his daughter became more stone-faced by the minute. "You have my sympathies, my good man."

"Chance is my husband, Papa. This is his house. You will speak to him with respect or you may leave," she said, her delicate shoulders shaking with anger.

"Tempest, darling, I was the one who invited him," Mathias said, giving her a silent warning that baiting him would not gain the old rogue's cooperation. "Your father and I have a few things to discuss. If you would prefer to go upstairs, I think we both would understand." He handed the marquess his glass of brandy.

Lord Norgrave sniffed it before he took a sip. Satisfied that he was not being offered inferior spirits, he took a healthy swallow. He nodded. "Fairlamb is right, Tempest," her father drawled. "Give me a little time to talk to your husband, and then we can leave."

"I am not going anywhere with you," she said, decisively walking to Mathias's side and touching his arm. "You chose Lord Warrilow; however, Chance is my choice. And now he is my husband."

"Still mad at me for cuffing you for your disobedience, I see." The marquess sighed. "I had good reason and the right to reprimand you, Daughter. However, the mark on your cheek offends me, so I offer my sincerest apologies for hurting you."

Tempest nodded, seemingly surprised by her father's remorse. "I think I will take my tea in the drawing room."

Mathias waited until she left the library before he sat down. Over the years, inherent curiosity had prompted him to observe Norgrave at a distance, but he had never spoken to him. They drank in companionable silence as each studied the other.

Finally, Norgrave said, "Your invitation was unexpected. It arrived while I was deliberating with my son about whether or not he should challenge you."

"Did you come to an agreement?" Mathias asked. He took a sip of his brandy, not particularly concerned about Marcroft.

"I am certain you are aware that Croft has been eager to put a bullet in your chest for some time," he said casually, his light blue eyes assessing his opponent.

"He may try, but I would regret shooting family." What Mathias didn't add was that he would make an exception for Marcroft.

"Ah, family," Norgrave said, savoring the word on his lips. "And where do your loyalties lie, Fairlamb? Your father? Your mother? Your lovely bride?"

"All three deserve my allegiance, Lord Norgrave," he

replied, suspecting that Tempest's father was playing word games with him.

"And your mother and father . . . they approve of this marriage?" he politely inquired.

Mathias tried not to choke on his brandy. "My family was surprised by my haste to claim my bride. Also hurt that I would marry without them at my side."

The pain in his mother's eyes still made him feel guilty. Mathias noticed his father-in-law's glass was empty, so he stood and walked over to the cabinet to retrieve the bottle. He removed the stopper and refilled the man's glass.

"And why did you do that?" He elaborated at Mathias's questioning glance. "Choose to hurt your family when it was within your power not to by simply declaring your intentions."

The older man had forced Mathias's hand and he knew it. Not only had Norgrave struck Tempest in anger, but there was also a risk that he might force her to marry Warrilow. "You know why."

"Aye, I do." Norgrave cocked his head to the side. "The real question is, do you?"

Mathias placed the bottle next to the marquess's glass of brandy. "No more games, Lord Norgrave. If you have something to say to me, be forthright about it."

Approval gleamed in the other man's eyes. "Very well. I want you to encourage Tempest to return home with me. In the morning, you will return to Doctors' Commons and put into motion a request for an annulment."

He snorted. "Impossible. Your daughter is my wife in every way."

Norgrave tipped his head back and laughed. "I'll wager she was yours in all ways before you secured that special license from the Archbishop of Canterbury." He raised his hand to silence Mathias's need to defend himself and Tempest. "Although he prefers to deny it, your father and I have known each other since we were boys. We discovered and shared women, and my instincts tell me that you are very much your father's son."

It was a fact he could not deny. "Bait me all you like, Norgrave. I am not seeking an annulment. Tempest is mine."

"It heartens me to see that my daughter has found a man strong enough to love and defend her, even to her father. Under different circumstances, I might have given her to you without demanding a price."

"What circumstances? The old feud with my father?" Mathias braced his palms on his knees and leaned forward. "Tempest loves you. I do not want to keep her from you and Lady Norgrave. There does not have to be animosity between us. You are dealing with me, not my father."

A flicker of admiration lit the gentleman's light blue eyes and then it faded. "Regrettably, there is just one problem."

The hairs on the back of Mathias's neck bristled in warning. "You are just like my father," he spit, disappointment rising within him. "You cannot let go of the past."

"Not quite, Fairlamb," he said, his forefinger tapping the edge of his glass. "The past won't let go of us. There is a reason why Blackbern and his beautiful duchess have kept you and their children away from me and my family. Blackbern knows the truth."

"What truth?" he pressed.

"You are *my* son, not his," he said succinctly.

His field of vision narrowed at the marquess's declaration. Mathias sat down in the nearest chair and glared at his companion. "I am impressed," Mathias said, a harsh laugh escaping his lips to dispel the ugliness of

Lord Norgrave's words. "Never have I heard a more brilliant and abhorrent reason to separate a wife from her husband. I congratulate you on your inventiveness, my lord."

The hint of pity in the older gentleman's eyes seemed genuine. "I cannot take credit for speaking the truth, Fairlamb."

"No." Mathias gripped both armrests to keep himself from slamming his fist into Norgrave's arrogant jaw. "I do not believe you."

Lord Norgrave idly stroked the scar on his cheek. "It appears Blackbern has not been honest about his debauched past and it is up to me to enlighten you. Perhaps it is fitting since you are my—"

Mathias pounded his fist against the armrest. "I will not be accountable for my actions if you finish that statement."

The marquess's eyelids narrowed at the promise of violence, but he possessed enough common sense to retreat. "Now where was I in my tale? Ah, yes, Blackbern. In his misspent youth, my friend bedded any female that caught his eye. We often placed wagers about which one of us would fuck the wench first. It mattered little who won, Blackbern and I just enjoyed the game. Our friendship had few boundaries. It was not unusual for us to share women."

Mathias thought of his mother, and his mind blanked. His father wasn't a saint, but he was not the man Norgrave was describing. He would never have shared Mathias's mother with this man.

"Did my father grow tired of your guile? Is that the reason why he cut his losses with you? I have not spent an hour in your company, and already I am bored with your lies," was his soft reply. "And everything you have said is a lie. My father loves my mother."

A wistful smile played across his generous mouth. "Yes."

Mathias stood and glared at the marquess. "The Duke of Blackbern is my father, you wily bastard. My mother would never have allowed you to touch her—"

Norgrave jumped to his feet so they stood face-to face. He realized they were the same height. Appalled at the direction of his thoughts, he stalked away from the man before he did punch him in his deceitful mouth.

"Oh, I did touch your mother, Fairlamb," the marquess said, circling around Mathias. "It was a night I will never forget. Imogene was so achingly beautiful." His eyelids lowered and his light blue eyes became unfocused as he recalled the past. "So eager for my touch. I can understand that a son does not wish to view his mother in such a carnal fashion, but you have demanded that I speak the truth. Your mother could not decide which one of us she desired most, so she gave herself to both of us. Even though Blackbern was my best and dearest friend, I could not refuse Imogene. Our passion could not be denied, nor do I regret it. Neither one of us considered the possibility of my seed taking root within her womb that night. When I found out that she was with child, I was prepared to marry her. Blackbern was also in love with her and determined to have her. We fought over her, and he gave me this scar. It is a constant reminder of what I lost when your mother chose him over me."

Mathias stared at the long-faded scar on the other man's face. He glared at Norgrave because his father— Blackbern—had refused to discuss the reasons for his feud with the marquess. Mute with rage, he was unable to refute the man's story.

"The man I once considered a brother married Imogene and cut all ties with me because he didn't want anyone to know that your mother was carrying my son."

"Enough. Just stop," Mathias pleaded, too shaken to listen to more. Had he unknowingly married his half sister? How many times had he pleasured her with his body and filled her with his seed? There was the possibility that she already carried his heir within her womb. The brandy in his stomach burned like acid at the unsavory thought. "You are not my father."

This time, there was little conviction in his strained voice.

Mathias scrubbed his face with his hands and felt the sting of unshed tears. He mentally cursed both Blackbern and Norgrave and their bloody debauchery—their secrets.

The notion of giving up Tempest stripped him of his soul.

The other man must have sensed the direction of his thoughts. "And this is why you have to let Tempest go," Norgrave said wearily. "You have to believe me. She is your half sister. However, I have a plan. With a hefty bribe, no one has to learn why you are seeking an annulment. Return her to her family. Warrilow is a good man and he cares for her. I will talk to him again. Once he knows you will not stand in his way, he can step in and marry Tempest. That way, if she is carrying your child, no one—"

A soft gagging noise drew their attention to the door. Tempest looked as sick as Mathias felt. She gagged into her cupped hand again. "It isn't true. You will say anything to hurt me."

"Daughter, why do you think the Rookes severed all connections, and that your mother and I honored their decision? An intimate connection between Chance and any of my daughters would be disastrous."

Mathias walked to his wife, and she cringed when he attempted to touch her. He did not want to call her father a liar, because his words were rather damning. "Do you believe him?"

"I don't know," she cried, the admission ripped from her chest. "What have we done?"

His jaw tensed and flexed as he swallowed his anger. "I need to speak to my mother and my father."

"What if I am your half sister, Chance? Let's face it, your parents have lied to you your entire life and refused to discuss the origins of the feud. Even you cannot deny that your family disapproves of our marriage and would support an annulment."

"Love, do not ask me to give you up," he begged, capturing her face with his hand and pressing his forehead to hers.

Tears coursed down her face and over his fingers. "I cannot stay here. I have to leave." Tempest pushed him away.

"No!" he shouted, intent on following her. "We only have *his* version of the truth. Give me time to meet with my parents."

Norgrave placed a firm hand on Mathias's shoulder. "Son, it is best for everyone if she leaves with me immediately."

Mathias shrugged off his touch. "You are not my father," he growled. A man could sense his own sire, could he not? "Tempest is staying with me. Damn it, she is my wife!"

"If the ton learns of your true parentage, you will ruin her. She is my daughter, Chance," Norgrave said, and when he opened his arms, Tempest rushed to him. He cradled her against his chest while she sobbed. "If you love her, you will allow me to protect her—and you."

The muscles in his throat were so tight, he could barely breathe. Tempest was crying and refusing to look at him, and he felt so helpless. "Take care of her. I need to—" He cleared his throat. "If an annulment is warranted, then I will see that it is done discreetly."

"And soon," Norgrave said, wordlessly reminding him that an annulment was needed so Tempest was free to marry Warrilow to stave off any speculation that she carried Mathias's child. "You know I speak the truth. There is no reason to dredge up the past for Blackbern and your mother. Give them some measure of peace by rectifying this mistake on your own."

Five minutes later, Tempest and the father he never suspected of having were gone. He felt sick and lost, and the thought of facing his parents with Norgrave's outrageous story and the risk of discovering it was true was starting to push him over the edge.

Mathias picked up one of the chairs and threw it at the wall. Stepping over the wreckage, he grabbed the bottle of brandy on the table and headed for his desk. He planned on getting drunk, and with any luck he would pass out so he could numb the agonizing pain in his heart.

# Chapter Twenty-Eight

"What have you done?" Charlotte demanded, following her husband down the staircase. Her skirt and petticoat prevented her from keeping pace with his long stride, but she was on his heels.

"I brought our daughter home," Norgrave replied. "I thought you would be pleased."

Tempest had locked herself in her bedchamber, and she refused to speak to anyone. The quiet sobs Charlotte heard on the other side of the door broke her heart.

"Did you say something to her? Threaten her?" She abruptly halted on the bottom step when her husband turned around to confront her.

"Threats were unnecessary. Tempest regrets her hasty marriage to Lord Fairlamb, and now that foolishness is over, she is prepared to accept Warrilow's offer of marriage," he explained, apparently quite pleased with his role in breaking up the young lovers.

"What about Fairlamb? Several people told me that boy was madly in love with our daughter." Her eyes narrowed. "You couldn't buy him off. What did you say that convinced him that he should divorce Tempest?"

"An annulment will suffice."

"I highly doubt Tempest and Fairlamb would be granted one. The normal circumstances would not apply.

You would have concocted something quite devious to separate them."

"You have a low opinion of me, Wife."

"Only because you have never sought to rise above it," she said, recalling that he had done everything he could to destroy the love she had felt for him.

The door to the billiards room closed, and she realized he had walked away.

Charlotte chased after him, cursing under her breath. When she opened the door, he was staring out one of the windows.

"So why specifically an annulment? What could you possibly tell Fairlamb that would cause him to—?" She paused and pondered for a moment what connection her husband had with the young marquess that he could exploit. "There is Tempest, but he had already outwitted you by marrying her. A virile young man would not delay in consummating the marriage."

With his back to her, Norgrave sipped a glass of port but remained silent.

"So not Tempest." Charlotte scowled, her anger renewing when she thought of her heartbroken daughter crying into her pillow. "You threatened Blackbern and his wife. No, Fairlamb would simply have challenged you. A bullet in your old hide would have discouraged you from—" No, there was another card her husband could play. One difficult to refute when the Rookes and Brants were so good at keeping their secrets. It made her nauseous to even consider. She marched over to him and tugged on his sleeve until he looked at her.

"You didn't. Even you wouldn't be that cruel."

"You will have to be more specific about my alleged misdeeds," he calmly informed her.

"Oh, not all your sins are mere speculation. Lady Imogene Sunter comes to mind." She leaned closer and whispered, "Have you forgotten that I was one of the few people who saw your face and bruised body when Blackbern was finished with you? He tried to kill you, and both of us know why."

Norgrave stroked his scar and grinned. "Blackbern tried his best to claim his pound of flesh."

"Do not deny the cost was much higher, and you were not the only one who paid for it in blood. Just as you know—Dear heavens," she said, taking a step away from him. "You told his son what happened twenty-four years ago. How could you? Have you not ruined enough lives?"

McKee opened the front door to the Rookes' residence to find an intoxicated Chance on the other side.

"Good evening, my lord," the butler said, noting the half-empty bottle of brandy in the marquess's hand. "Were you pounding on the door with the bottle?"

Mathias shrugged. "It was sturdy enough for the task. Is he home?"

"Who?"

"Blackbern," he chuckled, and rubbed the grit from his eyes. "The man who claims to be my father."

McKee stilled at the marquess's choice of words. "You mean your father."

"I want to talk to the man who lied to me my entire life!" he shouted, enjoying how his voice echoed in the front hall. "And let's not forget my mother, too."

"Chance?"

Mathias spun halfway, but the world tilted and twirled like a child's toy. He blinked and came face-to-face with his mother. She must have been in the conservatory. The delight in her expression faded into concern when she noticed the bottle in his hand, and his less-than-sober state.

"Has something happened? Where is Tempest?"

"She left me," Mathias said, the pain having welled

within him. "They are asking for an annulment, so you have to tell me the truth."

"Chance." Blackbern descended the stairs. "I am so happy you returned. I have been thinking about what I said—Where is your wife? I owe her an apology."

"Something is wrong, Tristan," his mother murmured. "Chance, why don't you give McKee the brandy—"

"Damn right you owe her an apology!" he yelled at them, waving the bottle of brandy about. "I bring home an angel, and you treat her as if she were a whore with the pox."

"You're drunk." The duke's lips twitched as he fought not to grin.

"Tristan, you aren't helping," his mother complained, and decided to take charge of the brandy herself. "There, there, give me this. I will have McKee—"

Mathias squinted at his mother. "Is that why you despise her?"

"Who?" She exchanged baffled looks with the duke and McKee. "Maybe we should have several servants carry him upstairs and put him to bed. That will give him a chance to sleep off all that brandy."

"Why didn't you tell me that Norgrave was my father?" he blurted out.

Two things occurred at once: First, the Duchess of Blackbern fainted dead away at his feet, and second, his father slammed his fist into Mathias's jaw with such force, he could have sworn he heard several teeth crack. He dropped to his knees and then landed face-first on the marble floor.

The next time he opened his eyes, he was lying on the chaise longue in his mother's sitting room. Someone had been kind enough to drape a wet cloth over his sore jaw. Mathias sat up and cursed.

"Good, you're awake," Blackbern said, looking stern and unapologetic that he had punched his son in the jaw. "Your mother was worried that you fractured your cheekbone on the marble."

Mathias touched his face. "What were you hoping?"

"That you had expired while I was tending to your mother. Then I wouldn't have to strangle you for upsetting her," he growled.

"Is he awake?" his mother asked, entering the sitting room. She sat down beside him and inspected his jaw and his bruised cheek. "Does it hurt?"

"Less than I deserve, I guess." The duke's punch and the nap had sobered him. "How long have I been napping?"

"An hour," his father said, prowling the sitting room. "Now that you have rejoined the living, I need to know one thing: How did you come to the asinine conclusion that the Marquess of Norgrave is your father?"

Blackbern was so furious, Mathias was reluctant to explain that hours of speculation fueled by brandy had sent him on his fool's errand. "I sent a message to Norgrave. You were too angry about my marriage to Tempest that I thought I might get answers about the feud from her father."

"All the wrong answers!" he shouted at Mathias. "What did he do? Hit you over the head with a bottle and steal your wife?"

"Tempest left me."

"Mathias, what happened?" His mother clasped his hand. "Did Tempest leave because of what was said in this house?"

"No, I assured her that once everyone calmed down, you and Father would eventually accept her as my wife."

His mother winced, and was probably embarrassed by her behavior.

"What did Norgrave say when you asked him about the feud?" his father asked.

Mathias stared at his mother, silently pleading with her to look at him. "He told me that you and Norgrave had an affair and that you knew you were carrying his child when you married my father."

His father cursed. "I should have challenged him years ago."

"At first, I was convinced he was lying." Mathias squeezed his mother's hand. "He entered my residence with the sole purpose of convincing Tempest to leave with him. I was prepared for his threats but the tale he told me—suffice to say, it left me speechless. You and Father refused to talk about what happened twenty-four years ago, and his version of events made a certain amount of sense. I didn't know what to believe, so I had planned to come to you and demand an explanation."

"Damn it, why didn't you!" His father glowered at his son.

"Everything happened so quickly my head is still spinning. Then I realized Tempest had overhead what her father said to me. Neither one of us took it very well that we might be half siblings. Norgrave took advantage of our doubts and pressed for the annulment. He was concerned that his daughter might be already carrying my child, so he insisted that she marry Lord Warrilow immediately to conceal the truth."

"Who is Lord Warrilow?" his mother asked.

"Norgrave handpicked him for his daughter." Blackbern and Mathias sneered. They had identical expressions, a fact that only his mother could appreciate. "I confess, I panicked and feared that I had ruined Tempest's life by marrying her. I vowed to fix things, even if that meant annulling the marriage."

"You are an honorable man. However, your father is correct," she said, and her lips trembled as she tried not to cry. "Norgrave lied. He is not your father, and Tempest is not your half sister."

"Have I ever given you a reason to doubt that I am your father?" the duke shouted at him, and Mathias winced. His doubts had hurt his father's feelings.

"No, sir." Mathias shook his head. "There was a note of sincerity in his eyes when he mentioned Mother that convinced me he was telling the truth. He spoke of love and loss. Of betrayal, and how Father scarred him during their fight."

The duchess's head shot up. She stared into her son's eyes. "Your father didn't give him the scar on his cheek. I did." She exchanged a quiet look with his father, and then she leaned forward until her lips were an inch from his ear. "I don't want you to say anything. Just close your eyes and listen."

Mathias dutifully shut his eyes, and his mother shared how she had been tricked by Norgrave into visiting the house he currently resided in with his cousin. More than twenty-four years had passed, but he could hear the pain in her voice as she told him what happened in the bedchamber that had been destroyed in a fire set by Blackbern years later.

Even though it cost her to speak of such intimate and humiliating details with her son, she wanted him to understand who the true villain was that day so he could see that any sentiment the marquess harbored in his heart regarding the lady he had brutalized was false. His goal had been to create doubt between father and son, and divide the Rooke family. He also was determined to end Tempest's marriage to Mathias by any means.

His mother pulled back so she could observe her son's

reaction when she said, "Initially, I feared I might be carrying Norgrave's child after his attack. He had planted the fear in my head, and when I realized I was indeed with child." She blinked back tears and shook her head. "Your father—Blackbern, never had a doubt. Not once. His belief was unflagging, and when you were born and I held you in my arms, I knew he was right. You could never be Norgrave's son. I swear it."

Mathias brought his hands to his face. His family had kept secrets. At first it had been done to protect her, and later it had been done out of love to spare him and his siblings the painful truth. Their silence had also given Tempest and her siblings a measure of peace.

No one wanted to believe that their father had the capacity for true evil.

He let his hands fall away and embraced his mother. He held her as she cried, and he stared at his father, his face filling with remorse.

Blackbern acknowledged his silent apology with a curt nod.

"You need to find your wife, Mathias," his father said, his voice raw and gruff from emotion. "Do whatever it takes to convince her that Norgrave lies to trick her into marrying this Warrilow fellow."

"Will you go with me?" His mother stiffened at the question, so he appealed to his father. "You have already spoken out against the marriage. Tempest left me convinced you and Mother are against our marriage because everything her father revealed is true. If both of you stand with me and openly challenge Norgrave's claims, she will believe us."

Her father's confession had devastated her, but Mathias knew Tempest was too stubborn to give up on them so easily. Almost from the beginning, she had trusted him—and found the courage to love him.

"We will help you," his mother said, her voice soft and apprehensive about their impending confrontation.

It was time to put an end to Norgrave's machinations and bring his wife home.

# Chapter Twenty-Nine

Norgrave and Blackbern had not spoken a kind word to each other in twenty-four years.

Mathias doubted their confrontation would change anything this evening.

Nevertheless, the Duke and Duchess of Blackbern stood beside their eldest son while Lord Norgrave stood alone at the base of his staircase. He didn't have a sword or a pistol in his hand as he stared at his unwelcomed guests. To add further insult, the marquess had not invited them upstairs to his formal drawing room or even into his library.

He wanted them to leave, but Mathias refused to walk out of the town house unless Tempest went with him.

"Blackbern, the gossipmongers will be wagging their tongues come morning when they learn that you called on me," Norgrave said, sensing he had the upper hand since the Rooke family had willingly entered the lion's den.

"I owe your daughter an apology," his father said; his stance looked as if he were relaxed, but Mathias knew differently.

"I have been waiting for an apology from you for twenty-four years," Norgrave said, managing to sound peevish, even though he had not offered one of his own.

"And I am content to keep you waiting," Blackbern said, his voice sharpening. "Tempest, on the other hand, does not deserve our condemnation for a past not of her making or the sins of her sire. Send one of your servants upstairs to fetch her so my wife and I can make amends, and then we will be on our way."

"A pity," the marquess drawled. "I was about to offer you refreshments."

"You are a gracious host, Lord Norgrave," his mother said, even though he could only guess what it cost her to be civil to a gentleman who had once been cruel and abusive to her. Mathias's estimation of the duchess increased tenfold. "I had hoped that I might pay my respects to your wife."

Lord Norgrave grinned, sensing they were playing some kind of game, but no one had told him the rules. "I regret my marchioness has been indisposed, but I will pass along your kind words."

"Excellent." His mother placed her hand on Blackbern's coat sleeve, an unspoken reminder of her loyalties. "And tell Lady Norgrave that I will pray for a speedy recovery. When I spoke to her at Lady Karmack's, your lady appeared to be in good health. I hope it will continue."

Lord Norgrave's expression grew contemplative. "I was unaware that you and Charlotte exchanged words recently."

"Well, I expected it will happen more often now that our son and your daughter have married," the duchess said her voice infused with feigned lightness. She glanced at Mathias and some of the stiffness in her expression eased.

"Chance?"

Mathias stared up at the top of the stairs in time to see Tempest descending with her mother. Her face bore evidence that she had been crying, but she appeared composed. "What are you doing here?" Her gaze slid to the Duke and Duchess of Blackbern with undisguised curiosity and wariness.

"Can we speak in private?" Mathias inquired, and inwardly flinched when she shook her head.

Lord Norgrave stepped forward to prevent Mathias from approaching his daughter. "Since everyone has agreed that an annulment is the sensible course, I think it is unwise for you and Tempest to be unchaperoned."

"Do you honestly think you can stop me from speaking privately with my wife?"

A door opened and Marcroft joined their small gathering.

"Is there a problem, Fairlamb?" his new brother-in-law asked, silently noting the swelling and discoloration on Mathias's face. At his father's command, the earl would gladly add a few more bruises.

"No, as long as your father steps aside so I can properly greet my wife," he replied, daring him or any other member of the Brant family to deny him his rights as Tempest's husband.

Movement caught his attention, and Mathias noticed that Arabella was slowly descending the stairs and stood next to her mother. She appeared to be bemused to find Rookes standing in the front hall. "Good heavens! Are we celebrating Tempest's marriage to Chance?"

"No," Lord Norgrave snapped.

"Why not? After all, it seems appropriate," Lady Norgrave countered. She nodded to the butler standing in the background. "Starling, bring up a few bottles of wine from the cellar while I escort our guests up to the drawing room."

"See here, Charlotte," he said, raising his arm when Tempest reached the bottom of the staircase. "Blackbern and his wife are leaving. There is no reason to invite them upstairs. And you—Tempest—I will not have you—"

Tempest stepped out of reach and walked over to greet her new in-laws. Pride swelled within Mathias's chest as his wife defied her father and curtsied. "Your Graces, I would be honored if you joined me and my family in the drawing room."

His father managed to startle Tempest when he clasped her hand and bowed over it. "We will accept your gracious invitation, if you will allow me to welcome you to our family."

"There's no reason to waste your breath on pleasantries, Blackbern, when the marriage will be annulled within a week," Lord Norgrave said, drawing Tempest away from the duke.

"I would not wager on the outcome," Mathias said, claiming Tempest's other hand. "Now if you would be so kind to release my wife's hand so I may speak with her alone."

Lord Norgrave scowled at Mathias. "We had an agreement."

"Only if you told me the truth—something I am told you are unfamiliar with," Mathias said, not bothering to conceal his annoyance as he slipped his arm around Tempest's waist and pulled her away from her father.

"Chance?" There was no hesitation as she moved into his arms, her expression filled with curiosity and hope.

"What is Fairlamb talking about, Father?" Marcroft asked.

Lord Norgrave glared at Blackbern. "Will you shut him up or shall I?"

"Remaining silent is the reason why your lies almost succeeded in destroying your daughter and my son's happiness," the duke replied, his anger toward the marquess barely leashed. "Is that what you were counting on? That Chance would be so horrified by your revelation that his shame would prevent him from confronting us while you swiftly secured an annulment for your daughter so she could marry this Warrilow character?"

"Father?"

"Later, Croft," the marquess bellowed at his son.

"Yes, Norgrave, why don't you tell Marcroft how you tried to convince me that I, too, am your son because you forced yourself on my mother because she fell in love with your closest friend," Mathias said, his voice thick with disgust. "How you were willing to let Tempest believe that she had married her half brother so you could manipulate her into a loveless marriage because it benefited you."

Arabella gasped. Beside her, Lady Norgrave did not appear shocked by the news. Perhaps she had already deduced what her husband had done to convince Tempest to leave Mathias.

Everyone seemed frozen.

Marcroft stared at his father in angry disbelief.

Mathias was startled by the grim amusement that rose within him. He silently wondered if it was the father's dark nature that troubled the earl or the realization that he might have been forced to acknowledge a gentleman he had spent half his life despising as a half brother.

"Chance, how can we be certain?" Tempest demanded.

"Your father lied, love," Mathias said, needing to relieve the torment and uncertainty he saw in her eyes.

Tempest glanced over her shoulder and stared at the Duchess of Blackbern. "He told the truth about your mother. That they had been lovers."

His mother covered her mouth with her hand and sobbed.

"They were *never* lovers, Tempest. Norgrave attacked

Imogene," the duke said, taking a threatening step toward his former friend. "To punish me and her, and I will never forgive him for it."

Mathias did not want to release Tempest, but he could not count on Marcroft to step in if his father decided to renew his friendship with Norgrave by engaging in fisticuffs.

Tempest brought her hands to her face. "Don't you see, Chance, it does not matter which version of what happened we choose to believe. My father may be right. You could be his son."

"No!"

Everyone turned at the duchess's vehement cry of denial.

His mother walked toward them. "Norgrave has an impressive proficiency at subterfuge," she said, casting a brief contemptuous look in his direction before dismissing him. Sadness etched her face as she held Tempest's tearful gaze. "That means you cannot trust him. However, I have no reason to lie to you. Chance is Blackbern's son. There is no reason why you cannot love my son and build a life with him." She offered her daughter-in-law a wistful smile. "Have children. Do not let your doubts destroy what you have found with him."

"Tempest, I love you," Norgrave said, his voice gruff. "I am only trying to protect you from getting your heart broken."

Tempest stared helplessly at Mathias, and he longed to strangle the marquess for not giving his daughter the words that would ease her concerns.

"Daughter, Imogene is telling you the truth," Lady Norgrave announced, accepting that her betrayal would earn her husband's wrath. "I assume the timing was all wrong. It was the one thing my husband could not control. Do you not agree, Your Grace?"

"Yes," his mother replied, struggling to maintain her composure. The duchess boldly walked up to Lord Norgrave while he observed her approach with an indulgent smile. It was gone fifteen seconds later when she slapped him. The crack of flesh meeting flesh echoed in the front hall.

"Ah, Starling," the marchioness said cheerfully when she saw the servant holding several bottles of wine. "In your absence, our thirst has increased. A few more bottles will be required."

"I need something stronger," Marcroft muttered before he retreated into the library in search of a bottle of brandy.

Norgrave had the good sense to keep his mouth shut. Without a word, he disappeared into the library and shut the door.

Mathias pulled Tempest in the opposite direction when the marchioness encouraged everyone to follow her upstairs. Impulsively, he captured her hand and brought her fingers to his lips. "Do you know how many hours we have been apart, my lady?" Mathias asked. He lowered his voice for her ears alone. "I have missed you."

Her face softened with tenderness. "I have been miserable without you."

"Lord Warrilow will have to find another lady to wed because there is nothing your father can say that will persuade me to give you up again." Mathias tangled his fingers with hers as he lowered his lips to hers and kissed her. "I thought I had lost—"

"I know," she whispered back. "I wanted to die when I overheard my father tell you—"

"Hush," he said, kissing her again to soothe away the pain they had both endured. "It is done. Your father's lies have no power over us any longer."

He and Tempest had his mother and father to thank

for exposing Norgrave's lies. If not for them, he would have bowed to the marquess's dictates and lost the woman he loved to another gentleman. Like his father, Mathias was not the forgiving sort.

As far as he was concerned, the Rookes and Brants could keep their secrets.

Mathias looked beyond Tempest and realized they were finally alone. He cuddled her closer. "Should we join our family?" he murmured, reluctant to share her with anyone else.

"I want to go home."

Home.

Mathias found it mildly amusing that his priorities had shifted once he'd encountered Tempest in London. On his arrival, his thoughts had been focused on the ephemeral pleasures that men often sought to ease the boredom.

He had not realized he had been waiting for Tempest all along.

His friends might think him mad for marrying so young, but he considered himself a truly fortunate gentleman. The woman in his arms had filled his life with laughter, was a balm to both mind and soul, and together they would turn his grandmother's old house into a home.

He nuzzled the top of his wife's head with his chin. "What would you say to escaping this madhouse and toasting our marriage in the privacy of our bedchamber? Preferably naked."

"It sounds like a brilliant plan," she said, casting a guilty glance at the stairs. "Although it would be rude not to tell anyone."

"Yes," Mathias said, grabbing her hand and leading her to the front door. "And if we are fortunate, no one will speak to us for a week . . . possibly two."

"Promise?" she teased.

The brief truce between the Rookes and Brants would

not last. There was too much anger and history between them.

Mathias cast a rueful glance at the library where father and son were slowly getting drunk on brandy.

No, two weeks would not be enough.

"We'll make each day count. That much I can promise you," he said, indulging both of them with a lingering kiss.

With Tempest in his arms and the enticing curves of her body pressing against him, he was already home.

*Coming soon. . .*

Look for the next novel in this wildly popular series!

# Waiting For an Earl Like You

Available in January 2017
from St. Martin's Paperbacks

**Don't miss Alexandra Hawkins's
Lords of Vice series!**

*A Duke But No Gentleman
Twilight with the Infamous Earl
Dusk with a Dangerous Duke
All Afternoon with a Scandalous Marquess
Sunrise with a Notorious Lord
After Dark with a Scoundrel
Till Dawn with the Devil
All Night with a Rogue*

**And look for these novels
written as Barbara Pierce!**

*Tempting the Heiress
Courting the Countess
Wicked Under the Covers
Sinful Between the Sheets
Naughty by Nature
Scandalous by Night*

*Available from St. Martin's Paperbacks*